Crown of Light and Shadows

COURTS OF AETHERIA, BOOK ONE

G.K. DEROSA

Print ISBN: 9798327477018

Cover Designer: Sanja Gombar

Published in 2024 by Mystic Rose Press
Palm Beach, Florida
www.gkderosa.com

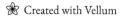 Created with Vellum

To my amazing PA, Sarah Jordan, without whom I would not survive! You're the best!

~ GK

CROWN
OF
LIGHT AND
SHADOWS

Contents

KINGDOM OF AETHERIA

DARKMANIA FALLS

COURT OF ETHEREAL LIGHT

LUMINOC RIVER

ARCANUM CITADEL

ALUCIAN MOUNTAINS

CONSERVATORY OF LUCE

COURT OF UMBRAL SHADOWS

THE SHADOWMERE SEA

FEYWOOD FORESTS

FEYWOOD

THE WILDS

Conservatory of Luce

Hall of Rais

Hall of Ether

Hall of Elysia

Hall of Luminesence

Hall of Enlightenment

Hall of Glory

Hall of Luce

Gymnasium & Training Field

CONSERVATORY OF LUCE
FORGED IN LIGHT · TEMPERED IN TRUTH

Chapter One

I pray to the goddess that the Fae lord who comes for me will be weak.

It was a silly prayer, but one that I'd repeated daily since the moment I discovered my inescapable fate as a magicless female Kin. I was destined to become the lifelong servant to a high Fae from one of the feuding courts upon my twentieth birthday. Tomorrow.

The setting sun crept across my bare shoulders, seeping into the light tunic from which I'd ripped the sleeves. I preferred to train in my leathers and the light frock, as opposed to the unwieldy sack-like dresses female Kin were supposed to wear. Balancing the worn hilt of the dagger Aidan had gifted me on my fifteenth birthday on my finger, I focused on keeping it upright with just the slightest movement of my hand. Only a few more seconds... Sweat beaded along my brow as I concentrated, my muscles tense from the strain. A strand of platinum hair fell across my forehead. Cursing, I blew it out of my face, and it settled atop my midnight locks. I'd been born with the strange white-blonde streak, and despite numerous attempts at tinting it with herbs of every shade of the rainbow, it refused to absorb color.

"Focus, Aelia." That gentle, sobering timbre centered my scattered thoughts.

For as long as I could remember, Aidan had drilled into my head the importance of not only brute strength, but also patience and control. I tended to ignore the latter. If I could simply outmaneuver my opponent with my sword or stealthy daggers, I could gain the upper hand. Which was exactly why I hoped for a weak Fae from whose clutches I could escape.

Beyond that, my plan was to return for Aidan, then travel to the Wilds, the desolate lands that stretched south of the courts of Aetheria. Surely, the mythical monsters that roamed the cursed territory would be preferable to returning to my home in Feywood and facing certain death. I didn't fear death, nor the god of eternal darkness, Noxus, but I would never risk Aidan's life, the man who selflessly raised me all these years.

"Very good, Aelia, and release." Aidan's voice drew me back to the present and the dagger I still precariously balanced. With a quick flip of my wrist, I sent it skyward, snatched it mid-air, and tossed it toward the target ten yards away. I watched as it sailed end-over-end before sinking into the straw figure across the field with a satisfying thwack.

"Always showing off." A moment later, Aidan appeared by my side with my dagger in his hand and a grin pulling at his chapped lips. His silver hair was neatly secured at his nape, despite the beads of sweat on his brow. Wisps of white hair mottled his upper lip and strong jawline, betraying his age.

A couple years ago, Aidan had confided he was nearing seventy years old. The confession had sent me reeling. Kin, like us, only lived to a hundred seasons—at most—unlike the Fae who could easily survive to three times that. It was the only moment in my life when I wished him to be one of them.

It was silly, much like the mantra I repeated daily. Fae were never weak; and powerless Kin did not become Fae. We lived only to serve the highborn, to toil at their fields or exist at their beck and call. Each of us served a purpose, our calling determined at birth. I would serve a Fae lord while Aidan would spend the rest of his existence working the fields. If we refused our caste in life, we would be killed along with every member of our family. The choice was simple really. In return for our obedience, the Fae protected us from the nightmarish beasts in the Wilds to our south.

Aidan handed me the dagger, patted me on the shoulder and directed me toward the small cottage I'd grown up in. I eyed my favorite weapon with its lethal blade and the once shimmery crystal encrusted in the ornate hilt, now dull from my incessant rubbing. It was one of a pair Aidan had given me. I rarely left home without one of them sheathed at my waist. Our cottage stood at the foot of the lush Feywood Forest which separated us from *them*, the two dueling courts that ruled our land.

An insect chirped in the distance and a few birds scattered overhead, signaling the onset of twilight. Not even the creatures of the woods lingered long once darkness fell. No one dared wander into Feywood Forest at night—especially not on a full moon.

This would be the last night I'd spend in the only home I had ever known; my final evening on the lumpy straw mattress with my feet hanging over the wooden footboard of the tiny bed. Tomorrow, one of the Fae lords would come for me, and I'd likely spend the following night in the kind of luxury I'd only ever dreamed of. Only, I wouldn't be basking in delight, because it wouldn't be mine to revel in, but rather mine to clean and keep tidy, to cater to every whim of the Fae to whom I would now belong.

I'd heard tales from females whose elder sisters had been

chosen. They were required not only to tend to the Fae lord's bed, but also frequently to warm it. The idea of giving my body to one of them... A bout of nausea crawled its way up my esophagus. I'd rather die. My fingers curled around the hilt of the dagger. Or kill him first.

"Do you think I'll end up in the Court of Ethereal Light or the Court of Umbral Shadows?" The question popped out as I followed Aidan to the front door of our old wooden hut. One would assume I'd be safer within the alabaster walls of the Light Court, but in truth, Light Fae were just as vicious as their dark counterparts.

Aidan's mouth twisted before it settled into a hard line. "I wish I knew, *estellira*." Despite the unsettling feeling in my chest, the hint of a smile tugged at my lips. *Estellira*. Aidan had called me that since I was a child, and somehow, it always settled the unease. He'd told me it was a word from the old Fae tongue of Faerish, meaning "little star." A distant memory scratched at the surface, a sweet, melodious voice singing. *Estellira*. It was as if that name had been a part of me all along. But it was impossible.

My mother had died at childbirth and my father had never come forward to claim me. Why Aidan had rescued me from a far darker fate in the hands of the local orphanage, I still didn't quite understand. He'd never given me a satisfactory answer other than "the goddess sent me to you." I supposed I'd done something incredible in a previous life to earn Raysa's favor. The goddess of light was clearly a kind and merciful one.

"Come, supper is waiting on the stove." He placed his hand on the small of my back and ushered me inside.

The savory scent of vegetable stew filled the small cabin and my stomach rumbled. I'd dug up the assortment of starchy tubers from our backyard this morning. Who would do that when I was gone? How would Aidan survive without me? The dismal thought incited the sting of hot tears.

Blinking quickly to keep them from rolling over, I slumped

into my seat at the small square table in the center of the cottage which served as our dining table, desk, workstation, and depository for miscellaneous items. I pushed aside a wooden carving of a dragon, the magnificent creatures now nearly extinct thanks to the ill-fated war. Aidan had been toiling over the little sculpture for days. I glanced at it fondly before spreading the two saucers on the table as he shuffled over, carrying the cast iron pot.

Aidan ladled a heaping portion into my bowl, but that unease simmering in my stomach made it impossible for me to lift the spoon to my mouth.

"What will you do when I'm gone?" I blurted once he was seated.

"Oh, I don't know, but I'm certain I'll manage somehow." He dipped his spoon into the bowl and twirled its contents around before his pale gray eyes lifted to meet mine. "You know, I was alive long before you came into my life, Aelia. I will not lie and say it will be easy without you, but please do not worry for me. I am not completely useless, just yet." He smirked and shoveled a heaping spoonful into his mouth.

"I know... and I'll come back to see you as soon as I can."

He nodded slowly, an unreadable expression on his face. "I'm certain you will." Dropping the spoon, he took my hand and squeezed. "Promise me you'll do as the Fae lord says. I know you have it in your head to escape, but trust me, there is no way out."

My stomach twisted. I hated lying to Aidan, but I would *never* succumb to the wishes of an arrogant Fae lord. I simply couldn't. Crossing my fingers like I did when I was a silly child, I dipped my head. "I promise." The old tales claimed the Fae couldn't lie and I thanked my lucky stars I wasn't born one of them. According to Aidan, it was a complete fabrication, but I hoped, regardless.

The remainder of dinner passed in a weighty silence. A tangle of spiraling thoughts was more than enough company for me, and Aidan, too, seemed preoccupied with his own demons. Two years ago, word came that Elian of Ether, the King of the Court of Ethereal Light, would be flying through our tiny corner of Feywood. As a naïve eighteen-year-old, I'd been thrilled with the chance to finally see one of the great kings of Aetheria. Aidan had refused to let me out of the cottage, but I managed to escape and steal a quick glance at the royal anyway. The following day, when I asked him why I had to hide, he went incredibly still and refused to say another word. It was the exact expression he wore now.

If a Light Fae appeared at our doorstep tomorrow to claim me, perhaps, I'd finally have the chance to have a better look at their king. There had been something about the royal that had called to me that day...

If not a Light Fae, I'd fall under the jurisdiction of Tenebris of Umbra, the King of the Court of Umbral Shadows. I wasn't sure which would be worse.

The pitter-patter of raindrops pivoted my gaze to the small square window above the stove. "Oh, the chickens!" I'd completely forgotten to cover their pen for the night. Despite the temperate spring weather, the rain was always icy in Feywood. "I'll be right back." I leapt to my feet, grabbed Aidan's cloak from the hook by the door and raced outside.

The last rays of sunlight dipped behind the forest as I rushed into the yard, illuminating the deep greens of the woods in a delicate glow. Racing around the back of the cottage with the dark hood over my head, I passed the small garden and found the hens and baby chicks huddled in the back of their pen.

Crouching in front of the wire enclosure, I squeezed a finger through the grating. "Sorry, little ones. I hope you didn't get too wet." I reached for the slabs of wood we kept behind the pen and positioned them over their home. "There, that should help keep you warm and dry."

When I was young, Aidan had never told me where the

roasted chicken on our plates had come from. The moment I learned the truth, I'd vowed never to eat meat again and I'd forced Aidan to become a vegetarian. Now, we had dozens of chickens and more eggs than we knew what to do with, but at least I could sleep with a clear conscience.

A flash of light streaked across my peripheral vision and I whipped my head around. "What the blazes?" Rising, I tiptoed around the corner of the hut, the crunch of grass beneath my boots suddenly deafening. I paused at the edge of the structure and peered around to the front yard.

A swirl of light hovered just beyond the front door. It danced through the dribble of rain and encroaching darkness in an ethereal display, like a thousand stars snaking through the sky. The hair on my nape rose as my heart picked up a manic rhythm. I'd never seen anything like it—and yet, still, I knew. There was something in the air, a distinctive scent that had my nostrils flaring. It was magic. Light magic.

My feet moved instinctively toward it, despite my brain urging me to stay far away. *Nothing good comes from Fae magic.* Aidan had drilled the refrain into my head since I was a child. And still, I couldn't help myself.

I reached for the sparkling light, my fingers wrapping around the glowing luminescence. It tickled, and a surprising giggle parted my lips. It swirled around my body, reaching up around my midnight locks and lifting them off my neck. Then it curled downward, illuminating my tattered tunic and umber pants. It crawled beneath my clothing causing tiny sparks to wriggle across my flesh.

Goddess, what was this?

The slight tickle became more insistent, until the prickle morphed into discomfort, and then, intense pain. I gritted my teeth, but in spite of my best efforts, a scream tore through my clenched lips.

Hot, fiery pain scorched my skin, despite the icy rain, racing across every inch of me. Liquid lightning surged through my veins and blinding light consumed the edges of my vision. *Oh, Goddess, it hurt.* I wanted to scream, I wanted to die, but only a wordless cry curved my mouth as my knees gave way and I collapsed onto the cold, wet earth.

My mind spun, the lawn blurring in a haze of green when I hit the ground. My cheek brushed the damp blades of grass, my entire body convulsing as a piercing ghostly blade carved into my heart. Steel bands wrapped around my failing organ, and I wasn't sure how it was possible, but I was certain I was having a heart attack. My chest was so tight, my lungs couldn't inflate properly. I drew in a desperate breath, then another, but my thoughts grew more foggy.

That fiery agony surged on, relentless as it consumed every inch of my being. Just when I was certain Noxus would appear to drag me to eternal slumber, the intense light finally began to fade, giving way to icy darkness. It crept into the corners of my vision until it annihilated the blinding light.

I should have fought harder, I shouldn't have given in—but in that moment, all I wanted was to disappear into the cold arms of murky oblivion.

So, I did...

Chapter Two

Stars, my head hurt. Slowly, I pried my eyes open to find a pair of light gray ones lingering over me. The familiar surroundings coalesced—the dark wood paneling, the small bed. I was still at home.

"Thank the goddess you are all right, *estellira*." Aidan's rough hand cupped my cheek, and I closed my palm over his. "What happened? I found you collapsed outside last night, and Raysa, you gave me such a fright."

I opened my mouth to reply, before snapping it shut once more. "I—I don't remember. I went outside to check on the chicks, and then everything after that is a bit hazy." A flash of light brushed across my subconscious thoughts. "I believe I may have been struck by lightning."

"Raysa forbid." An unreadable expression twisted Aidan's lips for an instant before the ever-patient mask slid back into place. "As long as you are all right, now."

I pushed myself up off the mattress and wobbled, my knees still slightly unsteady. Aidan took my hand, his silver brows puckered in concern.

"Are you certain you are all right?"

"If I said no, do you think the Fae lord will forget all about coming for me?"

A rueful chuckle slid through his lips. "I only wish, my child." He walked me toward the back of the cottage, to the small bathing chamber. "Now, go get dressed, I have a surprise for you. It is your birthday, after all."

A smile came unbidden, lifting the corners of my lips. I'd nearly forgotten in all the madness. My steps felt a little bit lighter and more sure as Aidan released me and I hurried into the dimly lit chamber. I vowed to enjoy this day for as long as possible and pretend it was a birthday like any other.

I flicked on the lantern and caught a glimpse of my reflection in the old, cracked mirror. My silver-blue eyes were bloodshot and weary, my hair a tangled mess, the streak of platinum running across my scalp like a skunk's tail. I tucked the errant locks beneath the dark curtain of black in a vain attempt to conceal it. With a frustrated sigh, I peeled off the leathers and tunic I still wore from yesterday, the stiff fabric brushing over a sensitive spot on my chest. Wincing, I glanced at the skin just below my collarbone and gasped.

Slashes appeared across inflamed, red skin.

Gingerly, I ran my finger across the strange markings engraved into my chest. "What in all the kingdoms?" I whispered aloud.

"Be quick, Aelia!" Aidan called out. "I am uncertain how much time we will have today."

With a quick glance at the empty basin and lukewarm water in a pail, I opted to forgo a bath this morning. Besides, the more unappealing the Fae lord found me, the better my chances to escape bedroom duties.

Running a brush through my hair, I splashed some water

on my face and pinched my cheeks for color. I seemed even paler than normal this morning. The odd markings caught my eye once more and my lips twisted at the sight of the unsightly burnt skin. It must have been lightning.

Reaching for the dress I'd hung on the door days ago, I fingered the soft, pale blue satin material. It was the finest frock I owned with puffy, translucent sleeves and a full skirt lined in crinoline. Aidan had scrimped and saved for an entire year to buy it. It was silly, really. Yes, it was my twentieth birthday, a cause for celebration, but it was also surely to be the worst day of my life, so far. A hint of unease swirled low in my belly, warning it was far from the last.

Carefully, I stepped into the dress and snuck a quick peek in the mirror, hoping it covered the angry red engraving on my chest. I barely recognized myself in the delicate gown, a marked difference to the worn tunic and leathers I typically wore. I almost looked beautiful. And thank Raysa, the sloping neckline just covered the angry red lacerations. The last thing I wanted was to worry Aidan. Crouching down, I rummaged through the pockets of my discarded leathers and found my daggers. Once I'd secured them to the sheaths around my thighs, I felt more like myself. I didn't often don this sort of gown while wearing my most favorite weapons, but I'd have to make do.

"Aelia, everything is ready!" Aidan's voice drew my attention away from my reflection.

"Coming!"

Blowing out the lantern, I stepped out into the main room where Aidan awaited. He stood at the table with a big grin lighting up his face. "Happy birthday, *estellira*." A small cake sat on a plate, covered in chocolate confection and wild berries. A lit candle stood in the middle, the flame flickering happily.

"Oh, Aidan, it's perfect."

"I hope so. It's been decades since I've made a cake from scratch." He ran a palm over the back of his neck with a sheepish grin as he regarded me. Handing me a knife, he slid into his worn wooden chair. "Go ahead, have a taste."

I sliced a heaping portion for myself and one for Aidan, my mouth already salivating. Sweets were a treat we couldn't often afford, even with our copious supply of eggs for trading. I took a big bite and couldn't keep the groan from seeping out.

"It's incredible, Aidan. How long have you been keeping this secret from me? Had I known you were such a talented confectionary, I would have saved all our extra gildings for sugar."

He smiled as he licked the fork. "That is exactly why I never told you." He wriggled in his seat, then withdrew a small pouch from his pocket. "There is one more thing."

I eyed the tiny leather sack curiously, a twinge tightening my chest.

Aidan handed it to me, an uncharacteristic sparkle in his eyes. "Well, go on, open it."

My fingers trembled as I unlaced the twine, pulled the draw-string open and upended its contents into my palm. A delicate gold necklace tumbled out, and my heart clenched at the sight of the braided chain and small medallion that hung from it. "It's beautiful," I whispered. I thumbed the warm metal and a faint etching caught my eye. Bringing it right up to my nose, I tried to make out the strange symbols. "What does it say?"

Aidan cleared his throat, his eyes dipping to his folded hands. "I'm afraid I'm not sure. I believe it is in the old tongue of Faerish. I wish I could say I had it made for you, Aelia, but I stumbled across it in the village a few months ago. Raysa must have guided me to your gift for this special day."

"Well, I love it, whatever it says." Handing it back to him, I turned around in the chair. "Will you help me put it on?"

"Of course." Lifting my hair, he closed the clasp and tucked it beneath my dress. The chain was so long the medallion disap-peared beneath the satin trim. I tried to pull it out from between my breasts, but Aidan slowly shook his head. "It's best to keep it out of sight, Aelia. We wouldn't want to draw too much attention."

I nodded slowly. He was right. Such a valuable item shouldn't be flaunted. Though I couldn't imagine there would be thieves at one of the courts. Out here in Feywood was a different story, though. Poverty and desperation pushed even the gentlest soul to do unthinkable things.

A sharp pounding at the door sent my heart leaping into my throat.

No... It's too soon. My panicked gaze lifted to Aidan's. His lips pulled into a scowl, then his hand found mine across the table. "Everything will work out in the end, *estellira*, I'm certain of it. The goddess is always watching, and she will keep you safe."

I ran my hand over the silky material of my dress and the hard, metal indentation hidden beneath. If the goddess didn't, my dagger would.

The sharp squeal of the chair legs scraping across the wooden floor jerked me into action. I had to keep my wits about me if I was to survive this. And I swore to myself that I would. Aidan trudged to the door, his steps slow and reluctant.

"Aidan, I'll be okay," I called out over my shoulder as I stood and moved across the small room to the niche beside my bed. I'd packed my bag days ago in preparation for the dreaded event.

"I know you will." He offered me a tight smile and marched the remaining distance to the door.

From the corner of the cottage, I watched, holding my breath as the door swung open to reveal my destiny.

A large, dark-haired male filled the doorway, a sneer curling his lips. Murky shadows danced across his arms, silent eerie whispers murmuring on the breeze. *Curses*, Shadow Court. Though I'd never seen a citizen of the Court of Umbral Shadows up close, the division between each kingdom was evident in not only his blatant powers, but also in his physical characteristics—the dark hair and eyes. All the Fae of the Light

Court had light complexions, blonde, silver or white hair, and pale irises. Kin like me were a mixed breed of light, dark, and everything in between. The male Fae towered over Aidan and, for the first time, I felt truly small. My adoptive father had always felt like the strongest male I knew, but compared to the giant in front of him, he appeared almost fragile.

"I am Lord Liander Nightkin, and I'm here for the girl," the male bellowed, glancing at a sheet of parchment clenched in his fist. "The female Kin, Aelia Ravenwood, is now my official property, per the Treatise of Aetheria." His dark eyes raked over me and a sinister smile spread his lips. Dread pooled in my gut at the hunger in his gaze.

My hand instinctively dropped to the blades tucked beneath my dress. So much for my daily plea. There was nothing weak about the male standing before me. It didn't matter; everyone had a weakness, and I'd find his.

Throwing my shoulders back, I marched toward him with my hand clenched around the one measly bag I was allotted. "I am Aelia Ravenwood," I replied, impressed with the coolness in my tone.

"You will do very nicely, woman."

An errant breeze lifted the long hair from the Fae lord's shoulders, and dark wisps lashed across his face. With a grunt, he swept the wayward locks behind his pointed ears. Gold circlets lined the sharp ends.

"I'm afraid not," a deep voice boomed from farther outside, compelling every tiny hair on my body to stand at attention.

The Fae lord spun around, wings made of shadows curling behind his back, his dark brows furrowing. "What is the meaning of this?" Liander growled.

Yes, what was the meaning of this? I crept toward the door, and Aidan followed.

Behind my new owner stood another male Fae with hair like liquid night. Bottomless midnight eyes met mine, causing my breath to hitch from the intensity of his stare. An unnamable force compelled my gaze until I took in every fiercely gorgeous inch of him. From the tousled dark hair to the stubble lining his strong jaw, down to the broadest shoulders I'd ever seen on a male. His black doublet molded to his form like a second skin, revealing the carved muscles of his chest and the hard planes of his body.

Good goddess, I'd never seen a more frighteningly beautiful male.

He stepped forward and shoved a rolled-up parchment into the Fae lord's chest. "Per the decree from King Elian of the Court of Ethereal Light, any Light Fae deemed worthy at the age of twenty years will be required to attend the Conservatory of Luce to train as a Royal Guardian of the Crown, at the sole discretion of the Royal Council."

The Shadow Fae let out a deep belly laugh, and I barely suppressed my own chuckle from bursting free.

"You must be mistaken, boy." Liander held up the yellowing sheet. "This female is no Fae worthy to protect the king or our realm, she is merely a lowly Kin, and she is mine."

"First of all, I am no *boy*," Dark and Dangerous snarled, closing the distance between them. Despite Liander's towering stature, there was something lethal about this Fae male. Darkness loomed across his broad shoulders, wrapping him in an aura of danger.

The Shadow Fae shrank back, blinking quickly, and something like recognition flashed across his dark eyes. Liander opened his mouth, but the male in front of him was already gone, reappearing an inch from my nose. "Second of all," he continued, that penetrating gaze chasing from my eyes down to my chest. His fingers closed around the neckline of my gown, and a gasp escaped as he slid the fabric aside and revealed a gilded symbol stamped across my flesh. The inflamed, grisly marks were gone, replaced by a shimmering, pattern of swirls seemingly forged from light itself. "She most certainly is Light Fae."

Chapter Three

My jaw dropped, my gaze bouncing between the glittering foreign mark that had appeared on my chest to the male's dark gaze. A male whose fingers still rested an inch from my breast, a previously unexplored area.

Impulsively, I slapped his hand away and leapt back.

Aidan and the Fae lord, Liander, gasped in nearly perfect unison, and deadly silence pervaded the chamber.

Dark and Dangerous's eyes flashed, but his mouth remained clenched in a hard line despite the blatant disrespect, as he stalked closer. Striking a Fae was a crime in Aetheria, punishable by ten lashes.

"I—I apologize," I murmured, as fear lanced through my heart. I could withstand the punishment... but I wasn't certain Aidan could.

The male's dark gaze seared to mine, and it was all I could

do to keep breathing. Stars, I'd never met a more intimidating Fae. "Never apologize for defending yourself. It makes you sound weak, and if there is anything the Fae despise, it is weakness."

I swallowed hard, trapped in that hypnotic gaze.

Aidan moved between us, and I was finally freed of that all-consuming stare. "Excuse me, but who exactly are you? Unless my senses deceive me, you are not Light Fae."

The male scrutinized my adoptive father, inciting a hint of fear that had me reaching for my dagger again. I wouldn't stand by and watch Aidan get hurt because of me. "How very astute of a simple Kin." A sinister grin revealed perfect, pearly white teeth. "My name is Reign Darkthorn and I am the professor of Shadow Arts at the Conservatory of Luce. I have come to escort your daughter back to the Conservatory."

"This must be a mistake..." I blurted.

My words trailed off as, again, those midnight, starlit eyes found mine, and my insides crumbled. "It is no mistake. The goddess herself selects the chosen Fae to attend the most prestigious university in the land to train as Royal Guardians to serve the Court of Ethereal Light, and you, Aelia Ravenwood, have been chosen."

My mind spun, his words floating in the air between us and bearing down on me like lead armor. How could any of this be?

"But she's Kin." Liander voiced the thoughts I couldn't quite yet manage as he skulked into the small cottage.

"Obviously not." Reign's eyes dipped dangerously low, nearly skimming my cleavage.

"But I am." I finally found my tongue and ran my finger over my clearly rounded ears. I'd spent my entire life in Feywood, under the boot of the haughty Fae who ruled our realm. "I would have known if I had magical powers."

Reign's unfairly perfect lips screwed into a grimace. "Fae do not have *magical powers*." He spat the words as if they were poison. "Light Fae are imbued with the spirit of the Goddess Raysa through *rais*, while Shadow Fae are blessed with *nox* by our god, Noxus."

I barely restrained an eyeroll, forcing my gaze to remain pinned to the arrogant Fae's. "As you say..." *Faery fool.* "Then again, how would *I* know since I'm just a simple mortal Kin, as I've tried to explain. I'm not a Fae princess from childish faery tales."

Reign inched closer and every nerve in my body lit up at his sudden inescapable proximity. "So you'd prefer to remain a powerless Kin, the property of this Shadow Fae for the rest of your days than explore the possibility that Raysa has blessed you?" He cocked his head toward the male lingering a few steps behind him, then leaned in so close, his warm breath brushed the shell of my ear. "From what I hear, Lord Liander has a rather pronounced foot fetish."

A gasp caught in my throat.

The very foot-loving Fae cast his gaze in our direction, dark brows drawing together in an angry twist. "Well? Has the mortal's status been confirmed yet?" He stomped closer. "I have every intention of taking this female home with me today." His hand jutted out, reaching for my upper arm.

"Over my dead body, Liander." Reign tossed him a feral smile and stepped between us.

The lord's eyes tapered at the edges as his irritated gaze bounced between mine and my new protector's. Dark shadows swirled around Liander's form, thickening the air between the two males.

"Try me, Nightkin," Reign snarled. A curved blade appeared in his palm and was pressed to the lord's throat in the space of a heartbeat.

Despite the professor's intimidating stature and clear mastery of weapons, I couldn't help but note that for an instructor of Shadow Arts, he didn't seem to wield any. The sinister dark tendrils that coiled around my would-be owner's failed to form around Reign.

The tense set of the professor's shoulders relaxed a smidge. "Go home, Lord Nightkin. I'll speak to the Council to ensure that a new Kin is assigned to your household."

Liander's mouth twisted as he regarded the male who'd clearly bested him without even using magical powers—or *rais* or *nox*, or whatever the gods it was called. "Will that be the Light or Shadow Council?" he sneered.

With Reign's broad shoulders to me, I couldn't make out his expression, but judging by the strain of every muscle along his back through the black doublet he wore, the lord had struck a nerve. "What does it matter to you as long as you get what you want?" he countered.

"Fair enough, *professor*." Liander spat the word with disgust then turned to me, murky irises scrutinizing. "Good luck, girl. You'll need it with this one." He spun on his heel, muttering curses, and slammed the door behind him. The entire cottage rattled from the force.

Reign heaved out a breath, his shoulders slowly falling before he turned around. His gaze dipped to the bag at my feet, the twine on the old canvas nearly bursting from the meager contents of my most favored mortal possessions. "I take it you're ready, then?"

My spine snapped straight. "Ready for what, exactly?"

He released a frustrated sigh. "Are all of you Kin so exasperatingly slow?"

"Are all of you Fae so exasperatingly rude?" The words escaped before I could stop them. Curses, I'd never survive in the world of the Fae if I kept this up.

Reign closed the space between us in one long stride and thick fingers curled around my neck. My breath caught, my heart kicking at my ribs.

"Please, no," Aidan cried out. "She didn't mean it—"

The professor silenced him with a biting glare before returning his attention to me. "Let me be clear about something, Aelia. You may have escaped the clutches of Lord Liander, but you are still property of the Fae. You are one of us now, and your fate will be determined at the Conservatory. You have two options: rise to the occasion and succeed or do nothing and spend the last few months of your miserable existence being tortured at the hands of Light and Shadow Fae much more powerful than you. And in case you had any grand delusions of escape, should you try to flee the confines of the academy and are caught, your life will be forfeit. More than that, your family"--his dark gaze drifted to Aidan— "will suffer the same fate. What do you say now, *princess*?" He hissed out my new pet name with such derision, I truly wished I were a princess so that I could strike him down with my extraordinary *magical powers*.

I swallowed hard, his fingers tightening so I was barely able to get the saliva down. "I. Will. Fight." I snarled.

A satisfied grin curled the corners of his lips. "Good girl."

His steel grip loosened and I took a giant step back. Eyeing the professor, I quickly assessed the likelihood of surviving an immediate escape. My daggers were strapped to my thighs, I could easily free at least one before he reached me. But then what? If I did manage to evade this Fae, what would become of Aidan?

I already knew the answer. He would be dead.

"You would never make it past the door." The lethal quiet with which Reign spoke the words had every hair on my nape rising.

"I never said—"

"You didn't have to." His brutal gaze raked down my chest and leveled between my thighs. "My guess is you're carrying a blade or two; small, lightweight and most likely useless against Fae."

"How did you..." Heat blossomed across my cheeks.

"It's obvious in the way you walk. You need to learn to

attach the sheaths at a better angle so that it doesn't interfere with your natural gait."

I caught a glimpse of Aidan over the professor's shoulder, and his mouth screwed into a frown. Realms, he'd noticed too. Damned fancy gown.

"There is no point in concealing weapons if everyone knows they're there."

"Noted," I mumbled.

"Now, say your goodbyes. This retrieval has already taken longer than it should have."

His command lanced across my heart as I lifted my gaze to Aidan. I'd barely had a moment to process what had happened. In a matter of a quarter of an hour, I'd gone from the future property of a Fae lord to the property of a Fae university and an enigmatic professor. But the bottom line remained the same, I was leaving Aidan and my home, and everything I'd ever known.

As if Aidan could feel my resolve crumbling, he stepped closer and swept me into his strong arms. Pressing his nose to my ear, he whispered, "You will not only survive this, Aelia, you will thrive. You will show those arrogant Fae who you truly are." He jabbed his thick finger to my chest, nearly skimming the glowing mark. "Do you understand?"

Realization raced through me as I peered into Aidan's pale gray eyes. "Did you know?" I murmured.

His gaze dropped to the top of my dress as if he could see the glistening symbol beneath, and his lips hardened into a thin line. Good goddess, he did know. What other secrets had he kept from me all these years?

"Aidan, please tell me—"

"It's time to go, *princess*." Reign's hand curled around my upper arm and jerked me away from Aidan's embrace.

"When will I return? When will I see him again?" I cast another lingering glance over my shoulder.

"If you survive the first term, you will be granted one week leave."

If I survive...

"I love you," I mouthed to my adoptive father as hot tears gathered. I blinked them back, convincing myself I'd never let one of these monsters see me cry. Fae hated the weak, and I'd prove myself strong or die trying. Those were the comforting thoughts that swirled through my mind as the dark beast dragged me from my home.

Chapter Four

At least a thousand questions spiraled through my jumbled thoughts as I followed Reign through the door, leaving my old life behind. How could I be Light Fae? Why didn't I have any powers? Why were my ears round? None of this made any sense at all.

"So how exactly—" My question was cut off as I took in the enormous avian creature over Reign's shoulder. "What in all the courts?"

He canted his head back, a devious grin pulling at his perfect bow-shaped lips. "You've never seen a phoenix, *princess*?"

"Stop calling me that," I hissed.

"Why? For a lowly Kin, you certainly behave like an entitled one."

"And for an arrogant Fae, I imagine you know nothing about spending all day tilling the fields, gathering turnips, and hauling them to the village market, or watching your fellow Kin die from overwork and starvation. You know nothing about me or my life, *professor*." I snarled his title with as much contempt as he did my new nickname.

His dark brows furrowed and he lifted the murky hood of the black cloak over his midnight locks. It only intensified his lethal beauty. "Get ready to mount." He stalked toward the majestic, feathered beast, who cocked its head at me, beady eyes studying. Fiery plumage in deep crimson and warm ochre covered its gigantic form, as if it were blanketed in flames itself.

"What's his name?"

"*Her* name is Pyra." He glanced up at the feathered fiend, a nearly gentle expression on his absurdly handsome face.

"And how does one ride this thing?" I dropped my canvas bag and stared up at the regal phoenix who easily surpassed the size of the draft horses they used to till the fields. "We lowly Kin don't have the luxury of riding astride such majestic animals."

Reign muttered something under his breath before offering his hand. "You'll have to learn to mount many large creatures in your time at the Conservatory, and not all will be willing."

The hint of a smile tugged at my lips as a completely inappropriate comment perched at the tip of my tongue. Thank the stars, I managed to restrain it.

Before I took his hand, the phoenix bowed to the ground, extending a magnificent fiery wing. I was fairly certain I could mount on my own, but the last thing I needed was to fall off the other side and make a complete fool of myself in front of the haughty professor. So I wrapped my hand around his palm, and tiny jolts of energy prickled my skin at the touch.

What the flying faeries?

I looked up, searching for any indication he'd felt the strange current too, but his face remained perfectly composed. It must have been a Light Fae thing. Who knew what sort of magical powers I'd have now? Finally, after years of being ordinary and mortal, I was something else.

A swirl of excitement quickened my breath as Reign's free hand closed around my hip and helped me onto the phoenix's back. Smoothing down my ruffled skirt, I settled onto the leather saddle strategically placed between her wings before spearing the tips of my boots through the irons. A large pommel sat between my thighs and I clutched onto it with shaky fingers. Not only had I never even ridden a horse, but I'd also certainly never left the relative safety of the ground. Which clearly, we were moments away from doing.

"Do you have a cloak in that bag?" He eyed the canvas slung over my shoulder as if it had been pulled straight from the rubbish pile.

"No." The weather in Feywood was temperate, when it wasn't scorching. I certainly never needed a heavy cover.

Muttering what I was certain were curses in a language I didn't recognize, Reign slid my bag off my shoulder from where I sat on the phoenix and attached it to the back of the saddle. Then he leapt onto the worn leather seat behind me and draped his dark cloak over us both. His imposing form curved around my body as he reached for the reins slung over the phoenix's proud neck. A glint of silver caught my eye, peeking out from beneath dark sleeves. But I simply couldn't focus. Heat surged through my form at each and every point of contact as a tangle of hypnotic scents impeded my synapses from firing. His firm biceps wrapped around my arms, the hard planes of his chest pressed against my back, his powerful thighs curled around my behind. *Oh, goddess, this cannot be normal.*

Then again, I'd had extremely limited experience with males. Perhaps, this was my body telling me it was time. I'd never felt the urge to explore relations with any of the male Kin I'd grown up with. Maybe, this was why. They'd never elicited any sort of sensation close to this.

"Ready?" Reign's warm breath skated across the shell of my ear, and goose bumps rippled down my arms in response.

Thank the goddess for the cloak that concealed the embarrassing physical reaction. "Hold on tight."

My fingers strangled the pommel and I squeezed my thighs around the supple leather of the saddle. Oh, please, Goddess, don't let me die such a tragically foolish death. Thrown by a phoenix on the way to the Court of Ethereal Light! My fellow Kin would have a good laugh about that one.

"*Volarys!*" Reign shouted over my head.

The creature's elegant wings stretched out, revealing a rainbow of fiery plumes. He took one step and then another, faster this time, and I hurtled back, right into Reign's chest. The powerful appendages flapped, and my stomach dropped to my toes. With another mighty thrust, we lifted off the ground. I squeezed my eyes closed as the air whipped strands of dark hair across my face and my insides leapt up my throat.

Once the flapping grew more steady—and I was fairly certain I would not lose the meager contents of my belly—I stared over the phoenix's shoulder as the yellowing grass grew smaller, and the insects flying below became non-existent.

I drew in a breath and stretched out my cramping fingers. My knuckles were white from the strain.

"Are you all right, princess?"

"Just fine, thank you."

"What did I say about thanking me?" he snapped.

"It makes me look weak?" I gritted out.

"Do you wish to look weak in front of your fellow classmates?"

"No."

"Then mind your tongue. And while we are on the subject, no apologizing to me or any Fae either. I've been more than lenient with you given your unusual circumstances, but I can guarantee no one else at the Conservatory will be."

Realms, if this was nice, I didn't want to know what worse was.

Reign lapsed into silence after that last remark, which I was thankful for, because I had more than enough spinning thoughts to contend with. Once the initial fear subsided, I allowed myself the opportunity to enjoy the beautiful scenery.

We soared across Aetheria and, for the first time in my life, I was able to revel in the enchanting lands beyond Feywood. I'd never ventured past the southern border which skirted the Wilds, the land inhabited by the terrifying beasts that should only live in the darkest corners of our imagination, according to Aidan. Thank the goddess for the Fae's protection against our enemies. Then to our north were the Fae lands: the Court of Ethereal Light lay to the west and the Court of Umbral Shadows to the east, where obsidian shadows blanketed the land, casting the entire court in menacing darkness.

A chill tiptoed up my spine and I couldn't suppress the tremor. With Reign's body hinged so tightly around mine, he must have felt it. He didn't say a word, but somehow the heat beneath his cloak intensified.

His surprisingly considerate action moved me to boldness and my lips began to move, blurting the first question that came to mind. "You are a Shadow Fae, correct?"

I felt his nod more than heard an actual reply.

"Then why are you a teacher at the Light Fae university? No job openings in the Shadow Court?"

He leaned forward so that I could just make out the sharp slope of his nose from behind the hood. "Let me explain something to you, *princess*," he hissed. "In our world, secrets are power, so hold yours close to your heart and keep that pert little nose out of everyone else's affairs."

My lips twisted at his icy tone, and I tried my best to scoot farther up the saddle so his body wasn't quite so attached to mine. It was in vain, but I felt a modicum of comfort at the passive-aggressive rebuff.

Reign jerked the reins to the left and, thank Raysa, we turned toward the west where the sun shone brightly over the horizon. I should've counted my blessings, at least I'd been chosen a Light Fae instead of being forced to endure the court of endless night. Resuming my perusal of the verdant lands below, I focused far ahead to where the other kingdoms within the continent of Crescentia lay, those ruled by Fae imbued by magic from the other gods: the wolvryn, immortalis, and spellbinders.

Being tied to one of those beasts could certainly have been much worse.

My shoulders dropped with a sigh, causing me to accidentally lean into Reign's unrelenting chest. "*Oh, Raysa,*" I cursed, before sitting straight up once again.

A dark chuckle vibrated behind me, carrying on the whipping winds until it surrounded me like a blanket. "It's a long ride to the Conservatory, princess. I suggest you get comfortable."

This time the derisive lilt to the pet name seemed slightly less jagged.

"I'm fine," I gritted out.

"Good, we wouldn't want Pyra to feel you tense up and decide you're a threat. You do know what happens when phoenixes feel threatened, right?" Without glancing back, I could almost feel the wicked grin on his face.

"No..."

"They shed their skin and are reborn in a sweltering pyre."

I gulped, the sound so loud I'm certain it rang out over the swirling winds.

Reign's steel hold tightened around me, forcing my shoulders to butt against the unforgiving planes of his chest. "So relax, unless you prefer to kill us both in a blazing inferno before you even set foot on Fae lands."

I held my shoulders stiff against his body, but I willed myself to relax somewhat. "From everything you've told me, it might be a kinder fate."

Another chuckle shook his chest against my back, the smooth sound surprisingly warm and inviting, like the warm tea with honey Aidan would make for me as a child when I was ill. I was rarely ever sick, but I'd often pretend to be only to get the sweet treat.

"Maybe for you," he murmured. His tone was quiet, the typical booming suddenly vanished. I wasn't even certain I'd heard him correctly.

All attempts at civil conversation died out at that point, and I spent the rest of the journey considering my new status as a Light Fae and imagining what life would bring at the Conservatory of Luce.

I must have nodded off because my stomach climbed into my throat, waking me from a fitful sleep. I lifted my head from Reign's chest to see we were descending, a line of saliva dribbling down my chin to my utter mortification.

"Rise and shine, princess." His rough voice moved like silky shadows across my eardrum. "We've arrived."

Chapter Five

A*elia*

Two sprawling fortresses stretched out below, divided by a meandering river. One radiated light like the most brilliant sunrise, while interminable darkness cloaked the other. Reign must have noticed my puckered brows because he pressed his lips to my ear as we continued our descent. "I suppose a little history lesson is in order. The Conservatory of Luce is on our left—"

"Clearly," I muttered, using the sarcasm as a shield against the traitorous sensations his mouth against the shell of my ear elicited.

"Well, if you already know everything, princess, then I'll save my breath."

"No," I blurted. "Tell me about the other one, the dark fortress across the river."

"That is Arcanum Citadel, where the finest minds and strongest hearts of the Court of Umbral Shadows study and train. *Strength from Darkness, Power through Pain* is the motto to which the students adhere."

From the corner of my eye, I caught his expression turning wistful, but it vanished before I was certain.

"And the motto of the Conservatory?"

"*Forged in Light, Tempered in Truth.* It doesn't quite have the same ominous ring to it, now does it?"

I slowly shook my head. Thank the stars. "And why are the two universities so close?" They appeared to sit right along the border of each court.

"Why do you think?"

I chewed on my lower lip as I considered. There would only be one logical reason to have enemies so close to one another. "To train against each other."

"Very good, princess."

A streak of murky shadows darted across the sky and Pyra banked left. My hands tightened around the pommel as I teetered off the saddle.

"By the gods' blood," he hissed. "Hold on!"

"I'm trying," I cried out, my palm instinctively lifting to my chest and the necklace hidden beneath my dress. *Oh, please do not die today.*

The beast wrapped in shadows circled closer, and this time I could make out a dark-haired rider perched atop the winged creature. The monster's head resembled that of a giant bird while its bottom half appeared similar to a muscled stallion.

"What is that?" I shouted against the wind.

Dark tendrils coiled around us, like icy fingers dancing across a grave. My instructor expertly guided our mount through the muddy haze until we re-emerged on the other side. The winged animal spun toward us and the shadows morphed again. A projectile careened toward us.

"Your introduction to life at the rival academies," Reign finally replied as he jerked the reins to the right and Pyra darted toward the ground, just missing the spear of shadows.

"Come on, old girl, *desentim*. We just need to get a little closer."

Pyra tucked her wings to her sides and we hurtled toward the ground, wind lashing the hair across my face. My heart catapulted up my throat with the breakneck speed of our downward climb. A golden orb encased the Conservatory just ahead.

"Almost there," Reign rasped out.

Another barrage of shadow daggers hurtled toward us, and squeezing my eyes closed, I waited for the impending sting of mystical blades. Pyra twisted and turned, Reign's muscular arms the only thing keeping me in the saddle. A sharp ping snapped my eyes open to the sight of a dagger bouncing off Reign's cloak and disintegrating to ash.

What in all the kingdoms?

Before I could draw in a steadying breath, the golden sphere settled over us and a wave of warmth blanketed my icy bones. Reign exhaled sharply and tugged on Pyra's reins, the phoenix leveling out.

"Relax, we're safe now." His deep voice sailed across the breeze as if his mouth were pressed to my ear again, only this time, it clearly was not. He sat up, tense behind me, the coiled muscles of his abdomen brushing my back.

"What was that thing?"

"The Shadow Fae skyrider or the hippogriff?"

"The second one."

"A hippogriff is half-eagle, half-horse. Surely, they taught you something at those primary schools for Kin?" I shook my head and he released a grunt of disgust. Like it was our fault we weren't educated. "All students at both universities are paired with a flying mount. You will be too."

My thoughts flickered back to Lord Liander and those wings of smoke. "But I thought Fae could fly." I eyed my professor who was lacking shadowed appendages of his own.

"Only the most powerful can summon wings. With some

Fae, it comes with time, and with others, never at all. Having a beast to ride for training is incredibly advantageous."

I tried to wrap my mind around the fact that I'd be riding one of these winged fiends by myself before long. Not only that, but I'd also be battling midair against Shadow Fae with actual powers. If I survived my first day...

The phoenix's talons hit the ground, curling into the lush lawn, and my body hurtled forward with the movement. If it weren't for the steel bands of flesh and blood draped around my middle, I would have flown over the pommel and fallen head-first into the expanse of verdant green.

Righting myself in a lame attempt to preserve a modicum of dignity, I heaved out an un-ladylike breath at the towering building standing at the edge of the enchanting forest.

The Conservatory loomed over us, a beacon of ethereal beauty amidst the wild greens. Its exterior was bathed in a soft, luminous glow that seemed to emanate from within the shimmery marble stone. Towering spires adorned with intricate carvings of celestial images reached towards the sky, catching the light of the sun in a dazzling display. The walls, crafted from shimmering white marble, veined with streams of iridescent crystal, reflected the vibrant colors of the surrounding flora, setting the entire fortress ablaze.

Elaborate gardens and water features cascaded around the perimeter, teeming with vibrant and exotic blooms that seemed to thrive under the radiance of the Conservatory's magic—or *rais*, I supposed. Graceful archways adorned with delicate vines and intricate filigree called to me, inviting me into this mystical academy. I could feel its power pulsating, like a tremor skimming across my skin.

It may have been beautiful, but a deep part of me knew it was just as equally deadly. That had been something else Aidan had drilled into me since I was a child. *Behind great beauty lies twisted, unfathomable darkness.* I vowed to remember that as

Reign drew his cloak over my head and leapt off Pyra. I wobbled on the back of the huge beast as soon as his hold fell away.

"Come, your destiny awaits." He unhooked my bag from the saddle and extended his hand once again, an unreadable expression crossing those bottomless, pitch orbs.

I chose to forgo his help this time. Sliding off Pyra's back while holding down my voluminous skirt, I managed to land on surprisingly steady feet, considering my legs felt like jelly after the aerial acrobatics, not to mention the hour aboard the phoenix before that. The sheaths strapped at my thighs had begun to dig into my skin, and I'd been fortunate my own daggers hadn't impaled me on the long journey. Perhaps, Reign was right about their placement.

My instructor handed me my bag then slid his arms behind his back, his face a mask of stone as he turned for the arched marble entryway. No guards manned the entrance, and there was no daunting gate as I'd imagined, only a faint hum and gentle glow surrounded the gilded doors of the Conservatory.

He moved up the steps, and my gaze finally dropped from the imposing ingress to the male in front of me. His cloak was gone, replaced by silky, shadow wings that spanned across his broad shoulders. They were much like the Shadow Fae's who'd come to claim me, only several times larger. They writhed and twirled across his form, whispering along an invisible breeze.

I stepped closer but an aura of sheer power hurtled me back.

Reign spun around, a wry grin on his lips. "Be careful not to stand too close, princess."

I barely restrained a dramatic eyeroll. "Where were your wings before?"

His shoulders lifted casually. "They come and go as they will." He ticked his head toward the elaborate gilded doors, made of what seemed like pure light. Glowing runes were engraved across the gleaming metal, the luminous symbols beginning to vibrate at our approach.

The doors glided open with a sharp keening sound that grated across my eardrums. He spun around again, those piercing irises raking over me, that look more lethal than any male's touch had any right to be. His brows pinched as he regarded me with that slow scrutinizing gaze. "May Raysa and Noxus be with you."

"Thank you," I muttered, oddly unnerved by his blessing. I forced my feet up the final step, and a surge of power crashed over me. Every nerve-ending in my body lit up and I could barely compel my legs forward. Crushing weight slammed into my chest, my shoulders, and my lungs stalled. What in all the worlds?

Heaving in a deep breath, I focused every ounce of power I had into my legs. I was strong, physically. I'd toiled the fields for the Fae nobles for years. Some silly magical door wasn't going to stop me now. My heart smashed against my ribs, my chest much too tight, but I fought anyway. Fighting was nothing new to me.

As quickly as it had come, the resistance vanished, and I careened through the opening right into Reign's waiting arms. My eyes lifted to meet his, an apology and a thank you on the tip of my tongue—but somehow, I managed to swallow down both.

He released me and took a measured step back, and again, that unreadable expression darkened the harsh beauty of his face. "You continue to surprise me, princess."

"Because I was able to walk across the threshold of the Conservatory?"

"Not just any threshold." He dipped his head toward the entrance, and the faint glow of some sort of mystical barrier coalesced. "The Veil of Judgement." My eyes widened as I waited for him to further explain the cryptic name. "Only those deemed worthy to attend the Conservatory are allowed to pass into the Hall of Glory."

"Oh." My hand reached out, fingers wiggling through the glittering veil. That must have been the resistance I'd felt. Though I'd never admit it to my arrogant professor, I'd barely made it through. That didn't seem promising.

I took a moment to gape at the expansive foyer and the majestic fountain at its center, its waters flowing with a gentle luminescence that cast shifting shadows across the room. A loud thud spun my head over my shoulder to the still open doors.

A monstrous silver hippogriff with two riders landed just beyond the steps on the lush lawn of the Conservatory, and I staggered back a few feet, right into the wall of Reign's chest.

"Don't worry, he's one of ours," he whispered.

I eyed the silver-haired, pointy-eared male as he dismounted. A flowing beard the same hue of his light hair nearly reached his silk tunic. The second male slid off the hippogriff, his inquisitive gaze alternating between the mystical doorway and me. A sneer curled his lip as his eyes ran over my softly curved ears. "Since when does the Conservatory of Luce allow mortals to grace its fine halls?"

"It is not up to you to question the goddess," Reign snapped at the young Fae.

"Yes, rightly so." The bearded male glanced over his spectacles before he ambled toward us, wings of pure radiant light shooting over his shoulders. The snooty young male paused at the entryway, the nostrils of his sharp nose flaring.

Did he know he was to be judged? That seemed like an unfair advantage. I suddenly hoped he was denied entrance because of that snooty remark, though the thought was pointless, really. I was certain I'd face the same prejudices from all the Fae I'd encounter at the university.

"Come on, then, Delius, cross over," the older male commanded.

With one last disdainful glare in my direction, he stepped up the marble stairs and across the threshold. The moment his boot reached the shimmering globe, a flare of brilliant light blasted from the male's torso and a soundless scream curved his fine lips. The explosion of light was so blinding, I was forced to shield my eyes from its scorching rays.

By the time I opened them again, nothing but a pile of sooty ash remained of the Fae.

Chapter Six

An odd, strangled sound erupted from my lips as I stared at the pristine silver-veined floor now marred by the ashy remains of the Light Fae.

The bearded male released a sigh, his shoulders rounding. "And he seemed to have such potential. One can never be too sure." With a shake of his head, he moved toward us nonchalantly, as if that Fae hadn't just disintegrated in an explosion of ethereal light right in front of us. He dipped his head, acknowledging Reign. "Professor Darkthorn, I'm pleased to see you had better luck with your most recent acquisition."

"Mmm, yes." Reign's dark gaze lifted to mine for an instant before returning to the elder male. "Aelia Ravenwood, this is Professor Litehaus, he is the Healing Light's instructor."

"Ravenwood?" The old professor's light brows knitted. "As in Feywood?" He lifted his spectacles from his aquiline nose and wiped both lenses with the hem of his tunic before replacing them. His slow scrutiny of my rounded ears had the hair on the back of my neck prickling. "Hmm, how very peculiar."

"I thought so as well, but she clearly bares the mark of the Court of Ethereal Light." Reign signaled to the neckline of my dress. "Show the professor, Aelia."

My lips screwed into a pout, the idea of baring my chest to this old man twisting my stomach, but this would not be the hill I died upon. Gingerly pushing aside the fabric to reveal a tiny corner of the mark, I held my breath as the professor moved closer to examine me.

"There is certainly no denying it, Reign. Rounded ears or not, the girl is imbued with *rais*." His eyes narrowed, a vein pulsing across his forehead. "It seems you've come across quite an interesting find, my boy. Well done."

Reign dipped his head. "I am merely a humble servant of Raysa and the King of Ethereal Light," he muttered.

"Blessed be their names," the old professor responded.

Humble? I nearly grunted aloud.

When Reign lifted his head, the tendon in his jaw twitched before that mask of calm slid back into place. "I must escort Aelia to the first-year dormitories. You'll have to excuse us."

"Oh yes, of course." Professor Litehaus signaled down the vast hallway and I moved into step beside Reign.

With everything that had happened since my arrival, I hadn't had a moment to take in the grand entrance of the Conservatory or the sprawling corridors that led deeper into the heart of the Fae institution. The arched ceiling towered over us, glass panes reflecting the golden sun's shimmering rays. It couldn't be possible, but somehow the sun seemed to shine brighter over the Light Court than Feywood. Perhaps, it was all part of Raysa's mystical powers.

As we crossed through the grand foyer adorned with intricate filigree and delicate archways, illuminated by the soft, ethereal glow of crystals embedded within the walls, I couldn't keep from gawking. The floor beneath my feet was a mosaic of shimmering marble tiles, reflecting the patterns of light that danced through the stained-glass windows overhead. It was incredible and completely unreal. Fragrant blooms and trailing vines cascaded from ornate planters, their vibrant colors adding to the magical ambiance of the space.

"Close your mouth, princess. Any Fae that walks these halls must act like they belong here."

"Right," I growled, adjusting the strap of my bag across my shoulders.

The slap of our footsteps across the marble resonated through the silent space, muffling my thundering heartbeat. For a university filled with blood-thirsty Fae students, I fully expected to see at least a few of them floating around the hallowed halls.

"Where is everyone?" I whispered, so as not to shatter the eerie silence.

"Still sleeping, likely. Classes go well into the evening so that the Light Fae may have a chance to train at twilight. It's never truly dark here, save a measly hour of dusk, while across the river, eternal night prevails."

A shiver crawled up my spine at the prospect of taking on one of those Shadow Fae in the dark without Reign's magical shadow-repelling cloak. Which reminded me...

"Is your cloak spelled against shadows?"

"Something like that," he muttered.

"How am I ever supposed to learn anything about the Shadow Arts with your cryptic responses?"

"It's your first day, princess. Relax. There will be plenty to learn in the next few years... if you survive that long." He muttered the last part under his breath, and irritation puckered my brow.

"I'll survive, don't you worry about that, *professor*." I hissed his title with the same disdain he typically used with my nickname.

Reign cast a sidelong glance in my direction, but the hint of a smirk curled the end of his lip. He led me around the corner of the glistening walls to a glass atrium. In the center, suspended in midair, a floating glass staircase spiraled all the way up to the soaring ceiling.

"The dormitories are that way." He pointed skyward. "The first floor is reserved for our most senior students, while the first-years are on the uppermost levels."

My head tipped back to the seemingly never-ending spiral. "How many floors up is that?"

"As you can imagine, first-years make up our largest number of students, especially at the beginning of the year." He ascended the first step, with me trailing after him. "Your birthday happens to fall close to the start of our next term, but due to the nature of our matriculation upon a Fae's twentieth year, we have a sort of rolling enrollment year-round. As such, the top four floors are reserved for our novices."

"Four out of?" I huffed out as we passed the second level.

"Eight. There are a few floors above, but they are of no concern to you."

Wonderful, so I'd be trudging up four stories at minimum, eight at the maximum. Considering my status as a powerless Kin, I'd likely be assigned to the highest level. As I followed him up the steps, I performed a quick calculation given the numbers he'd divulged.

"How many first-years do not make it to the second?"

"Roughly fifty percent."

"Stars, that's not too encouraging."

"It isn't meant to be, it's the brutal truth. Half of the novices at the Conservatory will return home in a gilded urn."

My breath caught as images of the Fae male drifted to the forefront of my mind. He hadn't even survived crossing the threshold. How many others suffered the same fate? Reign's whispered words as I lingered at the entrance upon our arrival echoed through my thoughts: *May Raysa and Noxus be with you.*

Professor Litehaus's prospective pupil had gotten no such blessing. I couldn't help but wonder what had earned me that benediction from the mercurial Professor of Shadows. I watched him from the corner of my eye as I trudged up the countless steps. Those wings of pure night clung to his body like silk, molding to his powerful shoulders.

And it wasn't only his wings, dark shadows now slithered across every inch of his finely sculpted form. Since he'd shed the cloak, every twitch of his muscled, tanned forearms caught my eye. Black runes ran up and down every inch of exposed flesh, only intensifying his dark aura.

"It's rude to stare, *princess.*"

I started, his booming voice echoing across the vast stairwell and shattering the tense silence. I dropped my gaze to my worn boots. "I wasn't staring," I grumbled.

He lifted a cocky brow. "No?"

"I was merely observing. Like you said, if I plan on surviving the next few years, I'll need to understand what I am up against. And in case it wasn't clear before, I haven't exactly spent much time with Light or Shadow Fae."

"It's certainly clear."

With a grunt, I looked away from my professor, grasped onto the straps of my bag, and focused my attention on the top of the landing. With each step, I gritted my teeth as my daggers slid precariously closer to my lady parts. I'd never be so careless about their placement again, assuming I'd be forced into another gown. I simply wanted this nightmare of a day to be over, and it was only mid-morning.

A thousand years later, we finally reached the top floor. I'd been right, eighth level for the lowly Kin turned Light Fae.

Reign led the way down the quiet hall, shards of light spearing through the stained-glass windows overhead and bathing every nook and cranny in an otherworldly luminescence. I wondered how the Fae could sleep with the constant sunshine streaming in. About mid-way down the corridor, my escort stopped in front of a door made of such pale wood it was practically white. A glowing rune hovered an inch off the door, in the spot where a knob might have normally been.

"Go ahead, let's see how deeply buried that *rais* truly is." He signaled toward the dancing rune.

I spun at him, brows scrunched together. "What exactly am I supposed to do?"

"Unlock the door."

"How?" I all but shrieked, dropping my bag.

"With the protective rune. It has been spelled to recognize your mystical signature."

He may have been speaking the language of the savage wolvryn who roam the Wilds. "Excuse me?"

Reign expelled a frustrated breath, as if I were the stupidest Kin ever to walk these hallowed halls. I almost pointed out I was probably the *only* Kin to do so. "When you crossed the threshold of the Conservatory, your unique mystical signature, or aura, if you will, was imprinted into the university's network. With that, this rune was created. Only you and your roommate, along with select faculty, will have access to your dormitory."

"Please tell me you're one of the select few." The moment the words were out, my cheeks flamed at the insinuation. "I only meant because... It's not that I wanted you to enter my room—"

Reign lifted a hand, cutting off my embarrassing ramblings. "No need to get so flustered, princess. I would never expect anything other than complete adherence to the rules from someone like you."

"What does that mean?" The embarrassment quickly morphed into irritation. He didn't know anything about me—and on the contrary, I was quite the rebel.

"Only that improper relations between faculty and students

are strictly forbidden and, if you're so intent on surviving, I'd never expect you to suggest something inappropriate."

"Of course I wouldn't." That gods' forsaken heat blanketed my cheeks, and the ghost of a smile flickered across my professor's dark countenance. "I don't plan on pursuing any sort of relationship—" Oh Raysa, what was wrong with my mouth? Why was I explaining my plans for my depressing future love life to my professor?

"Will you just try the door?"

Right. Clenching my teeth to keep any more ridiculousness from dribbling out, I squared off with the door. I eyed it for a long moment, waiting for some mystical energy to bubble up inside me. Defeated, I turned to my irritating escort. "What do I have to do, exactly?"

"Simply sweep your palm across the rune."

"Why didn't you just say so?"

"It seemed more entertaining this way." A lopsided smile parted his lips, and stars, my heart attempted to somersault right out of the safety of my ribcage.

Clapping my hand over my chest to smother the traitorous reaction, I inhaled a steadying breath. When had I become one of those simpering females, knees wobbling at the sight of a handsome male? This was not like me at all. Throwing my shoulders back, I focused my attention on the rune and slowly waved my palm over it.

A flicker of warmth tingled across my skin and the door squealed open. "I did it!" I rose to my tiptoes, about a second away from dancing a happy jig when I realized I had no one to celebrate the accomplishment with.

"Well done, princess, you opened a door." Reign's sarcasm was so thick I could slather it on an entire loaf of stale bread.

I bit back a nasty reply, reminding myself he was a professor and not one of my friends from the village, and took a step toward the threshold before pausing. Spinning back around to said professor, I lifted a wary brow. "Will I be judged again? Any possibility of being torched from the inside out?"

He slowly shook his head. "Your worth was established the moment you successfully crossed the entrance of the Conservatory, Aelia. No one can take that away from you."

There was something about the sincerity in his tone that momentarily chased away the ice that had settled in my veins upon my arrival. Dipping my head, I picked up my bag, threw my shoulders back and stepped across the threshold into my new life.

Chapter Seven

A^{elia}

Reign's fingertips lightly brushed beneath my chin before he exerted more pressure, and my jaw slammed closed with a sharp snap of teeth. Twisting free of his touch, I dropped my bag at the door and attempted a nonchalant perusal of my room, but I could not stop myself from gawking at the splendor rolling out before me. The room was so spacious it could hold our entire cottage within its walls. With high ceilings that seemed to stretch endlessly upwards, shimmering with a soft ethereal light that filtered in through the large ivy-framed windows, it was utterly enchanting.

The furniture was crafted from living light wood, grown and shaped by what could only be magic to fit perfectly into the room. Two beds were nestled in alcoves lined with moss and soft, luminescent flora, providing a dream-like quality. Each bed was draped with gossamer fabrics that fluttered gently on an invisible breeze.

A large, circular table made of polished stone sat at the center of the room, surrounded by chairs that seemed to have been formed from the roots of a great tree. Along the walls, shelves were carved into the very foundation holding an array of ancient books, mystical artifacts, and small glass vials filled with ingredients for what I could only assume was potion-making.

I circled the space, moving slowly to take it all in. I'd never seen such luxury, but more than that, I'd never felt so much power teeming from a chamber. It was as if its very walls exuded mystical energy. Had I simply been ignorant to it before this symbol engraved into my flesh, or had I never encountered it in Feywood?

As if Reign had read my mind—and who knew, perhaps he had—he cleared his throat, interrupting my wild mental musings. "You should begin to feel your *rais* now that you are on Light Fae soil. Most Fae develop their abilities slowly with age, but one of the first skills most Fae experience is illumination sight—the ability to see beyond the visible spectrum, allowing you to perceive things such as auras and energy patterns. Then later you'll develop abilities such as photokinesis, healing light, solar empowerment and so on."

"Well, that explains a lot." I turned toward my professor and the silky shadows that surrounded him. If I squinted and looked past the ever-moving midnight silhouettes, a murky haze emanated from his form.

I still wondered what had brought a Shadow Fae to teach at the most renowned Light Fae university of the entire Court of Ethereal Light. But after spending only a few hours alone with the male, I knew I wouldn't receive an answer any time soon.

Reign's piercing midnight orbs caught mine and I quickly pivoted my gaze to the bed he stood in front of.

"You mentioned a roommate?" I blurted.

"Yes, the female should be arriving tomorrow. My colleague was forced to travel to the far western corner of the realm to retrieve her. Some Fae choose to live in the outskirts of the territory to avoid the politics of court. I don't blame them really..." He spoke the last part under his breath, as if he hadn't meant to say the words aloud. "Nevertheless, she will be here soon. You will have the day to sort out your affairs, then tomorrow you will have orientation, and the following day, classes will begin." Motioning toward the nook in which my bed lay, his gaze landed on a scroll sitting atop the nightstand. "You will find your schedule there, along with the names of your teachers and the locations of your classes. The scroll will be updated daily with any new information you may need."

"Like magic?"

His lips twisted in amusement. "Yes, princess, magic."

I turned toward the bedstand a bit too eagerly, and as I did a sharp squeal burst through my clenched lips when one of my daggers cut into my thigh. *Curses!* I should have removed them the moment we entered this damned chamber.

Reign's nostrils flared as his dark gaze darted to my billowing skirts. A trickle of blood slid down my thigh, moving down my calf, before appearing from beneath the curtain of taffeta and silk.

"You're bleeding," he muttered, his voice holding a jagged edge that wasn't there a second ago. He stepped closer, and I took one back.

"You were right, okay?" Heat flushed my cheeks at the embarrassing confession. "It's not often I wear blades beneath a gown, and in my rush this morning, I didn't fasten the sheaths well."

"So you've impaled yourself with your own dagger?" A hint of delight laced his lips.

"Clearly not *impaled*!" I snarled. "It's just a scratch."

"Then why can I smell your blood from here?"

"Don't you Fae have superior senses?"

"Yes, *we* Fae do." He inched closer, and I prayed to Raysa to strike me down on the spot. "I did not bring my new acquisition safely all this way to lose you to bacteria from a common flesh wound." Reign dropped to his knees in front of me, and my jaw fell along with him. "Lift up your skirts."

"I will do no such thing." My fingers curled around the layers of lace.

"Aelia..." That growl sent the heat from my cheeks racing between my legs, to the very spot my professor was now trying to uncover.

"It's nothing, I'm sure. I'll be just fine."

His dark eyes lifted to mine, starlight blistering within the smoldering onyx. "Just allow me to check, and then I will leave you alone." A dark shadow slithered off his arm and snaked beneath the hem of my dress. "I forget what delicate sensibilities you mortals have."

A hiss parted my lips as icy fingers danced beneath my skirts. Devastatingly slowly, the shadows pulled up the layers of my dress, baring my legs up to the knees. Reign moved between my thighs and all the air caught in my throat. My heart kicked at my ribs, an anxious flutter sending my entire body into a fit of tremors. His hand drifted up my thigh and I clenched my bottom lip between my teeth. His fingers deftly worked at the soft leather sheaths, never once making actual contact with my skin. *To my dismay*?!

An instant later, he popped up, rising to his full height. An unreadable expression darkened his features for an endless moment before the icy mask slid back into place. "You were right. It's just a scratch. You'll find a tincture in the bathing chamber along with a bandage. I've adjusted the sheaths as they should sit on your thighs. Should you choose to continue to wear them beneath dresses, I suggest you position them as such."

"Thank you," I mumbled, before I could stop myself.

Dark brows slammed together, those ominous onyx shadows seeming to double in size. "By thanking a Fae, you are indebting yourself to them, and trust me, princess, I am the last person to whom you want to owe a favor."

"I take it back, then. Your modicum of kindness has gone completely unnoticed."

The hint of a smirk crossed his lips. "Good, it appears you're learning."

I didn't think I'd ever learn quickly enough to survive my first week at the university, let alone the next few years.

Reign turned toward the door, and it took every ounce of willpower and good sense to keep my mouth from pleading with him to stay. He was the only Fae I knew here, after all, and the idea of being left alone in this sprawling fortress had unbridled anxiety blossoming from every corner of my being.

His hand closed on the doorknob, but he canted his head over his shoulder, dark eyes finding mine. "Remember, the door is spelled shut. Only you or your roommate may enter uninvited. I suggest you keep it that way."

I nodded quickly, worrying my bottom lip between my teeth. With a stern nod, he slipped through the doorway. The moment the door sealed closed behind him, I slumped down at the foot of my bed and splayed out across the mattress. It was like sinking into a cloud.

A groan spilled out and a smile crept across my lips despite the day. Well, I'd been right about one thing last night. I would be living in the lap of luxury, only instead of warming a Fae lord's bed, I'd be fighting for survival against brutal Fae students.

I wasn't certain which held better odds.

There was still the option of escape. No... I could never risk Aidan's life like that.

Exhaustion bled through my bones and all I wanted was to close my eyes and fall into Noxus's arms of oblivion. A slight sting on my inner thigh kept my lids from drifting closed.

Stars! First, I'd tend to my wound, then sleep.

Pushing myself off the mattress, I forced my weary legs to the bathing room door Reign had pointed out earlier. I prayed to all the gods they had heated water.

I swung the door open and the rush of rippling cascades echoed across my eardrums. It was a good thing Reign was gone, because he would have clearly frowned upon my gaping maw. The bathing chamber wasn't a chamber at all, but rather a mystical space nestled within a lush, verdant grove. Towering trees with iridescent leaves formed a living canopy, filtering sunlight into soft, dappled patterns that danced across the ground and water.

The centerpiece of the bathing area was a series of miniature cascading waterfalls, flowing from one level to another in a symphony of crystal-clear ponds. The water flowed into the natural pools carved into the stone floor, their edges softened by centuries of flow, and lined with smooth pebbles and moss. My gaze darted from the crystalline pools to the walls of the bathing room which were covered in a tapestry of matching moss and ferns, interspersed with flowering vines that released a soothing, natural fragrance into the air.

The open sky above was just visible through the canopy, allowing me to gaze up at the sunlight streaming through the shifting patterns of clouds. How was any of this possible? Surely, I'd have a terrible ache in my jaw soon if I kept this up.

Focusing on the reason for my trip to the bathing room, I searched the stone vanity for the tincture and bandages, but the rippling waterfalls called to me. How could I not take a quick dip? Crouching down at the edge of the stone pond, I dipped my fingers through the tepid waters. Lifting my skirts, I crawled to a smaller pool with warm mist floating along the translucent surface. As expected, this one was deliciously heated.

Tossing all thoughts of my little scratch aside, I peeled off the cumbersome dress and allowed the soothing scents and sounds of the magical bathing area to chase everything else away.

Chapter Eight

Sunlight streamed in through the stained-glass windows, bathing the chamber in a heavenly glow of warm ochre, deep vermilion, and a brilliant jade. Reign hadn't been exaggerating about the endless light. The sun had crested the peaks of the Alucian Mountains to the west shortly after two in the morning, according to the sundial hung on the wall. I'd tossed and turned, riddled with anxiety ever since. The tranquility the steamy whirlpool had provided had been short-lived.

A golden spark drew my attention to the scroll perched on the nightstand. The swirl of glittering light danced along the rolled parchment, pushing it open until it stretched out across the pale wood. Black scrawling raced across the yellowing paper, and I gaped at the mystical message until the final word was inked.

Aelia Ravenwood
Designation: First-year

Squad: Flare
Squad Leader: Heaton Liteschild

Daily Instructions:
Report to the Hall of Luminescence for orientation at oh-nine hundred hours.

Tentative Classes:
Photokinesis
Illumination Sight
Healing Light
Combat
Shadow Arts

A crude sketch appeared beneath the note, presumably a map detailing the directions to the hall. I turned the scroll around trying to orient myself from what little I remembered from my arrival yesterday. I'd been so consumed with my spiraling thoughts that I'd barely paid any attention while Reign led us through the Conservatory.

I suppose I'll figure it out somehow.

Placing the scroll back on the nightstand, I pushed the silky coverlet back and forced my weary bones to the edge of the bed. One would think my body would have reveled in a night spent on such a fine mattress, but instead, my muscles ached from the soft cushion as opposed to the tough straw it had been accustomed to. My thoughts whirled to my home and my heart, too, ached for the only father I'd ever known. Would Aidan be all right without me? In all the chaos yesterday, I'd completely forgotten to ask about correspondence. Surely, the university would allow me to send letters to Aidan.

Tiptoeing across the quiet room so as not to shatter the

unearthly stillness, I stood at the arched windows and stared into the rolling countryside. If I squinted hard enough, I could just make out the deep greens of the Feywood Forest at a distance. Or maybe it was some other forest along the edges of the Court of Ethereal Light. Reign hadn't been exaggerating yesterday, the education of the average Kin was severely lacking. If Aidan hadn't insisted on instructing me himself in not only self-defense, but also countless tales from history books he'd bartered for, I would be utterly clueless as to the lands of the Fae. Either way, I pretended I could see Aidan tending to the chickens and gathering their eggs to be sold at the market. He'd be fine without me; he simply had to be.

A flicker of light drew my attention across the river to the pitch black that stretched across the Court of Umbral Shadows. A shiver raced up my spine as a winged creature sped through the interminable darkness. Perhaps, I'd been too quick to complain. Living in eternal night would have been a thousand times worse than putting up with the ever-creeping sunlight.

Forcing myself away from the window and pointless reminiscing of the past, I marched toward the closet I'd found yesterday. I'd spent the entire day locked in my room, too scared to venture beyond the safety of the warded door, but today would be different. Today, I'd be forced to find my way to the Hall of Luminescence and orientation.

To my relief, I'd found a variety of useful clothing, along with a smattering of fancy gowns within the wardrobe. My fingers found the silky material of one of the dresses, and I wondered why one would ever need such an extravagant ballgown at a university such as this. Surely, they didn't expect us to don something this elaborate for classes.

Pushing aside the lace and satin frocks, I found the familiar, worn leathers I'd hung last night. They were similar enough to the other ones hanging from the rod, only the material was soft and a little threadbare from continuous use. I grabbed them anyway, needing this little piece of home today. Spearing my legs into the supple dark leather, their feel brought the familiarity I desperately needed. Tugging my old tunic over my head and tucking my necklace beneath, I breathed in its musky scent coupled with the softer undertones of lavender I used to wash my clothes by the river.

Muffled voices in the hallway sent my heart catapulting up my throat. Yanking my tunic all the way down, I spun toward the entrance as the door whipped open. A blonde female appeared in the doorway, her wild, ashen curls shooting out in a dozen directions. Her pale blue eyes found mine, and her pert nose crinkled as she regarded me. "It's true, then!" She raced toward me, then stood on her tiptoes, her dainty little fingers reaching for my ears.

I leapt back, brows slamming together. "Excuse me!"

A sheepish smile crossed her heart-shaped face, and a flash of crimson coated her cheeks. "Oh, by the goddess, where are my manners? I'm Rue Liteschild, your new roommate. And you must be the new Kin..." A nervous energy fluttered all around the Light Fae as she regarded me with unbridled curiosity.

"My name is Aelia Ravenwood," I finally managed.

"Incredible!" She clapped her petite hands and lifted onto her tiptoes.

I practically towered over her, standing at least a head over the tiny female.

A male peered through the doorway, eyes intent on me— or rather my curved ears. "Is everyone decent? May I come in?"

"Of course you can, Heaton," my new roommate exclaimed. "Don't be so uptight and get in here."

I, for one, appreciated his sense of decorum. "I'm dressed," I murmured lamely.

His light blue eyes brushed over me as he entered. "You'll have to excuse my sister's excitement, but she's been waiting for this day her entire life."

Rue's head bounced up and down, her full head of flaxen hair nearly poking my eye out.

"Your sister?" I glanced between the siblings. Now that I took a minute to observe the pair more closely, I did notice a certain resemblance in their wide-set eyes and sloping noses. Though where Rue's hair was a mane of tight spiraled curls, her brother's was long and straight, held back in a neat tie at his nape.

Rue latched onto her sibling's arm and bounced a bit more. "This is my brother, Heaton, and he's squad leader this year. It's his fourth year at the Conservatory, and he's pretty much amazing."

A rosy hue darkened Heaton's cheeks, the color rushing all the way up to the tips of his pointed ears. Glittering hoops of gold lined the sharp extremities, glinting beneath the rays of sunlight pouring into the chamber. "My sister overexaggerates, as always." He ran his palm across the back of his neck.

"Well, I imagine you must be good to be selected squad leader." Whatever that meant. My thoughts flickered back to the parchment. That name... I grabbed the scroll from the nightstand and unrolled it. Pressing my finger to the dark ink, I glanced up at the tall male. "Heaton Liteschild. You're my squad leader."

"Oh, that means you must be mine, too, since she and I are roommates!" Rue began clapping again as she raced for the bed on the other side of the room. Sure enough, a scroll had appeared beside the faery light. Her luminous eyes widened as they scanned the parchment. "Flare Squad, led by the one and only Heaton Liteschild!" she cried.

Heaton's lips flipped into a scowl, darkening his friendly countenance.

"Oh, Heaton, erase that frown this instant." Rue swatted at her brother. "Don't tell me you're not happy to be my squad leader?"

"It's not that, Rue. I'm merely surprised. As head of the

squad, there are certain difficult decisions that I'll be forced to make, and I'm simply stunned that they would allow me to make those choices when a sibling is involved."

"Well, I'm not surprised at all. Clearly, they realize you won't be influenced by nepotism." She threw him a playful wink. "Unless it's something I really, really need, right, Heat?"

Shaking his head, he ran his hand through his sister's unruly locks. "I'll give you a minute to acclimate, Rue, and I'll see you both in orientation in an hour."

I glanced up at the sundial and nodded. A trickle of unease surged to life, but one look at Rue's smiling face swallowed up the trepidation. After all the horror stories about my new room-mate I'd conjured up in my head last night, I couldn't have been more surprised.

She seemed absolutely lovely.

Perhaps, I'd simply gotten the wrong impression yesterday. Reign with his gloom and doom and ominous shadows had painted a much darker picture of what my future at the Conservatory held. Maybe he was wrong.

Chapter Nine

No, I was wrong.

It seemed Rue was the only shred of light in this horrible place. I thanked my lucky stars I'd ended up with her as my new roommate as I walked beside my lively companion into the Hall of Luminescence. Not only would I have been terribly lost in the never-ending, winding hallways, but I'm also fairly certain some Fae would have thrown me from the spiral staircase, judging by their hateful sneers. Even now, dozens of scathing glares bored into the side of my face, from teachers and students alike. Only Rue was completely oblivious to their hostile stares.

My roommate ushered us to the front row of the cavernous hall, much to my dismay, right in front of a raised dais. In a sea of blonde, honey gold and silver, my raven hair stood out absurdly amongst the other students, even the streak of platinum only seemed to call more attention. The arched rafters of the soaring ceiling loomed above us, brilliant light cascading in and casting a spotlight right on my rounded ears. An older male stood at the pulpit, his flowing white beard trailing down past his chest. Dazzling golden wings, seemingly made of Raysa's light themselves, fluttered across his shoulders. His crushed velvet robe was lined in gold piping, the indigo so deep it reminded me of the eggplants we grew in our garden. His curious gaze razed over me as I settled into the chair beside Rue.

Muttered voices echoed across the hall as more students and faculty arrived. Professors walked up the steps onto the stage, each one blatantly staring at the mortal Kin disgracing their hallowed halls. A dark form caught my attention from the far corner of the room, and my breaths quickened before my lips formed his name. Reign.

A thick silence descended over the hall as Professor Darkthorn stalked to the platform. It wasn't just the students that gave him a wide berth, but every member of the staff, too, seemed to balk at his presence. It was oddly comforting to know I wasn't the only one who found the Shadow Fae so intimidating.

Slithering shadows crawled up and down Reign's menacing form as he scaled the steps to center stage. He sported a similar doublet to the one he wore yesterday, only today the black satin was embroidered with hints of gold that popped against the dark background that clung to his muscled form like a second skin. His dark gaze chased in my direction, those bottomless onyx irises searing into me. I held that piercing stare for only a moment before my eyes cast down to my tangled fingers.

Once the professor of Shadow Arts was seated in a high-backed leather chair, the quiet murmurs began once more, and the tension in the room slowly dissipated.

"I see you've met Professor Reign?" Rue whispered.

"Hmm?" I attempted nonchalant, but judging by the arc in Rue's light brow, I was failing miserably.

"It's not like he's one who is easily missed. He is the only

Shadow Fae at the university." Her lively eyes cast in Reign's direction.

Following her line of sight, I allowed myself a moment to take in the sharp lines of his handsome face. "Why is he here, anyway?"

"No one knows for certain, but Heaton said that according to rumors, our Headmaster, Draven Lightshade, found him half-dead along the border a few years ago. He was banished from the Court of Umbral Shadows, which usually means a death sentence here in Light, but for some reason, Lightshade petitioned the Court Council to keep him." She shrugged. "He's proven an invaluable asset to the Conservatory from what I understand." Then she ticked her head at Reign seated on stage with his hands folded. A glimmer of silver caught my eye peeking from beneath his long sleeves, and I immediately recognized the thick bangles I'd noticed on the flight over. Rue followed my gaze, and a wicked grin curled her lips. "It's rumored that those bracelets keep his *nox* in check. Without them, he could overpower nearly anyone on campus."

A tremor raced up my spine as the power I'd felt surrounding the professor rose to the forefront of my mind. I wouldn't be at all surprised. There was something dark and lethal about that male's presence.

The elder Fae standing atop the stage cleared his throat and his luminous wings snapped out, bathing the male in an unearthly radiance. The entire hall fell silent. "Welcome initiates. For those of you odd souls who do not know me, I am Headmaster Draven Lightshade. Acceptance into the Conservatory of Luce is the highest honor that can be bestowed upon a Light Fae young adult. You have been chosen among countless Fae and only the most gifted, most powerful have been selected by the goddess herself. You will spend your years at the university honing your skills to serve King Elian of Ether and the mighty Court of Ethereal Light as the next generation of Royal

Guardians of the Court." He paused with a dramatic flourish, his words echoing across the sprawling chamber.

"We have been fortunate to live in peace since the Two Hundred Years War ended nearly thirty years ago, when our enemies in the Court of Infernal Night were vanquished. It is our duty to keep our neighbors across the Luminoc River, the Court of Umbral Shadows, in check, and to ensure they never rise against us. And that is why we train, to preserve the fragile balance between the two remaining courts. You'll be honed to lethal perfection, to become the Crown's instruments of destruction. As you know, we are also tasked with the protection of the powerless Kin to our south. Without us, they would undoubtedly succumb to the blood-thirsty creatures hidden in the depths of the Wilds. And without the mortals, we would lose our pool of laborers. Our duty to the Crown is of the utmost importance. Therefore, I want to make this abundantly clear; your life belongs to *me* for the next four years unless Raysa chooses to call for it sooner."

A faint snicker echoed from a few rows back, and the head-master's pale mossy irises nearly doubled in size. His sharp eyes focused on an initiate in the last row. "You, what is your name, boy?"

The silver-haired male stood and dipped his head. "Isaac Glimmersky."

"You find these sacred proceedings comical?"

"No, sir."

"Then why did you laugh?"

"I simply don't understand how Raysa, in her infinite wisdom, could have made such a mistake as inviting a lowly Kin to join us at the Conservatory."

Every head in the hall whirled toward me, dozens of scrutinizing gazes fixed to my dark hair and curved ears. Questioning murmurs filled the air, all clearly wondering the exact same thing. They weren't the only ones if I was being perfectly honest.

"It is not your job to question the goddess," the headmaster hissed. "It's treasonous." Then he pivoted to Reign and dipped his head ever so slightly.

A sinister grin curled the Shadow Fae's lips, and the inky darkness that cloaked his form shot across the room. I gasped as the bolt of pure black whizzed by, nearly decapitating my head from my shoulders. The dark tendrils of power found the Fae male, coiled around his lithe form, and a wordless scream curved his mouth. The shadows wrapped tight around his silk tunic until his choked gasps filled the air.

The female seated in the chair beside him buckled over, the sounds of her retching overpowering the boy's final attempts at drawing in blessed oxygen. Dark, twisted veins crawled across his skin, and his knees wobbled for an instant before he dropped to the ground with a sickening slap.

Reign's shadows receded from their victim, returning to their master atop the stage. I sat there, mouth agape as horror iced my veins. He stole that Fae's life like it meant absolutely nothing, and at the command of the headmaster, no less.

"Let that be a lesson to all of you," Lightshade proclaimed. "Raysa's word is law at the Conservatory. Should you choose to question her will, you shall face a similar fate regardless of the circumstances." He shot a narrowed glare in my direction before he turned to Reign and barked, "See to it that the initiate's body is returned to his family in a nice urn."

"Of course," Reign snarled.

I couldn't help but lift my wide eyes to meet his. How could he be so cruel?

As if he could read the disgust in my gaze, those bottomless orbs pivoted away from mine. His fingers clenched around the silver cuff circling his wrist, and a scowl carved into his wide jaw.

"And now..." The headmaster continued his speech, diverting my attention from the haunted look in Reign's eyes. But try as I might, I simply couldn't focus on Lightshade's words. One small slip up and I'd be returning to Feywood in a box. If they'd treated a Light Fae so callously, I doubted they'd even bother with a gilded urn for a lowly Kin.

Once the headmaster and professors stepped off the stage, the tension in the air dispelled as the students began to move around the hall. Rue spun at me, a tight grin across her face. "That was intense."

"I can't believe *he* did that." I cast a quick glance in Reign's direction, but the Shadow Fae professor had disappeared.

"I know. Questioning Raysa is unforgiveable." She slowly shook her head.

"No, I meant the professor killing that male!"

Rue waved a nonchalant hand. "I forgot you didn't grow up here at court. I suppose it must seem quite callous." She leaned in close and whispered, "I'll let you in on a little secret, Heaton and I didn't grow up at court either. We live in the far outskirts of the realm, so before Heat ended up here, I was nearly as naïve as you. Don't worry, you'll learn the courtly ways quickly."

"I hope so."

"Speaking of Heaton, there he is." Her lively eyes lit up as her brother marched onto the stage.

"Listen up, first-years, I need all members of Flare Squad in the left corner of the hall."

The squeal of chair legs across tile urged my weary body to stand. The idea of meeting the rest of the students in our squad had anxiety brewing in the depths of my core.

"Come on, Aelia, that's us." Rue curled her arm beneath mine and dragged me to my feet. "This is so exciting."

I disagreed but forced a smile all the same.

"Let's go meet our team."

I followed my overly cheerful new roommate to the far

corner of the hall as instructed, ignoring the myriads of curious stares as I passed the other students. Perhaps, I should have worn one of those gowns, after all. I suddenly felt greatly underdressed in the sea of vibrant tulles.

Heaton stood in the back, surrounded by fawning females who giggled and circled the attractive male. If I didn't despise all these arrogant Fae, I'd admit how flawless each and every one was. Heaton, with his high cheekbones, straight nose and shimmering blue eyes was the picture of male perfection. Clearly, the other females had taken notice.

"Looks like we're going to have to push our way to the front." Rue cocked her head over her shoulder at me and grunted. "The girls have always flocked to Heaton like denga flies to unicorn manure."

A faint laugh tumbled out despite my best effort to keep it in.

"Most of these Fae grew up at court, so Heaton is somewhat of a novelty, I suppose. Since he's been at the Conservatory, I swear he wrote home about a new female every week." She crinkled her freckled nose in disgust.

"Oh, letters!" That reminded me. "Then we are permitted to write home?"

"Not for the first term, I'm afraid. Once we pass our first semester exams, then we are allowed correspondence."

All the hope evaporated in my chest and my shoulders rounded. I must have made a face because the sea of females who'd surrounded Heaton parted, his attention already turned in my direction.

"Everything all right, Aelia?" He flashed a perfect smile my way, and... okay, maybe now I understood why all the others were drooling over him.

All eyes pivoted toward me, and I could practically feel the hatred lancing into me at stealing the attractive squad leader's attention.

"Oh, yes, fine," I mumbled. Then I took a step back,

wanting nothing more than to disappear among my pointy-eared, light-haired classmates. Excited whispers swirled all around as a few more males and females joined our corner of the hall.

By a quick count, there seemed to be twenty of us in each squad, with eight squads of first-years in total. As I scrutinized my new team, I was relieved to discover I wasn't the only one without wings. In fact, even our squad leader was missing the luminous appendages.

At least that was one thing that wouldn't immediately mark me as different among the ocean of blondes. A tall male standing across the gaggle of students shot me a wink, a shock of golden blonde hair tumbling over twinkling lilac irises. Was he actually smiling at me or was I imagining it?

"All right, everyone." Heaton clapped his hands, and the hushed murmurs fell away. "Welcome to Flare Squad. For those of you that don't know me, I'm Heaton Liteschild, and I will be your squad leader. I want you all to look to your left, and now to your right." He paused until everyone did as he'd instructed. Rue stood to one side and another blonde female lingered a few feet away to my right. It was as if she were scared to stand too close and catch my Kin-ness. "Only one of the students beside you will survive the first year."

A gasp squeezed through my clenched teeth as my head whipped back and forth between both females. I sent a quick prayer to Raysa that it would be Rue who survived.

"The Crown needs only the best to serve as Royal Guardians of the realm. Though the methods at the Conservatory may seem brutal, it is to ensure only the strongest survive. The title of Royal Guardian is a highly coveted one. It is a great honor to serve the king and the Court of Ethereal Light. You must remember that."

"I give the Kin a week, tops," a male with long, blonde plaited hair snickered.

My hackles rose, and the desire to reach for my dagger and

show this arrogant Fae exactly what he was up against rushed my veins.

"Belmore Dawnbrook, correct?" Heaton growled, cutting off my dark musings.

The faery fool dipped his head.

"I wish to make this clear today. You are a team, and you will act as one. I expect you all to return to your rooms this afternoon and study the Conservatory manual and code of conduct. Until then, I will emphasize rule number one: Your squad comes above all else. As the famous quote goes, 'The strength of the team is each individual member. The strength of each member is the team.' You'll do well to remember that, Belmore, or you will suffer the consequences."

"If that quote is true, it's not fair we're stuck with *her*." The girl who stood beside me raised her long nose in my direction. "What can a powerless Kin bring to our team?"

"I'm not powerless," I gritted out.

"Your rounded ears say otherwise," the blonde male, Belmore, interjected.

Rue glanced up at me, a look of pity on her kind face. I knew she only wished to provide comfort with that glance, but it had the opposite effect. My entire life I'd been looked down upon, pitied by powerful Fae. This was my chance to prove them all wrong; I knew I could.

Before I could think on all the reasons why this was a terrible idea, I reached for the dagger strapped to my thigh and sent it sailing end-over-end at the cocky Fae male. The blade's tip caught the oversized golden hoop dangling from Belmore's ear and impaled him to the wall.

His eyes widened to the size of giant emeralds, mouth curved into a satisfying capital 'O'. "Noxus's nuts!" he cried out, his chest heaving.

Heaton turned his blazing gaze on me. "Aelia..." A flicker of a smile ghosted over his lips before he hardened his mouth into a thin line. "As impressive as that was, you'll have to refrain from attempting to skewer your teammates, despite their ignorant comments."

"That *was* refraining," I muttered. "I didn't aim for his chest, did I?"

A dark chuckle resonated behind me, and my entire body lit up at the sound. I hazarded a glance over my shoulder, but I already knew exactly who I'd find. Reign stood a few yards away, his arms crossed tight over his broad chest, those dark shadows slithering over his form like venomous snakes.

"Looks like you picked a good one, professor." Heaton shot Reign a smirk.

"Well, she's certainly not powerless." His dark eyes tapered as they razed over me.

That look, alone, had goose bumps rippling over every inch of my exposed flesh. He kept his gaze fixed to mine for an endless moment. Every second was torture. When I couldn't stand the intensity for an instant longer, I dropped my chin and clenched my fingers behind my back.

"As I was saying," Heaton continued as he pried my dagger from the wall, the crystal within the hilt shimmering beneath the sun's striking rays, and freed Belmore. "It is against student conduct to attack a fellow squad member." He leveled Belmore, then me with another glare. "I will allow a pass for both of you today since it's the first day and I appreciate you may not be familiar with the code, but tomorrow once classes start, you will be held accountable. Are we clear?"

I mumbled a half-hearted, "Yes," and Heaton handed me the dagger.

"That goes for all of you. And given that you may not know, that rule does not apply for the other students at the Conservatory. In an attempt to weed out the weak and strengthen their chances of survival, the other squads *will* attempt to eliminate the competition. Take advantage of your team and foster a relationship that will grow over the next few years. It will mean the difference between life and death."

Chapter Ten

"You *have* to teach me how you did that with the dagger!" Rue's pale blue eyes sparkled with excitement as she nibbled on a biscuit.

I couldn't get the flaky pastry into my mouth fast enough. It tasted like the glorious afterlife, the crusty dough melting into a puddle of honey on my tongue. I couldn't remember the last time I'd eaten something so delicious.

"Sure, I'd be happy to," I replied around a mouthful.

I sat across from my new friend in the sprawling banquet hall, the echo of excited chitter-chatter bouncing off the glass-domed ceiling. Like every chamber at the university, sunlight streamed in through the multitude of stained-glass windows, illuminating every crevice in ethereal light.

Beside us, but not too close, sat the rest of Flare Squad. Heaton had given us a grand tour of the Conservatory grounds, and we'd spent most of the day traipsing across the yards and yards of campus. It had been quite a blur, and I doubted I'd remember any of it by tomorrow.

I only hoped the mystical scroll would appear with an updated map. According to my schedule, I'd have Illumination Sight and Shadow Arts tomorrow morning. Unease prickled at the thought of an entire two-hour class with the broody Shadow Fae professor.

Rue leaned across the table, her expressive irises glittering with curiosity. "I've never met a Kin before in person, I just have so many questions. What is it like living in Feywood? What did you do all these years? And how did you not know you were a Light Fae?"

The questions spilled out, one after another, but unlike the scornful stares I received from the other students, no malice laced her tone. She simply seemed curious about my life. And to be honest, escaping this new, unreal existence for a few minutes to delve into the past didn't sound that awful.

"It was lovely," I finally answered. "And difficult. I can only imagine what life at court must be like, but in Feywood, everyone works hard. We're up at dawn and we work until the sun set—"

"Wait a second! The sun sets in Feywood?"

I nodded quickly. "And not in the middle of what should be the night, like here. We have about twelve hours of daytime and twelve of night."

"Wow... it's like a perfect mixture of the Light and Shadow Courts."

"I suppose so."

"And what about the Wilds? Is it as terrifying as I've heard? I do not relish the idea of being posted anywhere near there."

I shrugged. Though we lived in constant fear of the monsters to our south, I'd never encountered one in my twenty years. "One simply grows accustomed to the looming threat, and of course, we never wander south of the Feywood border."

"How frightening."

I took another bite of the biscuit and washed it down with a big gulp of honeyed wine.

"Oh, by the way, you better be careful with that." Rue motioned at the gilded goblet filled to the brim with the golden-hued wine.

I'd already admitted to never tasting the Fae special spirit when we'd strolled through the buffet line. "Careful, how?" I took another long sip. It was the most incredible thing I'd tasted —next to everything else I'd eaten since my arrival at the university.

"Its effects can be unpredictable if you're not accustomed to drinking it."

I glanced around the room at the dozens of other first-years enjoying the sweet beverage and shrugged. "Everyone else seems to be fine."

"Everyone else also grew up at court, living off the stuff." She grinned. "When my oldest brother, Lawson, came home for a visit after his first year, he brought a bottle of it, and I spent all night on our rooftop alternating between howling at the moon like a crazed wolvryn and belting out my favorite song while dancing a jig." A cackle burst free. "Pa had to drag me down when the neighboring dogs started joining in the chorus."

An unexpected laugh pealed out as I imagined the cute Fae dancing atop a thatched roof. Uncurling my fingers from the stem of the goblet, I searched the front of the hall for a less questionable beverage. "Maybe I *will* go find some water."

Still in the middle of a fit of the giggles, she nodded as I rose. Scanning the gilded hall, I moved between the long banquet tables to the front where the sprawling buffet sat. Beside the bottles of honeyed wine, I finally found a few silver pitchers of water. Or at least, what I assumed was water. I poured a bit into a cup and sniffed the clear liquid. Seemed okay, but one could never be too sure in this strange land.

A cool breeze lifted the tiny hairs on the back of my neck an instant before icy breath ghosted across the shell of my ear. "Are you worried about being poisoned already? That typically doesn't occur until at least a few weeks in."

I spun around as my heart rioted against its skeletal confines.

Reign leaned against the buffet table, back once again in a simple black tunic, highlighting the dark runes inked across his arms, and matching breeches. The hint of a smile teased up the corner of his lip, and goddess, it simply wasn't fair how someone so frightening could also be so beautiful.

Steeling my spine, I snapped my shoulders back and glared at the intimidating male. "It's clear no one wants me here, so I must stay vigilant."

"Good girl, you're already learning."

"Aidan always said I was a quick study."

He reached for my cup, and the shadows peeled away from his form before slithering across the liquid's surface. Then his fathomless eyes lifted to mine. "Perfectly palatable."

I eyed him warily as he handed the goblet back. "How do I know your shadows didn't just do something nefarious to my water?"

A crooked grin settled across his mouth. "Well, you could simply take my word for it, or I could let you in on a little secret." He inched closer, and my skin prickled at his proximity.

"Go ahead..." Raysa, why did I sound so breathless?

"Every term the professors wager on the initiates they are sent to collect. As you were my acquisition, I have an inherent interest in your success."

Interesting. That certainly was valuable knowledge to have.

"And after that move against Belmore" --a chuckle rumbled his broad shoulders --"the odds on you have gone up exponentially."

That explained Heaton's comment earlier after the dagger incident. *Looks like you picked a good one, professor.*

"I'm so thrilled to hear the esteemed staff makes wagers on our lives." It seemed awfully cruel, but then again, it did seem right in line with everything else I'd learned since my arrival.

He gave a lazy shrug before reaching for an applett off a serving platter and taking a big bite of the crisp, ripe fruit. My eyes fixed to his lips as he devoured it with an enthusiasm that had heat rushing below my navel.

What in all the realms?

My head suddenly spun, and my hand shot out to steady myself, gripping the edge of the table. Oh, no. My vision blurred, the bottles of Fae honeyed wine blinking in and out. The wine! Rue had said its effects were unpredictable. Darkness seeped into the corners of my vision, and I heaved in a steadying breath to keep from succumbing.

"Aelia, are you all right?" Reign's words were muffled, the concern on his face distorting as he stepped closer.

"I—um..." I keeled forward and strong arms laced around my waist.

My face was buried in his dark tunic and icy shadows pinned me to his chest. I should have been mortified, but instead, an embarrassing giggle pealed out. Then a hiccup. Oh, goddess, no.

Reign's head dipped, and he inhaled deeply, his nostrils flaring. "Oh, Noxus, princess, don't tell me you drank too much of the honeyed wine?"

"I didn't know," I tried to mumble lamely but my pitch was off, and it came out in a silly sing-song. I snapped my mouth closed before I could further embarrass myself.

"Come on, I'll take you back to your room." A steel band tightened around my waist before turning me toward the end of the banquet hall.

My knees wobbled with every step, cheeks heating as dozens of judging gazes abandoned their suppers to gawk at me. Why, oh, why didn't someone warn me about the wine sooner?

"Aelia?" A familiar, sweet voice echoed behind me. "Are you all right?" Soft footsteps pitter-pattered behind us.

"She's fine," Reign barked. "Finish eating first-year, you'll need your strength for tomorrow's class."

I could barely make out my roommate trailing behind us from the corner of my eye. "R—Rue?" My tongue felt like a hyppo sat atop it. It was heavy and sluggish, and I could barely form words.

"I'll make sure she gets back to her room safely," he called out over his shoulder.

At the end of the banquet hall, a vaguely familiar form coalesced, that long flowing beard reminding me of newly driven snow.

"Stand up straight," Reign snapped.

"Whhat?"

He hissed a curse between his clenched teeth and his hold around my waist loosened, only to be replaced by the support of icy shadows. They crept up my tunic until my spine snapped straight from the frosty chill.

I barely muffled a gasp as we reached the headmaster. The old Fae's face swam before me, twisting and turning like the image in a cracked mirror. I blinked quickly trying to clear my vision. Reign's hand on my lower back was nearly imperceptible through the haze of shadows surrounding us. Or maybe that was simply my scattered vision unable to focus.

"Everything all right, here?" Headmaster Draven asked, his mossy green eyes darting between us.

"Yes, fine," Reign replied before I could remember how to open my mouth. "I was merely escorting this initiate to her chambers. She nearly took Belmore Dawnbrook's ear off with a concealed dagger."

The ancient male's silver brow perked up. "Did she now?" The hint of a smile twisted his flowing mustache.

"Mmm. I will see to it that she spends the rest of the evening in her room studying the Conservatory's code of conduct."

"Very well." He nodded and Reign shuffled me through the door, his shadows nudging me across the threshold.

As soon as the gilded door closed behind us, my legs gave. Reign's arm encircled me once again, keeping my knees from crashing onto the cold, marble floor.

"Gods, princess," he snarled, heaving me up. "How much did you drink?"

"Not a l-lot," I stammered. "And why did you lie to the headmaster? You made it seem like—"

He pressed a finger to my lips, and all the words died on the tip of my tongue. "It's better that Draven sees you as a threat than weak. How many times must I tell you?"

"Blah, blah, blah..." I snapped my loose lips shut, but it was too late. *Curses*!

Reign's hold fell away, his shadows peeling off my form and the hallway whirled, the stained-glass ceiling spiraling. "If you prefer, you can crawl back to your chamber, princess."

"No, please," I spluttered, my hand reaching out for his. My fingertips brushed the silver cuff around his wrist, and his dark gaze chased to mine. "What are these?"

"None of your business," he snarled. His fingers wrapped around mine—a bit more enthusiastically than necessary, if you asked me—and he hauled me down the quiet corridor. "Now, hurry up, before anyone else sees you like this. Or more than have already witnessed the embarrassing spectacle, that is."

"What's the big deal? Does no one get inebriated at this great, sacred university?" Oh, my goddess, I simply couldn't control my tongue. Or my body apparently. I leaned into him, wobbling.

A dark chuckle rumbled his chest, vibrating through my own body as he held me tight against the hard planes of his form. "They do, princess, just not before the first day of classes." He paused for a moment, his expression pensive. "If you survive the first term, there will be quite a celebration on the Winter Solstice, the Night of the Longest Shadow."

"Don't sound so forlorn, professor." I slapped my hand across his chest, because clearly, I'd lost all sense of self-preservation, and my head snapped back at the unyielding muscle. Still, my mouth continued to spew nonsense without my control. "One would think you actually cared about your round-eared acquisition."

A feral grin crossed his face as he held me out to arm's length. "The only thing I care about is you surviving so I may win the hefty pot of gildings."

My traitorous smile must have faltered at his words because his jaw clenched, eyes searing into my own. If it wasn't for his iron grip on my shoulders, I would've hit the floor, my head spun so badly at the jostling movement. "You must understand something, Aelia. No one here is your friend. Not a soul here cares for you beyond what you can do for the Crown. The sooner you grasp that, the safer you'll be."

"You included?" *By the gods, please, someone strike me down already*!

His lips thinned, impenetrable darkness cloaking those fathomless spheres that seared into me, burrowing into the farthest depths of my soul. "Me, most of all."

Chapter Eleven

A*elia*

"Aelia, wake up! We can't be late for our first class!"

I forced my heavy lids open and grumbled a curse as pain pounded across my temples. My chamber mate flitted across the room, dragging a pair of suede breeches up her slender legs.

"Oh, goddess, Rue, please remind me never to drink that blasted wine again."

She plopped down on her bed, the ivy curling across the headboard turning toward her as if it hadn't appreciated being jostled. "It's all my fault. I never should've let you have any. I just didn't think..."

"No, it's not." I pushed the silky coverlet back and forced myself to the edge of the mattress. "Like you said, you've never had a Kin as a friend. How would you know I'd have such a terrible reaction?"

A silly grin crossed her face despite her best attempts at hiding it. "You were really quite funny, Aelia. When I returned to the room, you told me all about the time you and that Kin boy, Edgert, ran off in the woods to bathe in the pond—"

"Oh, no, I didn't!" Heat burned my cheeks as I recollected the embarrassing story of my first kiss. Why in all the courts would I have chosen that tale to share?

"Sometimes I forget how prudish non-Fae are." She smirked. "You had your first kiss at sixteen, and I'd already lain with three males by then."

"Three?" I squealed.

Goddess, I'd yet to have one. But now that the effects of the wine had worn off, I certainly would not be sharing that piece of private information with my new roommate.

"You forget, I had an older brother. Heaton's friends made for great company." She threw me a wink and a chuckle slid free despite the pounding in my skull. For a few glorious moments, I'd forgotten all about the blinding pain. "Enough about my conquests... you must get dressed!"

I forced myself off the bed and bypassed the bathing room all together. I'd have to enjoy the soothing sensations of the heated pools this evening. Assuming I survived the day.

As I yanked on a pair of new leathers from the closet, Rue darted over. "Don't forget that the rules of conduct come into play starting today."

Damn it, and I'd fallen asleep before reading a single page from the book of conduct last night.

"Can you give me a quick summary?" I speared my legs through the fine leather before dragging a light tunic over my head.

"The key is there aren't many rules, other than to survive. The other squads are permitted—nay, encouraged, to thin out the competition. If we can't stand up against other Light Fae, we'll never stand a chance against the Shadow Fae across the river. Only the strong survive."

"Wonderful." I gulped.

"Only our teammates are considered off limits."

"Then I suppose it's a good thing I chose Belmore to make an example of."

She grinned. "That cocky Fae lord deserved to be taken down a few notches."

"I only hope he sticks to the rules better than I did."

When Rue turned to the closet to search for her shoes, I tucked my daggers into each of my boots. I had a feeling I'd need these today.

A few minutes later, we were both dressed and meandering through the dormitory corridors. A swarm of bodies surrounded us, curious gazes swiveling in my direction. I wondered if the other students would ever tire of gawking. I wasn't certain I could endure it for my entire tenure at the Conservatory.

"There she is," someone whispered. "It's so unfortunate she's on your team."

"I know. How do they expect us to win with a powerless Kin?"

I canted my head over my shoulder to make out a female walking behind us with one of the members of Flare Squad. Ariadne, if memory served from roll call. The blonde had been the one standing next to me when Heaton gathered us all in the Hall of Luminescence.

"Just ignore them," said Rue, weaving an arm through mine in an unspoken gesture of reassurance as we reached the spiral glass staircase.

My fingers itched for my knives. I'd show Ariadne exactly how powerless I was. I didn't need *rais* or *nox* to prove myself to these arrogant ladies of court.

"Ariadne Bamberlight may seem all manners and sophistication, but don't be fooled, Aelia," Rue whispered. "She comes from an ancient line of powerful Light Fae. Her four older brothers have been through the Academy and Heaton says they're some of the best Royal Guardians he's seen."

I whirled to face my roommate and nearly stumbled on the

last step. "How did you know I was even considering..." My words fell away.

"It's your aura. It's usually a bright gold with hints of silver. When you were staring at her, it grew dark like an impending thunderstorm."

Wonderful, so now even my enemies would know when an attack was imminent. "I wasn't going to—"

She shrugged. "I don't blame you. Growing up on the outskirts, I've never quite fit in with the ladies of court myself, but just remember not to underestimate them."

"Noted." I heaved out a breath as we reached the immense, sunlit foyer in the Hall of Glory and paused in front of the sun-kissed fountain. "And thank you. You've been the only female here to show me a hint of kindness, and I appreciate it."

Rue giggled, her pale cheeks flushing a deep rosy hue. "Don't mention it. Like I said, I'm a bit of an outcast myself. And as for the aura reading, I'm sure you'll pick up on it quickly. It's typically one of the first abilities to manifest at maturity."

I certainly hoped so since our first class today was Illumination Sight. We would be harnessing our ability to see beyond the visible spectrum, allowing Light Fae to perceive things such as auras, energy patterns, and hidden magical forces. It seemed most of my fellow classmates had already mastered those skills, whereas I was hopelessly behind.

"Come on, through here." Rue led the way out of the grand hall and as we crossed the threshold, I couldn't help but remember that Fae male incinerated at the same threshold just two days ago. A chill skirted up my spine at the memory. How many lives had the Veil of Judgement claimed?

The moment we stepped outside, a temperate breeze flitted across my face, and I drew in a deep breath. The rush of waterfalls cascading into the river below soothed my churning nerves. It wasn't time to worry about that lost Fae soul, I needed to focus if I didn't want to join him in the afterlife.

"Where to?" I scanned the immense campus, trying to remember the map scrawled on the parchment this morning that would lead us to the Hall of Ether. I refused to remove the scroll from my satchel, which would only draw attention to my lowly, first-year status. As I'd assumed, no one else needed to carry them around to orient themselves.

Nodding her head in the direction we needed to go, Rue jerked me toward the pathway on the right around the Conservatory's main building, the Hall of Glory. The cobblestone road meandered through arched trellises of snaking vines and colorful blooms. I'd never seen such vibrant, lush flora. Beside the main hall, three domed buildings looped around the circle, each a dazzling spectacle of alabaster walls and endlessly climbing vines. "Don't you remember anything from our tour yesterday?"

I stared back at her, gaping, before finally shaking my head. It had all been such a whirlwind, I truly couldn't. Growing up in Feywood, where my entire home would fit into the dormitory we shared, this sort of sprawling grandeur was unheard of.

"Okay, the campus is simply a series of concentric circles. The pathways all eventually circle around to the main building. Even if you get lost, sooner or later you'll find your way back to the Hall of Glory."

"Which is where we came in, right?"

She nodded.

"And where our dormitories are located."

"You're getting it." Then she ticked her head at Ariadne and the silver-haired female who'd been whispering about me earlier. "And remember, all of Flare Squad has the same schedule so worst-case scenario, just follow us."

"Right." A scowl twisted my lips as I regarded the beautiful blonde. "I think I'd rather be hopelessly lost than ask Ariadne for anything."

"Well, there's always Belmore."

The Fae male with the blonde plaited hair darted after

Ariadne and swung his arm around her shoulder. If I could just manage to steer clear of both of them today, I'd be happy.

Rue stopped in front of a towering white stone building. The domed ceiling and elaborate columns reminded me of the great temple to Raysa in Feywood. It was the only structure that remotely compared in grandeur to the majestic edifices across the campus. "This is it. Are you ready?"

I swallowed hard, staring up at the magnificent structure. A tiny voice in my head surged to the surface. *What are you doing here? You don't belong with these Fae...* I shoved back the doubt and pinned my shoulders back. I could and *would* survive because I deserved to be here. I'd worked harder than any other Fae here, I was certain, and today, I would prove it to everyone.

✕

I'd been wrong, terribly wrong. So much for Illumination Sight being the easy class. Not a spark of awareness flitted to the surface as I stared blankly at each of my teammates, trying to discern their aura.

Ariadne didn't neglect to point out that she'd been reading auras since she was only fifteen years old. In fact, every single member of Flare Squad could do it but me.

"Don't get discouraged, Aelia," said Rue as she speared her arm through mine again. "It's only your first day."

"Even Professor Gleamer thought I was defective."

"No, she didn't."

"She pulled me aside and asked if I was certain I was Light Fae. I had to show her my mark in order for her to believe me."

"Oh, Aelia." My roommate released a rueful chuckle. "Surely, things will only get better from here."

As I scanned the floral pathway for the next building, I muttered an oath. "Oh, curses, I forgot my scroll in the auditorium." I'd pulled it out of my satchel to glimpse a sneak peek of the Hall of Rais and, of course, I'd forgotten it.

"Do you want me to go back with you to fetch it?" Rue offered.

"No, you go ahead, I'll meet you at Shadow Arts."

"Are you sure?" She eyed my skeptically.

The last thing I wanted was to become a burden for my one and only friend. "I'll be fine. I'll see you in a few minutes, save me a seat."

"Will do."

Spinning back toward the Hall of Ether, I quickened my pace as the crowd of students thinned out. Just my luck to be late to Reign's class on the first day. He'd likely blame it on the honeyed wine. Goddess, I couldn't remember much of anything of our encounter. I only prayed I hadn't said anything embarrassing.

What if I'd told him the Edgert story too?

Heat flushed my cheeks with shame. I'd never live that one down. And if what Rue said was true about the Fae's liberal ideals of sex, I couldn't imagine how many females the Shadow Fae must have claimed in his lifetime. A swirl of irritation pressed down on my shoulders at the idea of another female's hands on that firm chest, those strong arms—*stop it*! *Realms what is wrong with me*? I squeezed my eyes shut to dispel the vivid images, but those piercing midnight orbs flashed across my vision and my heart staggered on a beat.

I was so distracted, I nearly tripped over the first step leading up to the Hall of Ether. I threw my hands out and somehow managed to remain on my feet.

"Aww, the poor little Kin can't even walk." A male voice rasped behind me.

I spun around to find Belmore with two other males.

"How is she ever expected to fly?" said the silver-haired male.

"Can one even fly with those rounded ears?" The third Fae smirked.

Steeling my nerves, I glared at the three males as they walked toward me. With the hall at my back and perched precariously on the second step of the building, I wasn't exactly in a great position to take on a trio of attackers.

A group of females hurried down the steps, and I glanced over, my gaze pleading. "Um, excuse me—" They completely ignored me, rushing along to their next class.

"No one's going to help you now, little Kin," Belmore barked.

Clearly, I was on my own. "I don't see wings on any of you," I bit back.

"You were right, Belmore, she does have a quick tongue." The silver-haired male inched closer. "I wonder what else she can do with it." A slimy grin slid across his face.

"Take her and let us know, Kian." A wicked sneer curled the corners of Belmore's mouth. "I've never been with a Kin before, I'm sure they're feral in the bedroom."

Nausea crawled up my throat as I stared from one male to the other.

"I wish I could stay and watch this play out, but I cannot be late for Professor Darkthorn's class. He's quite the stickler for the rules I've heard." Belmore smirked as he sauntered past me before turning to his friends. "Show the Kin how we welcome fellow first-years to the Conservatory."

Chapter Twelve

Blood iced my veins as I watched Belmore saunter down the pathway, each footfall like a nail in my coffin. The bastard couldn't touch me according to the code of conduct, but that didn't mean he couldn't sic his friends on me. My hand lifted to my chest, unbidden, finding the gold necklace hidden beneath my tunic. Somehow, Aidan's gift provided a measure of comfort.

"Come here, little Kin." Kian's sing-song prickled the hair on the back of my neck.

"Why do you get the first taste?" said the other male. "If you ruin her, there will be nothing left for me."

"Quit your whining, Lucian." Kian stepped closer, and my heart kicked at my ribcage.

Come on, Aelia. You've trained for this your whole life. Make Aidan proud. Closing my eyes for an instant, I pictured the quiet meadow behind my home, my adoptive father's patient face as he rearranged the targets for the third time, the melodic chirping of insects, the warm sun on my shoulders, and I willed the familiar calm to emerge.

"Do you see that, Lucian?" Kian's smirk kicked up. "Her aura is darkening. We've upset the little Kin."

"Or maybe you're turning her on," he countered. "An aura can darken with lust."

The two males chuckled and bile oozed up my throat. I would rather die a thousand times over than allow either of these Fae to touch me. The two large males blocked the pathway toward the Hall of Rais. I could try to dart past, but I doubted I could outrun them both. Though I had to try. Jumping off the steps, I made a run for it. Kian reached out a long arm, but I dropped to a crouch and unsheathed the knife from my boot. I slashed my blade across his chest, but he moved like a wraith. He leapt back and the rip of fine material whooshed between us.

"You bitch," he hissed as he glanced down at his torn tunic. "This was new."

"Just leave me alone," I shouted. "Let me by so I can go to class and we can forget about all of this." Frantically, I scanned the lawn for other students, anyone. Raysa, where was everyone? Surely, there had to be someone else late for class!

"I don't think so, Kin," said Lucian, inching closer. He ran his hand through his shorn, pale blonde hair and licked his lips. "You embarrassed our friend and now, it's your turn to pay the price." He flashed his hand across my face, brilliant light streaking from his palm, blinding me.

As I blinked rapidly to clear the stars from my vision, a body pummeled into me, and we crashed to the ground. My knife came loose and the clatter of metal across stone sent all hope squeezing from my lungs.

"No!" I shrieked as one of the males pinned me to the roughhewn path. "Get *off* me!" The coarse stone sank into my shoulder blades as I squirmed beneath his weight. My vision was still hazy, his face a blur of muted colors.

"Stop wiggling, you worthless Kin." A palm cracked across my cheek, and the sharp sting rushed through every nerve-ending. The back of my head bounced against the unyielding stone and darkness etched into the corners of my vision.

"Son of Noxus!" I gritted out.

"Don't knock her out, you fool." A muffled voice echoed from above, but I couldn't tell if it was Kian or Lucian. My thoughts were scrambled, the bright blue and cottony clouds overhead spinning. "Let's have some fun with her first. Bring her back to the dorms."

Panic lanced through my chest, pushing back the darkness. *No.* I would never let them take me. If I could only reach my boot... Blinking again, the form hovering over me finally coalesced into a discernible figure. It was Kian leering down at me, strands of silver hair coming loose from the neat tie at his nape. He held both my wrists in one big hand. I struggled and kicked, attempting to buck him off, but the Fae was an immoveable force.

A whisper of heat kindled deep in my core, and I grasped onto the flicker with all I had. It swirled around my gut, like gauzy strands of energy I couldn't quite hold onto. It was a sensation I'd never felt before. *Raysa, help me.*

"Blazes, look at that aura," Lucian gasped. "I've never seen anything like it."

With my last ounce of energy, I planted my boots against the stone floor and vaulted my hips up. Kian bounced up allowing me to free one of my hands from his grip. I reached for my second blade and jabbed it into his thigh.

"Noxus's nuts!" Kian roared as he rolled off me. "She stabbed me!"

I leapt up, and my head spun, a slight throb at the back of my skull. My knees gave, and I dropped to the ground once again. I lifted my hand to my nape and my fingers came back sticky with blood. *Oh, no.* The Hall of Ether tilted, the blue of the sky flipped upside down, and my cheek hit the rough stone again. Lucian loomed over me, a satisfied grin twisting his mouth into something truly wicked.

Icy tendrils licked up my spine and I turned my head, slowly, trying to keep my world from whirling. A dark presence raised the hair on every inch of my body. Inky shadows zipped by, a tornado of umbral power thickening the air.

"Step. Away. From. Her. *Now.*" The ominous growl cut through the manic pounding of my pulse. Where everything else was muffled, Reign's voice rang out as clear as the blinding light streaming from the gods' celestial abode.

That piercing gaze found mine, where a storm brewed below the sleek obsidian surface. Tendrils of darkness curled around his form in a midnight cloud of sheer power. I might not have been able to read auras, but even I could see his.

Lucian twirled around, offering our professor a slick smile as Kian pushed himself off the floor, leaning on his good leg. Blood dripped from the wound in his thigh and despite the endless spinning, a faint smile pursed my lips.

Reign, too, noticed it, his murderous gaze dropping for an instant to my attacker's leg.

"Professor..." Lucian dipped his head.

"You're late for my class." Reign bared his teeth, and another chill skittered up my spine.

"We were detained with more pressing matters." Kian limped closer and leaned against his friend.

"Nothing is more pressing than my class." Reign's tone was calm, collected, and altogether lethal. His hand jutted out and a shadow streaked off his form, darting toward the male first-year.

Kian's eyes bulged, two saucers of icy blue widening to impossible widths as the shadow curled around him.

"Are you proficient in umbrakinesis?" Reign twisted his

fingers and the dark shadow snaked around Kian's throat. He twisted again and the darkness coiled like a rope, tightening around the male's neck. "What about fear induction? Umbral blades?" Another shadow shot from his splayed fingers and blades made of pure night whizzed across the few yards between them. One hummed by, millimeters from his stuck-up nose, while a second sliced across the tie at the back of his neck, and a clump of silver hair hit the ground.

"Blessed Raysa," Lucian rasped.

"Only Noxus can help you now, boy," Reign hissed as he released another onslaught of murky shadows. They surrounded Lucian, and a scream tore from his curled lips.

"Get them off! Get them off!" He jumped up and down, scratching and tearing at his clothes.

I watched, horrified, as the chaos unfolded.

"There's nothing on you," Kian shouted, but Lucian's eyes were vacant and wide, blind terror etched into his features.

"Fear induction," Reign snarled, as he closed in on both males. "Another important ability you would be learning if you were currently in my class instead of torturing a weak, fellow first-year."

My head snapped up at the insult. I wasn't *that* weak... I'd managed to land a few hits, at least.

Reign's arms opened wide and, like dogs returning to their master, the storm of darkness retreated, curling around the Shadow Fae's muscular form. He towered over the cowering males, his lethal glare fixed to the pair. "Get out of my sight," he growled. "Do not show your face in my class until I say so."

Lucian and Kian stood frozen, eyes wide and jaws unhinged.

"Go, now," he shouted.

"But..." Kian whimpered.

"Now!"

Both males scrambled toward the lawn, Kian limping

behind Lucian's speeding form. I drew in a breath as relief loosened the tense set of my shoulders, and I attempted to sit up. Until that ominous power slithered over me and shards of ice danced across my skin.

I swallowed hard and glanced up to meet those fathomless midnight orbs. Technically, I was also late to Reign's class. Would it matter that an assault prevented me from arriving on time? Probably not, knowing how things worked in this academy. Forcing my shoulders back, I faced the dark beast.

"Are you hurt?" he gritted out.

Well... that hadn't been what I'd expected at all. "Does my pride count?" I forced a smile, despite the pounding ache at the back of my head.

The ghost of a smile twitched at his lips. "I'm afraid pride does not count for much at the Conservatory unless it is well earned."

"Fair enough."

Reign crouched in front of me and offered a hand. Those shadows swirled around his palm, writhing like possessed wraiths. Again, my gaze drifted to the silver bangle hanging from his wrist, the metal gleaming beneath the sun's brilliant rays. *What secrets do they unlock?*

"I'm not going to bite, princess."

"I don't know if I believe you after what you just did to Kian and Lucian."

"That was different. They were late to my class."

"So am I." *Goddess, shut your mouth*! Why couldn't I stop myself from blurting out stupidities in front of this male?

He dropped lower so his eyes were level to mine. "You're my acquisition. I have an inherent stake in your survival. We've already gone over this. Do your rounded ears prevent you from hearing well?" An actual smile lifted the corners of his lips and Raysa, it was gorgeous. Shadow Fae or not, that grin was more radiant than the gods' blessed sun.

"Was that a joke?" I sputtered. "Is the dark and broody professor of Shadow Arts actually capable of humor?"

"There are many things I'm capable of, princess. Maybe one day, I'll grant you the honor of witnessing my *numerous* talents." A devious grin lit up his onyx irises, bathing them in pure starlight.

Goddess, and was that flirting? *Thank the realms I kept that thought to myself.*

Reign wrapped his hand around mine and hauled me off the stone walkway. All the blood rushed from my head at the sudden jolt and I crashed face-first into his firm chest, his arm encircling my waist as he held me up. I inhaled a mouthful of musky, frosty male, like the air after a thunderstorm, and another type of heat rushed low in my belly.

"You *are* hurt," he snarled, nostrils flaring. His hand moved from my back, up my neck until his fingers tangled in my hair. "Fuck, Aelia, you're bleeding."

"Right. I think I hit my head before—"

"Who did this to you?" he snapped. "Was it Kian or Lucian?"

My thoughts were still fuzzy from the attack, but I was ninety-nine percent certain... "Kian," I muttered.

"Hmm." His lips pursed, and the shadows darkened around him. That power expanded, pressing into me like a tidal wave. "Can you walk?" he all but growled.

"Of course, I can." I peeled my body away from his and attempted a step. Thankfully, I didn't fall on my rump and embarrass myself further.

"You're going the wrong way, princess."

I spun around, clearly too quickly given my head wound, and flopped into Reign's open arms. "Oh, Raysa, strike me down," I growled against his dark tunic, breathing in another lungful of his intoxicating scent.

"Be careful what you wish for." With a dark chuckle, Reign swept me into his arms before I could get a word out. His hard planes yielded to my soft ones, and despite the unearthly chill that clung to his shadows, his body felt warm against mine. Honestly, with my form pressed so close to his, my tongue was hopelessly tied. A completely new phenomenon for me.

Those omnipresent wisps of darkness wrapped tighter around me, cool and crisp like a dead lover's embrace. Another chill skittered up my spine, unbidden.

Reign dropped his gaze to mine. "Are you aware of what shadowtraveling is?"

My dark brows furrowed as I regarded my professor. "Excuse me?"

"Oh, Noxus, princess, did they not teach you anything at all in that Kin educational system?"

"Apparently not."

"Shadowtraveling is an advanced Shadow Fae ability to traverse space through shadows, allowing us to move swiftly from one shadow to another."

I gawked at my professor. He may as well have said he had the power to travel through time. "You can move through shadows?" I finally blurted.

"Correct."

The epically long journey aboard the phoenix tumbled to the forefront of my mind. "Wait a second, then why didn't we just do that when you found me in Feywood?"

His lips flipped into a scowl; clearly, I'd hit a nerve of some sort. "So many questions..." he muttered.

"That's a sign of intelligence," I countered.

"And extreme vexation."

I couldn't stop my eyes from rolling.

"If you must know, traveling such lengths takes an inordinate amount of power. So that is why we flew instead."

I shrugged. "Why was that so hard to admit? You wish for me not to know that even your impressive abilities have limits?"

A rueful smile flashed across his face, and I wanted to smack myself for noticing the perfect bow of his soft, pillowy lips.

"Something like that, princess." His arms wrapped tighter around me—no, not his arms, his shadows. "Get ready."

Endless black coiled around me, and a chill seeped into the depths of my bones. The bright sunny campus blurred, then disappeared altogether. A rush of air whipped dark and light strands of hair across my face as the void swallowed us whole.

Chapter Thirteen

elia

My fingers curled into Reign's tunic, my nails digging into the fine fabric as we catapulted through murky oblivion. My lungs constricted, ribs crushing my organs for an impossibly long moment. Then as quickly as it had begun, a flicker of light appeared, and a familiar hall coalesced before us.

The icy tendrils of darkness fell away, and the glimmering Hall of Luce stretched out in all its radiant splendor. Reign held me in front of a door with a familiar sign. *Healer.* How embarrassing. Not even three full days and I'd already found myself at the healer's chamber.

"Can you stand?"

I scoffed and wiggled to be put down though my fingers still clutched his tunic like he was the only remaining lifeboat in a turbulent sea.

Slowly, he lowered my feet to the ground, keeping a firm grip on my waist. I may have wobbled slightly, but somehow by the grace of Raysa, I remained standing. "See?" I threw him a cocky smile. Soon, that warm grip was replaced by icy tendrils I'd come to instantly recognize.

"Stay," Reign murmured before he lifted his knuckles to the door and an instant later, a smiling Fae appeared at the entrance.

"Well, hello there, Professor Reign." She offered him a flirty grin before her lips pulled into a pout as she took in my dark hair and rounded ears.

"Good morrow, Elisa, I have an injured student for you."

"Ah, this must be the infamous female Kin everyone's been buzzing about. I'm not surprised to see her so soon." They exchanged a smirk, and my fingers itched for my daggers. *My daggers*! I had to retrieve them along with my scroll and satchel. Clearly, I needed my weapons if I wished to survive even a day on this campus. "Bring her in."

Reign ushered me through the entrance, his cool shadows supporting part of my weight, and deposited me onto a cool metal table. Like all rooms at the Conservatory, light spilled in from the arched stained-glass windows bathing the healing chamber in a luminous glow. "She has a wound to the back of her head and has been dizzy, likely from blood loss. It needs mending. And if you could take care of it quickly, I'd be ever so pleased. We have a class to return to."

"Of course." The healer turned to a large basin of water and dipped her slender hands inside. "If you prefer, you may return to your lecture and I will send her back when I'm finished," she called out over her shoulder.

"No. I will remain with her."

"As you wish."

While she was preoccupied, I turned to Reign. "I left my daggers, my scroll and my satchel back there. I need to get them before someone else does." The blades were what I cared most about. They were a gift from Aidan, though I didn't share that bit of personal information. I was certain any sort of emotional attachment would be frowned upon here.

He squeezed his eyes closed as if my request were the most irritating thing ever. That darkness coiled around him, expanding until its murky presence filled the room and a whisper of dread pooled in my gut. Goodness, I'd just go back for them myself when I got out of here; it wasn't as if I'd expected him to retrieve them. I'd nearly opened my mouth to say as much when a shadow skimmed across my palm and dropped my missing knives into my hand.

My jaw went slack as I stared at the sharp blades, then back at Reign. A loud thump came next as my satchel appeared on the floor immersed in a cloud of black.

"You're welcome," he whispered, leaning in so close his cool breath brushed over the shell of my ear. "I'll save you the embarrassment of thanking me."

Something like emotion stung at the back of my eyes as I took in the feel of the familiar blades, but I blinked quickly, burying the rush of sentiments to the farthest corners of my mind. I was certain crying was tantamount to treason at the Conservatory.

"I'll wait outside," he said out loud as he stepped back, and I tucked the daggers back into their hiding spots within my boots.

"I'll have her mended in a few minutes, Reign." The healer turned to me, rubbing her hands. A warm glow seeped from her palms as she approached. "Don't worry, little one, it doesn't hurt a bit."

I could have been imagining it, or maybe it was the head trauma, but the healer didn't look at me with the same scorn as all the others. When she brought her luminescent palms to my head, a smile flashed across her serene face. I gritted my teeth as a flood of warmth bathed my skull and a gentle hum vibrated the air. I could practically feel my skin knitting back together. It was the strangest sensation.

"You have such beautiful hair," she murmured once she removed her hands a long moment later. "I've never seen anything quite like it. Is it typical among Kin like yourself?"

As if the dark raven hue didn't stand out enough amidst the fair-haired Fae, the streak of platinum blonde certainly was distinctive.

"Thank y—" I cut myself off before finishing the phrase. "And no, it's not typical." In fact, though a variety of shades of hair color existed among the residents of Feywood, I'd never encountered anyone with tresses like mine.

She offered a smile. "You're welcome," she whispered. "And may I offer a word of advice?"

I nodded. "You can simply say 'cheers' instead of thanking Fae."

"Cheers?"

"Yes, it doesn't hold the connotation of indebtedness, but it is an acknowledgement all the same."

"Okay, thank—cheers."

"Well done." She handed me my satchel from the marble floor. "Now go on, you mustn't keep the professor waiting. He's known to have quite a temper."

"Yes, I've come to realize that in my short time here."

Her eyes turned glossy, and a silly grin broadened her smile. "I'll let you in on a little secret: Reign is not as bad as he pretends to be."

I'd realized that, too, but thank the goddess I'd kept the revelation to myself. Of everything I'd gathered about the professor, his mercurial nature was the one consistency in his character.

"What are those silver bracelets he wears?" The question popped out before I could stop the words from tumbling free. "Since we're speaking of secrets..." I added.

"That, I'm afraid, is not mine to share." She motioned toward the door, and I took the gesture as my cue to leave.

I hopped off the table and was eternally thankful that my

world had finally stopped spinning. The Light Fae's healing power truly was exceptional. I only hoped I'd be able to master a hint of that power. Any Light power, really. Still, there was nothing I wanted more right now than to fall into my feathered bed, or even to take a dip in that divine bathing chamber.

Gingerly, I pulled open the door to the hallway, praying to all the gods that my dark escort had somehow vanished. A pair of bottomless obsidian orbs found mine as I peered through the opening.

No such luck.

"Ready?" he snapped.

"If I must be..." Crossing the threshold, I knotted my arms over my chest as I prepared for the broody professor to sweep me into his icy embrace once more. "Let's get this shadowtraveling over with already."

A devious smirk curled Reign's lips as he waggled a finger at me and tsked. "Uh, uh, uh, princess. That little treat was only because you were injured. I'm not in the habit of carrying lazy students around, even my own acquisitions."

"But how am I supposed to get to class?" I couldn't help the whiney twinge to my tone.

"With your feet, princess." He pointed two fingers down and wiggled them in a walking motion an inch from my nose. "Now, hurry. If I beat you there, you *will be* punished for tardiness." A wicked gleam brightened those endless obsidian orbs.

The rough edge to his tone sent burgeoning heat settling low in my core before I snapped myself out of it. "That's not fair, you can shadowtravel!"

"I will not use my powers, but you better move your little ass. I'll even give you a ten second head start, princess."

"Dunghead," I gritted through clenched teeth before spinning around and sprinting down the hall. Never mind that I had no idea where I was going. There was no celestial way I'd beat him back.

Unless...

Reaching around for my satchel, I pulled out the scroll Reign's shadows had delivered as I raced through the front door of the Hall of Luce. Luckily, I managed to avoid bumping into any students since the corridor was empty. Thank the goddess for small mercies.

Ah, ha! I thought so.

The crisp air swept hair across my face as I stopped at the verdant ledge that dropped at least twenty feet. I eyed the glistening depths of the meandering river that circled the Conservatory. I'd always been a strong swimmer and the current *did* surge in the right direction, straight for the Hall of Rais, according to my map. It was a good thing Rue had told me about the campus and its concentric circles.

All I had to do was survive the jump.

Indecision battled it out in my gut as I watched the churning rapids. Death by drowning or punishment by Reign? I wasn't certain which would be worse. My professor's murderous eyes flashed across my mind's eye as he tortured Kian and Lucian with his demonic shadows, and the answer came easily. I tightened the straps of my satchel over my shoulders and lifted myself over the golden balustrade.

Here goes nothing.

"Please welcome me into your open arms, Raysa," I prayed before I closed my eyes and leapt off the guardrail.

CONSERVATORY OF LUCE

FORGED IN LIGHT · TEMPERED IN TRUTH

Chapter Fourteen

A *elia*

The chilly rapids enveloped my body in a cocoon of sparkling azure ice as I plunged into the depths of the Luminoc River. *Stars!* It was frigid. The tide swept me under a few times before I managed to keep my head above the water. I drew in a frantic breath and focused on swimming.

Come on, Aelia. You can do this.

I bobbed amidst the swirling whirlpool, the current ushering me in my desired direction. As I moved, I glanced across the river at the looming darkness just over the border into the Court of Umbral Shadows. Arcanum Citadel stood a towering monstrosity of obsidian stone. Had Reign attended those sacred dark halls?

The tides grew stronger and I forced my attention away from the rival academy to my present predicament. I'd nearly reached the glistening marble bridge that served as a crossing point between the eastern and western sides of the campus. The rippling waves pushed me under the channel and once I cleared it, the radiant dome of the Hall of Rais soared ahead.

I was nearly there. It had been much faster than if I'd dared run. Not to mention safer than risking another encounter with bloodthirsty first-years.

Just a few yards ahead, an alabaster staircase emerged through the dense foliage of the cliff. That was it! I willed my frozen arms to move and dragged myself through the rapid current. Thank the gods Aidan had insisted I learned the useful skill while most Kin remained landbound.

A swathe of land jutted into the river, and I lunged for it, propelling my sodden self onto the makeshift dock. My fingers dug into the earth, nails splintering as the river tried to force my body deeper into the whirling rapids. "Come on," I gritted out.

I lost my grip, one hand falling free, and my body lurched into the spiraling eddies once more. My shoulder was nearly pulled out of its socket as I clung on with one hand. With my free one, I reached for my knife beneath the water, jerked it out of my boot, and jabbed it into the soil. With the solid grip the blade offered, I finally boosted myself out of the churning waves.

Sprawled across the lush greenery, I released a haggard breath. "I made it." My clothes were drenched, but I'd reached the other side of campus in record time. *No time to rest, Aelia.* Forcing my weary bones to stand, I took the steps two at a time, pumping my arms, until I reached the eastern edge of campus. The Hall of Rais's pristine dome surged into the heavens, like a beacon of radiant light.

Wringing out the excess water from my tunic, I traipsed up the steps and between the massive, gilded columns of the building. *Oh, please, let me have beaten Reign.* If not, that death-defying act would've been for naught.

I barreled into the hall, my boots squeaking against the marble and long, dark locks dribbling water across my shoulders. All eyes turned to me, faint chuckles ringing out as the other students took in my haggard appearance.

But I didn't care. Because the one scrutinizing gaze that was noticeably missing was Reign's.

I did it!

As if my thoughts had conjured my enigmatic professor, the door swung open behind me and his ominous presence pressed into my spine.

"Aelia, what happened?" Rue's cheery voice echoed across the cavernous space a second before she launched herself at me. "Raysa, you're soaked!"

Reign coalesced in front of me, that dark gaze cloaked in shadows. "Decided to go for a swim, princess?" Amusement flickered across those midnight spheres, and something else, too. Pride?

No, I must have imagined it.

"You continue to surprise me," he murmured beneath his breath. That piercing gaze finally released me and dropped to the floor, to the growing puddle around my boots. "Try not to inundate my classroom, first-year."

"Oh, I can help with that." Rue flashed me a smile, and a now familiar golden glow lit up her fingers. "I'll have you all dry in no time." As my roommate lifted her hands and warmth seeped from her palms, the chill that had overtaken my bones since my leap off the cliff finally began to dissipate.

Reign stepped behind me and leaned in, his nose nearly brushing the rounded tip of my ear. "It's a pity. I think I like you sopping wet, princess," he whispered.

A flare of heat kindled below my navel and traveled across my cheeks. I was so hot I was fairly certain I had no need for Rue's magic at all. He shot me a feral grin before stomping to the front of the classroom. "Now, finally," he announced. "We shall begin today's lesson in Shadow Arts."

Sweat beaded across my brow as I trudged down the steps of the Hall of Rais with Rue skipping along beside me. After two hours with the grueling professor of Shadow Arts, not to mention the assault and impromptu swim in the river, I could barely lift my feet.

"Are you okay?" Rue cast a worried glance in my direction. "Maybe the healer's *rais* wasn't strong enough."

"No, my head is fine." It was every other bone in my body that felt like it had been shadowmelded. "I'm just exhausted." I'd given my roommate a quick summary of what had transpired with Kian and Lucian. She'd been furious, her cheeks burning until her freckles nearly popped off her typically pallid skin.

Rue curled a slender arm across my shoulders and drew me into her side, which must have appeared quite comical considering our rather noticeable height disparity. "Should we grab a bite to eat then return to our chamber?"

I shook my head. "I'm too tired to even eat."

"Oh, sweet Raysa, it's clear you weren't raised at court." A male voice echoed behind us.

I spun around, my fingers an inch from reaching for one of the daggers concealed in my boots. But an unexpected smile flashed across the Fae male's face. He held out his hand and dipped into a bow. "A pleasure, ladies. Symon Lightspire here, but please call me Sy."

I vaguely recognized the light-haired male who'd winked at me when Flare Squad was first assembled in the Hall of Luminescence. And that name also struck a bell, but I couldn't quite place it. Dropping my guarded stance, I allowed my weary muscles to relax and returned a tight smile.

"Hi!" Rue bounced up and down on her tiptoes. "Lightspire... do you have an older sister?"

"I do. I believe Sissily is in Heaton's class."

"Yes, that's right. That's why I recognized the name." Rue

leaned in and whispered in my ear. "She and Heaton had a thing for a minute when they were first-years."

"Ah, I see."

"That practically makes us family." Symon wrapped an arm around each of us, and every muscle in my body tensed. I was not accustomed to being touched by Fae males, and especially not by ones I barely knew. "Shall we go dine at the banquet hall?"

"I was trying to convince Aelia, but she claims to be too tired."

"Now, that's nonsense. No one is ever too tired to eat, my new round-eared friend." He flicked my ear, almost tenderly. I shooed him away, but his smile only grew wider. "No disrespect intended, Aelia, I just find those rounded things so erotic."

I nearly choked on a laugh. "Excuse me?"

He chuckled. "Oh, apologies, I forget how easily flustered Kin can get about sexual matters. I've just never been with a mortal, so color me intrigued."

"Well, everything that you've heard is true. We do have incredibly delicate sensibilities, so I'd appreciate it if you didn't touch my ear. Or any other part of my rounded anatomy."

A wild cackle burst free, and his head fell back, tumbles of wild curly blonde hair spilling across his forehead. "Aelia, I think we are going to get along just splendidly."

"How do you know so much about Kin?" Rue asked.

Despite my best efforts to steer us to the dormitories, I found our threesome moving toward the banquet hall. With a grunt of irritation, I allowed Symon to usher us toward the scent of roasted meat and vegetables already tingeing the air. I reminded myself that I needed nourishment to keep my strength up if I was expected to survive more days like these.

"I spent a month in Feywood as part of my studies in secondary school," Symon replied, and my ears perked up.

"You did?"

His hold tightened around my shoulders as he drew me into

his side. "I did. Being so close to the Wilds was unnerving, and the living conditions were truly atrocious, but there was something calming and pleasant about the simple life." His slim shoulders lifted. "And despite my devastatingly charming personality, I was unable to bed a single Kin."

Rue giggled, but I couldn't suppress the dramatic eyeroll.

"Perhaps female Kin don't find you as irresistible as the Fae."

"Female, male, I do not discriminate, but neither would put out." His bottom lip pushed into what I had to admit was an adorable pout. Like most Fae, Symon was beautiful. With light lashes that fanned across high cheekbones and those mesmerizing lilac eyes that twinkled with each cheeky grin. "I blame my father. A large portion of the farmable lands in Feywood belong to our family. The Kin didn't simply dislike *me*, it was my last name they despised."

Lightspire! No wonder the name had seemed familiar. I'd spent the better part of my adulthood tilling their lands. "Thank the goddess I never ran into you," I muttered.

"You see!" Symon clucked his tongue. "Completely biased and unfair."

"Why would you even want to bed a Kin?" I blurted. "I'm sure we're very similar to Fae in the anatomical respect."

His light brow arched as he eyed my ear.

"Oh, Raysa," I gritted out, earning a chuckle from the surprisingly friendly male.

"It's not only that," he continued. "From what I understand, mortals feel things more acutely, something about their shortened lifespan enhances life's pleasures." He shrugged again.

I didn't dare announce I wouldn't know since I'd yet to have lain with a male, Kin or otherwise. It wasn't as if I'd never had the opportunity, it was simply that none of my suitors ever seemed that appealing. It was as if I'd been waiting and waiting for that special moment that just never came.

Symon paused in front of the Hall of Elysia, drawing all three of us to a halt. The mouthwatering scents perfumed the air and my stomach let out an embarrassing rumble.

"Well, it's clearly settled." Symon threw me a lopsided smile. "Aelia of Feywood, you *are* hungry, and we will all be dining together this evening so that you may tell me all the secrets of the Kin so that next time I find myself in your lands, I will be certain to cajole an innocent victim into my bed."

An embarrassing chuckle erupted at his ridiculousness. Rue was already grinning like mad.

"At worst, I will provide some entertainment before I accompany you lovely ladies to your chambers."

"To the door and no further," I interjected.

His hand jutted out, and long fingers gently caressed my ear as he sucked his lower lip between his teeth. For some inane reason, I let him. Perhaps it was simply because it was the first time a male Fae had showed me an inch of kindness or interest. Pathetic.

"You wound me so, Aelia." His smile grew downright wicked, but he finally released my ear with a sigh. "One day?" His brow lifted into a mischievous arch.

"Doubtful." I countered with a sweet smile.

He mimed a knife plunging into his heart and dramatically clutched at his chest. "Fine, fine, fine. I'll settle on friendship then."

My silly heart grew wings as I glanced between Rue and Symon. I had friends who were actually Light Fae. Reign had been wrong with his gloom and doom speech. Not everyone here was my enemy.

Chapter Fifteen

A*elia*

"Come now, Rue, we can't be late." I tugged my friend down the spiraling staircase, weaving between the crowd of Fae.

Miraculously, I'd survived my first week at the Conservatory of Luce, standing shoulder to shoulder against much more powerful Light Fae. I was still the only one without a hint of magic, or *rais*, as everyone continued to remind me, while all the other students had already manifested basic skills like illumination sight and photokinesis, even before setting foot on campus.

At least today, I hoped to level the playing field. Combat would surely be the one class I'd excel in. After all, I'd trained with Aidan nearly my entire life. I'd mastered a variety of weapons, I was strong, nimble and most of all, I couldn't wait to prove to my team that I wasn't just a worthless, magicless Kin.

We crossed through the enormous, gilded doorway of the

Hall of Glory, and the brilliant morning sun brushed my shoulders. I'd reverted to my old, worn tunic this morning. The sleeveless top would allow for freer usage of my arms when wielding weapons. And I needed every advantage I could get.

"Looking good today, Aelia," Symon called out from across the lawn. He stood beside a few of the male members of Flare Squad, Zephyr and Silvan, I believed were their names.

My cheeks heated as they always did when my new friend called unwanted attention to me. Though an entire week had passed, the glares that constantly followed hadn't subsided one bit. On the positive side, I hadn't been attacked, and I'd yet to see Lucian at all. Stranger still, according to rumors, Kian had been assaulted in his dormitory and had spent the past week recovering at the healer's.

Symon jogged up to meet us, toting the two males behind. Neither had been particularly nasty, but no one from the team besides Rue and Symon had bothered to speak more than a few words to me. In general, the males' curious glances paled in comparison to the females' wicked glares. I blamed my midnight hair with the freakish blonde streak. And of course, my ears. Symon eyed them like he was a second from reaching out and caressing the rounded curve.

"Don't you dare," I hissed. It was one thing when he fondled my ear when it was only Rue and me, but in front of the others? Absolutely not.

"You're no fun at all, Aelia."

"As it should be. Your years spent training at the Conservatory, especially as first-years, should be anything but fun." A deep voice vibrated the air behind me and Reign's booming presence pressed into my back. The man moved like a wraith. I twisted around, a pair of fathomless orbs capturing me in their mesmerizing gaze.

My heart pitched forward as if I'd suddenly taken flight. But, of course, that was impossible since I lacked the necessary luminescent appendages. Our Shadow Fae professor's wings of shadow were on full display, towering high above his shoulders and head. They were all at once terrifying and exquisite.

His eyes darted to Rue and the males, finally releasing me from their piercing gaze. "No dawdling, Flare Squad, I wouldn't want you to be late to my class. The punishment would be severe." A smirk hitched up the corners of his mouth as his gaze traveled to mine once more.

I swallowed hard as the terrifying images of what Reign had done to Kian and Lucian surged to the forefront of my mind. A tiny part of me wanted to believe he'd done it to protect me, but then the logical side told me to stop being so stupid.

I was nothing more than his acquisition.

When my scroll appeared late last night with today's schedule and I'd discovered Reign would also be my Combat instructor, a tangle of unease and excitement had assaulted my nerves. Much like I felt right now in his presence.

"See you all in class." Reign spun on his heel, those ominous shadows cloaking his muscular form. My traitorous gaze followed him until he disappeared in a shroud of night.

"I wish we could travel through sunbeams like they do with shadows," said the male with the closely shorn hair. I was ninety percent certain his name was Zephyr.

"Hmm, it would make traversing this enormous campus much easier," Symon replied.

"If you think about it, the Shadow Fae have much more impressive abilities than we do." The other Fae male pulled his long, ashen locks into a high bun.

"Bite your tongue, Silvan," Sy snapped. "If the headmaster hears you talking like that, you'll be succumbing to Reign's lethal shadows much like poor Isaac."

My stomach pitched.

"You do remember the first-year who was killed by Reign's corruptive touch on orientation day, right Sil?"

I would certainly never forget it.

"Corruptive touch?" I squeaked, the embarrassing sound erupting through my clenched lips.

"I thought it was his power of umbral constructs that did him in," Zephyr interjected.

Clearly, I needed to study my Shadow Arts manual more thoroughly this evening. Corruptive touch? Umbral constructs? How many abilities did the blasted Fae of the Umbral Court possess? After a week of class with the mercurial professor, I hadn't learned nearly enough about his powers.

Sy waved a dismissive hand. "Whatever it was, I have no desire to meet a similar fate."

Everyone in the circle nodded, myself included. It had seemed like a horrible way to go.

"Can you imagine the breadth of Reign's powers if those manacles ever came off?" Silvan's broad shoulders trembled.

"No, never." Sy's expression grew haunted.

"So it's true, then?" I asked. "Those silver cuffs inhibit his power?"

The males all nodded.

"My brother graduated from the Conservatory the year Reign arrived," said Zephyr. "He said the professor was like a wild animal. He'd used his umbral daggers to try to cut off his own wrists to remove them."

An icy chill zipped up my spine at the grisly image.

"If it hadn't been for the healer," Zephyr continued, "he would have bled out."

No wonder Reign had been so reticent when I'd asked about them.

"That's awful," said Rue, her lips screwing into a pout. "He scares the sun out of me, but no one deserves to have their abilities imprisoned like that."

"Imagine what that buildup of *nox* must be doing to him," Silvan whispered.

A long moment of silence settled over us. From what little I'd learned about Reign so far, his ill-tempered disposition began to make more sense. But if he was so powerful, why did he remain here? If he'd been banished from the Court of Umbral Shadows, surely, he could have found another territory to reside in beyond Aetheria. Crescentia was a large continent with varied peoples and lands.

"Anyway," said Sy, interrupting my musings. "I'm not looking forward to our first battle against our dark colleagues across the river. If any of them have powers even close to Reign's..."

"When will that be?" I blurted.

"At the end of the term. It's our final test to determine if we are allowed to remain at the Conservatory." Rue offered me a reassuring smile. "Don't worry, we'll all be much more advanced in our training by then."

Gods, I hoped so.

She threaded her arm through mine and tugged me toward the training field. To the west of the main building, the Hall of Glory, was the immense parcel of land dedicated to combat training. In addition to the acres of land outside, an indoor gymnasium stood at the center to house the myriads of weapons the Conservatory supplied, as well as serving as a secondary training location in the case of inclement weather.

From across the verdant field, a swirl of shadows coalesced at the door to the gymnasium. *Noxus*, we were going to be late.

"Hurry." I pulled Rue into a jog as Sy complained from behind us, huffing and puffing as he picked up the pace. We darted across the lush field as our fellow first-years lumbered toward the gymnasium.

According to the mystical scroll, we were to assemble here and await Reign for further instructions. Rue and I darted up the marble steps, through the gilded columns to the domed building with Sy, Zephyr and Silvan trailing right behind us.

The enormous metal doors were open, and across the gleaming parquet floor stood Reign, a hood cloaking his menacing form. "Ten seconds," he barked.

We raced through the threshold and filed into the massive chamber. No one spoke, a charged current weighing in the air. The doors began to close, the ominous creaking spiking my pulse. Two first-year females slid between the crack, right before the doors slammed closed with a depressing ring of finality.

I glanced around the crowded space at the eight teams made up of the initiates. By a quick count, all twenty of us from Flare Squad had made it, along with Heaton, who stood at the back of our group.

Some of the other squads weren't as lucky, with a few missing members.

"Now, let's begin." Reign's booming voice filled the gymnasium and all excited murmurs instantly fell away.

Sharp pounding at the door swiveled my gaze over my shoulder.

"Oh, no," Heaton muttered, shaking his head.

I pivoted just in time to see the swarm of shadows peeling from Reign's body. They zipped across the room, flying over our heads and slid through the cracks in the door. My heart rammed up my throat. An impossibly long moment later, a spine-tingling shriek echoed just outside the door.

A gasp escaped, and I squeezed my eyes closed, imagining that Isaac boy again and the look of sheer terror on his face. Before I could chase back the grisly images, Reign's shadows reappeared and once again coiled tightly around their master.

I glared across the chamber at the bloodthirsty Fae, all previous notions of understanding the twisted male vanishing. His gaze caught mine, and as if he could read the hatred in my expression, his dark eyes tapered.

They locked on mine, and for a moment, it was as if we were the only two beings in the room, as if he were speaking directly to me. "Some of you may not understand why it's necessary for brutal punishments to be inflicted. But you will once we cross that river."

His lethal gaze drifted from mine, releasing me from its

mesmerizing hold. I loosed a breath and glanced between Rue and Symon. Neither seemed as affected as I was. I didn't think I could ever get used to the rampant cruelty or its complete acceptance at this academy.

"Now, I need all of you to break up into your teams and find a partner. Then I will allow each of you by squad to choose your weapon of choice. Today, we will alternate between that chosen weapon and hand-to-hand combat."

I pushed down the inappropriate anger and reminded myself why I was here. I was not here to find a shred of decency in a male that clearly held none. I was not here to judge the brutal ways of the Light Fae. I was here to survive.

"Aelia, will you be my partner?" Rue stepped forward, an excited grin flashing across her face.

"I would love to."

CONSERVATORY OF LUCE

FORGED IN LIGHT · TEMPERED IN TRUTH

Chapter Sixteen

A*elia*

It was no wonder we only had two classes per day, because they each lasted an eternity. Sweat trickled down my spine and exhaustion seeped into muscles I didn't even know existed. Rue might have been small, but behind that sweet smile lay a fierce Fae female.

I should have known since her brother was our squad leader.

Heaton watched from beyond the circle, his gaze intent on both his sister and me. For the most part, he'd allowed us to figure it out, rarely stepping in. We'd moved past the weapons portion of the exercise, and now Rue and I circled, each waiting for the other to make a move.

I clearly had a size advantage over her, but after the past two hours of training with short swords, I'd come to realize not to underestimate my feisty friend.

G.K. DEROSA

"Come on, ladies, do something," Sy called out from the sideline.

We danced around the circle, a nervous tension tingeing the air. The object was simple, get your opponent outside of the red sphere. In theory, I should've been able to use my larger size to push her out, but I hadn't been able to get close enough to lay a single hand on her yet.

"Oh, hush," Rue hissed over her shoulder, but somehow, her bright blue eyes never deviated from mine.

"Make your move, princess." An icy tendril of darkness licked across the shell of my ear. I swatted it away, half-expecting to find Reign behind me. Only he was all the way across the room, glaring down one of the first-years from Solar Squad.

How was that possible?

A petite form pummeled into me while I was distracted, and I hit the floor with a smack. "Son of *Noxus*!" I bit out, my teeth gnashing on impact.

"Sorry, A." Rue tossed me a wink as she hovered over me, her small hands holding down my shoulders.

Goddess, for such a little thing, she was strong.

I squirmed beneath her, vaulting my hips like I'd done when Kian attacked me and sent her flying back. Nearly outside the red line.

"Let's see what you've got, princess." Reign's voice slithered over my ear once again, taunting. "We're not here for playtime. You are here to train to become one of the great Royal Guardians of the court, and only the strongest will claim that title. The rest of you will return to the dismal holes you emerged from or worst, you'll spend the rest of your days patrolling the Wilds."

The Wilds? How had no one mentioned that yet?

I wouldn't allow him to distract me this time. Before Rue could get back on her feet, I jumped on top of her and straddled her slim hips. The top of her head was only a yard away from the red line now. I just had to push her across.

114

I dropped down and wrapped my arms around her, planning to carry her across the line if that's what it took. But her little hand shot out, and a blinding light emanated from her palm. My lids snapped shut as stars danced across my vision, and I let out a curse. How could I fall for that again?

"If she were a Shadow Fae, you'd be dead, initiate." Reign's gravelly voice surged all around me, and my entire body lit up at his presence.

I forced my eyes open and found our combat professor looming just outside the circle. He must have shadowtraveled across the room.

"Well, it's a good thing we're just training," I hissed.

Reign snapped his fingers and icy wisps of darkness curled around my arms and hauled me off the floor. The bastard let me hang in the air, legs dangling for an endless moment before he dropped me.

Looming over me, his body a hairsbreadth from mine, he whispered, "Let me give you a word of advice, princess. Don't choose a friend as your sparring partner. Your weak mortal sensibilities will deter you from doing what is necessary to win." He spun on his heel and pointed at Belmore. "You, come here."

All the air squeezed from my lungs as the big male stalked into the ring.

No. Why him? Of all the members of Flare Squad, why did Reign have to choose the male that hated me the most? Perhaps, I should have shared Belmore's involvement in my attack with my professor, but I'd been too embarrassed to bring it up.

Belmore's thin lips curled into a savage smile.

"No daggers this time, Aelia," Reign announced, eyeing my boots, "or you will be disqualified." He moved to the edge of the ring, dark gaze intent on mine. "I want to see how you fare against a real opponent."

I stood there, frozen, toeing the red line. Belmore crooked a long finger in my direction and beckoned me forward. "Come on, little Kin, let's see what you can do without your weapons."

This was hardly fair. The male easily outweighed me by a few stones. Not to mention I had no magic to speak of, and basic *rais* was allowed in hand-to-hand combat.

"Today, Aelia," Reign growled. "We'd like to make it to the banquet hall before it closes for the evening."

Gritting my teeth, I tossed him a sneer and stepped inside the ring. *Please, Raysa, let it be quick.* The moment my boot crossed the line, Belmore lunged. I darted to the right, just barely missing the swipe of his meaty paw. He let out a growl as we circled each other, the air thick with anticipation. I could feel every muscle, every sense, primed for battle. For an instant, I was back on the field with Aidan, his patient voice guiding me through the steps. Belmore was formidable, his body honed with muscled precision, his eyes gleaming with challenge. More than that, this was his chance for revenge, to embarrass me as I'd embarrassed him.

He lunged again, the clash electric, as his fist slammed into my gut with a force that sent shockwaves through the air. I gasped, my jaw nearly unhinging. He was relentless, each strike a thunderbolt, aimed with lethal accuracy. I staggered back a few steps, all the wind knocked out of me before I planted the heel of my boot at the edge of the ring.

"Come on, Aelia!" Rue's voice echoed behind me.

He swung his foot and kicked my legs out from under me. I slammed into the floor with a crack, my backside absorbing most of the pain. "Mother Raysa," I hissed out.

Belmore was on me again before I had a chance to stand. His big hands clamped down on my shoulders as he attempted to drag me past the confines of the circle. I kicked and squirmed beneath him, landing a knee in his groin.

His head fell back and he released a volley of curses. "Bitch," he snarled, his eyes flashing.

"Kick him in the balls again!" Sy shouted from the sidelines. "Anything goes!"

I leapt to my feet as he circled me once again. If I could just

116

avoid him, maybe I'd be able to tire him out. My own muscles ached, the fatigue from the endless day of sparring boring into me. As the battle wore on, I danced on the edge of his reach, my movements a whisper against his storm. He was powerful, but I found power in agility, in the spaces between his strikes. It became a rhythm, a deadly dance of advance and retreat. One in which neither of us was winning.

Belmore finally grew tired of the waltz and charged, his arms spread wide as he barreled into me. The force of his weight sent me sprawling to the ground. My head smacked against the unyielding floor and pain ricocheted across my skull. Gritting my teeth through the agony, I attempted to scramble to my feet. My vision was hazy, and Belmore blurred in and out as he rushed toward me.

Oh no, not again.

Clenching my fist, I pulled my arm back and landed a punch to his exposed right side, just under his ribcage. Belmore let out a howl and buckled over, retreating a few steps. A shot to the liver was excruciatingly painful, Aidan had taught me that. A correctly placed hit could incapacitate even your strongest opponent. And I had something more than just strength; I had resolve, honed from years of being underestimated.

With the big giant still folded over, clutching his side, I launched my attack. In that split second with his guard dropped, and with all the force of my being, I unleashed a flurry of strikes, a tempest that he hadn't expected. He staggered back a step and then another. The red line loomed ominously less than a yard away. Dropping my shoulder, I released a feral growl and pummeled into him with the last shreds of my remaining strength. He teetered on the edge of the red circle for an endless moment before his heel inched across the line.

Rue and Sy let out a resounding whoop, wild applause drowning out the mad thumping of my heart. My chest caved, heaving in ragged breaths as I stood in the center of the circle.

Belmore glared at me from across the divide, defeat in his eyes as he muttered a curse and spun away, still gripping his side.

The moment he stalked away, I dropped to the ground. The gymnasium tilted again, and I blinked quickly to right the domed ceiling, which had suddenly dropped between my legs.

Reign's dark form coalesced before me, a glimmer of something unreadable in his midnight irises. "Do I need to send you to the healer again?"

I shook my head, slowly, so as not to aggravate the spinning. "I think once is enough for the week."

The ghost of a smile kissed his lips. "Well done, princess. I knew you could do it." He offered me his hand, and I eyed it skeptically for a long moment before my fingers closed around his palm.

Tiny jolts of awareness seeped into my hand and surged up my arm until goosebumps cascaded over my skin. Goddess, what sort of *nox* was that? I stared up at him for an endless moment, our gazes locked in an epic battle. The air became charged, the entire atmosphere thick with his oppressive power. Those shadows swirled across his form, growing larger and more potent with every exhale.

Rue suddenly bounced between us, throwing an arm across my shoulder, and Reign's hold fell away, both the physical and metaphysical one. With the connection severed, I dropped my gaze and drew in a lungful of much needed air.

"Well done, first-years," Reign barked from somewhere behind me. "We're finished for today."

From the corner of my eye, I watched as the prince of shadows stalked toward the door, his power thrusting in waves all around him.

"Do you feel that?" I whispered to Rue beside me.

"Feel what?" She followed my line of sight to Reign's retreating form.

"That overwhelming power any time he's in the room."

Her slim shoulders lifted. "Sure, a little. He's a formidable

Fae, Aelia, and as our illumination sight grows stronger, his aura will become more defined." She offered a smile and a pat on the back. "It's a good sign that you can already pick up on it."

My lips slid into a smile, but it didn't quite feel right. There was more to it, I was certain of it. I couldn't read anyone's aura as clearly as Reign's. It was as if I was somehow attuned to his power.

Symon threw his arm across my shoulders, pulling me into his side. Every muscle ached at the unexpected jostling. "Well done, my little Kin!" He pressed a kiss to the shell of my ear and the smack echoed across my eardrum. "Tonight, we celebrate your victory."

"What? No..." My head whipped back and forth as he steered me through the gymnasium doorway.

"Yes," Rue squealed, scampering beside us. "We must!"

"It's a Conservatory of Luce tradition," Sy interjected.

"What is?"

"Surviving the first ten days of the term."

I cocked a skeptical brow. "Seriously?"

Symon held up his hand, his expression one of utter solemnity. "If I'm lying, may the great goddess strike me down." He tipped his head up to the brilliant sunbeams crisscrossing the cerulean sky. "You see?" His smirk was contagious, and I found myself laughing at my ludicrous friend.

Rue bounced on her tiptoes as we crossed the lawn toward the Hall of Glory. "Oh, and Heaton smuggled in some laegar from our hometown."

"What's that?" My nose crinkled, because I already had a pretty good idea.

"It's a special brew distilled from the wheat native to our little corner of Aetheria."

Sy's lilac eyes lit up. "Oh, yes, girl! I've heard that draught is potent."

"It is. Especially the way my Pa makes it."

My thoughts whirled back to the honeyed wine, and my lips

puckered. "Sorry, friends, but I will not be indulging in any exotic Fae beverages again any time soon."

"Fine," Rue grumbled. "Just come with us to Heaton's tonight. It will only be Flare Squad and a few of my brother's closest friends. You don't have to drink a thing." She offered me her pinky, and I eyed it, thoroughly confused.

"What? It's a pinky promise. You don't have the Kin version? It's like a light form of a Fae bargain."

Oh, gods, no, even I knew never to strike a bargain with the Fae.

"Relax, A." Rue tossed me a smile. "Just come tonight. I swear it'll be fun."

Famous last words.

FORGED IN LIGHT · TEMPERED IN TRUTH

Chapter Seventeen

A *elia*

I squirmed nervously on the settee in Heaton's dormitory, an exact replica of our own. Only instead of two beds, the commander of Flare Squad only had one massive one in the center of the space. Gauzy lace curtains and climbing verdant vines hung from the four-poster bed. Brilliant light streamed in from the arched windows, casting light on the ensuing debauchery. Even if I hadn't promised myself not to partake in any suspect Fae beverages this evening, I wasn't certain I could have relaxed beneath the relentless sunshine. There was something about getting inebriated in the daytime that seemed wrong.

Perhaps it was just my *delicate Kin sensibilities*. Goddess, why did Reign affect me so? I shouldn't give two gildings about what he thought of me. And I didn't.

"Aelia!" Rue staggered over with a tankard of laegar in her hand. The immense mug was bigger than her head and already nearly empty. "Come dance with us." She tugged Silvan by the collar and wiggled her cute little body against his.

At some point, a dark corner of Heaton's chamber had become a raging mini dancefloor. The ivy curled over the tangle of bodies writhing to the hypnotic beats.

"I don't think so," I finally murmured.

"Oh, come on!" Rue leaned over the settee, her mouth only a few inches from my own, and the pungent scent of hops and alcohol made my nose twitch. "Sy is on the dancefloor too."

I glanced over her shoulder to see our friend grinding against one of Heaton's fourth-year classmates. The male was huge with glowing runes tattooed up and down his bare arms. Symon must have felt my curious gaze because he threw me a wink over the massive male's shoulder. Then he beckoned me over with a curl of his finger.

My head whipped back and forth, and I swiveled my gaze back to Rue. Silvan was rubbing up behind her, dancing to the intoxicating beats. Good goddess, what was in this laegar?

A tiny part of me was jealous of my new friends, of their uninhibitedness and the freedom it brought. I had to remind myself I didn't have that luxury. If I had any hopes of surviving at the Conservatory, I had to always be on top of my game. Which meant not giving into seductive nights like these.

"Go have fun," I whisper-shouted to my friend. "I'm having a great time watching you all."

Silvan tugged on Rue's arm, and with one last pouting glance, she scampered off toward the dancefloor.

It wasn't a complete lie, I really did enjoy watching my friends' drunken antics. It reminded me of another lifetime when I was just a young Kin gathering with a group of friends after we'd finished our schooling. It was nowhere near this luxury, of course, but we had fun all the same.

"Aelia, what are you doing just sitting there?" Heaton's warm breath danced across the shell of my ear. His long, blonde hair was tied back neatly at his nape, as he often wore it, blue eyes sparkling with the effects of the laegar. He held a tankard in one hand and a smaller stein in the other.

"I'm Fae-watching."

He leapt over the back of the sofa and folded down beside me before handing me the stein. "It's just water. Rue told me you weren't drinking tonight."

I took the offered mug, sniffing it before indulging in a big swallow. My throat was parched. After days of intense training, my entire body felt depleted.

He loosely hung his arm across my shoulders while I sipped the cool water and pierced me with a questioning glance.

"What?" I finally blurted when the silence became too thick.

"You've really impressed me, Aelia."

My cheeks burned at the compliment.

"I'll be very honest with you, I didn't think you'd make it past the first week."

"And here we are at day ten." I clinked my mug against his.

A rueful chuckle vibrated his broad chest. "It's better than many full-blooded Light Fae have fared."

My brows quirked at his word choice, and I placed my mug down on the gilded side table. "Full-blooded?"

His lips pinched as he regarded me. "Please don't take that as an insult. I only assumed that perhaps you were of mixed blood. Half-kin, half-Light Fae. I presumed that was why your *rais* hadn't manifested yet." His gaze lifted to my rounded appendages.

"And why my ears aren't pointed like yours."

He shrugged. "It's simply a thought."

It was a good one. I was surprised I hadn't even considered it sooner myself. Perhaps, it was because it was so rare for Fae and Kin to mix at all.

Heaton's warm hand landed on my thigh, distracting me from my swirling thoughts. "I apologize, I shouldn't have brought it up. Tonight is supposed to be an evening of fun and distractions." He leaned in closer and twirled a dark lock of hair around his finger. "I've never seen hair so beautiful," he whispered.

"Th—cheers."

His smile broadened. "I see you're learning quickly."

"I am. The last thing I need is to be indebted to my team leader." I reached for my mug and took a long pull to hide my smirk.

Another chuckle tumbled free. "I'm not the worst Fae to owe a debt to."

"Oh, I'm sure you're right about that." I scanned the room filled with my squad mates and a dozen other fourth-years I didn't recognize. Though Rue had assured me I'd be safe, I knew better than to ever let my guard down around these Fae.

"Come on, then, dance with me." His bright eyes lit up with excitement as he extended his hand, and I couldn't deny the faint stirring in my chest. Heaton was an extremely attractive male, and even my inexperienced lady parts could appreciate that.

"Fine, but just one dance."

"Challenge accepted." He smirked and took the drink from my hand, depositing it onto the table. He wrapped his hand around mine and led me to the impromptu dancefloor. A handful of jealous gazes flickered in my direction. I tried to ignore them and focused on Rue and Sy wiggling their behinds with their respective dance partners.

"Aelia!" Rue abandoned Silvan and threw her arms around my neck as I approached. "Finally!"

Symon rushed up behind me, pressing me into a Light Fae sandwich and a giggle burst free.

"Hey, you two," Heaton grumbled, "I was the one that did all the work of getting her on the dancefloor and now you get to reap the benefits?"

"Tough luck, brother." Rue tossed him a cheeky grin.

My two friends surrounded me, and the initial awkwardness

started to dwindle. As the music blared on, my body began to move to the rhythm. I recognized a few of the other members of the squad: Phoebia, Jacarta, and Ariadne. The females were among those who'd been staring as Heaton led me to the dance-floor. Besides them, Zephyr, Manon, and Dinan danced with a pair of females I didn't recognize, likely fourth-years and friends of Heaton.

After a few minutes, all the faces and bodies began to blur together as I wiggled and moved to the beats. My muscles felt looser and my hips swayed more easily, the time swimming by. The laegar flowed freely and more than once I wondered how my friends would survive class tomorrow morning. At least Combat wasn't on the schedule.

Sweat coated my brow and trickled down my spine as the night wore on and on. I was suddenly thankful that Rue had insisted I wore the light sheath dress with leggings as opposed to the thick tunic and leathers I'd originally planned on wearing.

"Isn't this the best?" Rue bounced on her tiptoes, grabbing my hands.

"It is!" I took another long pull from the tankard filled with water.

Heaton appeared behind me, enveloping me in his strong arms. "Finally, I found you," he whispered, the scent of laegar heavy on his breath. He'd clearly had too much to drink, which explained his sudden boldness, but I leaned into him despite myself. Rue's brother had been the first Fae to show even the slightest bit of interest in me—besides Symon, of course, but he simply had a rounded-ear fetish. A silly smile spread my lips at the thought of my friend. Heaton's hand drifted down to my waist and his firm fingers dug into my hip. A flare of heat kindled below, and all thoughts of Sy flew out the window.

"Heaton!" A shrill cry jerked me from the sultry song and the feel of my squad leader behind me.

He peeled himself off and turned to the irate silver-haired female.

"What are you doing with *her*?" she snarled, nostrils flared.

A rosy hue blanketed Heaton's cheeks as he faced off with the girl. "Oriah, calm down, we were only dancing."

"I *won't* calm down. Is this Kin the reason you broke up with me?"

Oh, Raysa. I staggered back a step, wishing I could disappear into the thick wall of ivy coiling behind me.

Rue stepped between her brother and the female, hands lifted palms up. "Oriah, I'm sure that's not what happened."

"Oh, Rue, stop defending him. You have no idea what he's like."

Her light eyes tapered at the edges, and a hint of the ruthless Fae I'd seen on the training mat surged to the surface. "Maybe I don't, but he's still my brother, and I won't simply stand here and watch you insult him or my friend." Her gaze swiveled toward me, and that unfamiliar warmth kindled in my chest.

"I can't believe this." Oriah lifted her perky little nose in the air, grabbed one of the other females and marched to the door. The sharp slam echoed across the chamber, cracking over the hum of music.

The moment she was gone, Heaton appeared by my side. "I'm sorry about that, Aelia."

I waved a dismissive hand. "No, please, there's nothing to be sorry about. You don't owe me anything." I was beyond stupid to think that just for one night I could be seen as one of them. I would not make that mistake again. "I—I have to go."

"No, don't leave." Rue bounded up beside me and squeezed my hand. "Oriah is a terribly jealous little thing. She and Heaton haven't been together for a while."

I glanced between both siblings, a whisper of embarrassment rearing up. "It's not that, I swear. I'm simply exhausted."

"I'll go back with you then," Rue offered.

"No, that is completely unnecessary; stay and have fun."

Silvan still lingered beside my friend, an eager look in his eye. He clearly was hoping to bed my roommate this evening, even I could see that.

"At least let me walk you to your room. As your squad leader, of course." Heaton's warm smile eased some of the awkwardness.

"Okay," I finally mumbled. With my luck, Oriah and her friend would be waiting to ambush me on the spiral staircase of death.

Heaton ushered me through the tangle of bodies littering his chamber. As soon as we reached the quiet hallway, I heaved in a breath of fresh air. I hadn't even noticed how suffocating it had gotten inside with so many people.

"I hope you had some fun this evening," Heaton whispered. The corridors were silent, and it only just occurred to me that his chamber must have been encased in some sort of silencing spell.

"I did." I glanced at Heaton who watched me with a hopeful smile. "It was certainly the most fun I've had since I arrived at the Conservatory."

"Well, that doesn't say much." A rueful grin parted his lips.

I wondered if he knew about the attack. Had Rue shared the embarrassing truth with her brother? I'd hate for him to pity me.

We reached the glass staircase and he offered his hand. "I've had more than my share of laegar tonight, Aelia, do you mind?" A playful smirk curved his lips and brightened the turquoise of his eyes.

"Don't worry, I'll keep you safe." I threw him back a grin.

The sharp crack of glass shattering sent my heart leaping up my throat and my eyes to the glass dome above. Dozens of dark shadows streaked through the gaping hole in the atrium.

"Shit," Heaton hissed. "Get down!"

Chapter Eighteen

A<small>elia</small>

"What is happening?" I shrieked as glass rained down on us, the tiny shards piercing my skin despite Heaton's attempt at blanketing my body with his own.

"Shadow Fae attack," he hissed.

"What? But I thought we were mostly at peace with the Court of Umbral Shadows?"

"We are. This is an unscheduled Arcanum Citadel exercise."

"What!?" I repeated, a few octaves higher this time. "Does this happen often?"

A second later, two sharp blares echoed across the blossoming chaos. I slapped my hands over my ears as the strident sound vibrated the entire atrium.

"Only a few times a year. Don't worry, they've triggered the alarms, the squads will be convening in no time."

I watched as a dark, murky shadow swooped in from the hole in the glass dome. I immediately recognized the hippogriff covered in tendrils of night from the day I'd arrived at the academy.

"Go back upstairs, Aelia, now!" Heaton shouted. "Find Rue and stay with her, you'll be safe."

"I can't just leave you here."

"The other teams will be here any second. I'll be fine." Heaton splayed his hands and flames danced across his palms.

Mother Raysa!

The fire blossomed across his skin, growing more and more brilliant until it formed a large sphere. He hurled it at the Shadow skyrider and nailed the hippogriff's long tail. The beast screeched and bucked mid-air, nearly sending his rider tumbling off.

"Aelia, go, I've got this!"

"But I can help." I bent down and unsheathed my daggers as another flying creature zipped overhead. With the body of a lion and a bird-like head, the animal released a beastly roar and banked straight for us. A gryphon?

"Get out of here, now, Aelia! As your squad leader, that's a direct order." Anger curled my fingers around the hilts of my daggers. "You're not ready for this; it's an exercise for upper-classmen only," he shouted over the turmoil.

I wanted to scream that I hadn't been ready for any of it, but I was here all the same.

A rush of footfalls echoed over the flap of mighty wings. Students spilled from the staircase, wielding a variety of weapons, and more importantly, *rais*. A female Light Fae reached the landing and stretched out her arms. A rainbow of light shot from her palms, twisting and turning until it surrounded the gryphon in a blinding swirl.

A male who'd appeared with the female brought his hands together and a glowing orb surrounded the female as she continued her spectacular light show. I willed my feet to move, but I was too entranced by the luminous spectacle.

A wave of darkness hurtled down the steps, swallowing up

the light, and every hair on my body prickled in awareness. From the murky shadows, a familiar form coalesced. Darkness draped over every inch of Reign's body as that murderous gaze locked on me.

"What is she doing here?" he bellowed at Heaton.

The team leader paled. His mouth opened but no sound came out.

"Heaton tried to force me to leave, but I can help," I shouted.

"Not if you're dead, you can't." Reign's shadows swirled around me, their icy fingers coaxing a chill up my spine.

A Shadow Fae zipped across the atrium on the back of another gryphon and disappeared into the darkness before reappearing an inch from the Light female with the rainbow powers. A blade made of pure onyx appeared in his palm slicing right through the gilded orb surrounding her before it sliced across her throat.

"No!" The cry ripped from my lips before I could stop it.

Blood gushed from the gaping wound at her neck, and her knees gave. She rolled down the staircase, toppling other Light Fae in her path.

"Watch out!" I shouted to the other students below.

The weight of the daggers in my palms spurred me to life. I pulled my arm back and hurled it at the Shadow Fae skyrider. Reign's shout sounded muffled and far away over the pounding drumbeat of my pulse. The blade flew end over end and sank into the gryphon's flank.

"Aelia!" Reign shouted. "What are you doing? Are you trying to draw their attention?" One of his shadows slithered from his fingertips and retrieved my dagger before it hit the ground.

"I'm not just going to stand here and watch the others die."

He handed me the dagger, those eyes smoldering as he regarded me. "No, you're right, you're not. I'm not losing my acquisition in a meaningless Shadow Fae exercise." Those shadows wrapped tighter around me, until I was suddenly weightless. They lifted me off the ground and I let out a shriek. Reign flicked his wrist, and I cursed again and again as they flew me over the bedlam ensuing across the floating staircase.

My instructor appeared beside me a moment later, his wings made of night flapping leisurely.

"Put me down," I hissed.

"Not until you learn to follow the orders of your commanding officers, princess."

"It's not fair," I gritted out as his shadows carried me away from the chaos and farther into the halls of the dormitories. He flew beside me, tension radiating from each pore, bathing his aura in pure black. "I'm not completely powerless. I could have helped the other students."

"Did you see any other first-years?" he snarled, stopping our forward momentum so his nose nearly touched mine as he loomed dangerously close.

"No," I snapped.

"There's a reason for that."

"But I was already there."

"And you shouldn't have been," he growled. "Did you see what they did to Talia?"

My lips pressed into a tight line as the girl's grisly image flickered to the forefront of my mind. I slid both daggers back into my boots, momentarily defeated.

"She's a fourth-year, Aelia. With abilities far more powerful than half her graduating class. And still, she fell... If that happened to you—" His words cut off as his jaw slammed shut. "I've devoted too much time on you already. I won't have you fail now."

Of course, because all I was to him was his prized acquisition. "So what do you get if I survive past ten days? It's something special, isn't it?"

His dark eyes tapered, a feral grin hitching up the corners of his lips. "I don't owe you any explanations, princess."

"I'm right, I know I am." Goddess, I hated him so much in that instant that I wanted to fail just to spite him. I wriggled and struggled against his shadowy binds, but they only tightened the more I fought.

"You're not going anywhere until I deliver you to your room safe and sound." Once we reached the eighth floor, the big brute's wings disintegrated and he stalked beside me.

"So I'm just supposed to pretend nothing is happening right downstairs?"

"Exactly. That's why your room is warded."

"This is insane. Students are dying only a few flights below, and I'm simply supposed to remain here and cower in fear?"

We reached my chamber and Reign's shadows released me, dropping me on the cold marble with a smack. The murky wisps slipped back, retreating into his dark form. "No one said you had to cower." He flashed me a savage grin as I glared up at him before waving his hand across the door.

It unlocked and swung open, and my jaw fell along with it. "How did you do that? I thought you said only Rue and I could access the ward."

"I added my own." His lips peeled back, and irritation blossomed across my already tense form as he stalked inside.

"You had no right." I jumped up and lunged at him, and he staggered back against the wall. The satisfaction was fleeting. His shadows unfurled, one dark tendril curling around my throat and swapping our positions so that I had my back against the wall and his body pinned me against the solid barrier in my room.

"I have every right." His voice was a lethal whisper as it ghosted across my cheeks. "You are my acquisition, and I will ensure your survival, whatever the cost." Those piercing eyes lanced into me with the fury of a tempest, raw and untamed.

I remained unmoving, locked in his mesmerizing gaze for an impossibly long moment. Then, without another word, he spun on his heel, marched out and slammed the door behind him. The moment he was gone, I slumped back to the floor, all the fight lurching right out of me.

Raysa, I hated that male.

I was sent to this goddess damned academy to be honed into an instrument of destruction... weren't those the headmaster's words? Then why was I forbidden to fight at my first chance? What good was a prized acquisition kept in a warded cage?

The creak of the knob turning sent my head whipping toward the entry. I leapt to my feet and yanked my dagger from my boot. If that infuriating instructor thought he could just walk into *my* chamber whenever he wanted—

"Oh, Aelia, thank the goddess you're safe!" Rue raced into the room and threw her arms around my neck. "I was so worried when I heard the alarms."

"I'm fine." I squeezed my friend.

"Where's Heaton?" Her eyes grew wide as she slipped to arm's length.

"He's down there fighting. I tried to help, but they wouldn't let me..."

Her lip quivered for an instant before she drew it between her teeth.

"He insisted he'd be fine."

Rue's head dipped. "And he will be. He's strong and he's survived this long."

"Absolutely." I pulled her into another tight embrace.

"It was so different before I came to the Conservatory. I had no idea what Heat was facing, but after less than two weeks here, I can't imagine how he survived all this time."

I couldn't imagine living with that fear for years, not knowing when and if you'd see your sibling again. As an only child, I knew little of that bond, but I felt her pain all the same. Having grown up without blood relatives, I'd always felt that absence, that terrible twinge of emptiness. The only upside was I had much less to lose.

My thoughts flickered to Aidan. How was he managing

without me? Had he been feeding the chickens? Tending the garden? He must have been ever so lonely without me. I couldn't wait until the first term ended so that I could send him a letter. I only hoped he knew I was still alive.

Rue sniffled, drawing my attention from my spiraling thoughts to the present. She pressed her fingers to her temples and groaned. "I never should have indulged in so much laegar."

Oh, stars, and Heaton had, too. I prayed the haze of alcohol wouldn't affect his abilities.

"Where's Silvan?" I waggled my brows at my friend, hoping to distract her.

"Probably back in his dormitory." A hint of a smile curved her lips. "Everyone scrambled when the alarm sounded."

"Why didn't they tell us about the possibility of attacks or the alarm system?" If I hadn't been with Heaton at the time, I wouldn't have had any idea what to do.

Rue shrugged. "Likely for the same reason they allow first-years to assault one another. They want us to be prepared for anything." She staggered to her bed and dropped down on the mattress with a sigh. "I don't know how I'll be able to get any sleep tonight."

A yawn was already building at the back of my throat, but I swallowed, keeping it at bay. "We don't have to sleep. I'll wait up with you until Heaton returns."

"You don't have to do that. You need to be rested for tomorrow. We have Combat first thing in the morning."

"No, we don't have Combat tomorrow."

"Oh, you probably haven't seen it yet, but the scrolls updated, and Combat was put on for first thing in the morning, probably because of the attack."

My stomach churned at the thought of facing Belmore again. And even worse, Reign.

I crossed the space between us in two long strides and folded down onto the mattress beside her. "Who needs sleep? Tell me more about this new development with you and Silvan."

A cackle burst from my friend's pinched lips. "It's nothing, really. He is quite attractive though, and with all the stress from the past ten days, the idea of a little release was pretty enticing."

I couldn't agree more. Since I'd arrived at the Conservatory, it felt as if a bubble of energy had been building in my core, growing and growing until it threatened to crack my ribcage. I drew in a breath, willing the unnerving sensation down.

"How about you, A?" She lifted a mischievous brow. "I saw you and Heaton dancing..."

Warmth flooded my cheeks at the memory of his hands on my waist. "Oh, Rue, don't be silly. We're just friends. Besides, the last thing I need is to find myself in Oriah's crosshairs. I already have enough Fae who despise me."

A rueful chuckle parted my roommate's lips. "Fair enough. But for what it's worth, I think Heaton really does like you."

"Maybe. Along with half a dozen other females." I released a breath and lay back on Rue's bed. She plopped back beside me. A sea of mossy vines climbed overhead, nearly blocking the remaining shards of light. The hour or so of rare twilight was nearly upon us. "Regardless, I don't have the luxury of focusing on trivial matters of the heart. If I have any hope of survival here, I need to maintain all my focus on training." Tonight was a clear reminder of that.

Rue's mouth twisted into a pout. "That sounds terribly boring."

"Then I'll simply have to live vicariously through you." I tossed my friend a smile.

Chapter Nineteen

A*elia*

Another week came and went in a flurry of classes and training. After the attack from Arcanum Citadel, in which we'd luckily only lost the one Light Fae female, I'd doubled my efforts. I had more bruises than I could count splattered across my body, but at least I was becoming physically stronger. The one aspect in which I hadn't progressed at all was my *rais*.

I was no closer to successfully reading an aura than I was summoning a radiant shield, all basics that every other student at the Conservatory had already mastered. I was hopeless. My fingers drifted through the rippling crystalline water of the bathing pool as I stared to the open sky above. The canopy of ferns and mosses shielded me from most of the sun's brilliant rays. The bathing chamber was decidedly my favorite spot on campus. I spent any free moment I had floating in the tepid stone pools.

"Aelia!" Rue's voice shattered the peaceful tranquility an instant before she bounded into the lush space.

I dropped down below the water, so the whirling eddies covered my bare breasts.

"Oops, sorry! I still forget how prudish you are when it comes to nudity." She kept her eyes fixed to mine as she held out a scroll. "We've been summoned to the Hall of Luminescence by the headmaster."

"Right now?" I groaned. We only had one free day a week, and it seemed nearly every single one was interrupted somehow.

"Yes. The message just came through on the scroll."

"Oh, fine." I dipped my head beneath the warm water, dreading whatever news the headmaster was to impart.

Rue stood there watching expectantly.

"Well, give me a second so I can get out!"

She laughed. "Oh, come on, Aelia, I've seen your plentiful breasts on many an occasion."

That blasted heat tinged my cheeks. And I'd thought I had become accustomed to the Fae's liberal ways. My roommate frequently paraded around our chambers completely nude.

"You are beautiful and there is no need to hide that perfect form from anyone, least of all me."

"Is that why you're all so comfortable with nudity?" It made sense since most Fae were unfairly striking. "It's an issue of pride?"

"Honestly, I've never thought about it, but I suppose so. We should be proud of our bodies. They were created by Raysa herself, after all. And you are one of us now, so it's time to embrace it!"

My thoughts flickered to Reign, unbidden. Noxus had certainly gone above and beyond when he created that perfect male specimen. *Stop it*! Since the night of the attack, my professor had become oddly cold and unreadable, even for him. He'd maintained a larger distance between us, which I convinced myself was for the best.

And, still, I found myself ogling the male every time an inch of his flawless skin was on display. Which happened often in Combat class. He'd forced me to continue sparring with Belmore, which I despised. I would never admit it to my professor, but he'd been right. The reason I'd come as far as I had in combat was due to my utter hatred of the Light Fae male. I never would've been able to accomplish that with Rue.

Pinning my shoulders back, I swept my hair over my shoulders and stood. The water sluiced from my long locks in tiny rivulets across my breasts. Fighting the overwhelming desire to cover myself, I stepped out of the stone pool and faced my friend.

"You see? Was that so bad?" A satisfied smirk curled her lips. "You'll thank me for this one day, Aelia."

I didn't exactly see how being comfortable in my own skin would assist me in surviving my tenure at the Conservatory or accepting my Fae-ness, but for now, it was a small win. "Can you hand me a towel already?"

Rue laughed as she reached for the thick terry cloth and offered it to me. "Of course. Now hurry, we cannot be late."

An hour later, Rue and I were back beneath the arched rafters of the soaring ceiling of the Hall of Luminescence. Quiet murmurs echoed across the sprawling chamber as the initiates filed in. From the looks of it, our numbers had already dwindled from the original hundred and sixty. Eighteen of the twenty from Flare Squad were still standing. I could hardly believe it was approaching a month since my arrival.

"Look at Spark Squad," Rue whispered as we moved through the crowd to find a seat. "They're down to only ten members."

I gulped as I took in their weary gazes and slumped forms. Their squad leader, Jase, was known for his brutal tactics. I'd certainly lucked out being placed under Heaton's command. Our team leader was tough but fair, and I could confidently say everyone in the squad respected, if not admired him.

As if my thoughts had summoned him, Heaton appeared in the midst of the other Light Fae. His light blue-eyed gaze swung in our direction. With a tight smile, he summoned us to the front. Apparently, he'd saved us the entire second row. *Curses.*

"So glad you could join us, ladies." Heaton's smile widened as we approached.

"Sorry we're late," I whispered. "I got us a little turned around on the way over."

He shook his head, but the smile remained steady and unfaltering, much like our squad leader's character.

I scooted past Heaton, down the aisle behind Rue, and we settled in between Silvan and Phoebia. As Rue folded down beside the ashen-haired Fae male, I wondered if anything more had happened between them since the night of Heaton's party.

Most nights, after hours of training, Rue and I were so exhausted we collapsed in our beds without more than a quick goodnight. Surely, my friend would have told me if she'd been seeing the male, right?

"What do you think this is about?" Phoebia's whisper tore me from my thoughts. The Fae female from our squad wasn't quite as horrible as Ariadne, but still, she hardly ever spoke to me.

"I have no idea," I murmured back.

Ariadne, who sat on her opposite side, craned her neck in my direction. "It's probably about the trials."

"What trials?" I blurted, earning a glare from the row in front of us. Mumbling an apology, I pivoted my attention back to Ariadne.

"There are a series of trials we must pass in order to advance to the second term. My sister told me about them. Amely is a Royal Guardian of the Court. She graduated from the Conservatory of Luce with highest honors two years ago." A smug smile curled her glossy pink lips.

Of course, she did.

"I thought everything that went on at the Conservatory was supposed to remain a secret," Phoebia replied.

Ariadne shrugged. "Oops."

The sound of approaching footfalls sent my gaze to the entryway. Headmaster Draven, dressed in a trailing velvet robe, shuffled toward the stage, with Reign following a few steps behind the ancient Light Fae. A midnight tunic melded to his form, much like his shadows, and the dark leathers highlighted the defined muscles of his thighs. As if the mysterious professor had sensed my scrutiny, his dark eyes narrowed in on mine. The instant our gazes touched, a prickle of awareness zipped across my skin.

Mother Raysa, what the sun was that?

I'd hoped that with the increased distance between us as of late, the strange sensations this male incited would have dwindled. Instead, they seemed only more powerful. My lungs tightened as he stalked closer, and every breath became more difficult than the last.

Draven swiveled his head over his shoulder, his cascading white beard caressing the long sleeves of his robe as he turned to Reign, and my professor's gaze released mine. Now freed from that piercing stare, my lungs began to function once more. Was he using his abilities of fear induction? I wasn't frightened, not really. What sort of power did this male hold over me?

The hushed murmurs fell away as the headmaster crossed the stage and stood at the pulpit. "Good morrow, first-years. I am pleased to see so many of you have survived the first month of your tenure within these hallowed halls. Now that you've passed the initial probationary period, the real work will begin."

I barely suppressed a groan.

"For the next four months, you will train for the Ethereal Trials. These trials will prepare you for your first battle against

Arcanum Citadel at the end of the term. I will warn you now, many of you will fall during the trials. Still more will not survive past the first battle."

"Such a positive fellow, isn't he?" Rue whispered.

I clapped my hand over my mouth to keep the inappropriate chuckle from slipping free. No wonder Heaton and Reign had been so angry when I'd wanted to fight the night of the party. The dismal picture the headmaster painted made it seem truly hopeless.

"I commend all of you for making it this far. You have outlived fifteen percent of your classmates. Well done. But now is not the time to celebrate. The stakes are now higher than ever. I have recently spoken with the King of Ethereal Light, Elian of Ether, and I'm afraid he has grave news." He paused as faint gasps rolled across the great chamber.

"Our enemies to the east, the Court of Umbral Shadows, grow restless, and the creatures of the Wilds are growing more bold by the day." The headmaster cast a sidelong glance in Reign's direction. "The attack a fortnight ago only confirms the king's belief that the Shadow Fae are fortifying their offenses. Therefore, we must do the same. No—we must do better."

A cheer erupted across the crowd of students, but a sliver of fear wiggled its way into my heart. Aidan was so close to the Wilds in Feywood. Was it true about the beasts of the Wilds? It almost seemed as if the Fae held the threat over us as merely a way to keep us in line.

"Our peace only endures as long as we remain vigilant against our foes. We must not let this false sense of security lull us into inaction." The headmaster paused again, swinging his bright eyes toward the only Shadow Fae in the room. "Don't you agree, Professor? You, of all people, have suffered the most at the hands of your Shadow brethren."

Even from this distance, I could make out the flutter of the coiled tendon in Reign's jaw as he nodded.

"The Court of Umbral Shadows is ruthless," the headmaster continued. "King Tenebris and Queen Vespera are complete savages. They will stop at nothing to ensure their supremacy and spill endless night upon all of us. It is up to you to keep that from happening."

Another round of whoops echoed across the chamber.

A twinge of pity speared my chest as I watched Reign. The proud slope of his shoulders softened, his dark gaze pinned to the floor. What had they done to him? Why had he been banished from his home court?

I vowed to find out somehow.

"In a week's time, you will each take part in a Conservatory tradition: the Choosing Ceremony."

A flurry of excited voices whispered all around.

"What's that?" I murmured to Rue.

"You'll see, listen." Her light eyes sparkled with excitement.

"Since the majority of you will not develop wings, and those that do, not until the age of maturity at around twenty-five, you'll need some way to combat our neighbors to the east on battle day."

My thoughts soared to the winged creatures the Shadow Fae arrived upon when they ransacked the dormitories and the beautiful phoenix that Reign had brought me to the Conservatory on. No... it couldn't be, could it?

Rue thrummed with so much excitement, she was practically vibrating in her seat.

"Each of you will be assigned a skyrider—or rather, by the power of Raysa, they will choose you. Should you not be chosen, your time at the Conservatory will come to an end."

Chapter Twenty

A *elia*

"Again, Aelia!" Reign barked from across the lawn.

A torrent of darkness swept over me, icy fingernails clawing at my exposed flesh.

"I can't!" I gritted out. Sweat coated my brow and stained my tunic. My bastard professor had been drilling me for hours. All the other squads had been dismissed except for ours. "I can't even read an aura, how am I supposed to summon a protective shield against your blasted shadows?"

That wasn't entirely true. I could read his aura just fine, and right now, judging by the globe of pitch black surrounding the male, he seemed about a second away from murdering me.

"Try harder!"

Heaton and the rest of Flare Squad stood a few yards away, watching. Every single member of the team had managed to at least summon the radiant shield. Reign's shadows had easily sliced through them, but their *rais* had at least made an effort.

While mine remained locked within a skeletal prison of my own making.

Reign stalked closer, his onyx irises blazing as they fixed on mine. The umbral shadows slid from his form, twisting and turning until they formed half a dozen blades. They floated in the air only a few feet away. "Summon the shield or die."

A gasp caught in my throat.

"Professor," Heaton interjected, "she is trying—"

His words were abruptly cut off when a shot of darkness zipped across the field and curled around our squad leader's mouth.

"You're not helping by taking it easy on her, Heaton," Reign snarled. "I've seen how you coddle her. That ends today. The preliminary period is over, and the trials will be upon us before long. Aelia must succeed or die trying."

Rue's faint whimper reached my ears, a true feat over the wild thrashing of my heart. Gritting my teeth, I focused again. *For her*. Not for the dickish Shadow Fae shooting lethal glares in my direction.

"This blasted prize for the best acquisition better be worth it," I snapped.

Reign cocked a challenging brow. "You have no idea, princess." His words traveled across the space between us, and again it was as if he stood an inch from my ear instead of yards away. "Now. Summon. That. Shield." His command crackled through the thickening air.

I squeezed my eyes closed and searched for that thrum of energy that had been growing in my gut since the day I arrived. Like tiny gossamer wings, it fluttered across my insides, too faint to grasp.

"Aelia, watch out!"

Shadows blossomed in the space between Reign and me, cloaking us in a muddy darkness. My eyes snapped open as a pair of shadow blades whizzed toward me. Without a radiant shield in sight, I dropped to the ground and freed my own daggers. In a vain attempt, I sliced at the dark air with my sharp blades. As the metal slid through the first, the ghostly missiles disintegrated. I stared unbelieving. I'd never seen a weapon forged of metal have any effect on Reign's shadows. Masking the shock, I sliced again, and the second one fell.

I glanced up and met a pair of astonished starlit, midnight orbs.

"Good Noxus," he murmured as his shadows dissipated, exposing us once again. His voice sailed straight to my ears. "You're all dismissed," he growled at the rest of the team. "Except for you, Aelia."

"But—" Heaton's rebuttal was swallowed up by Reign's intimidating glare.

"Leave, now," he snarled.

I watched as my teammates evacuated the field, leaving me alone with the fuming Fae.

Reign ate up the distance between us in two long strides, his immense wings and midnight shadows coiling and uncoiling around him in a fevered pitch. His thick fingers encircled my wrist and the breath caught in my throat as he squeezed.

His eyes were pinned to the weapons clenched in my fists. "What sort of blades are these?"

My brows furrowed as I regarded the sudden shift in his aura, from the typical black to swirls of ochre brightening the impenetrable darkness.

"Aelia!"

My gaze jumped up to meet his. "I have no idea. They were a gift from Aidan, my adoptive father. They're the same ones I've been using since I arrived here."

"Give them to me."

My fingers clenched around the hilts, thumbs sweeping across the warm crystal embedded within the ornate handle of each dagger. A faint electric current hummed across my skin at the familiar feel. "No."

"Princess, don't provoke me." His eyes flashed as his lips pulled into a wicked snarl. "Let me see those daggers."

His hold tightened around my wrists and a cloud of pure night closed around us. The suffocating shadows crawled across my flesh, pushing against me from all angles. I was trapped. Reign pressed closer, pinning me against the wall of deadly silhouettes. His lips inched toward my ear, his breath tickling the sensitive area. "Drop them, now." His musky, frosty scent enveloped me, and a tremor shot up my spine.

I wish it were only fear, but it was an emotion far worse overtaking my body. "They're mine," I hissed, the embarrassing breathlessness only exacerbating the irritation puckering my brow.

He inched back, his nose now nearly grazing mine. "I promise to return them, okay?"

"You swear?" A promise was much like an oath, and if the folktales were true, Fae took vows such as these extremely seriously.

Reign heaved out a frustrated breath and a growl vibrated his entire torso, the beastly rumble echoing through my own ribcage. "Yes, I swear, princess." He extended his hand and lifted a challenging brow.

In order for me to shake his hand, it would require me to release the dagger. Tricky little Shadow Fae. But I certainly wasn't stupid. Sliding one dagger beneath the waistband of my leathers, I took his hand.

His fingers tightened around my palm as he eyed the blade, precariously pointing at my lady parts, and released a low whistle. "Risky move, princess."

"Oh, shut up and make the promise."

"As you wish." A swirl of energy ignited between our pressed palms and heat kindled over my flesh. "I, Reign Darkthorn of the Court of Umbral Shadows, vow to return to you, Aelia Ravenwood of Feywood, the aforementioned daggers. Should I fail to do so, may Noxus strike me down on the spot."

A prickle of light danced over our joined hands before a tendril of darkness joined the tangle. A jolt of awareness spread from my fingertips, up my arms, and zipped straight to my heart. An invisible tether laced around my thundering organ, the odd sensation only escalating the tempo.

"And it's done," Reign breathed. "Now, give me those sun-cursed daggers."

Despite the binding vow, a part of me was still reluctant to release my weapons. Slowly, I handed him one, leaving the other tucked in my waistband. The circle of shadows still surrounded us, concealing us from the meandering students walking across campus. I almost asked why he kept the shield up, but as his fingers closed around my dagger, an odd pulse thrummed across my veins.

My professor eyed the hilt of the first dagger, running his thumb over the crystal. Then it skated across the blade. His brows furrowed as he moved over the precisely honed steel. "You have no idea what metal this is?" he repeated, without looking up.

"No." I shrugged. "It never really mattered before today."

"I've never seen a weapon cut through my umbral blades," he murmured. I had a feeling he was speaking more to himself than me. A long minute later, his gaze lifted to mine, and he held out his other hand. "May I see the other one?"

I must have hesitated for a moment longer than he appreciated, because he reached into my waistband and slid the dagger free.

A sharp gasp escaped as the blade swept across my most sensitive area. "Watch it," I hissed.

An evil glint sparked in his eyes. "Trust me, princess, I know my way around the female anatomy."

Heat scorched across my cheeks, and a wicked chuckle vibrated our cloud of darkness. I was suddenly acutely aware of our close proximity. And the fact that not a soul could see us. He must have realized it as well within the same instant because his eyes chased to mine as he continued to stroke the blade in his hands, almost lovingly. I swallowed hard as the air crackled between us.

Reign inched closer, and my chest heaved, my lungs suddenly fighting for air.

"Do you mind if I keep one?" he breathed.

My entire body slumped forward and I urged my lungs to keep functioning. Daggers. Right. *Focus*! "For how long?" I rasped.

"I'll have it back to you by tomorrow, at the latest." He paused, eyes intent on mine. "You'll still have the one, princess. And from what I've seen, you're more than capable of defending yourself with that."

"That is true."

He smirked. That bastard was resorting to flattery, and I was playing right into his hands.

Despite every cell in my body urging me to keep the dagger, I couldn't help the streak of curiosity. Plus, he had sworn an oath... "Fine, take it, but if you don't return it to me by tomorrow, forget Noxus, *I'll* be coming for you."

A dark chuckle parted his lips, and I hated how the deep sound was more powerful than any heated caress. One day, I vowed to put this male in his place. If I could only get my wild emotions under control.

Chapter Twenty-One

A *elia*

Blasted never-ending light. The constant invasive glow from above made it nearly impossible to be stealthy. I'd trailed Reign after he abandoned his supper at the banquet hall and descended the steps toward the circular pathway that weaved across campus. Sticking to the shadows of the towering hedges, I followed my mysterious professor as he stalked toward the Hall of Enlightenment. *Of course, the library*! I should have known. I may have agreed to let him borrow my dagger, but that certainly did not mean he could have free reign over it.

Since I'd entrusted him with my most favored possession, he'd kept it on his body, tucked into his waistband. I'd watched him scrutinize it over supper for endless minutes before he finally gave up. Which brought me here.

Reign marched up the steps of the grand hall, the brilliant shards of light dancing over the alabaster marble columns as he skulked through the door. I waited a few seconds in the shadow of the towering pillar before trailing behind him.

A wave of dense silence descended over me as I crossed the threshold into the grand library. Soaring bookshelves filled the cavernous space, ascending at least six or seven stories high. My jaw dropped as my head tilted back to take it all in. In the past weeks at the Conservatory, it was the first time I'd entered the immense archive.

The enormous space must hold every tome ever produced in all of Aetheria, perhaps even the entire continent of Crescentia. The inner bookworm inside me was filled with glee. I resolved to return and dive into the shelves the first free moment I had. Unfortunately, it didn't seem as if I would get many of those in the weeks to come.

A whisper of movement called my attention to the far corner of endless soaring shelves. Dark tendrils coiled around a corner, and I forced my feet to move more quickly. The library was empty, not a soul in sight. The intense solitude pricked at the hairs on the back of my neck.

What if I ran into Belmore, or worse, his friends—or even some other student set on thinning out the competition? Kian and Lucian had practically disappeared, but it didn't mean they weren't plotting revenge. Reaching for my remaining blade, I held it tightly in my fist as I maneuvered through the maze of long mahogany tables and row after row of bookstands.

Where are you going Reign?

I trailed his shadows across the sprawling chamber until they disappeared around yet another corner. Following on tiptoes, I prayed to the goddess I wouldn't be swallowed up by this never-ending labyrinth.

A deep grunt halted my footsteps. Backing up against a towering rack, I peered around the edge. Reign hoisted an enormous, ancient tome from a shelf and folded into a chair at a long table. I watched as he flipped through the weathered, yellowing pages, then came to a stop. "It's not possible," he hissed and slammed the book closed.

Rising, he stomped away from the table and disappeared between another row of shelving. I waited a long moment before creeping from the shadows, my breaths shallow. I eyed the golden-foiled title across the worn leather tome and ran my finger over the words: *The Fae Compendium of Mythic Weaponry*.

I waffled for a long moment as I debated pilfering the book or following Reign. Already, I could somehow sense his aura moving farther away. *Curses*! Whirling around, I double-backed toward the entrance—or at least what I believed to be the entrance.

Ten minutes later and I was hopelessly lost within the tangle of ancient texts. I muttered a curse as I circled the table, I'd found Reign at for the second time. With a frustrated huff, I grabbed the massive book and tucked it under my arm. Perhaps, I could find whatever he'd been researching, and the entire mission wouldn't end up a complete disaster.

"Young lady," a sharp voice resounded behind me.

I whirled around and met an elderly Fae female with silver hair pulled into a severe bun.

"The library is closed. You must leave."

"Right, I'm sor—" I snapped my jaw closed and dipped my head. "If you could just direct me to the exit, I'd be happy to be on my way."

Shaking her head, the female led me toward the double doors I'd entered through nearly an hour ago. Irritation raged through my system as I marched out into the brilliant sunlight. Sure enough, Reign was nowhere to be found.

Where did the staff sleep, anyway? I marched across the circular path in front of the Hall of Enlightenment. There must have been a designated dormitory for the administration. Perhaps I could find it... *And then what, Aelia*? That irksome voice of logic questioned. It wasn't as if I could simply knock on Reign's door and ask what he was up to, right?

"There you are, Aelia!" Rue's cheerful voice drew me from my insane musings. "I thought you said you were going back to the dormitory?"

My cheeks burned at keeping the truth from my friend. I'd lied to her when I'd fled the banquet hall after Reign. I held up the book tucked under my arm. "Just took a quick detour to the library."

"Oh." Her lips puckered. "You probably shouldn't wander around campus by yourself, Aelia. With the preliminary period over, Heaton said things would start to get brutal."

"Fantastic," I mumbled.

She weaved her arm through mine, the now familiar move instantly comforting. "Come on, let's go to our chambers. I'll keep us safe."

I gave my roommate an appreciative smile. "Thank you, Rue. I know I'm not supposed to say that, but I truly am thankful for you."

She stood on her tiptoes and pressed her head to mine. "Cheers, my dear."

Darkness curled around me, endless night wrapping me in its icy embrace. A wave of warm light seeped from my bones and danced across my skin until it swallowed up the void of black. A tangle of energy filled my chest, pummeling my insides.

My eyes snapped open and I jolted straight up in bed. An erratic symphony of heartbeats resounded through my chest. A faint glow rippled beneath my nightgown, illuminating the dim room. *What in all the realms?*

Running my hand down the silky material, I unlaced the tie and peered at my bare skin. Nothing. The necklace Aidan gifted me hung loose, right above my heart. I fingered the pattern of swirls engraved across the medallion. Could it have been that? Perhaps, it had reflected the light from somewhere...

I glanced out the window to the gloomy night below. Somehow, I'd managed to wake up during the rare hour of twilight that existed in this sun-kissed court. I slid to the edge of the mattress and peered out the crystalline glass onto the lush grounds below.

A swirl of darkness caught my eye, and a familiar form coalesced from the shadows moving across the lawn.

Reign!

Squinting, I followed his shadowed figure as he moved toward the river. His aura burned pure midnight. What was he doing at this time of night? And did it have anything to do with my dagger?

For some reason, I just knew it did.

Before I could stop myself, I reached for my discarded leathers, tucked my nightgown into the waistband, and then pulled my boots on. I raced for the door, grabbing a jacket on the way out. I'd never been out at night since I'd arrived at court. Maybe with the sun's rays hidden, the night air would be chilly, not to mention the fact that I needed something to conceal my nightdress.

I raced down the floating staircase, my feet moving faster and faster with each spiraling turn. When I finally reached the ground floor, I sprinted through the doors of the great hall where I'd first entered and been deemed worthy. Sometimes in moments like these, I wondered if the great Raysa had made a terrible mistake.

Through the murky twilight, I could just make out Reign's dark form cloaked in shadows as he stalked to the foot of the Luminoc River that separated the Court of Ethereal Light from our dark neighbors across the water. He paused at the edge, giving me time to close the considerable distance between us. I skirted the hedges that ran across the campus, wrapped in shadows much like the ones that writhed across my professor's hulking form.

Those enormous midnight wings materialized across his shoulders, and I paused, holding my breath. With a powerful flap, he shot into the night sky.

My head tipped back, following the elegant curves of his body as he ascended. A glimmer of moonlight brushed against a blade tucked into his dark leathers.

My pulse skyrocketed as I recognized the familiar glint of my dagger. Why was he going across the river... and more importantly, why was he taking my blade with him?

As soon as he was far overhead, I emerged from the shadows and stood at the river's edge, much like he had a moment ago. His dark form sailed through the sky, toward the looming citadel on the other side. What if he was selling my dagger to the enemy? They could destroy the one weapon we could use to annihilate the Court of Umbral Shadows.

I had to go after him. I wouldn't lose one of the few possessions Aidan had gifted me. Especially not after witnessing what they'd done to Reign's shadows.

Steeling my nerves, I drew in a deep breath and plunged into the icy river.

Chapter Twenty-Two

R *eign*

Noxus, that female was persistent, and as stubborn as an ancient oak rooted deep in the mystical earth of Feywood Forest. I was certain I'd lost Aelia in the maze of the library earlier today, and yet, there she was hours later, chasing me across campus in the middle of the night.

She must know more about these blades than she's letting on. Why else would she resort to stalking me?

A ridiculous grin ghosted across my lips as I imagined the obstinate girl braving the Luminoc River to come after me. Aelia was nothing like I'd expected.

A cool breeze rushed through my hair as I flew higher, the full moon shimmering above. I forced back all thoughts of the female Kin I'd been tasked to observe. Already, she had appropriated too much terrain in my mind. Drawing in a breath to clear my thoughts, I scanned the quiet fortress below.

Arcanum Citadel loomed ominously at the edge of the

Luminoc River, its presence a whispered legend among the Shadow Fae. Wrapped in the embrace of eternal twilight, the academy was an architectural marvel of obsidian stone and shadowglass; a castle that appeared to drink in the scant moonlight, shimmering with an otherworldly iridescence. Its spires reached toward the dusky sky like the fingers of Noxus himself weaving spells into the heavens and casting silhouettes that danced with the ever-present mists.

Gods, it had been too long since I'd been across the river. My shadows vibrated in delight, coming alive at the buzz of *nox* that pervaded the atmosphere of the Court of Umbral Shadows. The ancient rune on my chest prickled, calling my attention to the symbol carved just above my heart. The mark of the banished. Running my finger over the crude design beneath my tunic, I began to descend.

And barely in time.

My wings of shadow and smoke began to flicker, disintegrating in the blossoming nightfall. I hissed out a curse, glaring at the silver bangles latched around my wrists. Their blasted *rais* prevented me from using the full scope of my powers the moment I stepped foot away from the Conservatory borders.

Or, at least, that was their intent.

Fortunately for me, Headmaster Draven had no inkling of the extent of my abilities. It was incredibly draining, but I could overpower the oppressive manacles when absolutely necessary. Angling my faltering wings, I descended the final yards.

My boots touched down on the hardpacked earth on the edge of the Nightbloom Gardens. The labyrinth of flora that thrived in the gloom, emitting a soft luminescence and exuding fragrances that soothed my spirit and chilled my bones, was a favorite refuge of mine when I attended the academy. I breathed in the familiar scents, sparking memories of the past, of youthful trysts, of sprints in the darkness ringed in laughter.

Gods, everything was so much simpler then.

I stood in the shadows of the immense citadel, waiting... And waiting...

My thoughts flickered to Aelia, unbidden. Had she made it across the river? A prickle of unease tightened my chest. I knew she was a strong swimmer after that stunt she pulled in order to beat me to class a few weeks ago, but still... From my current vantage point, the citadel blocked the river's crossing. Maybe, I should check on her. Gideon was certainly taking his sweet time.

Closing my eyes, I focused my energy on the manacles' incessant throbbing. Summoning my own *nox*, I visualized blanketing its suffocating power. My shadows spilled forth, mist and darkness floating on the faint breeze. *Find her.*

The midnight tendrils streaked across the gloom, my obedient hunters fixed on their prey. Clearing my mind, I pictured Aelia, that unique raven hair with the streak of pale gold, the fire in her eyes and that constant pucker of her lips, as if everything I did or said was the most irritating thing on this gods' damned earth. That hint of a smile threatened to overtake my mouth again, but I pressed my lips into a hard line.

Where are you, Aelia?

That brilliant aura of hers a deep gold threaded in silver washed over my shadows, invading the black and penetrating all the way to my bone marrow. I could feel her. She was certainly alive, and angry by the sensations swimming through my core.

Recalling my shadows, I drew in a breath of relief. She was safe and not too far away.

Now, where in the realms was Gideon?

Gently, I withdrew the dagger from my waistband and studied the intricate carvings along the hilt. It was unlike any ancient language I was familiar with. More than that, the crystal embedded within the metal was one I'd never encountered. Even in the endless gloom of this court, it radiated an ethereal light, twisting and dancing within the prism.

Soft footfalls lifted my gaze to the male sauntering toward

me. I emerged from the shadows and smirked at my friend. "It's about time, Gideon. It wasn't as though I was risking being discovered every second that I waited for you."

My old friend dipped into an elaborate bow, his ebony hair pulled into a high bun and streaks of navy spilling from the nest of wild hair. "My apologies, my—"

I lifted my hand, cutting him off. "No time for pleasantries, Gid. I must return to the Conservatory before someone discovers I'm gone."

"Well then, let's see the dagger." His lively eyes sparkled with curiosity. I'd sent word of my arrival, along with my little discovery, earlier today. Gideon was a bit of a history buff, and if anyone knew anything about these blades, it would be him. Or, at the least, with the vast wealth of knowledge contained within the Citadel's walls, I hoped he could find it.

I handed over the weapon, my fingers oddly reluctant to release it. "Tell no one, Gideon. I cannot stress this point enough." The existence of this sort of blade was life-altering for the Shadow Fae. It could change the delicate balance upon which the two rival courts had existed for centuries. We were literally perched upon a knife's edge, and this discovery could throw our world into devastation.

"I understand. Your blasted shadows sent your message at least a dozen times." He eyed the dagger, slowly flipping it over in his palm. "It's certainly unique, that's for sure. I've never seen this crystal before."

"Neither had I."

He ran his fingertip across the smooth surface and sparks ignited along the path. "Whoa, did it do that for you?"

"No." I moved closer, and he held out the dagger so it sat flat across his palm. "Let me try." I retrieved the dagger and traced my fingertip over the crystalline surface, the light flickered and hissed, but it clearly did not react to my presence as it had to Gideon.

"Well, that's odd." My friend repeated the procedure where

I now held the blade, and again, the spark followed his movements. "It seems to like me." He smirked. "Then again, compared to you, I'm far more likeable."

"Oh, shut it, Gid." I tossed the dagger back at him, and he winced before catching it by the hilt. "Take it, study it, and tell me what you can find. I need it back by tomorrow."

"You cannot be serious? How do you expect me to find anything concrete that quickly?"

"I am completely serious. I made a vow, so there is little room for fenagling."

"You're kidding me? The great Reign has forged a binding vow with a female Kin? You truly must be desperate."

A twinge of irritation furrowed my brow. "You know as well as I how crucial this weapon could be for the sake of peace within the courts."

"I know, I know."

"Speaking of the courts, is Ruhl making friends amongst the first-years?"

"Of course, he is. You know what you lack in personality, he more than abounds in."

"You're such an ass," I grumbled.

"But I'm the only one who puts up with you."

"True enough, my friend. I am truly blessed by Noxus." I flashed him a sarcastic smile.

"From your lips to the gods' ears."

"Very well, I must go." I patted Gideon on the shoulder. "Oh, one more thing. How is Phantom?"

"Miserable without you. She's a moody, terribly insufferable beast. On a good day." He shot me a smirk. "Much like her master."

"You're just full of enlightening quips this evening, Gid. I hope that means all is well within those obsidian walls." I ticked my head at the looming fortress at his back.

"The headmaster is still an ass, but he leaves me be most of the time."

"I'm glad to hear it." Spinning on my heel, I turned toward the river. "Now, I truly must go before the blasted sun rises across the river."

"Ah, to be a slave to the sun." He threw me a wicked grin and pocketed the dagger. "Noxus, be with you, my friend."

A sharp scream echoed across the Nightbloom Gardens, in the direction of the Sombra Forest that surrounded the Citadel. My heart ratcheted up my throat, the pounding vibrating my entire skull. *Fuck, Aelia.*

"What is that?" Gideon howled.

Reaching for my shadows, I extended their reach until I could sense her aura. "My acquisition."

"You let her follow you across the Luminoc?"

"I didn't *let* her do anything. She's the most stubborn female I've ever encountered. I assumed she would give up once she reached the Citadel's wards." Instead, the obstinate woman tried to go around them through the forest. "I have to go!"

"I'll go with you." He took off behind me, but I whirled around and shoved him back. "You can't. Your presence would only make this situation more difficult to explain."

His hand wrapped around my upper arm, and my shadows writhed beneath his touch. "But those cuffs..."

"I'll be fine, Gideon. Now let me go to her."

Chapter Twenty-Three

A*elia*

For the love of Raysa, what had I gotten myself into?

The terrifying Shadow Fae creature stood tall, with limbs elongated and fingers ending in talons sharp enough to slice through the massive trunk I currently cowered behind. My damp locks fell over my forehead, blurring its form. I squeezed my dagger tight in my fist, waiting for an opportune moment to strike. The problem was that its body, ethereal and shifting, seemed to be made of shadowstuff, with a texture that oscillated between smoke and solid darkness. It was nearly impossible to focus on or predict its movements.

Its eyes, if one could call them that, were two glowing embers of hatred that pierced through the dark forest. They scanned the thick copse, searching for its prey. I heaved in a breath and pressed my back against the rough bark as it moved closer. The monster's face coalesced around the trunk, a mask of sorrow and rage shrouded by the cloak of shadows it wore.

My fingers itched to loose my dagger on the beast. If I could make a clean hit to its head, I could, in theory, kill it. If my blades impacted Reign's shadows, then surely, they must be lethal to this monster as well. But what if my reasoning was mistaken?

Reign already had one of my daggers, I couldn't risk losing the second.

Stars, I never should have followed him here.

The creature let out a resounding hiss, and the blood froze in my veins. The most terrifying aspect of the beast stalking me was not its appearance, but rather, its voice. It hissed in hushed tones, a cacophony of whispers that seemed to come from all directions. Oddly enough, it reminded me of Reign's strange power of communicating through shadows.

The hisses grew more insistent, penetrating every corner of the forest. My head spun, the echoing sound pushing my thoughts to madness. I clapped my hands over my ears to drown out the incessant sound, but it was useless. The continuous droning pierced my senses and scrambled my thoughts.

The creature's murky shadows once more coalesced now right beside me, and an embarrassing squeal squeezed through my clenched lips. I swung my arm in a wide arc and sliced through the spectral form.

The beast recoiled, a sharp hiss escaping through what I assumed was a mouth. A trickle of dark liquid oozed from its torso and pooled on the ground. Was that blood? Had my dagger managed to wound the shadow fiend?

The dark tendrils whipped and spun, recomposing themselves into its giant form. A snarl rent the air, flashing me a sneer full of pointed teeth. It swung a clawed hand at me and a long talon sliced through my jacket all the way to the nightgown underneath. The scorching sting seared across my shoulder, and I hissed out a curse as I ducked, just barely darting out of the way to avoid the brunt of the hit.

It lunged again, swiping those feral claws. I staggered back, the burn in my shoulder reaching a fevered pitch. I gritted my teeth as I leapt out of the way again. With my good hand, I attempted to staunch the blood now free-flowing from the wound. A thick dark substance coated the crimson, and a bout of unease twisted my gut.

The spiraling veins of darkness continued to twirl around me, despite my dagger's strikes. The blade cut through the umbral wisps, each one earning a hiss from the creature. At least I succeeded in wounding it, but with the pain coursing through my shoulder, I wasn't sure how much longer I could hold it off.

A coil of pure night extended from the beast's form and wrapped around the hilt of my dagger. "No!" I shouted as it pried my weapon free and tossed it to the ground. Dropping on all fours, I crawled, reaching and pawing blindly through the shadows at the dark earth in a desperate attempt to find it.

I felt it the moment before it happened.

The atmosphere bristled with intensity, and I could sense the faint shift in the air as a clawed hand reached for me. An unnamable force buried deep inside shimmered to life. A rush of energy swept over me, like liquid lightning through my veins. I squeezed my eyes closed as the jagged talons aimed for my throat, and I waited for the sharp sting, for the accompanying darkness that would surely come.

Only, instead of darkness, I was surrounded by blinding light. The glow was so powerful the glare pierced through my closed lids. Sneaking a peek through narrowed slits, my heart danced a delighted jig. A radiant shield. After weeks of struggle, I'd finally summoned a radiant shield!

"Aelia!" A familiar voice boomed through the chaos, and a prickle of awareness surged through my being. Reign appeared amidst a tornado of shadows, the fierce tendrils spinning and churning with untamed fury in the chaotic rhythm of a wild tempest.

His overwhelming power pressed into me, his aura spirals of pure midnight. The instant he materialized, the creature staggered back. Its head dipped, and the vines of darkness that made up its spectral form began to waver.

I glanced up at my professor through the shimmering gold and relief flooded my system. The truest thing to a smile I'd yet to see from the broody male flitted across his lips, and the glowing orb encasing me in pure *rais* suddenly popped.

Returning his attention to the shadow fiend, Reign barked something in the old tongue, and the Shadow creature moved farther into the forest, until it disappeared into the night. The moment it was gone, he dropped to the ground beside me. Those starlit irises locked on mine and, for an instant, they were all I could see, all I could feel. A tempest stirred beneath the moonlit surface as unreadable emotion played across his handsome face.

A long moment of silence passed between us as my heart drummed out a frantic beat against my ribs. Not because of the monster who'd nearly killed me, but for the one kneeling in front of me. "For fuck's sake, princess," he growled, "what in the realms were you thinking, following me here?"

Every ounce of warmth evaporated at that tone. Irritation puckered my brow and I narrowed my eyes at the mercurial male. "What am *I* doing here?" I spat. "What are *you* doing here? Isn't banishment the act of expelling someone from a specific territory, typically as a form of punishment?"

"Thank you for that, Miss Dictionary. I wasn't quite aware of the precise terminology." His glare morphed into something downright murderous as it landed on my shoulder. "Did the Gloomwhisper do that?"

"Excuse me?"

He hovered over me, his presence much too consuming at this close proximity. "That creature I just chased away, did it wound you?"

Actually, how did he chase it away? And why not kill it? If it wasn't for the desperate look in his eye, I would have voiced my question. Instead, I nodded reluctantly. "But I got him too, and did you see my radiant shield? I finally summoned it, and apparently, my blades—"

"Fuck, Aelia!"

Goddess, why did he keep saying that?

He scooped me into his arms as I squealed my displeasure.

"Put me down!" I kicked and squirmed, but his hold only tightened around my middle, and he started to move.

"Do you want to die?" he hissed, piercing irises searing into my own.

All the air caught in my lungs and an embarrassing choking sound squeezed out. "... What?"

"The gloomwhisper's claws are coated in poison from the nyxen tree. It's lethal to Light Fae." His Adam's apple jerked down the column of his throat as he spoke the final sentence.

"Lethal? But I feel fine..." Except for the slight piercing pain in my shoulder.

Reign's head dipped, and a look I would have sworn I'd never see on my professor's face swept across his tense jaw. Fear.

"Then why are you running if I'm as good as dead?" We were moving so quickly it felt as if we were flying, but Reign's shadow wings had vanished.

"If we can reach the Nightbloom Gardens, there may be a chance. There is a pond created from the very waters that feed the nyxen tree, along with all the other deadly flora of this court. For Shadow Fae, the poison is only a nuisance, so the pond was created long ago as a healing pool."

"But I'm a Light Fae, right?"

He shook his head slowly. "To be perfectly honest, Aelia, I have no idea what you are." His lips twisted into a scowl, a tendon in his jaw fluttering like mad. The ache in my shoulder had begun to dissipate, which as pleasant as it was, I knew was not a good thing. "So we must try."

The forest whipped by in a blur of spectral shadows and bedtime horrors. The gloomwhisper, or whatever it was, couldn't be the only deadly creature looming in the ominous silhouettes of the towering trees.

My eyelids drooped, exhaustion suddenly setting in.

"Hold on, Aelia, we're nearly there."

Why did I ever follow this man to this ungodly place? Poor Aidan. He'd be crushed when he found out I was dead. Killed by a Shadow fiend while chasing after his treasured gift.

"Aelia!" Reign's voice towed me back from the brink of sweet oblivion. A sharp sting lanced across my cheek.

"Ow!" I shrieked. "You slapped me."

"Keep your eyes open."

"I'm sorry you won't win the grand prize, Reign," I murmured, my voice strange to my own ears. "I tried my best. You just didn't pick a good acquisition." Numbness spread down my arm, nearly reaching my fingertips.

"You're wrong," he snarled, his fingers digging into my cheeks with unyielding resolve as he wrenched my gaze to meet the fire in his. "You are the strongest female I have encountered across this great continent, Aelia Ravenwood, and you will *not* die today. Just like you did not succumb to the icy embrace of the river, nor when those Light Fae bastards attacked you, or when you strode through the threshold of the Veil of Judgement. I do *not* pick losers, Aelia. Now fight, *princess.*"

Chapter Twenty-Four

A *elia*

The fire in Reign's words kindled something deep inside. Once again, that long-buried power ignited, warming my icy bones. A sliver of moonlight slipped between the thick copse of trees overhead, illuminating the necklace Aidan had given me. It seemed like years had passed since my birthday. I thumbed the warm metal, the slow circles an anchor in the storm of poison ravaging my body. Exhaustion's feral claws wrapped around my chest, again threatening to pull me beneath its dark depths, but I refused to surrender. Reign was right. I'd come this far, and I would *not* die like this.

Reign's frantic footfalls began to slow, and I tore my gaze from the medallion. The twisted oaks and gnarled banyans of the forest gave way to a lush moonlit garden where the rainbow of flowers defied the sun, unfurling their petals under the caress of moonlight. Midnight roses with velvet petals as deep and dark as the night sky, ethereal moonflowers glowing with a luminescent sheen, casting a soft, silvery light that illuminated the winding paths. The elusive shadow orchids thrived in the muted light, their black and purple hues a vibrant contrast against the dark foliage.

Despite the anguish tearing through my veins, I couldn't help but gawk at the nocturnal splendor. Twisting vines adorned with star-shaped blossoms climbed over elegant arches and trellises, creating quiet nooks. At the heart of the garden lay a tranquil pond, its surface still and reflective as obsidian glass.

"Is that it?" I whispered, my voice oddly hollow given the beauty surrounding me.

"Yes." Reign gently lowered me onto the silky blades of grass beside the pond, removed my torn jacket, and began unlacing my nightgown from behind.

It took my foggy brain a moment to process what was happening. "What are you doing?" I squeaked, fumbling to keep the shreds of fabric across my breasts.

"The waters must have direct skin contact in order for the healing to occur."

"If it works at all..."

"Would you truly risk your life rather than allow me to see your bare form?" He dragged his hand through his unruly midnight hair, and it occurred to me that I'd never seen the perfect professor so disheveled. Sweat beaded across his brow and a thin layer of dirt darkened his cheeks. But that wild look in his eyes... I'd never seen anything like it. "We don't have time to argue about this."

I pinned my good arm across my chest, using what little energy I had, despite knowing how foolishly I was behaving. "Well, you said yourself the likelihood of this pond healing me is slim."

"Aelia," he growled, those fathomless orbs lancing into me and broaching no further argument.

"Fine," I grumbled.

He kneeled behind me, untying the final laces. As the light

linen fell to the grass, I kept my arm tight across my chest. My breathing grew haggard, coming faster, each inhale more of a struggle as he crawled around me and began to unlace my boots. He kept his head down, his eyes intent on the dark thread weaving through the leather.

My shoulder throbbed and the piercing ache now climbed higher, up to my neck, then doubled back down through my fingertips. I hazarded a quick glance and found that dark vines of pure black now crisscrossed my pale skin. Not only could I see the poison spreading, I could feel it, numbing every inch as it surged through my veins.

Once he finished with my boots, those starlit irises lifted to mine. Despite the tangle of fiery pain and icy numbness, an uncontrollable flutter battered my chest when those eyes locked on my own. "Can you manage with the leathers?" he rasped. The rough edge to his tone stoking the burning embers in my core.

Tearing my eyes away from his, I glanced down at the laces and groaned. I could untie them, but that would likely be the most I could accomplish with one hand. I'd never be able to shimmy the wet leathers down my hips unassisted. Slowly, I shook my head.

A feral smile carved across his face, lifting the corners of his mouth into a wicked promise, and with the moonlight glistening across those midnight orbs, his eyes sparkled like a glittering night sky. Gods, I should not be this aroused so close to the brink of death.

Reign's fingers slid beneath my waistband as I undid the ties, revealing my damp undergarments. Heat traveled up and down my core, scorching my lower half before traveling back up and burning my cheeks. As he slid my leathers down my body, he kept his eyes pinned to mine.

I inhaled a ragged breath when nothing but my scant underclothes remained between us.

Reign abruptly stood and tore his tunic over his head, then

shimmied out of his pants. The flimsy linen underdrawers he wore beneath left little to the imagination. I swallowed hard and tore my gaze away from the clear outline of his arousal.

"What are you doing?" I breathed.

"Damn it, Aelia, we don't have time to argue logistics. The pond is deep and the mystical current strong. In your condition, I doubt you'll be able to stand, much less swim. I'll have to hold you, and I'd rather not have to suffer wet clothes the entire flight home."

If my damned *rais* would simply cooperate, I would be able to dry him. At this rate, I might be dead by the time we've finished here, so this entire internal conversation was moot.

"I'll get in first, then I'll help you. Once you're beneath the water, you can remove your underthings."

I squeezed my eyes closed and nodded, muffling the faint gasp that threatened to erupt at mention of my most personal articles of clothing. At least he didn't mock my delicate mortal sensibilities this time. A faint splash encouraged my eyes to open, and I caught a glimpse of Reign sliding into the pond, his agile movements barely disrupting the dark ripples. Once he was immersed up to his neck, he held his hand out. I scooted to the edge of the pond, the subtle movement sending searing pain up my shoulder.

I must have winced, because without uttering a word, Reign's arms weaved around my waist. His fingers dug into my hips and pops of energy skimmed across my bare flesh as he lifted me for an instant before lowering me into the surprisingly heated water and positioning me in front of him, chest to chest. I could barely muster the strength to look him in the eye at this close proximity.

A groan escaped as the warmth enveloped me, the combination of the tepid waters and the heat of Reign's body chasing away the chill that had pervaded my bones.

"Now take off your undergarments."

Suddenly, the lack of heat was no longer an issue. That

jagged edge to his voice had fire burning through every inch of me. I opened my mouth to object—surely, it couldn't have been that important to be completely naked—but Reign's murderous glare cut me off.

"Must I do it for you in order to ensure compliance?"

"No," I murmured as I reached around my back with my good arm to unhook the fastener. The brassiere sloughed off before floating between us for an agonizing moment. Plowing through the embarrassment, I tossed it to the lawn along with my other discarded clothing before reaching beneath the waters for my final undergarment, the delicate lace that covered my most private area nothing more than a scrap.

Reign's nostrils flared as I revealed the lacy fabric and lobbed it beside the other garments on the dark earth. A sparkle of mischief lit up those fathomless orbs, and a shudder raced up my spine as he held me against his unyielding chest. His legs kicked beneath the murky waves, keeping us both afloat.

"How long should this healing take?" I stammered, trying my damnedest to keep my eyes averted from his piercing ones. The current *was* strong, abnormally so for a pond. I'd greatly underestimated its power beneath the smooth glass façade. It only served to remind me of the perilous nature of all things Shadow Fae. I did my best to attempt to flutter my feet to keep from relying completely on Reign, but I could barely keep my head above water. If it wasn't for his solid hold, I'd be clinging onto the edge with one arm for dear life.

"For Shadow Fae, not long at all, but for you, I have no idea." His eyes drifted to my shoulder, and his mouth twisted into a frown.

"Not good?" I whispered. I was having a harder time keeping my eyes open, let alone forming words.

He released a noncommittal grunt and his arms tightened around my middle, pressing me even more firmly against the hard planes of his torso. His musky, frosty scent filled my nostrils, wrapping me in a soothing cocoon. I must have been near delirium because I'd nearly forgotten I was completely naked, flush against my moody professor. It felt oddly comfortable—natural, even. It was entirely not what I'd expected for my first time bared before a male.

"Now what?" I murmured.

"Fuck, Aelia, I don't know." His harsh tone snapped my gaze up to meet his. Those pitch globes were completely unreadable, a dark tunnel of endless night. His mouth quivered, then it flattened into a tight line. "I'm sorry," he mumbled. "I didn't mean to shout; I simply do not have an answer, and I'm not accustomed to this feeling of utter loss of control. I despise it."

The surprising confession, not to mention the apology, was enough to momentarily clear my foggy mind. I truly must have been moments away from Noxus's waiting arms for Reign to be acting in this manner. "You did all that you could. You went above and beyond, really." I lifted my good shoulder. "You definitely deserve the prize."

"Damn it, Aelia, it isn't simply about the prize," he gritted out, his expression savage. His dark brows pinched as his heated gaze razed over me.

"It isn't?" Goddess, I hated how weak I sounded.

A heavy silence descended over us as Reign contemplated his answer for an endless moment. "No," he finally whispered. "I'm impressed by how far you've come. You've outlasted dozens of other Light Fae students with years of *rais* training, and tonight, you finally summoned your own power. As your professor, I'm proud of you."

Right, of course. *As my professor.* What had I expected him to say?

"I'm dying, aren't I?" I fixed my eyes to his luminous ones. "That's why you are suddenly being kind to me."

A rueful smile slid across his lips, and his head tipped forward so that our mouths were a mere heartbeat away. "Maybe," he sighed. His cool breath sailed across my lips, and my pulse thumped more quickly. "You have no idea the immense amount of willpower this is requiring of me, princess..."

My brows knitted as I lifted my eyes to his. "Willpower?" I'd assumed this was taxing on his *nox*, but his will?

"To be completely naked and wet in the cover of darkness with a beautiful female? I deserve a direct pass from Noxus straight to the heavenly afterlife."

My cheeks burned beneath that heated stare, a look that had likely done in dozens of females before me. My mouth curved to form a reply, but not a single word took shape.

A long minute later, he unraveled one arm from my waist and brushed a finger across my shoulder. His brows furrowed as he traced a path along my skin. "Does this hurt?"

I slowly shook my head to keep it from spinning. Wrapped in his arms, I'd momentarily forgotten all about the pain.

His dark gaze traveled up my neck, then down along my collarbone. He traced the invisible line his eyes had drawn with his finger, and goose bumps exploded across my flesh.

"Hmm," he murmured.

"What?"

I dipped my chin to survey the damage at the same time Reign's head dropped. Our noses brushed, and my breath hitched, the sharp intake of air vibrating the dense air between us. He licked his bottom lip and slanted his mouth toward mine. My entire body clenched in anticipation.

"Oh princess..." A low growl rumbled his chest, the vibrations echoing through my ribcage. "If you really were dying and these truly were the final moments between us, the things I'd do to you..."

My chest heaved, and my bare breasts nearly popped up above the surface as my body propelled me closer to his. I stared up at Reign, each inhale more difficult than the last as he trapped me in that mesmerizing gaze, drawing me further into the abyss.

He shifted and his now hard as steel arousal pressed against my belly through the thin linen of his underdrawers. Heat pooled between my thighs and I was certain I'd combust if he didn't release me at once.

"But alas," he murmured, his lips brushing mine. The touch so faint it was no more than the delicate flutter of pixie wings and, still, it set my heart galloping. "I believe the poison has stopped spreading."

"It has?" I squeaked. Following his line of sight, I trailed the inky tendrils that had spread across my flesh and now halted at my elbow.

"You see?"

I nodded, then Reign clasped my chin and tipped it up before trailing his finger down my neck and pausing at the sensitive skin of my collarbone. "And it's stopped here too."

"That's fantastic news." Then why did I sound so dejected? Was the idea of his heated promise worth more than my life? Raysa, the toxins surely must have spread to my brain. "So now what? Do we have to stay in this pool forever?" *Please say yes — No!*

"Elisa should have an antidote among her potions at the Conservatory. Now that the immediate threat has passed, we should have enough time to get you to her."

Ah, yes, the healer.

I waited for an endless moment as he watched me, willing words to spring free from his bowed lips. The almost kiss? His wicked desires? Was he simply going to pretend none of it happened?

I pushed back an inch, putting some much-needed space between our heated bodies when no further explanation came and breathed in a breath of air not tainted in Reign's heady scent. I supposed he would pretend. Then so would I. Clearing my scrambled thoughts, my mind instantly jumped to a startling conclusion. "If I were full Light Fae, I would be dead right now."

"Mmm." He nodded slowly. "Perhaps there truly is some Kin in you. It would explain the ears and the latent development of *rais*."

"So this toxin isn't lethal to Kin?" He could have led with that to begin with.

"I'm not certain of its effects on non-Fae, Aelia. To my knowledge, none have been exposed to it before today." He shrugged. "I don't claim to be the expert on the subject, but in my time at the Citadel, it had never been documented."

"You attended Arcanum Citadel?" I didn't know why it was such a difficult fact to swallow. He was Shadow Fae, after all, and clearly powerful. I'd already considered it more than once.

Again, his head dipped.

"Is that why you came tonight?" All the questions I'd wanted to ask before encountering that damned gloomwhisper pushed to the front of my mind. "And why did you bring my dagger?"

Reign pressed a finger against my lips, scrambling every thought fighting for dominance. "Not that I mind spending the evening with you in the nude, but you may want to save your questions for later, once we are safely back on Conservatory grounds."

My entire body stiffened as those scrutinizing eyes lanced over me, crawling beneath the dark surface of the pond. His hands were still molded to my hips, his grip like steel. How had I forgotten I was naked again? "Right, yes, of course." I attempted to cross my arms over my chest and this time succeeded without much pain. He was right, the mystical pool had helped.

"Shall I help you out?" Those midnight orbs glittered in amusement.

"No, thank you. I'll be just fine getting out on my own."

Reign swam me right up to the ledge. Once I had a solid grip on the earth, his hands unraveled from my waist. My body immediately reacted to the loss of his, that unearthly chill ravaging my bones. What in all the realms?

Twisting my head over my shoulder, I met a pair of lively, expectant orbs. "Close your eyes until I'm dressed."

"You must be joking," he growled.

"I am not."

"But I've already seen you—"

"No, you haven't," I gritted out.

"For the love of Noxus..."

"Just do it, Reign."

"Fine," he grumbled. "You know, you're not fully healed yet. If you collapse from the effort it takes you to get dressed, it will be your own fault."

"I think I'll take the chance."

"Insufferable, modest Kin," he hissed through clenched teeth.

"Insufferable, arrogant Fae," I muttered right back as I heaved myself out of the pond. My head spun from the exertion, so instead of standing once I reached solid ground, I crawled to my damp clothes. He wasn't wrong, simply getting out of the water had taken a lot out of me. I hated when he was right.

Once I was fully clothed, I slowly pivoted to face him. To my surprise, he still remained in the pond with his eyes closed. "You can come out now."

"Thank the gods. I thought I'd shrivel up and die in here."

"Very funny, professor."

He planted his palms on the lawn and heaved himself out of the mystical pool. Water sluiced down his perfectly sculpted torso, droplets collecting along the defined ridges of his abdomen. I'd been so preoccupied with nearly dying earlier, I hadn't noticed the symbol carved into the flesh right above his heart. The mark of the banished. I only recognized it because I'd done copious research at the library once I'd heard about

Reign's predicament. It was a crude design of slashes and swirls puckering his skin. Gods, it looked horribly painful.

He loomed closer as I stared, unable to tear my gaze away from the dark symbol. "You know," he whispered, when he stood only inches away, "I could have had you back in those clothes and out again in half the time."

My eyes snapped up to meet his, and his lips curved into a devious smile.

"Too bad you'll never have the opportunity to test that theory," I bit back.

He dragged his sodden underdrawers down his muscled legs, and a gasp squeezed through the hard line of my lips as I diverted my gaze. A deep chuckle rumbled his broad chest, lifting his shoulders. "Oh, princess, if only we'd met under different circumstances..." He let the end of the sentence hang in the air between us, and I was oddly thankful for it.

I whirled around to face the towering Citadel as he dressed. This thing growing between Reign and me could go no further. Besides despising him most of the time, he was my professor and, per the Conservatory's rules, there was no fraternizing permitted between students and staff. It was a directive I'd quickly skimmed over upon my first perusal of the rules of conduct, as it had no bearing on my tenure at the academy.

"I'm finished dressing, you can turn around now."

Slowly, I rotated my body, and as I glanced up at Reign watching me, I convinced myself it still didn't.

"Now what?" I finally asked.

"Now we go home, princess."

Chapter Twenty-Five

A *elia*

"Great." Internally, my core clenched. The idea of a flight across the river cradled in Reign's arms again was too much for my weary heart to endure. Still, I drew in a steadying breath and slipped on a smile. "Will your wings be making their grand appearance?" At least, I'd finally have a chance to get some answers.

He clucked his tongue. "I'm afraid not tonight. I've burned out the majority of my *nox* saving your lovely ass." He lifted his hands, showcasing the silver manacles on his wrists. "I'm sure you've heard the rumors. These sparkling bracelets suppress my power when I'm beyond the Conservatory's wards."

That was how they worked? I remained silent, shocked he'd shared such a crucial tidbit of information with me.

Despite every ounce of me wanting to ask more about them, I kept my mouth closed, choosing to savor the odd moment of intimacy between us. "So how will we return?" I was certainly feeling better, but I wasn't sure I could muster another swim across the Luminoc.

"Another secret, princess." His obsidian eyes glistened beneath the pale moonlight. "Can I trust you?"

"Well, considering you just saved my life, I suppose I owe you."

"Good girl."

Reign lifted his hand and plunged two fingers into his mouth. A low whistle vibrated the air, the frequency a sharp pitch I could barely discern. A few seconds later, thunder pounded through the night sky. I glanced up in search of the storm rolling in, but instead of the ominous clouds, an enormous creature blocked the moonlight, magnificent wings spread across the endless night.

"Is... that... a dragon?" I choked out. To my understanding, there were less than a dozen left on the entire continent. They had been dangerously near extinction as a result of the Two Hundred Years War. The ruthless creatures had been used as mystical aircraft and lethal weapons on all sides of the courts.

An answering roar echoed through the whipping winds an instant later. A torrent of white flames lit up the pitch sky as the beast soared overhead. It took every ounce of willpower I had to keep still when every nerve in my body urged me to flee.

Reign moved beside me, his gaze tilted to the sky. "That's not just any dragon, princess, that's *my* dragon. I'd like to introduce Phantom, the Death of Dawn."

The enormous obsidian monster banked right then angled her wings toward the earth, and fear's claws dug into my lungs. I'd barely recovered from this wound, and yet again, my body was fighting for survival.

As I watched the dragon descend, Reign's smile grew brighter and his intent became clear. "Wait a second... we are not riding that thing back to campus, are we?"

"We most certainly are."

My head whipped back and forth as that fear froze the blood in my veins.

"Well, *I'm* riding Phantom back. How you choose to return to the Conservatory is up to you." His teeth flashed a brilliant white beneath the moonlight.

"You're an ass," I gritted out.

"Maybe, but I'm also your only way home."

The ground rumbled beneath my feet, jerking my attention to the monstrous creature who'd alighted at the foot of the garden, partially hidden by the looming forest beyond.

Reign held out his hand, and I stared at his palm as if touching it might actually kill me. "Come on, princess. I promise she won't bite."

"So... she's your pet or something?"

He snorted on a laugh. "Don't let her hear you say that. Dragons are incredibly proud creatures and would never suffer the indignity of being called the pet of any Fae, no matter how powerful. Phantom is my bonded skyrider. She chose me when I attended the Citadel."

His words from earlier drifted to the forefront of my mind. "Why is she a secret?"

"Dragons are a priceless commodity in Aetheria. Only a few trusted friends know of Phantom's existence, and no one across the river, which is why we must move quickly before my loud friend wakes the entire campus. If others knew she still resided within the Umbral Court's borders, they'd seek only to exploit her powers." Reign stared across the garden in the direction of the massive creature. His expression was tender, almost loving.

I'd never seen anything like it on the sullen male, and I did not appreciate the feelings it incited through my insides.

"Now, are you coming or not?" His hand twitched impatiently. "We do not have much time until full light descends across the river. Getting Phantom through unseen at night is difficult enough. We will never stand a chance in the daytime."

I hazarded a glance at the enormous beast, and beady, onyx

eyes, burning with fierce intelligence, seared into mine. The dragon snorted and plumes of silver smoke expelled from its vast nostrils. "Fine," I grumbled, wrapping my hand around Reign's palm. "If I end up dying today, after all, please tell Aidan it wasn't for a lack of trying."

His strong fingers tightened around my own and those mesmerizing irises met mine. "You are not dying today, princess. Of all the horrible ways you could perish within the confines of these two courts, Phantom is the least of your worries." He tugged me forward and somehow, my weary legs complied.

"How can you be so sure?" I moved warily beside Reign, one eye fixed on the obsidian dragon and my free hand closed around my dagger.

"Simple. She told me."

I glared up at the grinning bastard for a long moment before I realized I'd stopped walking. "Excuse me?"

"Good gods, they really taught you nothing at that Kin school, did they?"

"I think I would have remembered a lesson on talking dragons."

Reign released my hand and marched closer to the lumbering beast. I nearly begged him not to leave me. "Did you hear that, Phantom? Aelia believes you can speak."

The dragon's lips peeled back, baring razor-sharp incisors and row upon row of jagged teeth. Was that a smile? "Is she laughing at me?" I squealed.

The animal prowled forward, moving with a sinister elegance, its very presence commanding awe and terror. She lowered her head and nudged Reign in the stomach with her giant snout. It was a complete mystery to me how he avoided being impaled by the crown of horns circling the dragon's massive skull. Its colossal, serpentine body was covered in thick, obsidian scales that gleamed with an oily sheen, as if absorbing all light that dared to touch it.

"Not laughing, simply amused," Reign responded as he

patted the beast's head, strategically avoiding the sharp points. "And Phantom does not actually speak. When Fae are bonded to their skyriders, a spell is cast which allows us to hear each other's thoughts."

"Oh." Well, that made more sense. "So all the bonded riders can communicate with their mounts?"

"That's correct."

"Why didn't you tell me that when we rode Pyra the phoenix?"

"Because she and I are not bonded. She allows me to ride her as I must to fulfill my duties as professor at the Conservatory. The mental link can only exist with one creature at a time."

"Interesting." I watched the giant dragon nuzzling Reign, and still, I couldn't *not* think of a dog with its master. He seemed almost gentle with her.

"Now, are you ready?" Reign raised an impatient brow, and I could have sworn the dragon's expression mirrored her master's.

"I suppose." I eyed the intimidating monster, silently pondering how in the realms I was to mount the thing.

The dragon's expansive, bat-like wings unfurled with an intimidating span, the webbing between their spiny bones as dark as a moonless midnight. Its muscular tail, lined with spines, twitched back and forth, a deadly weapon in its own right. It seemed more than capable of crushing stone *and* bone without much effort.

"Come now, Phantom, give her a hand."

With an annoyed huff that sent columns of smoke into the air, the dragon dropped its belly to the ground and extended a leg. A clawed talon stretched before my boots, and my wide eyes followed the sleek, obsidian scales up a knobby limb covered in spikey protrusions. On the positive side, the nubs served as hand and foot holds—if only I could manage not to impale myself on their jagged points.

"Now, I climb?" I cocked a brow at my professor.

"Now, you climb, princess."

The typical scowl carved into his square jaw was annoyingly absent as he watched me. A spark of mirth lit up the endless midnight of his eyes.

Reaching for a scaly nub, my fingers closed around her thick skin, and I attempted to haul myself up. A sharp pang scorched across my shoulder as the wound from the gloomwhisper tore open. Biting out a curse, I miraculously held on. Thank the goddess the soles of my boots gripped the dragon's tough flesh, and I somehow managed to slowly crawl up its leg, despite the searing pain. "I would just like to remind you I almost died only a few minutes ago," I gritted out, clinging onto what I assumed was the beast's knee joint.

Reign heaved out a frustrated breath. "For the love of *nox*, Phantom, help her, or we'll never make it across the river in time."

A clawed talon, showcasing dagger-like nails, appeared over my head, and the scream died in my throat. Rough fingers—or toes?—closed around my torso, and I was suddenly weightless.

By the time my eyes opened—I wasn't sure when they'd closed—Phantom had deposited me onto her back, right between her shoulder blades and the ridge of her wing bones. My thighs instinctively closed around the big beast's body and warmth bled through my tattered clothes, reaching all the way to my marrow. My fatigued body nearly groaned in pleasure.

Until another familiar form appeared behind me, and my entire body tensed once again.

Reign's icy shadows curled around me, pinning me to his torso.

"Is that really necessary?" I hissed, squirming beneath their frosty touch.

He leaned in close, his heated breath tickling the shell of my ear. "I suppose that depends on whether you would still like to survive the flight home, princess?"

Raysa, I hated him.

With a resigned sigh, I sat back, allowing his shadows to curl around me, bindings of smoke and darkness. I wished I could say I hated it, despised their icy feel, but instead, I leaned into their ethereal touch.

"Hold on." Reign's sharp words jerked me from the brief moment of calm.

"To what?" I screeched as the dragon's powerful wings began to whip the air into a frenzy.

"Her wing bones!"

I could barely make out his reply over the thunderous flapping and the tornado of air thrashing around us. Strands of dark and light hair lashed across my face, the sharp sting bringing tears to my eyes.

Reign's shadows extended, cocooning me in a cloud of midnight, and the wild winds subsided. His arms tightened around my middle, and my body melted into his, just as a powerful thrust sent us shooting into the pitch sky. My stomach dropped to my toes and a groan fled through the gaping curve of my lips.

I squeezed my eyes closed and focused on my breaths, praying to all the gods I wouldn't pass out and fall to my doom. Once we leveled out, I hazarded a glance through slitted lids. The Court of Ethereal Light stretched before us, twilight blanketing the mystical, lush lands ahead.

When Reign had fetched me from Feywood all those weeks ago, I'd been so overwhelmed I hadn't truly had a chance to admire the breathtaking scenery. The soaring turrets of the Conservatory glittered with the moonlight at our backs and the first rays of sunlight dispersing across Aetheria. It was a truly splendid sight.

After skirting the arms of death, I needed a moment to appreciate it, to take it all in.

"Thank you for saving me," I whispered to the wind. I was well aware Reign hated when I thanked him for anything, but it needed to be said. With a quick glance over my shoulder, I caught a smirk ghosting across his lips.

"I'm simply going to ignore that remark."

"Do with it what you will." Releasing a breath, the tense set of my shoulders slackened, and I rested my head against Reign's shoulder. Every muscle, bone, and nerve in my body ached, and I was simply too exhausted to fight any longer.

Chapter Twenty-Six

I was a complete embarrassment. In only a few months, it was my second visit to the healer. Elisa was kind enough, but still the humiliation burned my cheeks when Reign once again dropped me off at her door.

More than that, I hated lying.

Reign had concocted a story about the gloomwhisper crossing the banks of the Luminoc in search of a tasty Kin treat while he gave me a private lesson outside regular class hours. There was something about the look in her eye that made me certain she didn't buy into the lie. Nonetheless, she smiled and nodded, offering my professor a flirty wink when he left.

And I hated her for that.

Which made no sense, whatsoever. Elisa was one of the only members of the staff who was kind to me, and still, the jealousy that had churned through my insides at that coquette gesture had been startling.

"You are very fortunate that you must have a significant amount of Kin blood coursing through your veins."

"Said no one ever." I shifted on the stiff mattress and stared through the dome of glass overhead.

A rueful smile parted the healer's lips. "Well, in this case, it was fortunate. I've never seen a Light Fae survive the gloomwhisper's poison unless the antidote was administered practically instantly."

"Lucky me."

Narrowing her eyes, she examined the nearly healed wound across my shoulder. "It's remarkable, really. The rate of healing is also much faster than I've ever seen."

"I suppose being a Kin is good for something, then." In truth, I did feel much better this morning. I'd only slept a few hours on this uncomfortable bed with Elisa fussing over me most of the night. "When can I return to class?"

Reign's Combat class was this afternoon, and after the ride on Phantom and learning about bonded skyriders, I was eager to earn my own. Not to mention the fact that Reign still owed me an explanation for last night's excursion into Shadow Fae territory. Now less than a week remained until the Choosing Ceremony. Would I get a phoenix, or maybe a hippogriff? I'd have to ask Rue what my other options were. A pit of dread sank to the bottom of my stomach. What if I wasn't chosen at all? Would one of these creatures have qualms about bonding with a lowly Kin?

"With the way you're progressing," Elisa replied, returning my thoughts to the present, "you should be able to return by tomorrow."

My lips twisted into a pout. "How about this afternoon? I really hate to miss Professor Reign's class."

Her mouth curved into a knowing smile. "I bet."

That damned heat spread across my cheeks again, and I hoped I could blame the embarrassing flush on a fever from the gloomwhisper's poison. "Oh, it's not like that," I stammered,

"Reign, I mean, the professor, said the Choosing Ceremony was near, and I simply wouldn't want to miss anything important—"

She lifted her hand, cutting off my nervous ramblings. "Relax, Aelia. I'm not insinuating anything. I would never question the undue attention Reign bestows upon you."

"I'm his acquisition," I mumbled lamely.

"And there have been a countless number before you, my dear." Her lips tightened into a firm line. "And I've never seen him fuss over any of the others like he does with you." She stepped closer and sat on the edge of the bed. Lowering her voice, she whispered, "I only wish to offer a word of advice: be careful. You must remember, above all else, Reign is Shadow Fae, and a powerful one at that. He may find himself on this side of the Luminoc for now, but I doubt it will remain that way forever."

There was something about the slight tremble in her voice that had waves of unease crashing through my insides. Had she guessed we'd lied? Did she know we'd been in the Court of Umbral Shadows only last night?

I nodded quickly, biting back the thank you. "Cheers," I managed sullenly.

She patted my leg and offered a fuller smile. "Get some rest. If your wound is sufficiently healed by this afternoon, I will *consider* allowing you to return to class."

"Great." But even I could hear the hint of dread in my tone.

Reign owed me answers. In the chaos of my first dragon flight, I'd neglected to wrestle out the truth from my professor. Why had he returned to the Shadow Court—and what did my daggers have to do with it?

"Oh, Aelia, I was so worried!" Rue jumped to her tiptoes and her slender arms wrapped around my neck as I approached the training field.

Elisa had finally allowed me to leave the confines of her healing sanctuary, but by the looks of it, I'd already missed the majority of Combat.

Reign's eyes chased to mine from across the grounds, and he offered a quick dip of his chin before he continued pelting waves of darkness at one of the other first-years. Darla, I believed was her name, from Flash Squad and she'd at least mustered a radiant shield as protection.

Which reminded me... I needed to attempt another one myself.

Rue held me out to arm's length, her light eyes scrutinizing every inch of my exposed flesh. "I can't believe that gloomwhisper crossed the river to get to you. That's perfectly horrifying!"

"It was." I swallowed down the lie, the untruth bitter on my tongue. I hated keeping the truth from my best friend.

Symon raced over a moment later, abandoning his hand-to-hand combat session with Zephyr to croon condolences at me. "Thank the goddess you survived, little Kin." He pressed a kiss to my forehead and brushed the tip of my ear on the way down.

"Sy!" I squealed.

"My apologies, Aelia. I simply couldn't help myself. The mere idea of never touching that sexy, curvy tip had me to the point of hysterics."

A laugh bubbled out despite my best attempts at a scowl. "You're completely incorrigible."

"Ladies and gentleFae," Reign's voice boomed across the field, his power pressing into my being. "Get back to work!" An instant later, he coalesced from the shadows an inch from my face. "If you are fully healed, I expect you to practice summoning that radiant shield, otherwise, if you are only here to distract your teammates, leave my class." The big brute towered over me, and all warm and fuzzy feelings for the male who saved my life only yesterday disappeared.

"I'm ready," I growled back.

"Good." He retreated a step before releasing a whirlwind of shadows. I dropped to the ground, barely avoiding the onslaught. Focusing my scrambled thoughts, I searched for that flicker of power I'd felt when the gloomwhisper had attacked, but only a vacant hole filled my core.

"Come on, come on," I muttered as the shadows swung back in a circle for a second attack.

Reign's dark gaze locked on mine, the intensity more fearsome than his enormous dragon. What I saw in those midnight orbs ignited something far below the surface. Not anger. Not disappointment. Not pity. Confidence. He really believed I could do this.

And I could.

Somehow, I'd called upon my latent powers last night, which meant I could do it again. What was different yesterday? My thoughts swirled back in time to the frightening creature... I was terrified. And right now, I wasn't. Reign might have been slightly unhinged, but I knew he wouldn't truly hurt me.

That was the difference.

The midnight shadows zipped closer, writhing like venomous snakes, coiled to strike. Closing my eyes, I latched onto the flicker of light, a tiny flame luminescing in the impenetrable darkness. *Come on, come on, Raysa, help me.*

"Shield up, princess!" Reign growled, and my lids snapped open as his shadows spun into a fury of night.

With my eyes fixed to his, I inhaled a deep breath, and the tiny flicker of gold swelled. It blossomed in my core, growing, rising, until it poured through my veins. Brilliant light consumed my vision, blotting out those midnight orbs still locked on mine. The shield expanded until it blanketed my entire body, enclosing me in a shimmering bubble.

Reign's shadows slammed into the luminescent orb and were hurled back.

"Way to go, Aelia!" Rue shouted.

Through the glowing orb and the encroaching darkness, I could just make out the pleased smile crawling across Reign's mouth.

"That's my girl!" Symon called out a moment later. "You show them; you show everybody!"

Beads of sweat collected along my brow as I held the shield while Reign's shadows poked and prodded, determined to find a way in. My professor stalked closer, the smile morphing into something wicked. The tendrils of darkness pressed harder, my skull pounding from the effort to keep them at bay.

Despite the chaos around me, Reign's voice brushed my ear as if he stood beside me. "Impressive, princess. It appears you've been holding out." The heat from his breath skidded across my ear, and a tremor rolled through my body. I lost focus.

Completely and utterly.

The shield burst, and Reign's shadows swirled around me in a maddening tempo. Coils of silky darkness caressed my skin, and I reveled in their ghostly touch. I was fairly certain this was supposed to be a punishment, and yet... I couldn't get enough.

As if Reign noticed, he stepped closer, dark brows furrowed and voice lowered. "My powers seem to be having less and less effect on you," he murmured.

"Or maybe I'm simply growing stronger," I countered with a smirk.

"Perhaps..." He drew his tongue across his bottom lip, and all focus was lost, once again. "You know, I was thinking we should begin private training sessions."

I swallowed hard, the idea of spending one-on-one time with my professor sounding like a terrible one. "Why?" I finally mustered.

"Because I think it will serve you well."

I crept closer, keeping my voice low. "Only if you promise

to tell me what you were doing last night, and what my daggers have to do with it."

A deep chuckle rumbled through Reign's powerful chest. "It's funny you think you have a choice in this. I didn't ask if you agreed to it or not." He dropped his head, so his lips were inches from my ear. "And if you think I'm simply going to spill all my secrets because we've seen each other in the nude, you are gravely mistaken."

Heat licked up my spine, settling across my cheeks before diving low between my thighs. *Oh, Raysa.*

"Meet me at the bank of the Luminoc tomorrow night after supper, I have a theory I'd like to test."

I willed my mouth to form the word *no*, but instead my head dipped like a fool, acquiescing. Good goddess, it was like I lost all self-control when I was around this male. Before I could utter another word, Reign and his ominous shadows twirled away in a cloud of darkness.

The moment he was gone, Rue bounded toward me with a devious smile. "What was that about?"

Sy moved into step beside me before I could answer. "What was what about?" He cocked a light brow, curiosity splayed across his handsome face.

"It was nothing," I blurted to my two friends.

"It sure looked like something to me." Rue's light brow arched. "And why didn't you tell me Reign was training you privately?"

"We just started." I shrugged nonchalantly. "And apparently, we'll be continuing for the foreseeable future."

"You're so lucky," Sy chanted. "To be personally trained by a Shadow Fae? And one as powerful and gorgeous as Reign? I'm sure he'll have your *rais* singing in no time."

"Her *rais* and her—" Rue's mischievous gaze dropped to the apex of my thighs.

"Rue!" I cried, an inferno of heat smothering my cheeks

and my lower half at her insinuation. "It is not even remotely like that."

She lifted a slim shoulder and grinned. "A girl can dream, can't she?"

Gods, if she only knew how Reign had plagued my dreams last night after the encounter in the dark pond nestled within the Nightbloom Gardens, she would die.

It had been nearly an entire day later, and still, I couldn't erase the vivid, heated memories or the lingering effects of his touch. I would never survive days of private training sessions...

Chapter Twenty-Seven

A*elia*

My fingers squeezed around the dagger's hilt, trembling from the strain, the muscles in my back screaming in agony, but I widened my stance and prepared for the onslaught of shadows, all the same.

Reign had been relentless for the past two hours, battering me with wave after wave of his unstoppable *nox*. But I'd held my own. Even my radiant shield had made a reluctant appearance. Currently the only thing that kept me from keeling over was the satisfaction of seeing his fatigued expression. Wild strands of dark hair tumbled over his brow, and a mixture of sweat and dirt darkened his features. On any other male, it would have been repulsive, but on him, that unkempt state only accentuated his brutal beauty.

Half a dozen umbral knives whizzed toward me, and with the exhaustion bone deep, I couldn't summon my shield fast enough. Relying on my dagger instead, I arced my blade across the air, slicing through two of the spectral weapons before dropping to the ground to evade the remaining ones.

"Again," Reign barked from a few yards away.

To my relief, he'd kept the hand-to-hand combat at a minimum today, relying almost entirely on the use of our mystical powers, which thankfully left us at a safe distance from one another.

Pushing myself off the grass, I tried to lift my weary bones, but only made it up to my knees before I fell back on my haunches. "I need a break," I complained.

"Breaks are for formidable Light Fae, and you have yet to prove yourself as one."

"Fae you." I lifted my index finger in a foul gesture, because apparently, I'd lost my mind.

Reign stomped toward me, erasing the distance between us in two long strides. His tunic flapped on a light breeze, dark shadows melding to his intimidating form. "If you could produce flames at will like other Light Fae, I would be more than happy to give you a rest, but since you cannot, and the Choosing Ceremony is only a few days away, we shall continue."

I glared up at the infuriating male looming over me. "If I die from exertion, it won't really matter now, will it?"

"Don't be so exaggerative."

"I'm not," I whined, the embarrassing sound squeezing out.

Reign crouched in front of me, balancing on the balls of his feet as he dragged a hand through his untamed locks. "Aelia, I am going to be perfectly honest with you. You have been here for over three months, and you are the only student of your year who can barely summon a radiant shield. I've seen tiny tots barely weaned from their mother's breast do it with less issue."

Something snapped as the arrogant bastard stared down at me. "I never asked to be here, gods' damn it," I hissed. "I was perfectly content living my quiet life on the farm as a Kin. I didn't request to have my life turned upside down, or to be honed into a warrior to serve the Crown. I didn't want any of this."

His dark brow arched, midnight eyes flashing, and a deep rumble vibrated his thick chest.

Perhaps, I'd gone too far. At times, I forgot Reign was a professor, a person of authority at the Conservatory, and not merely one of my difficult peers.

"You are a liar," he snarled. "I saw you in that miserable cottage, a second away from being hauled away by that Shadow Fae lord. You cannot tell me you would have been happier occupying his bed."

Heat flushed my cheeks, indignation sending my pulse skipping. "Who are you to judge? You have no idea what I truly desire. You know nothing about me." Goddess, I wished I could storm off, but my legs jiggled like jelly, and I was fairly certain if I attempted to stand, I'd end up flat on my face.

"That's entirely untrue, princess. I've seen you fight; I've witnessed the fire in your eyes and that indomitable will to survive." Reign's hand stretched out, fingers lifting my chin so I could feel the burn of his gaze. "You may not have chosen this destiny, but Raysa set you upon this path, nonetheless. You have the heart of a warrior, Aelia, and the spirit of the phoenix who rises anew from ash and flame. The trials you've overcome are merely the forging of your soul, sculpting you into the champion you are destined to become. Trust not in the fate that was given, but in the fate *you* will shape, with iron will and a courage that even the stars shall envy."

All the air fled my lungs, stolen by the force of his words. Gods, did he truly think so highly of me?

His fingers fell away, but that piercing gaze lingered for an interminable moment longer. Drawing on strength I was certain I did not possess, I forced myself to stand. Once I was certain I was steady, I lifted my chin to my enigmatic professor, matching the intensity I saw in his eyes.

"Okay, I'm ready."

"Good girl." His savage expression softened into a smile. "Because we have yet to test that theory I mentioned earlier."

Right. "How could I have forgotten?"

The storm of darkness curled around his shoulders until massive wings unfurled. He held out his arms and eyed me expectantly.

"Where are we going?"

His gaze lifted over my head to the dark waters swirling between the two rival academies. "Just across the river."

"Again?" I squealed, my head whipping back and forth.

"Only to the edge of Shadow Fae territory. Trust me, it will be quick, and we will go unnoticed."

"I don't know..."

"I will be retrieving your dagger."

A twitch of excitement curled the corners of my lips. "Well, why didn't you say that in the first place?" Before he could answer, I wrapped my hand around the back of his neck and leapt into his arms.

Reign grunted, staggering back. "A little warning would have been nice, princess."

"Surely, with those impressive muscles, carrying me should be no more trying than lifting a feather."

A deep chuckle bubbled up from his throat, the smooth, melodious sound like a warm caress. "Why, princess, are you trying to stroke my ego?" A devious smirk lit up the deep pools of darkness. "Not that I mind, but there are other parts I'd prefer stroked—"

A gasp cut off his wicked words as scorching heat descended over my face.

Another howl of laughter echoed between us as he pushed off the earth and his wings propelled us skyward. With my stomach plummeting, all thoughts of his mischievous humor vanished as I clung on for dear life.

We soared over the veranda separating the campus from the Luminoc River below and floated over the choppy waters.

From this point along the bank, the distance to the Court of Umbral Shadows was minimal; it was exactly where I'd chosen to jump from that ill-fated night.

A few powerful thrusts of his wings and we crossed the expanse. As we hovered between both courts, the brilliant light gave way to shimmery night. I'd hoped for a moment to pry more information out of my reticent professor, but before I could gather the courage, his wings angled downward, and we began our descent into darkness.

Reign's boots hit the soft earth with surprising grace for such an immense male, his wings almost immediately evaporating into the night. I wondered how difficult it was to fight the effects of the manacles. Gently, he lowered me to the ground, keeping one hand on my waist until I proved steady.

My thoughts darted back in time to our conversation the last time we were here. "How is it possible for you to stand on Shadow Fae soil with that mark on your chest?" It was my understanding that a symbol such as that was carved to prevent the traitor from returning to their homeland.

The sloping curve of his lips screwed into a distasteful pucker. He remained silent for a long moment before his Adam's apple jogged down his throat, and his quiet reply filled the air between us. "It's much like these cuffs. I can fight its effects for short periods of time."

Goddess, he must have been inhumanly strong.

"Which is why it's necessary we make this quick." He ticked his head to a swathe of nightbloom bushes along the bank, its deep lavender blossoms glistening beneath the moonlight. "We should find your dagger there."

Before the last word was out, I darted toward the lush hedges. A white bundle caught my eye about a yard away from where we stood. My pulse quickened as I hurried forward, the medallion of the necklace Aidan had given me bouncing on my chest.

"There!" I dropped to my knees and reached for the

package beneath the lush vegetation. Despite the bulky cloth wrapped around it, a familiar pulse called to me. Clearly, Reign had pushed me too hard at training because I was nearly delusional.

He appeared beside me a moment later as I ripped open the bundle. Nestled in the center was my dagger, a brilliant sheen coating the blade and the hilt more lustrous than I'd ever seen it.

"Well, that was kind of Gideon to give it a polish." Reign eyed my favorite weapon from over my shoulder.

"Who is Gideon?"

"A good friend."

"I still can't believe you left my dagger in the hands of the enemy," I grumbled.

"I told you he is a friend, and I can count my true friends on one hand. Your precious weapon was never in any danger, princess."

As I fondled my dagger, Reign reached for the slip of parchment I'd missed in my eagerness. His brows furrowed as he read over the dark scrawling.

I whirled around and stood on my tiptoes, trying to see over him. "What does it say?"

"Give me a second to read it."

From what I could see, it was only a few sentences. How long could it possibly take to read? With every second that passed, Reign's expression grew darker.

"Reign!" I hissed and snatched the note from his hand.

I scanned the neat penmanship before releasing a groan. "I can't read this."

"That's exactly the point, princess."

"Well, what does it say?"

He released a breath, a tendon fluttering like mad across his clenched jaw. "Gideon believes the blade is crafted from infernium vein."

"What in the realms is that?"

"A metal mined only within the Court of Infernal Night,

the former third Fae court, which to our best knowledge, should no longer exist."

Chapter Twenty-Eight

A elia

"But that's not possible." The words rushed out on a single breath. The Court of Infernal Night no longer existed. The Two Hundred Years War had ensured the extermination of all Night Fae, as well as the complete destruction of their lands to the south.

Reign's gaze remained fixed to the blade balanced on my palm. "It shouldn't be. All Night Fae weapons were supposed to have been incinerated by dragon fire." He reached for my dagger, but I pulled my hand away and tucked it behind my back. The corners of his eyes tapered as disapproval carved into the hard set of his jaw. "And yet, this one remains."

"I'm certain Aidan had no idea when he gifted it to me."

His brows furrowed, dark lines etching into his forehead. "If you say so..."

"How would he? Kin were not permitted to fight in the

Two Hundred Years War. We only sat on the outskirts and starved."

"Mmm." Reign's expression turned pensive as he eyed the silhouette of the other dagger tucked into my waistband. "Aelia, if Gideon is correct, that blade is extremely rare; not only does it counteract Shadow Fae *nox*, but also Light Fae *rais*."

"*If* he's correct…"

He nodded. "There's one more thing." He turned his palm up and crooked a long finger. I reluctantly pulled the dagger out from behind my back but refused to hand it over. "That crystal embedded in the hilt, Gideon's never seen anything like it, nor could he find any information about it in the archives. Its origins are not of the Court of Infernal Night. He said he did detect some sort of power emanating from the gem, and strangely enough, it was a mix of *nox* and *rais*."

How was that possible? And where in all the realms had Aidan procured this extinct artifact? Amidst the deluge of questions, one thing was clear, I had to protect these daggers and keep their survival a secret.

Tucking the weapon into my waistband on the side opposite it's twin, I lifted my gaze to his conflicted one. "Reign, you cannot tell anyone else of their existence, please, you must promise me."

He heaved out a breath, his head slowly twisting from side to side. "I cannot, Aelia. Do you have any idea what this could mean?"

"We don't know anything for certain yet. Your friend could be wrong."

"Doubtful," he murmured.

I reached for his hands, squeezing them between my own. My skin tingled at the contact with his rough, calloused flesh. "I'll do anything."

"Princess," he snarled and jerked free of my hold, "I warned you about this. Never make a deal you will not be able to carry through."

"I'm not."

Those pools of inky black sparked with excitement, and Reign's typically obscure aura lit up so vividly that barely a dark shadow remained. He captured me in that hypnotic gaze, a wicked grin teasing at his lips. "Anything?"

I nodded, anything to be free of that overpowering scrutiny.

"This deal will be binding for as long as we each draw breath. You understand that? And you agree to allow me to call in this promise at any time and for whatever reason I see fit?"

My chin dipped again, and I prayed to the goddess I was doing the right thing to keep my precious daggers from falling into the wrong hands. What could my professor possibly ask of me?

"So be it," he grumbled. "Repeat after me... I, Aelia Ravenwood of Feywood, vow to submit to any request at any time made by Reign Darkthorn of the Court of Umbral Shadows in exchange for the aforementioned secret about the daggers. Should I fail to do so, may Raysa strike me down on the spot."

I repeated the words as Reign took my hand, and a swirl of energy surged between our palms. A tangle of light and murky shadow enveloped our interlaced hands and invisible binds laced around my heart, tightening until my manic pulse slowed to nearly a standstill.

"I, Reign Darkthorn of the Court of Umbral Shadows," he murmured, "vow to keep your secret, Aelia Ravenwood of Feywood, regarding the aforementioned daggers. In exchange, you owe me a favor I may claim at my discretion. Should I fail to keep the secret, may Noxus strike me down on the spot."

We remained perfectly still for a long moment after we'd both spoken our vows, a weighty silence lingering between our interlocked hands.

"It's done," he finally whispered and withdrew his hand.

My fingers twitched at the loss of his warmth, and I reached for my dagger out of habit. I certainly hoped all of this would be worth it. Only the gods would know what I'd committed myself to. I thumbed the smooth crystal and a flicker of energy danced across my skin. When I removed my finger, a swirl of darkness spiraled around a spark of light. Aidan had gifted me these daggers at the age of sixteen, and they had *never* done that in the four years since.

"It's reacting to your *rais*."

I barely contained a snort. "You said yourself I have no more *rais* than a tiny tot." I bristled at his earlier insult. Why did I care so much what he thought, anyway?

"That was not what I said, princess. I said you could not summon your *rais*, not that you did not possess it."

"Semantics."

"Not at all." He loomed dangerously close, those starlit orbs pinned to mine. "There are a few possible reasons why you would not be able to access your powers. For example, they may be bound—"

"Bound? But why?"

"I have no idea, it's only a theory. But since your arrival in the Court of Ethereal Light, it does seem as if the binds seem to be loosening, which brings me to my second theory."

"Which is?"

"Try to summon your shield now."

I eyed him warily. He knew very well the only times I'd been able to coax it out were when I felt truly afraid.

"When was the first time you managed a shield?"

"With the gloomwhisper."

"On Shadow Fae land," he countered.

My brows puckered at his insinuation. "Because I was a moment away from being devoured by that monster."

"And you were healed by the pond's mystical power."

My heart fluttered like the whipping wings of a hemming-byrd, battering my ribs. "Because I'm Kin."

"Maybe, or maybe not."

"What are you saying?" I blurted, a tornado spiraling through my insides at what I was certain he was getting at.

"For Noxus's sake, Aelia, just humor me and try to summon your shield."

"It's not going to work," I hissed, my fingers tightening around the dagger's hilt.

Reign's shadows shot out and tendrils of darkness snaked around my throat. Their silky touch incited a ripple of goosebumps down my arms. Until the whispers of night began to constrict.

"Reign," I choked out. "Stop..."

"No," he snarled, and another band of shadow wraiths circled my form, lifting me off the ground.

"Let go!"

He stalked closer, inky darkness pouring off his form. "Make me!"

I jerked my dagger out and slashed at the umbral forms wrapped around my torso, and each one disintegrated with the slice of my blade.

"Use your shield, damn it," he growled.

Squeezing my eyes closed, I cursed the son of Noxus from here to kingdom come. Then I felt it. That tiny familiar flicker of energy in my core. Reaching for it, the well of power blossomed, growing more quickly with each ragged breath.

A golden glow, so brilliant I could sense it through my closed lids, exploded around me. Reign's shadows fell away and I dropped to the ground, my boots sinking into the hardpacked earth. My eyes snapped open to a radiant gilded orb surrounding my form.

Reign's umbral minions poked and prodded at the mystical shield, but it held against their onslaught. A smile crawled across my lips at the frustration in his eyes as he released torrent after torrent of dark energy.

An endless moment later, sweat trickled down my spine and a tremor raced through my body. Perhaps, my newfound power wasn't exactly limitless. As if Reign could feel my strength falter, he folded his arms, recalling his shadow minions into his form. The scowl of frustration softened, and something like pride gleamed from within the bottomless depths of onyx.

"Why are you smiling?" I gritted out as the shield sputtered out.

"Because I was right." His grin grew wider. "Your *rais* reacts to the *nox* in Shadow Fae soil."

"So what are you saying?" I rasped.

He paused and licked his lips, and I could practically see the gears spinning in that twisted head of his. "Two possible explanations come to mind."

My stomach churned as my own head reeled with the possibilities.

"The first and more likely scenario is that your abilities were bound by a powerful *rais* spell and the *nox* in the Court of Umbral Shadows somehow counteracts it."

"Or?" I held my breath as I waited for his response.

He crept closer and every nerve screamed at his proximity as his obsidian shadows folded around me. "Or..." He tipped my chin up with one long finger and trapped me in his mesmerizing gaze. "You have some Shadow Fae blood coursing through your veins, princess."

THE CONSERVATORY OF LUCE

FORGED IN LIGHT • TEMPERED IN TRUTH

Chapter Twenty-Nine

A *elia*

I followed Rue and Sy out of the gilded doors of the Hall of Rais after a fairly uneventful hour of Illumination Sight. I could still barely make out an aura, let alone a magical forcefield. My radiant shield was still my weapon of choice, and in the last few days, it appeared and disappeared as it saw fit, with little control on my part.

The Choosing Ceremony was only a day away, and I was terrified my time at the Conservatory was about to come to an embarrassing end.

"Why so glum my little round-eared friend?" Sy swung his arm across my shoulders and drew me into his side. His finger made a move toward the shell of my ear, but I swatted him away.

"Oh, nothing," I mumbled. "Just tired."

"From all those late-night training sessions with Professor Reign?" Rue offered a wicked grin.

"Ha. Ha." I was exhausted and perpetually nervous. Every time I saw the ominous Shadow Fae professor, I was certain he would call in the favor. A tangle of anxiety and thrill battered my insides any time I was within his proximity.

We had yet to test my daggers against Light Fae magic—except for my own, of course. That had been a disaster. The blades had bounced against my shield and nearly impaled Reign in the process. The hint of a smile ghosted over my lips at the memory of the surprise carved into his jaw as he dropped to the ground to avoid the mystical missile.

"There's that smile." Sy pinched my cheek as we strolled toward the banquet hall.

I barely managed to eat these days with the anxiety of one-on-one training looming over my shoulder after every evening meal.

When we reached the hall, Rue led us to our team table where platters of food already awaited. The heady scent of roasted vegetables coaxed a grumble low in my belly. Maybe I was a little hungry. Belmore and Ariadne tossed me matching scowls as I settled in at the opposite end of the table. Thank the goddess I hadn't had any run-ins with his blood-thirsty companions, Kian or Lucian. In fact, both males had avoided me at all costs ever since that day, and when Kian had finally emerged from the healer after that mysterious attack months ago, a gruesome scar bisected his face, running from his left temple, across his upper lip.

Now the monster outside reflected the one within.

Heaton appeared a moment later, distracting me from my thoughts, and folded down beside me. "Aelia." He dipped his head in acknowledgement and speared a massive chunk of meat onto his plate. I hadn't seen much of our team leader lately since I'd been overwhelmed with Reign's constant training.

"Where's Dinan?" Rue's bright eyes circled the table.

Heaton's gentle smile flipped upside down. "He's resting in Noxus's arms."

My eyes bulged as I regarded our team leader. "He's dead? How?" A twinge of pity ignited in my chest. I didn't know Dinan well; I'd barely spoken a few words to him, but he'd never been cruel like some of the others.

His shoulders rounded, drooping over his heaping platter. "I'm not certain. We found his body in the river this morning."

"Damned Arcanum students," Belmore hissed.

"How do you know it was Shadow Fae? It could have just as easily been one of our own." I threw the insufferable Fae a meaningful glare.

"Aelia's right," said Heaton. "Until the healer's examination is complete, we will not know the cause of death with any certainty."

"But you will after?" I blurted.

"Yes, both *rais* and *nox* carry a mystical signature. Hopefully, Elisa will be able to determine which was involved in his untimely demise."

Hmm, interesting.

"I'm certain the healer will find *rais*." Reign's voice drifted across my eardrum an instant before he emerged from the shadows. He loomed over me, those smoky fingers dancing across every inch of exposed flesh. A shudder raged through my body as his presence lit up every cell.

"Why do you say that, professor?" Heaton asked.

"Because I haven't detected any Shadow Fae movement across the river in the last few weeks, with the exception of the gloomwhisper who attacked Aelia."

"Not since the assault on the dormitory."

"Exactly." He pressed his lips together, gaze glossing over as if he'd traveled to another time. "It won't be long now, though. Their Choosing Ceremony will likely also take place this week."

A dribble of dread constricted my chest at the reminder.

"By the way, the king has decided to make an impromptu visit to the Conservatory tomorrow." Despite Reign standing over me, I could feel his heated gaze boring into the top of my head.

"King Elian of Ether will attend the Choosing Ceremony?" Rue squealed.

"Mmm." I caught Reign's head dip from the corner of my eye. "I suppose he's come to assess our newest class."

I swallowed hard, and my professor's gaze chased to mine.

"On that note, Aelia, are you ready?"

I stared at my empty plate and my stomach roiled. Gods' damn it, why did I stuff myself? Now that the king was to attend the ceremony, Reign's methods would surely be twice as brutal this evening.

Nodding slowly, I offered my friends a quick wave before reluctantly standing and following Reign out the doors of the hall. As soon as the hushed murmurs of my classmates fell away, I quickened my pace. The fresh evening air wafted over my face and the tight set of my shoulder blades relaxed a notch.

When we reached the training field, Reign finally turned to face me. "The king's appearance tomorrow changes everything, Aelia."

My brows shot up at the intensity in his gaze. "What do you mean?"

"King Elian does not often grace us with his ethereal presence. There's a reason he's decided to come, and it cannot be a good one."

"What do you know about the affairs of the King of Ethereal Light?"

He loosed a slow breath and dragged his hand through his dark locks, hidden beneath the hood of his cloak. "I know that he only cares about one thing: creating soldiers for his army."

"But we are at peace."

Reign barked out a laugh, the sharp sound reaching to the very marrow of my bones. "There is no such thing as peace between the Fae Courts, princess. It would serve you well to understand that now." He eyed the daggers tucked along my waistband. "We must discover if those blades truly have power over *rais*."

"I thought we determined they didn't—"

"No. We determined they do not affect *your* powers. Whatever those may be." He mumbled the last part, and if I hadn't been so attuned to him, I doubted I would have made out the words.

"Then let's test them out on Rue, like I suggested."

"We can't simply trust anyone with this secret, princess."

"Rue isn't just anyone. She's my roommate and my friend."

"How many times must I remind you not to trust anyone here?"

I threw him a dramatic eyeroll. "I, unlike you, am not so untrusting of the entire Fae and Kin races."

"Then you're more foolish than I thought."

Ouch. The remark stung. Goddess, just when I thought he wasn't as awful as I'd originally imagined. "Fae you," I grumbled.

A smile twitched the corners of his lips. "Oh, you wound me so with your foul curses."

"Reign..."

"Fine, Aelia. You trust the Liteschild girl so much, then we'll do it. It's your ass on the line anyway."

But it wasn't, and he knew it. He'd be as culpable as I was for keeping this secret, possibly more so as a professor. We even had a binding vow to prove it. A tiny part of me felt guilty for forcing him to keep this from everyone, but I shoved the errant thought far down. He was the one that had insisted on having my dagger examined. Technically, he brought this upon both of us.

Those ominous shadows peeled off his form, his dark minions sailing through the air back toward the Hall of Luce, presumably to collect my friend.

"Rue won't tell anyone," I finally murmured as we stood in the middle of the field locked in an epic battle of silence.

He stalked closer, erasing the space between us. "You're much too trusting, princess. You must rid yourself of that fatal Kin flaw."

"I trusted you with my dagger, and you returned it to me as promised."

Reign snorted, his upper lip curling.

I inched closer, rising onto the balls of my feet so his aggressive looming wasn't quite so overpowering. "I trusted you when I went into that mystical pond, and again when you forced me upon your rather large and dangerous *pet*." I paused, fixing my gaze to his blazing one before dropping back down to my heels. "It would even seem as if you trusted me since you did not require a vow in exchange for the knowledge of your beastly friend's existence."

The perfect bow of his lip twisted, then curved as he fought a reluctant smile.

"You trust me, Reign Darkthorn." I jabbed my finger into his tunic and hit a wall of unyielding muscle. "And I trust you." Gnawing on my lower lip to keep from wincing, I withdrew my finger. "So trust in my judgement. Rue will keep our secret."

The line between his dark brows puckered before he released a sigh. "I hope you're right, for both our sakes." His wary gaze remained locked to mine, his aura a smoky gray instead of the typical endless night.

"Reign, about that vow..."

His lip twitched. "I will call in the favor when the time is right."

"Wonderful."

Reign's icy breath skated across my lips. When had he gotten so close? I attempted to take a much-needed step back, but a vein of shadow slithered off his arm, crawled around my back and held me in place. "Are you worried you won't be able to fulfill your promise, princess?"

I gulped, the sound audible over the suddenly increasing tempo of my pulse. "No," I finally managed, steeling my spine. "As long as your *favor* is of an appropriate nature."

An unexpected chuckle curved Reign's mouth. "Noxus, princess, what sort of request are you expecting? I am nothing but a proper gentleFae."

My cheeks burned, dragonfire racing up my neck and blossoming across my face. "That's not what I meant—"

He laughed harder, his massive form hinging at the waist until he was practically doubled over. Even his shadows seemed to vibrate with mirth.

"Are you quite done?" I snarled.

Reign finally straightened, unshed tears glistening in his eyes. His expression darkened, the amused twinkle morphing into something dangerous. He captured my chin in his strong fingers and tipped it up, forcing my gaze to his starlit one. "Trust me, princess, if anything were to ever happen between us, it would *never* be forced upon you."

My traitorous thoughts flew back to the pond and the feel of his bare body wrapped around my own. Raysa, I didn't think I could ever erase that memory. It would be permanently emblazoned in my mind for all eternity.

"And as you know..." His voice softened, the sound like smooth velvet caressing my skin. "Relations between students and faculty are strictly forbidden."

"You don't strike me as much of a rule follower, professor." Good goddess, what sorcery had taken over my mouth? I snapped my jaw shut before it dribbled out any more insanity.

"An accurate observation, princess, but there are many reasons why we should maintain a professional distance, as much as it pains me to say."

As much as it pains him? I couldn't quite believe we were having this discussion. As if this thing between us were real. Worse, there was something about the smolder in his eyes, the

213

intense clench of his jaw and the deep trench between his dark brows that compelled me to believe it truly did pain him.

My thoughts whirled back in time to each lingering touch, every dark, heated gaze. To all the times he'd protected me, acted as if the cold, brutal Fae actually cared. My breath hitched as my heart pounded out a manic tempo. Reign actually desired me. The near confession was exhilarating and altogether unexpected.

His eyes tapered at the edges as he took a step back, his shadows withdrawing their hold over me. "In fact, it would serve you best to stay well away from me, princess." Those words cut deeper than I would ever admit.

In my time at the academy, Reign had been my captor, then my mentor, and had now become the forbidden desire that I dared not confess. "I wish I could," I snapped, "but with the never-ending training sessions, how can I?"

His head dipped, the typical twinkle in his eyes dimming. "You're right. Perhaps, I'll speak to Heaton and see if he can take over your training after the Choosing Ceremony."

"Why are you doing this?" The question popped out before I could stop it, morphing into a demand. "Because I said I trusted you? Because you realize you trust me, and you do not believe I fit on your one hand of friends?"

The tendon in his jaw fluttered beneath the dark line of stubble. "No," he growled.

"Then why?"

The crunch of grass beneath light footfalls swung Reign's gaze up and over my shoulder. Rue. I could practically feel her Light energy surging through the thick atmosphere of my professor's shadows. I hadn't even noticed them circling until this instant.

Emerging from the dense cloud of darkness, I offered my friend a smile. "Thank you for coming."

She hitched her thumb at her escort, a tornado of nightmarish shadows. "They didn't exactly give me a choice. I was barely able to finish my dinner before they dragged me here."

"I appreciate your expediency," Reign muttered.

"Anything for you, professor." Rue smiled sweetly at the scowling male.

"I have a favor to ask."

Chapter Thirty

R *eign*

Noxus, this female had learned nothing in her time at the Conservatory. A favor? Was she out of her mind framing it as such to a Fae?

I stepped between the two before Aelia condemned us both to the treacherous Wilds by some slip of the tongue. "What she means is I have a theory to test for class, and you've been chosen as the lucky participant to assist us."

The Light Fae female's gaze darted to Aelia before circling back to meet mine. Or rather, to fix her eyes at my forehead or my nose or the top of my head. No one ever quite dared to meet my eyes, not the way Aelia did.

Despite my boorish temper and cruel methods, that feisty little Kin never seemed frightened of me.

"It'll be fine, Rue, I promise," said Aelia, those silver-blue eyes alight.

"For Noxus's sake, hold your tongue!"

She tossed her silky raven hair over her shoulder and rolled her eyes. "Rue is my friend. She will keep this secret. Won't you?"

The girl's head bounced up and down. "Absolutely."

I never should have allowed this. Her brother, Heaton, was team leader, which meant he must have had a close relationship with the headmaster. If word reached his ears...

Aelia's slender fingers curled around my upper arm and the raging turmoil subsided. At a simple touch. "Calm down, everything will be fine."

I hadn't even noticed the whirlwind of shadows vibrating across my body. The swell of darkness immediately settled at that soothing, feminine voice. At that simple touch. Gods, my powers have never reacted to anyone the way they do around this female. Maybe the years spent in these damned cuffs were finally dampening my *nox*.

"Let's just get this over with." I jerked a dagger free from Aelia's waistband, earning a satisfying gasp from those pretty pink lips. "Rue, summon a radiant shield."

Her head dipped, ash-blonde bangs curtaining the fear in her pale blue eyes. The golden orb sputtered to life, faint at first, before blossoming to enclose her petite form.

"I will try to break through the barrier with this dagger, understand?"

"Yes, professor." Her voice sounded muffled through the protective bubble.

Bringing the dagger down in a small arc, I sliced at the mystical orb. The blade hit the Fae's *rais* and deflected, sending a twinge up my forearm. *Odd*. If Gideon was correct about the weapon's origins, it should wield power over both Light and Shadow Fae.

Perhaps, he was wrong, after all.

My eyes chased to Aelia's, to the thoughts clearly churning in that lively mind. Her aura brightened, a tangle of the most brilliant gold, marred only by an occasional flash of darkness.

She stepped toward me and held out her hand. "May I try?"

"Of course, princess." I handed the dagger over and took a step back.

Ever so gently, she pressed the tip of the blade into the shimmering orb encasing her friend. The glowing sphere popped, and the *rais* disintegrated into a pile of luminous dust.

"Whoa..." Rue's eyes widened as she glanced between her friend and me.

Good gods. She did it. A whirlwind of questions raced through my mind as I stood there frozen for a long moment. Only Aelia could wield its power, but why?

Slipping on the practiced mask, I forced my expression to neutral despite the tornado of thoughts spinning in my mind. It only took me an instant to make my decision. It had to be done.

My shadows slithered from my fingertips and wrapped around the Light Fae's head. Those luminous light eyes bulged as panic darkened her aura.

"Reign, no!" Aelia shouted. "What are you doing?" Her hands curled around my bicep, jerking my arm as her shrieks echoed across my eardrum.

Ignoring her and focusing on my powers, I directed my dark minions through the girl's mind. I'd long ago mastered nightmare weaving, a skill only very powerful Shadow Fae possess; but along with it, I'd discovered I was able to manipulate memories by placing new ones over the old.

Squeezing my eyes closed, I replayed the scene from only moments ago and replaced the last few minutes with another one of my making: Aelia attempting to slash through her friend's radiant shield and the dagger deflected, much like it had done when I had wielded it.

My shadows hissed and whispered the new memory, weaving through her mind. Pain seared through my temples, and the silver cuffs around my wrists heated, activated by the hefty use of *nox*. Fire scorched the skin around my wrists and I bit down the howl building in my throat.

I'd grown accustomed to the pain, to the torture every time I wielded too much *nox*. That bastard Draven and his manacles that attempted to keep me on a leash only allotted for so much energy. Just enough to make me useful, but not quite enough to make me a threat. Or at least, that's what the fool believed.

I felt it the moment my new memories supplanted the girl's. She stopped fighting, and the tense scrunch of her face softened. Aelia's nails still bit into my arm, her screams still echoing. Releasing my hold over the girl, I called my shadows back, and Rue slumped down to the ground.

Aelia's steel grip fell away and she slid down to the grass beside her friend. "Rue, Rue, are you all right?"

The girl blinked slowly, her light eyes focusing on her friend. "Whoa, that was quite a rush." A smile eased across her lips.

Aelia lifted her murderous gaze to mine. "What did you do?" she hissed.

I released one of my shadows and it curled around her rounded ear, whispering my will. "I did what I had to in order to ensure your secret remained safe. She will have no memory of your dagger piercing her shield."

Her dark brows lifted, but her eyes remained tapered at the edges as she regarded me.

"No harm came to your friend," I added.

Still, that piercing look of distrust lanced through my chest. Why did I care if Aelia trusted me or not? In fact, it would be better for her if she didn't. If my suspicions proved correct, she'd despise me once the truth came out any way. Why delay the inevitable?

Find out everything you can about the Kin girl. Draven's gravelly voice replayed through my mind from the night I'd ushered my newest acquisition to the Conservatory.

I heaved out a breath, my hatred for the headmaster only growing with every day I spent trapped on this side of the Luminoc. Noxus, I despised that man. Much like Aelia now despised me. She fussed over her friend, one eye shooting daggers in my direction. I should put some distance between Aelia and me, and having Heaton take over her training would be a good option. I simply couldn't seem to keep away from her.

"Let me walk you back to the dormitory." Aelia's voice drew me from my inner musings. She helped Rue to her feet and directed her toward the path back to the Hall of Glory.

"Aelia, wait. We aren't finished."

She whirled on me, those silvery blue eyes glowing with hatred. "We are. I must tend to my friend."

Rue waved a dismissive hand. "Oh, I'm fine. I simply had a little head rush." She turned her smile on me and a hint of guilt pricked at my insides. "The professor's *nox* was stronger than I expected, that's all. Stay, finish your training."

"No, trust me, I do not wish to." Aelia's hand closed around her friend's.

"Ms. Feywood," I barked, "you are not dismissed. There is much more to be discussed."

Her eyes grew impossibly wide at my frosty tone. *Good, you should hate me.* "I was not aware that this training was part of my obligatory curriculum, Professor Darkthorn," she bit back.

"Your curriculum is whatever I say it is."

"Go on, Aelia," Rue whispered. "We'll catch up when you're finished." With that, she squirmed free of her roommate's hold and darted across the lawn.

The moment she was out of earshot, Aelia spun at me, a lethal scowl entrenched across those full lips. "How could you do that to her?" she spat.

"I didn't do anything to her," I growled right back. "I simply replaced her memories to ensure your safety, damn it."

"Oh, *my* safety? This is all about me, then." She barked out a laugh. "Don't tell me it has nothing to do with protecting your ass. You are a professor, and keeping this knowledge from

Headmaster Draven would surely have you dismissed, if not worse. Are you not his little lapdog?"

Fury coursed through my veins, inciting my *nox* and whipping it into a frenzy. Before the fool girl blurted something a passerby could catch, I summoned my shadows and cloaked us in darkness. If she noticed the swell of night, she certainly didn't act like it. Instead, she jabbed her finger into my chest, completely unaffected by the looming tendrils of *nox*. "You have no idea what you speak of, no notion of where my loyalties lie." I stalked closer, pinning her against a wall of shadows. "I don't give a sun's ray about Draven. But you—"

"Me, what?" She lifted to her tiptoes, the heat in her eyes so gods' damned tempting.

"Fuck it." Aelia was right, I *wasn't* a rule follower. I never had been. I was a powerful, selfish Fae who took what he wanted. My hand snaked around her neck and yanked her lips to mine. A gasp escaped, swallowed up in the tangle of rage and desire. Noxus, I'd been dying for a taste since the moment she glared up at me so defiantly through those sooty, dark lashes the day I'd collected her from Feywood.

My mouth moved over hers as my fingers delved into the silky hair at her nape. Gods, she tasted like sunshine and the most glorious starlit night. I laced my free hand around her waist and brought her flush against me. My arousal bit at my trousers at the familiar feel of her soft curves. That night in the pond had been pure torture. The attraction I felt for this female was nothing like anything I'd ever experienced before. In my four years at the academy, I'd never craved a single student, Noxus, in my thirty years on this earth I'd never desired anyone like this, despite many brazen attempts by the female Fae, as well as a few of the males.

What was this between us?

"Reign..." she whispered against my mouth. My name on her lips only fanned the flames building in my core.

"Mmm, princess. You have no idea what you do to me."

As I tilted her head to deepen the kiss, a tether laced around my heart. The mystical bind squeezed the air from my lungs. I sucked in a desperate breath and ripped my mouth free of hers. Noxus, what in all the realms was that? What had I done?

Aelia stared up at me, cheeks a mesmerizing crimson hue, her chest heaving and breasts straining against the smooth fabric of her fighting leathers. "Reign?" Her swollen lips formed my name, snapping me back to my senses. I couldn't do this... I had responsibilities, vows I'd made.

"I—I'm sorry." I pressed a gentle kiss to her forehead, and my shadows slithered across her form, twisting and churning around her. "I never should have—"

"What are you doing?" Her eyes widened in panic.

"It won't hurt, I promise."

Her lips pursed, and I realized I'd lied. I could already see the hurt plastered across her heart-shaped face, and gods, it bored right into the depths of my soul.

My shadows slid through her mind, and I weaved a new memory, one that annihilated the heated kiss and would surely keep her at arm's length. As I planted the new scene, one in which she insinuated feelings for me and I brutally rebuffed her, my chest constricted, each lie I sewed a painful blade. By the time I was finished, she would surely despise me.

And it was the way it had to be.

Chapter Thirty-One

Oh, stars, my head hurt. I pressed my fingers to my temples as I forced myself to sit up. The canopy of vines hung over my bed, weaving a tapestry of blooms that tickled my nostrils. I breathed in the fragrant scents and the pounding in my skull tapered a notch. Glancing over at Rue's nook, I found my roommate still asleep.

Thank the sun, she's okay.

Memories of the night before assaulted my mind, and the thrashing across my forehead quickened once again. Gods, I hated him. Why did I ever admit to having feelings for him? His cruel rejection was mortifying. Never again... I needed to erase that male's existence from my thoughts.

And how could Reign have wiped my friend's memories without even consulting me?

What if he'd hurt her somehow? I'd already witnessed what those lethal shadows were capable of. If he had harmed one of

223

my only friends at the Conservatory, my best friend, I would have hunted him down and killed him myself.

I reached for my nightstand and pulled open the drawer. The familiar dagger immediately quelled the rising tension in my chest. I fingered the smooth blade and then traced the lines of the ornate, engraved hilt, ending along the luminous crystal. The translucent gem ignited at my touch, a flicker of light dancing across the shadows.

"Ugh…" Rue's groan sent my gaze swiveling from my dagger to my roommate. "I have such a terrible headache."

"Me too," I grumbled.

"And today is the worst possible day for it." Rue pushed the silky coverlet back and slid to the edge of the mattress.

Goddess, I'd nearly forgotten. Today was the Choosing Ceremony.

Fear twined around my heart, and my thoughts immediately flickered to Reign. I needed to—No. Gritting my teeth, I focused on his embarrassing rejection and deplorable behavior toward my friend. If he wanted to cut me out of his life, then so be it. I was certain Heaton would make a much better instructor anyway.

"Hurry, Aelia, we can*not* be late." Rue emerged from the bathing chamber and bounced around the room as she dragged on a pair of tights.

"Right." Shooting out of bed, I darted into the washroom then, after a quick visit, raced to my closet, ignoring the consistent throbbing through my skull. As I stared at the vast array of foreign clothing, I settled on a simple classic. A soft linen tunic and my suede leathers. As I slipped the familiar strappings on, I reached for my dagger and sheath. Once I'd secured it at my waistband, the fingers of my free hand twitched as if something were missing.

How odd.

"Ready?" Rue stood at the doorway, her hand wrapped around the knob.

I didn't think I'd ever seen my roommate so tense. Her knuckles gleamed white beneath the sun's lustrous rays.

"Yes," I blurted as I tugged on my boots and hurried behind her.

Dozens of first-years swarmed the halls as we all made our way toward the Hall of Luminescence. From what little Reign had shared of the secretive ceremony, each team would enter the hall separately.

"Why is everyone going at the same time?" I whisper-shouted at Rue over the trample of footfalls down the floating staircase.

"Maybe because the king's here. I imagine he'll speak to all of us before the ceremony."

Right, that made sense. "Does he often come for the Choosing?"

Rue shook her head. "No, not at all. In fact, Heaton said this is the first time he's visited in his four years at the academy."

I swallowed hard, gulping past the forming knot in my throat as Reign's words from yesterday's training resurfaced. *I know that he only cares about one thing: creating soldiers for his army.*

"Rue, your eldest brother is a Royal Guardian of the Court, correct?"

She nodded, her bright eyes dimming.

"Do you hear from him often about the state of affairs in Aetheria?"

My roommate's expression grew darker still. "Unfortunately, not. Lawson's battalion was deployed to the northernmost region of the Court of Umbral Shadows along the Shadowmere Sea over a month ago, and we've yet to receive a single letter."

"But we're at peace with the Shadow King, right?"

"That's what they tell us." A weak smile crawled across her weary face.

"Maybe King Elian will tell us more today," I offered.

"I hope so."

Squeezing her hand, I led her through the crowd of first-years. I was still the frequent recipient of curious and often hate-filled gazes, but once word had spread about my proficiency with my dagger, most of the other students gave me a wide berth.

Or maybe it was the terrifying Shadow Fae who constantly trailed behind me that had earned me some peace. I supposed I'd find out the true cause now that he'd drawn this imaginary line between us.

A storm of anger and hurt churned in my gut as we descended the final steps. *No.* I wouldn't let Reign occupy any more space in my mind. I needed to focus. If I didn't prove I deserved to be here today, I'd be sent back to Feywood, and likely shipped off to warm the bed of the next needy Fae lord.

Radiant light spilled across the grand hall, the rainbow of hues from the stained glass settling over the blonde heads of the already-gathered students.

"Psst, over here!" Symon waved from the third row.

Blast it, why we must we always sit so close to the front?

Heaton stood as we approached, offering his seat so Rue and I could sit beside each other. "I thought you were going to be late," he hissed at his sister.

"We almost were," she muttered back, fingers pressed to her temples. "My head hasn't been right all morning."

Heaton's brows twisted as he regarded her for a long moment before sinking down beside me. "Are you ready, Aelia?"

"I suppose I must be."

"I have faith in Raysa's wisdom. If she chose you, you were meant to be here."

His kind words brought a smile to my face, despite the nerves roiling in my gut.

"So what happens now?" I whispered.

Heaton leaned in close, lacing his arm around the back of

my chair to murmur in my ear. "This is different than the other years, with the king being here and addressing us all together first, but I assume after he speaks, we will be divided into squads and taken to the hatchlings."

"Hatchlings...?" The remainder of my question sputtered out on my tongue as that dark presence plowed into me.

My head spun toward the entrance despite my best efforts to keep my gaze trained on my team leader. Reign stalked in, a tornado of shadows whipping around him, driving his wild hair into a fury. The chatter immediately subsided as all eyes cast in his direction. It was as if the entire room collectively held its breath. He lifted his hood over his head and stalked past without so much as a passing glance.

Bastard, mercurial Fae.

He darted up the steps to the dais and joined Headmaster Draven who already lounged in his throne-like chair. The head of the Conservatory whispered something to the Shadow Fae and his midnight eyes lifted to mine. His brows puckered, and a tempest of emotions flashed through those impossibly dark orbs. His aura flared from a murky gray to the angriest pitch night.

Stop staring at him, Aelia. Clenching my hands into fists, I forced my gaze away from those invisible snares.

Another presence filled the room, a lighter, more airy one, drawing my attention to the back of the hall. The entire hall rose as one, with me as the exception. I quickly stood, heat tingeing my cheeks.

The tall, lithe form of King Elian of Ether glided toward us bathed in a sea of brilliant light. With an ageless countenance, his features seemed crafted from the purest light, casting an aura of soft luminescence. His glistening platinum hair flowed like liquid gold, spilling over his shoulders. Twin suns of pure turquoise caught my attention, gleaming with a wisdom that spanned centuries of strife. Their luminosity was otherworldly. His dazzling turquoise orbs swiveled in my direction as he paraded past, and the faintest pucker drew his light brows together. It wasn't surprising since, with the exception of Reign, I was the only Fae in the hall with hair like night.

"Bow," Heaton hissed.

I dipped my head as the king, adorned in the finest regal attire seemingly woven from the glistening threads of morning mist, and at least a dozen Royal Guardians marched past, each donning the pristine uniforms adorned in gold piping of the Court of Ethereal Light. When I straightened, I finally noticed everyone in the hall hinged at the waist in reverence.

In my defense, King Elian only became my sovereign a few months ago upon my acceptance to the academy. The great ruler of the Court of Ethereal Light had only once made an appearance in Feywood, and Aidan had forbidden me to attend. Which I had obeyed... sort of.

The king and his entourage swept up the steps and settled along the dais. The headmaster, Reign, and the other professors stood and bowed at the royal's approach. Draven dipped so far down I was afraid he wouldn't be able to straighten.

To my surprise, he managed fine, snapping straight up as soon as the royal took his seat. "Everyone please be seated," the headmaster called out. "We are honored to have His Royal Highness, King Elian of Ether, in our presence. May Raysa be with you, my king."

The tall, willowy male inclined his head. "And you." His voice held the soft, yet commanding resonance of a gentle stream.

"Will you do us the honor of addressing the first-years, Your Ethereal Highness?"

The king rose once again, his sweeping presence descending across the hall. From his elevated angle, I could just make out a scepter held tightly in his fist, seemingly wrought from the sun itself. Even from this distance and with my limited *rais*, I could feel its power pulsing.

"My esteemed initiates of the Light, today marks the

commencement of your journey as Royal Guardians of our great realm. With the Choosing Ceremony upon you, you stand at the threshold of destiny. It is no ordinary path you tread, for to wear the mantle of a Royal Guardian is to become the very soul of the Court of Ethereal Light."

He paused, that radiant gaze gliding over every student in the hall.

"Today you become warriors, protecting this great realm against those who would wish us harm. As you embark upon this sacred education within the hallowed walls of the Conservatory of Luce, let the light you bear within be a guiding star, unwavering, even amidst the tempest's wrath. May it kindle courage when shadows across the river loom and fortitude when the horizon dims."

I stole a quick glance at Reign, his expression an icy mask but his aura hiding nothing. His disdain for the king was evident. Why couldn't anyone else see it?

"Together, we are the everlasting dawn. Go forth, and let the light guide you."

Wild applause rang out through the silent hall, the abrupt noise jarring.

"Isn't he incredible?" Rue shouted over the cacophony.

The king hadn't really said much at all, but simply spurted pretty platitudes. He hadn't explained the situation on the front lines, at the border of the Wilds, or what it was exactly we were expected to do as Royal Guardians.

Headmaster Draven rose, his alabaster robes swirling a shimmering gold beneath the sunlight. "Good luck initiates, each squadron may now proceed to the hatchling site."

My entire team leapt up, and if it weren't for Rue's hand jerking me to my feet, I would've been swallowed up in the onrush. Heaton urged me forward as the mass of initiates rushed toward the doors of the great hall.

"Why is everyone running?" I hissed at Rue as she dragged me down the circular stone pathway.

At the far corner of the training lawn, eight tents had been erected, each with the name of our teams. The students flooded the field, racing toward their designated area.

"It's just exciting," Rue bellowed.

"Are we going to miss our chance if we don't get their first?"

"No, the hatchlings, guided by Raysa, make their choices regardless of who arrives first."

Then why, by all the gods, were we running so fast?

When we finally reached our tent, Belmore and Ariadne had already arrived and each stood staring at something in the middle of the grass.

"Come on, Aelia, hurry." Rue towed me to the center of the tent to join the others.

Peering over Belmore's shoulder, I could just make out a massive ring of light hovering over the lush lawn.

"What in all the realms is that?" I blurted as I squeezed past Belmore and stood between Rue and Symon.

"It's the hatchling site."

"But I don't see any eggs."

"Just wait," Rue whispered.

The spherical glow burned brighter and a pulse of energy skimmed over my flesh. Raw power pressed into me, reminding me of my first day at the Conservatory when I fought past the Veil of Judgement. I pushed back as the overwhelming presence sank into my very bones.

I could feel Rue fighting beside me, her tense shoulder brushing mine and sending an electric pulse across my skin. Another presence filled the air, this one so familiar I didn't need to glance over my shoulder to know who it was. I recognized Reign's *nox* more easily than my own.

Despite every muscle in my body urging my eyes to his, I kept them fixed straight ahead to the ethereal circle. The air vibrated, the light bending and fracturing in sharp edges, then more than a dozen objects coalesced from the brilliant surge.

Eggs... fourteen of them of varied sizes and hues.

Chapter Thirty-Two

A *elia*

"Oh, my goddess." I stared, awestruck, at the unearthly apparition, the collection of eggs seeming to have appeared from the ether. Hazarding a quick glance at the circle of tents surrounding us, I found the same marvel occurring across the field.

"Isn't it amazing?" Rue purred.

I scanned the assortment of hatchlings, my eyes immediately drawn to the largest one in the center. A deep emerald pattern was inked across the smooth surface, as if painted by the goddess's hand herself. It was striking. A vibrant golden aura curled around the egg, pulsing with power. Incredible. A long moment later, I continued my careful scrutiny over the remaining hatchlings. After a quick recount, I confirmed there were only fourteen eggs, but sixteen of us remained. "Wait, why are we missing two?"

The excitement in my roommate's eyes fizzled, and she

slowly lifted her shoulders. "It looks like the goddess only deemed fourteen of us worthy."

Fear blasted through my heart, devouring my weary organ with razor-sharp teeth. Oh, stars, this was it, I would be returning to Feywood. My chest ached with the certainty, and for the first time since I arrived at this dreadful academy, I longed to stay. I'd made a new home for myself here, had forged friendships, and I was finally beginning to scratch the surface of my reluctant *rais*. I wasn't ready to leave.

Unbidden, my gaze drifted over my shoulder. A pair of endless obsidian eyes latched onto mine, and my heart performed a hasty pirouette. Blasted Shadow Fae sorcery. If Reign was so intent on keeping his distance, why in the name of all things blessed wasn't he? Forcing my traitorous gaze away, I drew in deep breaths to still my thundering pulse. At least I'd be rid of my constant dark shadow. And I'd get to see Aidan. Hopefully I'd have a chance to spend time with him before I was whirled off to spend the rest of my days as a servant to an arrogant Fae lord.

"Flare Squad," Heaton barked, forcing me free of my dismal musings. "The time has come. You shall each come forward and be claimed. May Raysa be with you."

How can one be claimed by an egg? The absurd thought flickered through my mind as our team leader droned on.

"Belmore Dawnbrook, step forward."

"I hope that snooty Fae is the one going home today," Rue whispered.

I couldn't agree more. Though he'd been slightly less terrible lately, he was the obvious choice.

The male took a wary step into the circle of shimmering gold and the entire tent vibrated with energy. The faint hum began low, crawling over my skin like a thousand wild spaider legs before intensifying to a fevered pitch. I barely restrained the urge to clap my hands over my ears, and instead, focused on the goddess's magic unfolding right before our eyes.

Even Belmore seemed nervous, the typical arrogant smirk wiped clean. He took another measured step into the circle, and the eggs began to vibrate along with the incessant hum.

"Ooh, it's happening," Rue squealed. "I wonder what he'll get... hopefully not a phoenix. I don't trust that male with a beast that can spontaneously combust."

Memories of my first flight with Reign aboard Pyra sprang to the surface. I was certain he'd been joking when he mentioned bursting into fiery flames. I wasn't sure *I* wanted a phoenix—but then again, beggars couldn't be too choosy.

A sharp crack resounded, jerking my attention to a medium-sized pale, yellow egg. It jumped and the fissure widened, until a tiny beak poked out. The little creature strained against the shell until it split open, revealing the squawking animal within.

"A gryphon!" Rue squealed.

The hatchling staggered toward Belmore on four wobbly furry legs, squealing its protests. The Light Fae dropped to his knees and gently stroked the creature's pink bald head. Its feathers hadn't come in yet, and to be perfectly honest, he was the ugliest little thing I'd ever seen. But judging by the proud gleam in Belmore's eyes, you would believe it to be the grandest gryphon to ever grace the sacred halls of the Conservatory.

"Aw, he's so cute," Rue crooned.

"He won't be for long," Symon interjected. "Gryphons are among the most ruthless of the hatchlings."

"Then it seems that Raysa chose well for Belmore." I ticked my head at the pair.

"Exactly." Symon eyed Belmore as he lifted the baby beast into his arms and carried him out of the tent.

"Now what?" I asked. I couldn't imagine caring for a hatchling would become part of our duties.

"The bond forms the moment we are chosen," Rue explained, "and we will begin training with our skyrider immediately."

"But how? They're babies..."

"Not for long." A smirk drifted across Symon's face. "By the power of Raysa, our mounts will be full-grown within a week."

"What? That makes no sense. Then why go through all the trouble of a hatchling? Why not give us an adult from the beginning?"

"Because that week is essential to bond with the animal," Sy replied. "A full-grown wild gryphon or phoenix would be nearly impossible to tame."

"I suppose that makes sense."

"Symon Lightspire, you are next." Heaton's deep voice sent my heart catapulting against my ribs.

"Good luck!" Rue whispered as Sy approached the gilded sphere.

An hour later and each member of Flare Squad had had their turn, except for me. Symon was chosen by a feisty hippogriff, which according to Rue fit his personality perfectly, fierce and loyal, while my roommate bonded with an adorable silver Pegasus. Veridian and Galina, two members of the squad I barely knew, had been rebuffed by the goddess. Not a single egg trembled at their turn.

A part of me felt so damned guilty, but relief had flooded my system the moment they'd trudged out of the tent empty-handed. I was safe. Raysa had deemed me worthy of a skyrider, and only the heavens knew why.

The vibrant emerald egg called to me as I lingered just beyond the luminescent orb, waiting for my name to be called. What if it had been a mistake? Perhaps this hatchling belonged to no one...

That achingly familiar presence bored into my spine, and a shadow slithered across the shell of my ear. "Get ready, princess." That smooth, deep tenor sent heat spilling down my neck, despite the fact Reign remained yards away.

"I thought you were keeping your distance," I whisper-hissed at the invasive shadow.

"I'm afraid that won't be possible anymore."

What did that mean? I cursed my luck for being forced into this academy with the most infuriating male I'd ever had the displeasure of meeting.

"Aelia Feywood, step forward." Heaton's voice tore me from the thrill of Reign's words.

I cocked my head over my shoulder and met my capricious professor's dark gaze across the field. Always watching. Always waiting. But for what? And what caused this sudden change of heart?

Shaking my head out and focusing on the enormous egg in the center of the iridescent sphere of light, I stepped inside. That hum crawled across my flesh, pops of energy assaulting every single nerve ending. Power like I'd never felt before blossomed and pulsed within the ethereal orb.

A sharp crack whipped my head toward the vibrating egg. An enormous fracture raced across the smooth surface and a high-pitched squeal rang out. Gasps echoed beyond the gilded bubble as I strained to make out the creature forcing its way out. Tiny claws curled around the eggshell and a reptilian head peered out, intense warm golden eyes locking on mine.

My breath hitched, all the air siphoning from my lungs. *By the gods.*

A baby dragon.

Chapter Thirty-Three

A *elia*

"Just breathe, princess. You are a powerful Light Fae and your new *pet* must believe it if he's chosen you." Reign's voice slithered across the shell of my ear, only this time, instead of the icy shadows, his warm breath sent goose bumps spilling down my bare shoulder. He suddenly stood beside me, his eyes locked on the baby dragon staggering to its feet.

"Raysa's tits," Belmore hissed, toting his squawking gryphon in his arms. "The Kin was claimed by a dragon? How is that possible? There hasn't been one at the academy in ages."

The rest of Flare team, who had meandered beyond the confines of the tent to begin bonding with their skyriders, all reappeared, filling the pavilion to gawk at my hatchling. They weren't the only ones. I couldn't keep my eyes off the scraggly little brown dragonette.

It scrambled forward on wobbly legs, its talons seemingly

too big for its body while its leathery russet wings were tiny. It was no bigger than a wild dog and twice as mangy looking.

Belmore released a belly laugh. "Now I understand why Raysa chose this dragon for Aelia. It's clearly a dud. I doubt it'll ever be able to fly with those wings."

Ariadne giggled, hanging on his shoulder with her hippogriff at her feet.

"Oh, shut it," Rue snarled. "It's just a baby."

"He," I murmured.

"What?" Belmore barked, fixing his cold eyes on me, then my dragon.

"His name is Solanthus, the Sun Chaser." The name popped out of its own accord, as if someone had plucked it from my brain and placed it on the tip of my tongue.

I crept forward, slowly so as to not startle the little thing. Warm golden eyes found mine, and a tiny screech erupted between pointy fangs. "Hello, Solanthus," I crooned and reached out my hand. "That's quite a name for such a little guy. I think I'll call you Sol for short."

His oversized head was tipped with an array of jagged horns, so I opted for the soft skin under his chin. Solanthus lifted his head appreciatively, and a soft purring sound rumbled his throat.

"You like that?"

More purring.

"Open your thoughts to him, Aelia." Reign appeared once again at my side. "You should be able to speak to each other through your mental link."

Right. Squeezing my eyes closed, I cleared my mind and imagined a stream of light rushing between my new little friend and me. *Solanthus? Can you hear me?*

A presence filled a small, dark corner of my thoughts, but somehow, I couldn't quite latch onto it. *Solanthus, are you there?*

Blast it! Why couldn't anything come easily for me?

Snapping my lids wide open, I stared at the bumbling drag-onette. He stumbled along the grass, swatting at a swarm of beezus. "Oh, Sol..." I crouched beside him and giggled as he snapped at the flying insects.

My looming instructor dropped down beside me, his unreadable gaze flickering between the dragonette and me. "Has the bond been formed?" he whispered.

"No," I huffed out. "I can't hear a thing."

His lips pursed as he regarded me. "It must be whatever is blocking your powers."

That again. In his grand effort to put space between us, he'd never explained more on his theory.

"By the goddess, I cannot believe my eyes." A booming voice drowned out all mental musings and I scrambled to my feet as the Royal Guardians filed into the pavilion.

King Elian towered over me, luminous turquoise eyes alight in awe as he ogled my dragon. An unexpected streak of protec-tiveness zipped through my chest, and I stepped closer to Sol, blocking the royal's view.

The king's light brows puckered as he regarded me, his scru-tinizing gaze drawing over every inch of me, finally settling on my rounded ears. Even behind that practiced mask, I caught the flicker of surprise.

Headmaster Draven stepped out from behind the king's lustrous shadow, eyes wider than the midday sun. "Raysa be damned," he mumbled.

"This is the girl? The Kin you spoke of?" King Elian eyed me with barely veiled contempt.

"Yes, Your Ethereal Highness."

An endless moment later, he released me from his careful scrutiny and turned to the headmaster. "When was the last time a dragon appeared among the hatchlings?" The king's ominous whisper reached my rounded ears.

"It's been decades. Though I heard there was one across the river at Arcanum Citadel in the last decade." The headmaster's pale green eyes flitted to Reign before returning to rest on the royal.

"It's an odd-looking beast with those frail wings and enormous talons, but perhaps he'll grow into his body."

"Undoubtedly, Your Highness." Draven's sharp gaze scanned over Sol, and it took all my restraint to keep from shouting at the male to stop.

"Do you have a professor equipped to train a student on a dragon?"

"Well of course—"

"I'll do it." Reign stepped forward, his expression carved from stone. His shadow wings emerged, adding to the professor's already impressive height.

"You?" King Elian's light brow arched, a platinum rainbow nearly reaching his hairline. "Is this not the banished Shadow Fae?" His lip curled in disgust as if Reign were unworthy to step within his sun-blessed gaze.

"It is, Your Highness, but as I've mentioned before, Professor Darkthorn has proven to be quite useful over the years."

"What makes you capable of training a female Kin, nonetheless, on a dragon?"

Reign's piercing gaze chased to mine for an instant before he gritted his teeth, the tendon in his jaw fluttering at his tell. The incessant shadows circling his form grew denser, and he pivoted his attention back to the king. From within the looming midnight cloud, he leveled the royal with an icy glare. "Only the fact that I trained my own."

My eyes nearly popped out of my head at the admission. Why would he give up a secret he held so close to his heart?

"You did what?" Draven hissed.

The hint of a smile threatened across my lips. Apparently, the headmaster didn't know his lapdog as well as he thought.

"How could you not mention that... for years?" The headmaster's glare was palpable, and yet Reign kept his expression neutral.

"It was of no importance until now." His head swiveled toward Sol and that streak of overprotectiveness blossomed, inflating my chest.

"Does this dragon still live?" King Elian's hateful demeanor completely changed toward the Shadow Fae.

I held my breath as Reign's broad shoulders slowly lifted. "I do not know. I have not seen the beast since I was banished from the Court of Umbral Shadows."

Not a twitch, not a single tell. The male was an expert liar. I'd have to remind myself of that important fact going forward.

"But the bond?" Draven questioned.

"It was broken by the mark of the banished."

King Elian's thin lips pressed into a tight line. "It's a shame..." He turned to the headmaster, a vein fluttering across the porcelain skin of his brow. "Have any of the other Light Fae professors mastered dragonmanship?"

"In theory, yes. Many were alive during the war, but none have bonded with a dragon."

"Then I suppose the professor is right. He should be the one to train the girl." The king's curious gaze razed over me once again, and each and every hair on my body stood at attention. There was something about the male... "And I'd like to be kept apprised of the situation, Draven. A dragon would give the Royal Guardians a tremendous advantage over our enemy across the river."

"But I thought we were at peace, Your Highness." The words spilled out before I could stop them. A curtain of silence descended over the tent as Reign and the headmaster's glares bored into the side of my face.

"There is no such thing as peace, initiate. If you'd grown up at Court instead of in the wilderness of Feywood, you'd understand that. We must be constantly on guard against our foes."

A rebuttal sat perched on my tongue, specifically about the

terrible creatures of the Wilds at our doorstep, but I was rather fond of my head, and I preferred for it to remain attached to my neck. So, I bit back the retort, earning a sigh of relief from my professor.

"Come, Your Ethereal Highness, there are a number of promising students I would still like to present."

The king nodded and the Royal Guardians fell into line around him. As the headmaster led the royal away, faint murmurs drifted across the confines of the tent. The rest of the squad surrounded Sol and me, a circle of curious gazes following every twitch. Reign still stood beside me, his ever-looming presence oddly comforting now despite yesterday's brutal rejection.

I'd seen him with Phantom first-hand, witnessed their bond. As much as I hated to admit it, I needed him. I had no idea how to train a dragon. And though Sol didn't look like much at the moment, in only a week he would be an enormous, flying, fire-breathing dragon.

The little dragonette peered up at me, golden irises blazing around narrowed pupils, and let out a tiny roar.

My heart just about melted into a puddle. I may not have been able to mystically bond with the creature yet, but I felt a connection all the same.

"Are you hungry, Sol?" A long, reptilian tongue snaked out and wagged between a row of tiny, sharp teeth. "Well then, we'll have to get you some food, won't we?"

Reign's shoulder bumped mine, and those icy tendrils of night drifted over my skin. When had he gotten so close? Good goddess, I needed to put a bell on him.

Sol inched closer to Reign and sniffed at his black boots. A growl vibrated the hatchling's throat and he bared his teeth.

"Don't you dare," Reign snapped.

The dragon's eyes lifted to mine, and he flashed what I could have sworn was a smile, before he chomped down on the toe of my professor's shiny boot.

Reign let out a satisfying yelp followed by a string of curses that had the rest of Flare Squad swiveling in our direction. "That mangy little—"

"Watch your tongue, professor," I snapped. "You're talking about my bonded skyrider."

He rolled his eyes and lifted his boot to assess the damage. A row of teeth marks was imprinted into the front of his boot, and I simply couldn't restrain the laugh from tittering out.

"Oh, you think this is funny, princess?" he whisper-hissed.

"Just a bit."

He wagged a finger at Sol. "Do that again and I'll see to it that you don't eat for a week."

The little dragon curled into a ball at my feet, growling his displeasure.

"Don't listen to him, Sol, I'd never let that happen." I patted his horned head, careful to avoid the nastier spikes. His eyelids drifted closed moments later.

"So much for keeping our distance, professor," I muttered at the male bathed in shadows.

"Mmm, yes. It appears as if we're stuck together for the foreseeable future."

Chapter Thirty-Four

R *eign*

"Your task has become critical, Darkthorn, now more than ever." Headmaster Draven prowled the length of his grand desk, made from the very wood surrounding the small village of Feywood. "There is something about that Kin, and you must discover what it is before it's too late."

Noxus, I hated this obnoxious, blustering male.

"I've already told you I understand, Draven."

"Do you, boy?" He crossed the space between us and loomed over the leather chair I was sprawled upon. "Do you truly understand what is at stake here?"

I lifted my arms and flashed the gleaming silver cuffs around my wrists. "Trust me, I am well aware and counting down the days."

"Don't be so selfish, Reign. This isn't simply about you. This is about the fate of Aetheria."

"I know," I gritted out, sitting straight up in the chair to meet his furious gaze.

"Raysa, in her infinite wisdom, must have chosen the girl for a reason. The king has been relentless in his inquisition, and

I have no answers to provide. And now that she's been chosen by a dragon…"

"I've already told you, there is nothing unique about the girl. She is a mere Kin with barely enough *rais* to summon a radiant shield. You worry too much, Draven." The lies fell easily from my lips. I'd been living another life for so long now, I barely remembered who I was anymore. I could barely distinguish between truth and falsehoods, it all blended together as one.

The only thing that was painstakingly clear was Aelia. The hold she had over me was as inexplicable as a spell of starlight and shadow. Soon my threads of restraint would snap and then, the true risk would emerge. And now with the appearance of Solanthus, keeping my distance was no longer an option.

An initiate harnessing the power of a dragon was incredibly risky to a full-blooded Light Fae, but for Aelia, the ramifications were completely unknown.

"She cannot be a mere Kin!" Draven roared, returning my meandering thoughts to the present. "I want you at her side at all times, Reign. A Kin with a dragon is unheard of!"

"I have been," I gritted out.

"Then clearly you are failing in your duties if you've discovered nothing." He seared his watery gaze to my own. "Do whatever it takes to gain her trust and unearth her secrets."

"She doesn't know anything," I growled, unable to keep the anger at bay any longer. I believed her about the daggers. She truly had no idea of the infernium vein until Gideon discovered the truth.

"How can you be so certain?"

As Draven believed his silver trinkets to all but vanquish my powers, I couldn't quite admit my shadows had seen bits and pieces of Aelia's thoughts, had been able to decipher the truth from her aura.

"Just call it a feeling," I rasped.

He inched closer, his aquiline nose inches from my own.

"Well, your feelings don't mean beetle dung to me." Saliva sprayed across my face, and my nails dug into my palms to keep from striking the old Fae down. "I need proof, something to deliver to the king."

"Proof of what, exactly?"

From the moment Draven tasked me with retrieving Aelia, I'd wondered how much he knew of her mysterious origins. He'd never mentioned the Twilight Prophecy, not once. Unlike my father who'd drilled it into my head from the moment I started my lessons in language arts.

My thoughts flickered to the past to a chamber of obsidian walls, the stone so dark it abolished all shreds of light.

"Reign! Are you paying attention, lad?" Hard eyes glared down at me, nothing but frosty, endless black razing over me. "You have few options now. If you fail me, I will have no further use for you. Do you understand?"

"Yes, Father."

"Now memorize this. Finding the aforementioned child will be your duty to your realm. Do so and you will be greatly rewarded."

I stared at the ancient scrawling across the parchment, committing the foreign words to memory.

A child of twilight, born from the dance of light and dark, shall emerge with the power to reshape destinies. From the celestial embrace and the shadow's whisper, a harbinger of cosmic balance shall be brought forth.

A fateful choice awaits her - to heal or to harm, to nurture or annihilate. Her every step shall resonate through realms, influencing the very fabric of existence.

When the child of twilight shall come of age, her choices, guided by the celestial and obscured by shadows, shall determine the fate of worlds. Whether she becomes a beacon of hope or a harbinger of oblivion, the child of twilight shall be the catalyst of an epochal choice - to bring forth a new dawn or plunge all into eternal dusk.

"But Father, how will I find the child?"

"Noxus will guide you."

My brows furrowed as I stared at the words so intently, they began to blur.

"Are you up to the task, Reign?"

"Yes, Father."

"Good boy." His big hand patted the top of my head, the touch so surprising I flinched.

Blinking quickly, I banished the memories of the past to the dark corners of my mind where they permanently resided, except for the prophecy. Those words resonated across my skull constantly, a never-ending battle cry promising a future I'd been, up until now, denied.

Could Aelia Ravenwood truly be the child of twilight?

From the first moment I saw her standing in the threshold of that old cottage, I'd felt something. Was it in fact Noxus guiding me as Father had promised?

"Proof that our fate is changing." Draven's sharp words chased away the spiraling questions.

I was not the only Fae in this room concealing secrets. If Draven was aware of the prophecy, he too, was guarding it closely. But why?

Either way, it was clear the headmaster would not give me the answer today. Sliding to the edge of the cushion, I waved the odious Draven back and rose to my feet. "I will continue in my efforts with Aelia."

"Good. The end of the term will be here before long, and it is essential the Kin has mastered her mount by the battle with Arcanum Citadel. I cannot wait to see King Tenebris of Umbra's face when he sees our dragon." A sinister smile lifted the tips of his snowy mustache.

"Yes, that will be quite a sight." I hadn't laid eyes on the Shadow Fae royal in years. I hadn't missed him one bit. Dipping my head, I turned for the door. "I must go, I cannot be late for class. It's the first with the initiates and their hatchlings."

"More like babysitting this week." He scoffed.

"You know as well as I how important the initial bonding period is."

Draven grunted and flopped down on the grand chair behind his desk, his alabaster robes flurrying around his tall, slender form.

"As a matter of fact, I'd like to suggest something unique for Aelia and Solanthus. May I have your approval to take her off campus for the day? Professor Lumen could cover for me? As you said, it's only babysitting..."

He waved a dismissive hand. "Yes, yes, whatever you feel will help the process."

"Wonderful."

I raced out of the headmaster's office in the Hall of Luminescence before he could rope me into further conversation. How I'd put up with this blowhard male for three entire years only Noxus knew. But it would seem Father's intuition coupled with the seer's warning that the time was upon us had been right. What better place to find the child of twilight than at a prestigious university for the most powerful Fae?

Father had enough eyes across the river should the child pop up there, but here in the Court of Ethereal Light? That was the true test.

My feet carried me through the gilded halls and out the shimmering double doors into the blasted eternal sunlight. Some days I craved the cooling darkness so intensely I spent the morning huddled in the closet of my chamber. Nothing empowered my dwindling *nox* like the frosty arms of night.

As I emerged onto the training field, the sun's incessant rays drilling through my tunic, my footsteps quickened, an invisible tether drawing me forward. My boots caught the gleaming light as I moved, drawing my attention to the bite mark across the left toe. The hint of a smile slid across my face at the reminder of Aelia's skyrider. That little beast would be a handful.

Perhaps when he was full grown, I would introduce Solanthus to Phantom, if they weren't acquainted already. I worried about the solitary life she was forced to lead.

A flash of raven hair streaked across my periphery, and my strides lengthened instinctively. Aelia ran across the lush grass with Sol scampering behind her, the unwieldy little thing tumbling from side to side. My shadows buzzed with excitement, a slight hum coursing through my veins at the sight of her. Noxus, what could it mean that a so-called Kin had such an effect on me?

As if she'd sensed my approach, she spun toward me, her smile falling. Her eyes narrowed when they latched onto mine and pops of energy lit up my flesh. My reactions to her were growing stronger by the day, despite my best efforts. And now, this wonderful idea I had would only put us in closer proximity.

Noxus, help me.

My shadows slithered away before I gave the command, wrapping their silky tendrils around Aelia. I threw my voice with my whispering shadows, and her brows slammed together, as they often did when I used my powers. "Come, princess, we have training to do."

Chapter Thirty-Five

A *elia*

Holding Sol firmly against my chest as we rocketed through Reign's shadows of endless night, I whispered soothing words of encouragement. Only a day with my dragon and already I was using baby-talk around the hatchling. I had to remind myself in a week he'd be a full-grown, fire-breathing beast capable of devouring me in one bite.

But right now, he clung onto me, claws digging into my leather breastplate as we shadowtraveled to only Noxus knew where. "We're almost there, little guy," I crooned. My arms already felt like lead weights after holding the dragonette for only a few minutes. I hazarded a quick peek over my shoulder at Reign who toted both of us within his cloak of shadows. Barely perceptible droplets of perspiration beaded across his brow and upper lip.

The moment we'd abandoned the Conservatory's wards, I'd felt Reign's powers dampen. The throbbing, pulsing *nox* that

249

typically emanated from the male diminished, gradually leaking away the farther we traveled.

How far were we going?

The last time I'd shadowtraveled with my professor, we'd gone across campus and the trip had lasted mere seconds. This time, it felt like we'd been trapped in murky oblivion for decades.

I was mere seconds from asking Reign *are we there yet*? when a glimmer of light flickered at the end of the tunnel of fathomless obscurity. The shadows melted away and night coalesced around us, shimmering moonlight bathing the mountainous land in an ethereal glow.

As I placed Sol onto the dark earth, the steady rush of water spun my head around to a glittering waterfall. The cascade tumbled gently over a crescent of jagged onyx rock, softened by centuries of travel. The water somehow gathered the scant light, shimmering with hues of deep indigo and silver, as if moonlight had liquefied into a gentle stream.

I drew in a breath, unable to tear my eyes away from nature's beauty. "Where are we?" I whispered.

"The Darkmania Falls on the border of the Court of Umbral Shadows. It's a quiet stretch of land where we won't be disturbed." He ticked his head over the rocky crags towering above the quaint waterfall and wisps of dawn scattered through the murky night. "I used to come here to escape the demands of the Citadel."

I peered over his shoulder and could just make out the looming turrets at a good distance to the southeast. I supposed when you could shadowtravel or fly, it made exploration much easier.

"And why are we here now?"

The moonlight danced across Reign's dark hair as he cocked his head, casting it aglow in shades of silver and navy. "Why to train, princess." His unfathomable irises sparkled, more radiant than the starlit sky overhead. "I have another theory to test."

"You and your theories..." I grumbled as I crouched down and absentmindedly stroked Sol's bumpy head. He was entirely entertained by the bevy of insects crawling across the fertile earth.

"I would like you to attempt to access the bond between you and your skyrider upon Shadow Fae soil."

"You're still so adamant that my powers are being blocked somehow?"

"Yes. Especially now. There is no earthly reason that Raysa would grant you, a powerless Kin, a mighty dragon otherwise."

I bristled at the insult, but I held my tongue, fully aware he was simply baiting me. Knotting my arms across my chest, I glared up at Reign. "So what exactly do you want me to do, professor?"

Shadows shot from his fingertips, curling up my legs, their icy touch sending goosebumps rippling across my flesh. My knees hinged, and I dropped to the cool grass on my behind. With an excited squeal, Sol leapt into my lap and nuzzled my breastplate.

"You could have just asked me to sit," I snapped, rubbing my tender backside.

"But wasn't it much more fun this way?" He cocked a mischievous brow.

Not for the first time I noticed the volatile professor seemed to be in a better mood the moment we crossed into Shadow Fae lands. I wondered if it was a result of simply missing his home or if it had more to do with access to his *nox*.

He crouched down in front of me and reached for my hands. One was occupied with rubbing the scaly nubs atop Sol's head and the other dug into the blades of grass at my side. Neither moved at his offer.

"Princess..." he growled.

"What? I don't believe that touching is going to help with your *keeping our distance* decree."

"Damn it, Aelia." He grabbed for my free hand and squeezed it between his strong fingers.

Sol wiggled in my lap, whirled on my attacker and released a pitiful roar.

I had no control over the laugh that bubbled out despite the irritation at my professor. "Oh, Sol..." I laughed again as he flashed Reign his jagged little teeth.

"For the love of Noxus, Solanthus, I'm only trying to help you. We don't have much time." Reign dipped his gaze to the dragonette's eyelevel. "Trust me."

My little dragon snorted and plumes of silver smoke escaped his tiny nostrils.

"I don't disagree with you, little buddy," I whispered into what I assumed was his ear.

"Aelia, if this is to work, you must trust me. Despite your shaky bond with Solanthus, I'm certain he can feel you and sense your emotions. If you do not believe in me, then neither will he."

"Well, how can I?" I snapped. "You're kind with me one instant, and then a bastard the next. You treat me a certain, special way, then you're cold and distant. You abandon me, brutally reject me—. How can I put my faith in someone who guards his emotions with an impenetrable obsidian wall?"

Reign loosed a frustrated breath and dragged his fingers through his wild, midnight locks. "I don't know how else to be around you, Aelia," he rasped out. "The tethers of my restraint grow more tenuous with every moment we spend together." His jaw snapped shut as if he'd never intended for that confession to see the light of day.

He shot to his feet and paced a quick circle, the sudden silence overshadowed by the quiet murmurs of the cascades.

"I cannot be what you want me to be, princess," he whispered a long minute later, dark gaze fixed to his shiny boots. How could he know what I wanted when *I* certainly didn't? He finally lifted his chin, smoldering, unreadable orbs meeting mine. "But I will do my best to help you survive, if you'll let me."

I nodded slowly, the intensity in his gaze dropping my chin. He'd said it from the very beginning: we could never be together. It was forbidden. Despite what he may have felt, he'd been clear. I needed to get over my ridiculous, childish daydreams and face reality. I needed his help.

"The Ethereal Trials will begin at the end of the week, once your skyriders are full grown, and will culminate at the year-end battle with Arcanum Citadel. It is paramount you succeed in both if you wish to live."

Good gods, only a week—where had the time gone? "Fine," I gritted out. Lifting Sol so his fiery golden eyes met mine, I announced, "Solanthus, the Sun Chaser, Reign is our friend, and he will help us. He has a dragon, too, just like you, but that's our little secret. Can you trust him?"

My little dragon let out a happy chuff and wiggled until I released him. I tried to search the faint bond between us, and a faint pulse vibrated between the gossamer strands. Holding out my hand to Reign, I grumbled, "Okay, we're ready."

He knelt in front of me and wrapped his big hands around mine. That familiar pulse of Reign's energy whipped through me and lashed at my veins.

"Goddess, did you feel that?" I cried.

Reign's head dipped, but that unreadable expression remained carved into his stubborn jaw.

"What was that?"

"I assume it's your *rais* attempting to rise to the surface."

Wow, it was incredible.

"Now, focus on the bond between you and Solanthus. It should be a shimmery strand deep within your core."

"Yes, I know..." Squeezing my eyes closed, I locked onto the gauzy strings fluttering wildly within my chest. That faint presence blossomed and filled my heart so fully I wondered how I'd ever lived without it. *Sol. Sol, can you hear me?*

Reign's hands tightened around my own and warmth flooded my veins. Tiny sparks danced across my palms and a swirl of power tangled with my own, beating against my ribs.

Sol?

Aelia Ravenwood? A rough, beastly sound like waves across gravel caressed my mind. It sounded nothing like the cute, little creature in my lap.

Is that you, Sol?

It is I, Solanthus, the Sun Chaser.

You sound so different...

Though my body is new, Aelia, my soul has wandered these lands for many lifetimes. As I'm certain you know, very few dragons remain in existence today. Our souls reincarnate by the powers of the gods, the perfect balance of light and dark, and now Raysa has delivered me to you.

I did *not* know that. Gods, I needed to study more. *How can I hear you now?*

The little dragon lifted his chin toward Reign. *I imagine it's his* nox *flooding your system that is giving you access.*

So we won't be able to speak once he releases me? The thought alone had a gaping hole opening deep in my chest.

I'm not certain, Aelia. Everything seems different about you, but I suppose that is what will make our bond unique.

Reign's grip softened, then his fingers untangled from mine. I blinked quickly, the air whooshing from my lungs as Sol's presence was torn away.

"What happened?" I snapped.

My instructor heaved out a breath, his complexion a shade lighter than normal. "I couldn't sustain the connection any longer."

"But I heard him, Reign, I finally heard him! Can't we try again?"

"I said it was enough for now," he barked before he marched off to the edge of the glistening lagoon. Crouching in front of the water, he dipped a hand in and splashed the crystalline liquid across his face.

I eyed him as he stretched out across the bank and closed his eyes, as if he were moonbathing beneath the twinkling stars. "I thought we came to train."

"We did, princess."

"Then what are you doing?"

"I'm getting a good view." He cocked his head, leaned into his palm and smirked. "Start practicing your radiant shield. You must be able to summon it as easily as taking your next breath. I will time you."

Sol darted across the clearing, flapping his small wings as he chased yet another nocturnal creature.

"You better get started, princess. Once you manage that, I'll have you shield your skyrider as well. And trust me, once Solanthus reaches his full size, it will become much more difficult, so I suggest you master it now."

"Unbelievable," I grumbled as I squeezed my eyes closed and searched for the tiny hint of *rais* that flickered at the pit of my stomach. I focused on the swirl of energy and imagined it growing inside me, until it filled every inch of my being. Then I pushed it outward until it flowed from my pores like the rushing waterfall cascading down the cliff.

A flash of golden light crept across my periphery until it blossomed into an enormous, gilded orb encompassing my entire body and extending around Sol who frolicked in the grass a few yards away.

My gaze darted to meet Reign's wide-eyed one.

Energy unlike anything I'd ever experienced before punched through my system, emanating from the very soles of my boots and shooting through my veins to every inch of my flesh. The sphere grew larger, the power intensifying until a tremor raced through my body.

"Aelia?" Reign appeared beside me, his black tunic aglow with my protective shield. "Are you all right?"

A flicker of heat ignited in my core, a slow trickle before it intensified and expanded outward until it felt as if fire consumed my entire being. The scorching flames surged like liquid lightning and a scream tore through my clenched teeth.

Hands so cold they felt like ice closed around my own, and frosty tendrils of darkness curled around my body. Another tremor rolled up my spine, my teeth chattering from the strain. My heart pounded, an incessant drumbeat drowning out all else. My lungs constricted as the sizzling inferno scorched my insides and made it impossible to draw in a breath.

"Aelia!" Those icy fingers squeezed my shoulders and gave me a rough shake. Blazing midnight spheres met mine, and somehow that voice, Reign's voice, crept through the chaos of my mind. "Let go, Aelia, release the energy before it kills you."

Reign's soothing darkness infiltrated the fiery dawn, weaving shadows between the light.

Shut it down, Aelia, before it is too late. That rough, beastly voice snaked through my frazzled thoughts.

Sol?

Well done, child, now rein the power in before it consumes us all.

I blinked quickly, drawing free of the mental conversation with Sol and just caught the whites of my professor's eyes as they rolled back into his head an instant before he crumpled to the ground.

Chapter Thirty-Six

"Reign!" I shrieked.

With a loud pop, the golden sphere disintegrated as I dropped to the ground and crawled toward my professor. "Reign, are you all right?" My heart punched at my ribcage at the sight of his still form. Lifting his head into my lap, I hovered over him, desperately scanning his body for injury.

Nothing. He seemed wholly unharmed.

Had I done this to him? Had my *rais* somehow knocked him out?

The slow rise and fall of his chest momentarily eased the building panic. He was breathing. Well, that was a good sign at least. Then why was he so still? And his eyes closed? "Reign, wake up!" I slapped his cheek—perhaps a bit harder than intended—but the tremor in my hand and the fear blossoming in my chest had me at the point of hysterics. "Reign, please..." I murmured.

Sol ambled over, chasing a silkworm weaving through the tall blades of grass. His oversized feet and tiny wings threw off his balance, and his prey managed an escape. Now that I'd heard his commanding voice in my mind, I couldn't quite reconcile the deep timbre with the bumbling little hatchling.

"Sol, what's wrong with him?"

The dragonette sniffed at Reign's head, then moved further down his motionless body until he reached his hand. He released a sharp squeal and bared his sharp little fangs before chomping down on the silver bracelet.

"Sol!"

Grinding his teeth, he attempted to tear the cuff from Reign's wrist. Even though his teeth were small, irrational fear gripped my chest. What if he bit off his hand by accident?

"Sol, don't!"

The little dragon peered up at me with the manacle clenched between his fangs and warm golden irises aflame beneath the silver of moonlight.

"You're trying to help him, aren't you?"

He dipped his head.

"The cuffs are draining his *nox*, that's it, isn't it?"

He nodded once more.

Oh gods, Reign must have drained his energy to shadow-travel us both here, and again when helping me communicate with Sol. Then whatever I just did must have fully depleted it. Even his extraordinary powers weren't limitless.

Cradling Reign's head, I brushed my thumb across his cheek, the fine hairs tickling my sensitive fingertip. Dark midnight lashes fanned across porcelain skin, the moonlight bathing his face in an otherworldly glow. Strands of dark hair swept across his furrowed brow and I brushed them behind his ear, tracing the sharp point; I never would have dared if he'd been conscious. His lids fluttered as I lingered over the tip, and a faint sigh parted his lips.

"Princess," he whispered, eyes still closed, "if you keep that up, I'll never get the rest I need to recover."

I jerked my fingers away from his ear, my entire body stiffening.

Rolling over in my lap, his weary eyes lifted to mine. "I'm fine, Aelia, it takes much more than that to kill me, trust me. I simply overdid it and drained my *nox* because of these damned manacles. I will not be able to shadowtravel until my *nox* has been replenished, so we'll have to remain here for the night."

"All night?" I squealed. Technically, it was always night, but still.

"Remaining on Shadow Fae soil for longer will speed up the process." He glanced around the clearing then toward the cliffs behind the glistening falls. "There is a small cave at the foot of the cascades. It will make a fine spot to rest."

Rest in a cave with him? Right.

"But first, keep working on summoning your *rais*. I'll watch from here." That hint of amusement sparked as he glanced up at me, still nestled in my lap.

"Very funny." Gently, I lifted his head and rolled him off onto the blanket of lush grass. Sol ambled over and nudged his cheek with his tiny snout. "I heard him in my head again." I patted the dragonette right between his small wing bones. "When my *rais* was growing uncontrollable..."

He propped his head up on his palm and nodded. "I knew you had it in you, princess. We simply had to find a way to let it out."

"But what will we do when I return to Light Fae lands and whatever is blocking my power continues to do so?"

"That's precisely why I want you to practice so that it becomes second nature. How do you think I fight these lovely bangles?" He flashed me his wrists, a sneer on his lips. "Now, no more stalling, start training."

A curtain of moisture descended across my aching form as I crept into the dark cave with Sol in my arms, the brilliant gold of his eyes illuminating the murky space. I'd trained for hours, summoning shield after shield as my professor watched leisurely sprawled across the bank of the lagoon. To say I was a little aggravated, hungry and exhausted was putting it lightly. "Reign?" I called out, my voice echoing through the endless black.

"Back here."

An earthy scent clung to my nostrils the farther I moved into the tight cavern. Hidden by the rushing waterfalls, if Reign hadn't guided me here, I would've never found it. I supposed that was why he'd chosen this spot.

Squinting, I crept through the narrow tunnel, praying to all the gods I wouldn't bash my head against a jagged wall. "I can barely see anything," I grumbled.

"Then why don't you try summoning a spark of light?"

I followed the sound of his annoying voice. "Don't you think I would if I could?"

"A few weeks ago, you couldn't summon a radiant shield, and today, you knocked me on my ass with one."

Good point. A flicker of a smile crawled across my lips. Cradling Sol in one arm, I turned my hand palm up and searched the well of untapped power slowly blooming in my gut. Focusing on my fingertips, I willed the light to appear as I'd seen Rue and Symon do a hundred times. Most of my teammates had a good handle on basic photokinesis and could manipulate and control light with ease. But there wasn't a shred of light to be had in this murky cave.

There are other ways to create light, Aelia. Sol's deep voice cut through my thoughts.

Like what?

You need not name it to feel it.

I glanced down at the wiggly thing in my arms. Could he be a little less cryptic?

My mind wandered back to the hours of classes I'd endured, and the litany of powers Light Fae should be able to manifest. Most were advanced techniques, but I mentally scanned the list regardless. *Solar flare burst*. Hmm...

Focusing on my fingertips once more, I visualized light dancing across my flesh and illuminating the gloomy chamber. Raysa, guide me. Diving deep into my core, I found a burning ember of *rais*. Holding onto it with all my strength, I willed it to the surface. Heat flared from my belly outward, and a surge of lightning rushed my veins. Flames ignited on my fingertips and brilliant light bathed the entire cave.

Reign's dark form coalesced from the shadows, his eyes wide and glossy beneath the vivid display of lights. "Well done, princess. Now please, turn it down a notch before you burn my irises."

"You say that as if it were easy." I lowered Sol to the ground, and he immediately darted after a winged insect.

Reign stalked closer, shielding his eyes from the light with one arm. His inky shadows recoiled from the glaring glow emanating from my fingertips. "Just focus on your *rais*. Imagine a balloon in the farthest depths of your core. You can blow harder to inflate it, or you can release some of that air so that it becomes more manageable."

I nodded and attempted to do as he instructed.

"Close your eyes," he whispered.

My lids slid shut and I imagined the balloon, then pictured releasing a bit of air, then a little more. The glare just beyond the curtain of my lids diminished. Slowly, I opened my eyes and, instead of the overpowering light, a tiny flicker pirouetted across my fingertips.

Reign's shadows surrounded us, the coils of darkness weaving around our bodies.

I glanced up to meet hooded orbs. "Did you help me, or did I do it by myself?"

"It was all you, princess."

"Then why are your shadows circling like a starved animal?"

His dark brow rose into an incredulous arc. "Sometimes they have a mind of their own." He loosed an exasperated breath and inched closer. "And they simply can't stay away from you. It's as if they're drawn to your light."

With those fathomless irises locked onto mine, I couldn't quite summon the words to put together a response.

An endless moment later, his gaze dropped to his entangled fingers. "We should get some rest. A few hours of sleep, and I should be able to shadowtravel us back home."

"We could just walk. It's not that far, is it?" A night alone with Reign in this cave had warning bells resounding in my head.

"It would be about half a night's journey. I can make it, but can you and Solanthus?" He ticked his head at the baby dragon who was already snoring quietly, curled up against the wall.

I hated to wake him. "Fine, I suppose a little sleep wouldn't hurt." Truth be told, I was exhausted.

"If you sleep in the far corner by the wood I gathered, you'll be warmest."

I gaped at the pile of twigs. "Why didn't you say you had a fire before?"

"I don't have a fire; I only have a mountain of wood." He took my hand and flicked it toward the makeshift hearth. A spark flew from my fingertips and ignited the timber. Within seconds, it burned a deep ochre and warmth flooded the cavern. "Now, we have a fire."

With an arrogant grin, he sauntered to the corner and peeled off his cloak, then tunic, revealing his perfectly carved torso. Then he began to unlace his leathers, and I forced my traitorous eyes up as they sloughed down to the ground.

"Must you?" I hissed.

"I typically sleep completely bare. Would you prefer that instead?" Mischief churned across those fathomless orbs.

"No!" I squealed.

"Besides, I'd rather sleep atop my clothing than the dirt floor."

A fair point. Too bad I didn't find myself with a spare layer of clothing.

He lay his cloak across the dusty earth, then his tunic beside it. With a wry grin, he motioned toward the improvised bed. "If you'd like it, it's yours."

"And where will you sleep?"

He shrugged, his broad shoulders lifting and calling my eye to the mark of the banished just above his heart. "I don't need sleep to rest."

"But your *nox*..."

"Will replenish either way."

I was honestly too tired to argue anymore, so instead, I dropped down onto the soft material and curled into a ball. Reign's musky, frosty scent permeated the fabric and brought with it a surprising sense of peace.

I must have nodded off within seconds, because hours later when I awoke, my muscles no longer burned and the well of *rais* deep in my core spilled over. I only hoped it would remain once we returned to Light Fae soil. My lids fluttered slowly open as I peeled back the haze of sleep, warmth blanketing every inch of me. That was odd. I'd been so cold...

My eyes snapped open when a familiar presence stirred behind me and the blanket of pure darkness coalesced. Reign's arm was flung across my torso, his leg entangled with my own.

My breath hitched at the scandalous proximity of our bodies, and I tried to extricate myself from his hold before he awoke. To no avail. He squirmed behind me, his front pressed against my back and a very hard part of his lower anatomy digging into my backside.

Oh goddess, help me.

How did we keep finding ourselves in these appalling positions when Reign had made it *abundantly* clear we were to stay away from each other?

"Good morning, princess." Reign's rough voice slithered across my ear, his chin practically pressed against my shoulder.

"What are you doing?" I hissed as I attempted to pry his arm off me.

"You were shivering in the night. I decided to be a gentleFae and warm you up."

"You could have just re-lit the fire." I eyed the cold, ashy embers.

"No, I couldn't have because I'm not the one with Light powers. I would have had to wake you and at the time, this seemed the kinder option."

"I don't know if I agree." Again, I attempted to jerk free of his embrace, but his hold only tightened. "I'm perfectly warm now, if you'd kindly let go."

"Are you sure?"

I could just see his wicked smile from the corner of my eye.

"Why do you insist on teasing me like this? Especially after what you said--" I blurted, the words flying out before I could stop them.

Reign's entire body stiffened behind me before his arm retreated, then his leg, and he jerked up to a sitting position. I did the same, tucking me knees into my chest and staring into the dusky remains of the fire.

I didn't expect an answer. I wasn't sure I wanted one.

"I cannot help myself," he gritted out a long moment later, as if dragging out each word were physically painful. "Gods, Aelia, don't you understand the desire I feel for you is forbidden? To surrender would be to betray the trust placed upon me, to forsake the very essence of my duty. More than that, there are secrets, dark and intricate; truths I cannot unveil. So, I must resist. This is the constant fight I battle, my sacrifice—for you, for the academy, for the courts that teeter unknowingly on the brink of chaos."

I stared at Reign, at the desperation carved into his handsome face, my mouth unable to form words after that declaration.

"It's time to go."

"But—"

"No, Aelia. I've already said too much. Noxus only knows what happens to my tongue when I find myself in your presence." Shaking his head, he gathered his clothing from the floor and stalked out.

Chapter Thirty-Seven

A elia

I stared across the grassy field at Sol towering over all the other hatchlings—stars, towering over the *buildings* of the Conservatory. At nearly a week old, he was already shoulder to shoulder with the Hall of Glory. And he was gorgeous. He'd shed his murky brown scales and they'd been replaced by glistening golden ones that radiated the glorious rays from above. His wings had expanded by leaps and bounds and were now in perfect proportion to his enormous body. He'd even grown into his awkward, bumbling talons.

"Noxus's nuts, did that beast double in size overnight?" Symon sauntered toward Rue and me with Griffinclaw at his side. The hippogriff was nearly full grown, standing tall beside his rider. His beady eyes scanned the field, before turning his anxious gaze on Sol.

As did most of the other hatchlings.

Though I'd insisted Sol would never hurt any of the other

266

skyriders, tension remained high whenever my dragon appeared. Now that he was nearing maturity, he spent most nights scouring the court's lands for prey. It wasn't easy keeping that giant belly full.

"Thank the goddess he's nearly reached maturity," said Rue. Her pegasus, Winddancer, floated just overhead, eagerly neighing and whinnying at Griff to join her.

A part of me felt badly for Sol. He didn't have anyone to play with like the others did. My gaze flickered to Reign's unwittingly. Maybe someday he could meet Phantom... My volatile professor had barely spoken to me since our night in the cave. Not that I'd expected anything less after that stunning confession.

"I can't believe we begin our flying lessons today." Rue's gaze was fixed to the sky, watching her mount dart between the clouds.

"And then the Ethereal Trials begin shortly after," Sy added.

"And before we know it, the term will be over." Rue's expression turned pensive as she pivoted to face me. "Any luck with your *rais*?"

I hated keeping the truth from my friend, but Reign had sworn me to secrecy regarding our late-night romps with Sol to the Shadow Fae lands. My *rais* was becoming easier to summon, but it was nothing like the power I held when I crossed the river. "Getting better every day," I managed.

Symon slid his arm around my shoulders and tucked me into his side. "I'm so proud of my little Kin. How about this, when you ace the trials, you let me touch your sexy, rounded ear for a few minutes?"

"Sy!" I shoved him aside, laughing.

"Fine, then at least promise me that you'll take me to Feywood and introduce me to some of your Kin friends when we are allowed time off at the end of the term."

"Maybe... if you behave." I waggled a finger at my ridiculous friend.

"Let's begin, first-years, these skyriders are not going to train themselves." Professor Lumen, the flight instructor who'd recently joined our Combat class, marched to the middle of the field. "Now that you've had a week to bond with your hatchlings, flying should come as naturally as walking to most of you." His sharp eyes settled on me, and his lips twisted. "Now, there are always exceptions, and some beasts prove more difficult than others to bring to heel."

Did you hear that, Sol? He's talking about you.

My dragon's presence overpowered my own, filling my being until my skeletal confines became almost too tight for two. *I've been doing this for centuries, little Kin. No need to worry.* Warm golden eyes met mine from across the field and plumes of light smoke drifted from his nostrils. *I have yet to lose a rider, and I certainly do not intend for you to be my first.*

Well, that was comforting.

Another familiar presence bumped into me, the overwhelming darkness pushing against my light. I slanted Reign an uninterested glance as he stalked closer. "Are you ready?" he mumbled.

"Oh, so you're speaking to me again?"

Rue giggled and Sy bounced on his toes uncomfortably when Reign's unreadable mask twisted into something wicked.

"Leave," he growled at my friends.

Before I could open my mouth to object, my cowardly teammates darted toward their mounts. "You can't just treat them like that," I hissed.

"I can do whatever I want. I am their professor, and I require a moment alone with another student."

The hair on my arms lifted at the bite to his tone. Knotting my arms across my chest in a defensive maneuver, I glared up at my professor. "Fine, what is it?"

"Have you solidified the link between you and Solanthus?"

I nodded. "I've been able to speak to him all week. You

would have known that if you'd bothered to look in my direction even once during Combat class."

"Aelia..." he gritted out and raked his fingers through his wild hair. "We've already been over this—"

"Yes, yes, you're right, we have. No need to dredge it up again."

"Good." He heaved out a breath and motioned to Sol. "You've already ridden a dragon, so I hope that will give you an advantage," he whispered. "Only this time, my shadows and I won't be there to keep you seated." The hint of a smirk played across his mouth, and there was nothing I wanted more than to wipe that smug look right off his unfairly handsome face.

"I'm certain I'll do just fine. I've been strengthening my quadriceps all week."

"You should have told me, I could have helped." That wicked grin flashed brighter.

"Goddess, I despise you."

"Very good, use that anger to strengthen your resolve. That always worked for me."

"So you're purposely trying to piss me off?" I snarled.

Again, that veiled look.

"Aelia Ravenwood!" Professor Lumen's voice whirled my head over my shoulder. "Your turn to mount."

I swallowed hard, and as much as I hated myself for doing so, I found myself turning to Reign once more. "Any last bit of advice?"

"Don't die, princess."

Why was I so stupid to even bother asking?

I shot him a scathing glare and marched to the center of the field where Solanthus stood. Even Professor Lumen gave my dragon a wide berth. The old Light Fae peered up at the giant, a hint of envy in his gaze.

"Are you ready, Aelia?"

"You've got this!" Rue whisper-shouted from atop Winddancer. Her steed circled anxiously, ready to take to the skies.

Or maybe it was still Sol who was making all the other hatchlings nervous.

"Yes," I murmured and inched closer to my skyrider. "You ready?"

Always, Aelia. The magnificent golden dragon dropped to his belly, the ground trembling beneath my boots. A few of the other students let out shrieks of surprise at the unexpected tremor. Sol extended one long leg and I began the climb.

I moved gingerly, careful to avoid the spikey protrusions across his flesh, and whispers abounded.

"She'll never make it."

"My bet is that beast will toss her off the minute he's airborne."

"How in the realms did the Kin get a dragon anyway?"

Squeezing my eyes closed, I attempted to drown out their voices and focused on the only one that mattered. *Sol?*

Yes, Aelia?

You promise not to drop me, right?

Not on purpose.

That's not overly reassuring. I reached for another nub and hauled myself fully onto his back.

A deep rumble vibrated his throat, and I was fairly certain the big beast was laughing at me.

Sit all the way at the front, between my wing bones. You'll be shielded from the worst of the backdraft and the curve of my bones will provide a seat of sorts.

"Got it." I crawled across his spine and settled into the designated spot, finding two thick nubs at the end of his reptilian neck to hold onto.

"Now take your mount to the skies," Professor Lumen shouted from below.

I glanced down and my head spun. Good goddess, I was high up.

"Today we will simply focus on remaining aboard. Understand?"

"Yes, professor," I called out.

"Whenever you are ready."

You heard him, Sol.

His massive wings unfurled, and a few shrieks erupted below. I couldn't help the satisfied smile when I noticed one came from Ariadne. She and Belmore were apparently dating now, and she'd become even more arrogant and spiteful than ever.

Sol's wings beat at the air and all other thoughts vanished as the thunderous thrashing drowned out all else. He took a step forward, then another and we catapulted into the sky. My stomach dropped, then my lungs constricted as I gripped the bony nubs so hard my fingers cramped.

Hold on.

I'm trying. I clamped my thighs around Sol's neckbone, praying to all the gods that months of training had strengthened my muscles enough to keep me seated.

A blast of air lashed dark hair across my face, then a streak of blonde whipped into my eyes. I blinked quickly to rid myself of the tears as we lifted off the ground and soared over the top of the Conservatory.

"Oh, my gods!" I cried out. The thrill of flight took hold and a giddy burst of laughter squeezed through my lips. "This is incredible."

Yes... Sol's voice sounded almost wistful as it dribbled through the excitement.

He banked left and soared over the training field, then past the Hall of Luce, and drifted over the Luminoc River. The curtain of darkness at the edge of the border sent a chill up my spine.

Sol, have you participated in many battles with the students of the Citadel? We had little more than a month remaining before the final contest that determined our fate.

More than I care to remember.

That bad?

A muffled grunt seeped through my mind.

Then why do they force the first-years to compete?

To weed out the weak and prepare you for what's to come...

But we are at peace with the Court of Umbral Shadows. We have been for decades.

A peace that is flimsy, at best. It's nothing more than a fragile façade stretched thinly over the simmering unrest, threatening to snap at the slightest provocation.

Why was it that the more I learned about the Fae courts, the more I felt everything I knew was wrong?

What do you know, Sol?

It's nothing substantial, little one, only a feeling, a sense of foreboding deep in my old soul.

My brows knitted as we circled the training field and above the heads of dozens of students below. I wondered what had Sol suddenly waxing poetic.

Aelia, surely you know that dragons are known for our intelligence and strength, but were you also aware that we are the perfect mixture of dark and light? That we are blessed by the gods with rais *and* nox, *while most beasts are neutral, carrying the gifts of neither god?*

"No, I didn't." The answer popped out aloud. My thoughts fled back in time to what Reign's Shadow Fae friend had said about the crystal encrusted in my dagger's hilt—it, too, held *rais* and *nox*.

It is because of this blend of powers that we are so attuned to the world around us. His enormous neck curled around so that his eyes met mine. *And why we are so wise.* His lips peeled back, and I was certain of the smile this time.

Well then, I'm certainly lucky that the goddess chose you for me.

I am afraid you are mistaken, little Kin. She chose you for me.

Chapter Thirty-Eight

A elia

Professor Lumen's finger glided across the air leaving a trail of golden dust that formed words. I had yet to master that trick of photokinesis. And those manipulations of light were not just any words, they were the names of the trials we would have to pass in the next four weeks to continue onto the end of term battle with Arcanum Citadel.

I heaved in a breath, forcing my lungs to continue their struggle despite the anxiety, amidst the other initiates assembled in the sprawling Hall of Luminescence. The shimmery gold handwriting floated in the air, each swipe of his finger bringing on another massive swell of unease.

The Luminous Maze
The Dusk and Dawn Duel
The Shadows Whisper
Ethereal Light Sculpting
Skyrider Flight

273

Celestial Glyphs Exam

By the time he was finished, the six components of the Ethereal Trials hovered just over our heads, almost mocking in their shimmering beauty.

"Is he going to explain what each of them are?" I leaned closer to Rue, whispering.

"Yes, surely, he'll go over the expectations for each one."

"Some are fairly self-explanatory," Sy chimed in from the other side of me.

"Well, aren't you just a Fae know-it-all."

My friend shot me a smirk. "I'm most excited about The Shadows Whisper trial. We'll finally have a chance to cross the Luminoc into the Court of Umbral Shadows. In my twenty years on this continent, I have yet to see the fabled dark lands."

"Me too!" Rue squealed.

I supposed I was at an advantage, then, since Reign had toted me back and forth across the forbidden boundary a few times already. "Is there any particular reason Light Fae are not permitted to cross?"

Rue shrugged. "It was part of the treaty after the Two Hundred Years War. I suppose it was just to keep the peace. Crossing is only permitted for official academy-approved activities, and of course, the Royal Guardians move as necessary."

"What about that attack at the beginning of the year?" The horrific death of the female Light Fae student would be permanently emblazoned in my mind.

"A certain number of unscheduled exercises are permitted."

"From what I understand," Sy interjected, "the two head-masters convene at the beginning of the year to determine the amount."

"So you think Draven knew that assault was coming?" I blurted causing a few of the students' gazes to whirl in my direction.

"Not an assault, a Citadel-condoned exercise," Rue replied.

In which students were killed! How could my friends not see how wrong that was? I folded my hands in my lap, nails digging into my own skin to keep from blurting something completely inappropriate.

Professor Lumen cleared his throat, drawing my attention back to the ancient Fae. "There will be two trials held per week so that you may have enough time to recover between events. The two trials held in the classroom, the Celestial Glyphs Exam and Ethereal Light Sculpting, will be interspersed within the more physically demanding ones. The Dusk and Dawn Duel will be held at the narrowest point along the Luminoc River so that you may become habituated to fighting without the benefit of light. Some of you will notice quite a difference when you traverse that boundary. As Light Fae, our abilities come from the goddess, Raysa, and the embodiment of that power, the blessed sun. Without it, you may become more easily depleted of *rais*, so please be aware."

Hmm. How strange. And yet for me, the moment I crossed the border, my *rais* seemed fortified. Perhaps Reign was right and my abilities were somehow bound by more powerful *rais*. I chewed on the inside of my cheek as I considered.

"For The Shadows Whisper trial, Professor Reign"—he motioned toward the Shadow Arts professor who stood a few paces behind him on the dais— "has been granted a special dispensation to accompany you to the Twilight Forest, just past the border into Shadow Fae lands to ensure your relative safety."

The hair on my nape prickled as he paused on the word "relative." After my first excursion into the Court of Umbral Shadows, I'd wager there was not much safe about the forest at all. Not if gloomwhispers abounded.

Again, I hated being unable to share the truth with my friends. Somehow, I'd make it a point to warn them of the creature once we were away from curious gazes and pointy ears.

A hand went up just a few seats down, and Ariadne stood when the professor called her name. "I've heard that the Luminous Maze is the most difficult and typically results in the most deaths. Will that be at the end of the trials or the beginning?"

The professor cleared his throat and the nervous mutterings that began at her question quickly dissipated. "That is not always the case, Miss Bamberlight. And regardless, the order of the trials will vary depending on the squad. It is the most efficient way of organizing the event."

"Great," Symon muttered. "I hope it's last for us."

"Wouldn't you just rather die and have it over with?" Belmore's nasally voice from the row behind sent goosebumps prickling my flesh.

I twisted my head over my shoulder and regretted it immediately.

"I was speaking to you, Kin. With your measly powers, you would think a swift death would be preferable. You'll never survive the maze or the duel."

"I wouldn't be so sure about that." I flashed a toothy smile and patted the dagger at my thigh. "As I recall, of the two of us, I'm the more proficient one with blades."

"We'll see, won't we?" he snarled and sat back in his chair.

"Do we battle each other for the trials?" I asked Rue once I'd turned back around. *Please say no.*

"No, the other teams," Sy responded.

"Which is both good and bad," Rue added. "They're more likely to kill us since they aren't constrained by the rules of conduct. But I also won't feel so badly about taking one of their lives." My sweet friend's lips curled into a vicious smile.

It was so easy to forget she was one of them. Despite her kind demeanor and acceptance of me as a roommate and friend, she grew up in this ruthless world. I would fight for my life if I was forced to, but I preferred not to take a life if it was at all avoidable.

As if the prince of shadows had yanked the thoughts

straight from my mind, his dark gaze pivoted to mine. Those dark coils of night whirled around him, and a wisp hurtled in my direction. As a whisper of darkness curled around the back of my neck, I hazarded a glance at Rue. Couldn't she see the shadow?

"You'll have to be careful when we are in Shadow Fae lands." Reign's voice drifted across the shell of my ear as if he stood right beside me. "If your classmates see the astounding difference in your abilities, they will become wary."

"So you want me to lose?" I whispered.

Rue's head spun toward me. "Of course, I don't want you to lose. Why would you ever say that?"

Heat burned my cheeks, and I slowly shook my head. "Sorry, I was just thinking out loud."

"Or you could have said you were speaking to Solanthus," Reign murmured.

Ah, yes, that would have made more sense.

"How about we continue this conversation later," I whispered so quietly, even Rue didn't flinch this time.

"As you wish, princess."

Reign's shadow slithered back to its master, and a mixture of relief tangled with a hint of dismay coursed through my system. Gods, I hated that unflinching hold he possessed over me.

"Now, with the aid of your team leaders," said Professor Lumen, his voice echoing across the hall, "you will divide into squads and begin training for each event."

All the first-years began to move, but somehow, my behind remained anchored to my seat. Up until now, most of our training had been theoretical. How to *theoretically* kill an opponent... now everything would change.

"Are you coming, Aelia?" Heaton appeared at the end of the row, waving me out of my seat.

It was only then I noticed the hall had emptied out with the exception of only a few lingering professors. Heaton crept closer, his gaze on mine, as if I were some sort of skittish prey about to bolt. His assessment wasn't entirely unfounded.

"You will do just fine, Aelia, I'm certain of it." Heaton extended his hand, and a reassuring smile split his lips.

I allowed him to pull me out of my seat, but I didn't move far. "It's not something you can guarantee, now, is it?" How would I explain I was less afraid about risking my life and more about losing my humanity?

Heaton inched closer, a sad smile skimming across his porcelain skin. "There are very few guarantees in this life, Aelia. I wish I could lie and tell you otherwise, but that would only be a disservice to you." He drew in a labored breath, and his warm hand closed around my shoulder. "The next few weeks will be difficult, but they are essential if you wish to succeed in this life..."

"Are you happy with your choice?" This was Heaton's final year. Who knew where he'd find himself as a Royal Guardian a year from now. The question hung in the air for a long moment before his Adam's apple bobbed, and he began to speak.

"You certainly ask difficult questions, Aelia." A rueful smile lingered across his lips. "I am only one of a long line of Liteschilds who have followed in this path. It isn't quite a choice anymore." He paused and sucked in his lower lip. "I suppose I'll know the answer once I've been sent to the frontlines. Lawson seems happy enough."

"Your brother?"

He nodded. Rue had said they hadn't heard word since he had been dispatched to the northernmost province of the Shadow Court.

"Have you heard from him?" Perhaps the team leaders were privy to information that we were not.

His expression darkened, answering my question without a word. Heaton was a wonderful team leader, but he wore his emotions like a shield forged from the depths of his heart for all to see.

"Does Rue know?" I quickly asked so that he didn't feel obligated to answer.

"No," he murmured. "There are some truths a little sister should not have to hear."

"So why do you allow her to remain?"

A snort slipped out. "*Allow* is a very broad term, Aelia. As Light Fae not born in court, we are very limited in our choices. The good King Elian makes certain of that." He loosed a frustrated breath and swept a lock of stray blonde hair behind his pointed ear. "Anyway, we must go, Aelia. The others will be waiting for us." His hand dropped to the small of my back as he steered me between the chairs.

When we reached the double doors that led out to the training field, that dark presence skidded across my flesh. I lifted my gaze in time to find Reign storming up the steps of the hall. "Incoming!" he shouted.

Lifting my eyes to the sky, all the air squeezed from my lungs as I focused on the mass of pure darkness barreling toward us.

elia

"Get Aelia out of here!" Reign roared.

Heaton stiffened beside me, his hand sliding right off my back at the venom in Reign's tone, which is to say nothing of the murderous gleam in his eyes. "What about the other first-years?" he finally managed.

"I've already sent them to the catacombs in the library."

Aelia, do you need me? Sol's deep voice resounded through the impending chaos.

No, I'm safe. Reign is currently forbidding me from exiting the hall.

Good. At least that Shadow Fae is good for something.

I grinned despite myself. *Where are you?*

Hunting along the border of the Wilds.

So far? A gaping hole opened up in my chest at the mere thought of the great distance between us.

I can be back in no time if you need me.

No, I'm fine. Go have fun and fill your belly. I'll keep you updated should the training exercise worsen.

The sharp blare of a horn resounded across the hall, tearing my thoughts from Sol, and my heart flung itself into my throat. The warning bell. The upperclassmen would be racing down the steps any minute now, and I should have been running in the opposite direction. But for some unearthly reason, the soles of my boots were rooted to the ground.

The dagger at my waist called to me, my fingers itching to test the blade against another Shadow Fae. What if its strange power only worked against Reign?

As usual, it seemed as if my professor had read my thoughts. His dark gaze settled on the sheath strapped across my hips. He slowly shook his head. "No…"

"I must know the truth."

Thundering footfalls echoed behind us as students armed to the teeth spilled from the hall. Heaton squirmed beside me, his eyes intent on his classmates. "Professor, can you see to Aelia's safety? I should fight with my class. It could be one of the final exercises for the term."

Reign muttered a curse, but his head dipped all the same. "Fine, go and may the goddess be with you."

"And may her Light shine upon you." Heaton offered a quick nod, then his gaze pivoted to me, lingering for a long moment before he took off.

"Of course, he's smitten," Reign grumbled as his hand came around my forearm, jerking me up the steps of the hall.

Ignoring his comment, I made my best effort to wriggle free of his hold. "Reign, please, I have my own theory to test."

"Absolutely not, Aelia. You're not ready."

"That's absurd! I'll be battling Arcanum in a month. What is the difference?"

He halted midstride, and his glare turned lethal. "You will be performing a Conservatory-approved exercise against first-years from the Citadel, not this!" He threw his hands up and motioned at the chaos erupting in the sky.

A shrill cry blasted over our heads, and that now familiar pounding of air thundered from above. Reign tipped his head back and muttered another curse as he glanced through the clear dome ceiling. "For Noxus's sake, another dragon?" He squinted, his cheeks gone sallow. "And what the blazes is he doing here?"

An enormous slate dragon darted toward us, tearing through our aerial defenses. It let out a shriek and a torrent of white flames shot from its gaping maw.

"Oh, my gods," I hissed. "I thought you said there weren't any other dragons at the Citadel?"

"There weren't..." he murmured.

"Arcanum Choosing Ceremony?"

He nodded. "Must be." His gaze remained pinned to the sky, the brilliant light of day illuminating the creature's sleek scales, revealing every terrifying inch, from its crown of horns to its barbed tail.

I'd never felt a hint of fear around Sol, but this beast... Goosebumps rippled down my bare arms.

"Come on, princess, we're going. Now." Reign's hand closed around mine before he yanked me to the doorway, but my eyes never deviated from the sky. I could just barely make out the dragon's rider—a dark-haired male blanketed in shadows—before crossing the threshold.

"Wait." I dug my heels into the marble floor at the landing just before the doors leading into the hall. "I thought you said first-years didn't fight yet. If that Arcanum student was just chosen by that dragon, why is he in the battle?"

"Excellent question, princess. One I do not have the answer to; but it does not change the fact that you must get farther inside *now*."

"Fine," I gritted out and stepped through the threshold. The moment I passed, the doors slammed closed behind us, cutting off the raging sounds of the battle beyond. A dark shadow crossed over the glass dome overhead, turning my attention skyward once more. The giant dragon flew just over the academy's cupola, revealing the beast's soft underbelly.

"Is there somewhere I could at least watch?" I ticked my head to the stained glass above. "Perhaps, I could learn something."

A rueful smile flitted across Reign's mouth before it morphed into a hard line. "There's a covered balcony on the top floor. I suppose it could be safe enough."

I took off toward the floating staircase before my professor could reconsider my wellbeing—which for the life of me I still didn't understand why it mattered so. Except, perhaps, for whatever the grand prize may be for my survival.

Taking the steps two at a time, I reached the top floor only slightly winded. Apparently, my endless training sessions did account for something. Reign moved in front of me, taking the lead down the narrow corridor. I had never been to this level, my eighth-floor dormitory was the farthest up I'd dared.

At the end of the hall, a rainbow of light spilled from the stained-glass windows etched into a narrow door. Reign reached for the ornate handle and canted his head over his shoulder. "Let me go first to ensure it is clear."

My head bobbed instinctively.

A torrent of wind sent hair whipping across my face as the door swung open. Holding onto the doorframe, I stepped out onto the small balcony behind my professor. The gray dragon zipped by us, and my gaze followed Reign's skyward.

"He's nearly as large as Sol," he muttered.

"How do you know it's a he?" I followed the dragon's path across the sky, then focused on the rider. From this height, I could make out his features a bit more clearly. Like all Fae, he was gorgeous, with the same liquid midnight hair as Reign.

"Male dragons tend to be larger than females. Phantom is one of the biggest females I've ever heard of, and this one appears larger, still." Though he spoke of the animal, his gaze never deviated from the rider.

"Do you know him?"

"Hmm?" His head slowly turned toward me as if having to force his attention away from the Shadow Fae rider. An unreadable mask slipped over his handsome face.

"The rider, do you know him?"

"How would I, if he clearly seems to be a first-year?"

It never occurred to me to wonder how many friends, or at least acquaintances, Reign must have been forced to abandon when he'd been run out of Shadow Fae territory. And what of his family? Consorting with a traitor was treasonous and punishable by death. Did his family have any idea what had become of him? A pinch of pity stabbed at my heart.

"Aelia, watch out!" Reign's shout pierced my eardrum, sending all thoughts scrambling.

I dropped to the ground as a gryphon whizzed by and dark tendrils of power exploded around me. Reaching for my dagger, I clenched it tight in my fist as I pushed myself up in time to see an Arcanum student land on the edge of the balcony.

Shadows whipped around the male, a sinister glint in his eyes as he scanned Reign, then me. "Ah, the traitor..."

"Get back on your skyrider, boy, before you regret it," Reign snarled.

The Shadow Fae's powers circled his form and a pair of umbral blades coalesced in his fists. I fingered the hilt of my own dagger and slowly pulled back my arm. It was time to test my theory.

As Reign kept the male occupied, I released my dagger. I held my breath as it flew end over end in seemingly slow motion. From the corner of my eye, I could just make out Reign and the expression of horror carving into his jaw. The blade ripped right through the shadows and the student's mystical weapons disintegrated right in his hands. The male's eyes lifted to meet mine, his mouth curving into a capital O. "What in all the realms...?"

It worked!

"Damn it, Aelia," Reign hissed. His shadows shot from his fingertips and curled around the Fae, wrapping him in a cloud of pure night.

The Arcanum student released a sharp cry as the coils of darkness seeped into every orifice before dragging him off the balcony and back into the halls of the building.

"What are you doing?" I cried out as I followed behind them.

"He saw your dagger, Aelia. If we let him go now, he'll go straight to the headmaster at the Citadel and your secret will be no more."

The boy writhed on the marble floor, his dark hair and black uniform a stark contrast to the pristine white marble. Reign's shadows constricted, tightening around the male like serpents.

"So you're going to kill him?"

His hard eyes met mine. "What other choice do I have? I must protect you—your secret."

"But he's only a boy..."

"He's a second-year, Aelia, and he knew exactly what he was getting into the moment he set foot upon that balcony."

The Fae paled as the shadows laced around his throat, and he let out a strangled cry.

My hand gripped Reign's forearm, and his tense muscles twitched beneath my touch. "Please, don't do this."

His expression hardened, those bottomless pupils like obsidian stone. "I must. It's my duty to keep you safe. You are *my* acquisition, and I'd ravage this entire battalion of Shadow Fae if it meant your survival."

Of course. His precious *acquisition*. One day I'd have to ask him what he stood to win...

A shriek filled the quiet hallway, and I spun around in time to watch the life drain out of the male's eyes. His body spasmed, then went completely still.

"Why couldn't you simply change his memories like you did with Rue?" I shrieked.

"Tampering with the mind of a Shadow Fae is trickier, especially an elite student from the Citadel. There was a chance his memories would return. I couldn't risk, damn it, Aelia, not with you."

Oh, goddess. This was my fault.

My feet took off of their own accord, pushing me past the dead Fae.

"Aelia!" Reign's voice echoed across the narrow corridor, but I refused to stop.

That boy was dead because of me.

Chapter Forty

A elia

The following day continued as if nothing had happened. As if Arcanum hadn't skulked onto our campus and stolen our students' lives. No one cared that we had lost nearly a dozen Light Fae the night before, or that their bodies were already being shipped home to their families in sun-cursed blessed urns.

Heaton stood in front of our squad in the Hall of Ether, his battle wounds already on the mend thanks to our talented healer. Only two of his classmates had been killed, the majority of the dead having been unseasoned second- and third-years. He'd been speaking of the Ethereal Trials for a while now, but somehow, I could not seem to focus on his lengthy monologue.

"We will begin with Ethereal Light Sculpting, as it is one of the easier trials. The point of the exercise is to mold and shape pure Light energy into intricate sculptures or structures, demonstrating control and creativity."

"That should be an easy one for you, Aelia." Rue nudged

me with her elbow. She sat beside me, doodling on the parchment spread across the desk. My roommate had already started studying for the Celestial Glyphs exam last night, while I'd been too consumed with guilt to do anything but wallow in the warm baths.

"Aelia?" My friend speared me with her pointy elbow again.

"Right, yes, easy."

Nothing ever seemed easy with my *rais*. One day my insides blossomed with power, and the next it was an empty void. But Heaton was correct, light manipulation should have been an easy one to begin with.

I scanned the massive auditorium in search of a certain temperamental Shadow Fae, but Reign was nowhere in sight. I convinced myself this was for the best after yesterday's outburst. I hated how cruel he could be, how easily he could take a life, even if it was to save my own.

Symon flicked Rue's braid and signaled at the parchment. "Shall we study tonight? Celestial Glyphs is one we should all pass easily, even you my little round-eared friend."

I threw him a good eyeroll, but the edges of my lips curled all the same. He was right. The written tests were the ones I'd likely excel in since they mostly only required memorization and little *rais*. I'd already mastered a few of the celestial glyphs, which imbued us with additional strength: the ability to hear at great distances, throw our voices, and other such useful abilities.

"Or are you too busy training with your gorgeous, broody professor?" Sy waggled his brows and heat ravaged my cheeks.

"Not too busy," I hissed. "And don't you mean *our* broody professor?" I couldn't very well tell them what happened with Reign and the Shadow Fae yesterday, which I hated more and more each day. I had never been good at keeping secrets, and hiding things from my only friends was painstaking.

"Let's begin," Heaton announced. "You'll have two days to prepare for this trial, then on Wednesday, you will present to Professor Gleamer. Each team will receive points for their display, which will count toward your final scores for the Ethereal Trials."

"Let's do this, ladies." Sy scooted his chair back and leapt up. Radiant light illuminated his palms, and as he twirled them around, a dazzling display lit up the back of the chamber.

"Show off," I muttered.

"Oh, come on, little Kin, show us what you can do." He threw me a playful smirk. "After all that after-hours practicing, you must have something to show for it."

Flashing my teeth, I sent my friend into a fit of hysterics. When his laughter finally fell away, I pushed myself out of my chair and drew in a deep breath. *Come on, Aelia, you can do this.* My skittish *rais* still only preferred to make an appearance when I was truly in danger—or apparently, on Shadow Fae soil. If I had any hopes of passing the trials, I needed to find another way to coax out my reluctant magic that *didn't* require Reign's assistance. I'd become entirely too dependent on my professor.

That is true. Sol's voice interrupted my internal musings.

Are you listening in on me?

Trust me, it's not on purpose. I'm still new to this body, and it will take me a while to build my mental barriers.

So you can hear everything? Oh stars, my lusty thoughts too?

Yes, those too.

A flare of embarrassment coated my cheeks, and I was certain my face radiated a rosy hue. Luckily, my friends were distracted and paid no attention to the internal conversation with my dragon.

Sol, it's complicated with Reign... Goddess, I couldn't believe I was trying to explain this thing with my professor to a dragon. It felt worse than having to admit the truth to Aidan.

I'm well aware, Aelia—likely even more so than you.

What does that mean?

I suppose you'll find out when the time is right.

Sol? Sol? The connection cut off and a snarl pursed my lips.

"Everything all right, Aelia?" Rue waved her hand about an inch from my nose.

"Yes, sorry, just checking in on Sol."

Rue's expression turned downright swoony. She was so smitten by her Pegasus it was adorable. "I chat with Windy nearly all day. The connection we share, it's just incredible."

"Griff is quite the chatterbox too," Sy added. "If he's not sleeping or hunting, he's prattling away. It's rather distracting, actually."

"At least you're lucky that your skyriders remain on campus. Sol is so big and his appetite so uncontrollable, he's forced to nest in the surrounding Alucian Mountains." It was pitiful, but I missed him. For the short week he was a dragonette, he slept at the foot of my bed.

"He's a dragon, what did you expect?" Sy shrugged as he tossed a sphere of pure light between his palms.

"Less talking, more training," Heaton called out.

Rue whirled on her brother and rolled her eyes. "We are!"

Our team leader marched toward us and I muttered a curse. I hadn't summoned an ounce of *rais* since we'd been here chatting.

Heaton's warm cobalt eyes chased to mine, and an encouraging smile curled his lips. "Let's see what you've got, Aelia."

Pressing my palms together, I visualized the goddess's power igniting and flowing through my veins. A flicker of energy sparked, and I attempted to fan the flames. The feeling sputtered, then died all together.

Curses.

Squeezing my eyes shut, I tried again, searching for that mystical power. Even beneath my closed lids, I could feel Heaton's expectant gaze. *Gods, I would never get this!* A prickle of ice skated across my nape, a chill coursing up my spine in response.

"Now that your bond has formed with Sol, you can draw upon his power when yours fails." Reign's deep tenor sailed across my eardrum. My eyes snapped open and I searched the auditorium for my professor. He emerged from the shadows in the far corner of the hall an instant later, his penetrating gaze intent on me.

"Aelia, any progress?" Heaton's question jerked my attention back to the male standing in front of me.

"Sorry, just another minute."

He nodded, a patient smile on his face, unlike the one of the Shadow Fae glaring at me from across the chamber. Closing my eyes once more, I focused on the shimmery strands linking me to Sol. I imagined drawing from that powerful force and amplifying the tiny embers buried deep in my core.

The flicker immediately burned brighter, and I summoned the energy to my palms. Opening my eyes, I released a breath of relief as a brilliant glow lit up my fingertips.

"Good, Aelia," Heaton purred. "Now let's see what you can make with it."

I started slowly, molding the luminous light into a small sphere, then a larger one. Sol's energy blossomed, filling my chest with warmth. The sphere grew, encapsulating first me, then Heaton, and extending over Rue and Symon.

"It's a radiant shield," Rue exclaimed as she poked at the shimmery edges.

"Excellent, Aelia. That's quite a shield, but I'm asking for something else. Create an object, something that can take physical form."

Right. After spending the past few months at the academy writhing with jealousy over Reign's umbral blades, the idea came easily. Moving my palms, I twisted the light until it formed the shape of a weapon.

Symon let out a low whistle. "Aelia and her daggers..." He chuckled.

Daggers... plural. A faint memory niggled at the back of my mind. I hazarded a glance at the dagger strapped to my waistband and something felt wrong. Only one? And this wasn't the first time something felt off.

"Nicely done!" Heaton clapped, jerking my attention back to the ethereal dagger I held between my palms. "Now, let's see if it will hold." He motioned to the alabaster column behind Rue.

Focusing on the weapon hovering over my palm, I wrapped my fingers around the ghostly hilt and felt substance beneath my skin.

"Now throw it."

Excitement thrummed through my veins as I pulled my arm back and released. The glowing dagger flew end over end and plunged into the column with a satisfying *thwack*.

Rue spun at me with a beaming smile. "You did it!"

"Looks like all that extra practice with Professor Reign is paying off." Sy's light eyes sparkled with mischief.

As if Symon's words had summoned him, or he was using his shadows to eavesdrop on the conversation, Reign stalked up to our semi-circle. His eyes chased to the glowing dagger hanging from the alabaster. "Well done," he murmured.

I dipped my head, my cheeks heating for some unknown reason. Maybe because his praises were so infrequent—or worse, because his mere proximity had me flustered. "Thank—" I snapped my mouth shut before the whole forbidden phrase was out. "The last-minute tip was... helpful," I murmured instead.

"That's what I'm here for."

"Well, whatever you are doing with Aelia, keep it up, professor." Heaton patted Reign on the shoulder and the Shadow Fae stiffened, his entire body going as taut as a bow. His shadows vibrated around him, that aura darkening, and I wondered if anyone else was as attuned to his sudden change of mood.

"And you, Aelia, keep practicing." Heaton rewarded me with a warm smile. "If you continue in this direction, you'll pass the first trial with flying colors."

"And then the next and the next!" Rue added.

"Then we'll finally get to celebrate the Winter Solstice once the dreaded trials are complete."

"Winter Solstice?" My thoughts flew back in time to my arrival at the academy. Reign had mentioned it would be at the end of the term. I'd nearly forgotten all about it.

"It's a huge celebration," Rue replied. "It's part of our Fae ancient traditions, marking the longest night and the rebirth of light. It is a time when we honor the cyclical nature of life, death, and rebirth, acknowledging the darkness but celebrating the return of the light. There will be music and dancing, and so much food and wine you'll explode!"

"Sounds lovely."

Reign smirked, his dark eyes flashing.

"It typically occurs right after the Ethereal Trials and before the final battle with Arcanum," said Heaton.

That didn't make sense. "Why not celebrate at the end?"

Heaton's easy smile fell away, and his gaze swiveled to meet Reign's dark one.

"Because not many survive to the end."

Chapter Forty-One

R *eign*

Well done, princess. A smile threatened across my lips as Aelia dazzled Professor Gleamer with her luminous daggers, which proved not only mesmerizing but also lethal. She'd managed to impale an iguanid with the ethereal blade and received a round of applause from the old Fae. One trial down, five more to go.

Ethereal Light Sculpting would be the easiest, by far.

The Shadows Whisper, which would take place in the Court of Umbral Shadows, had become my biggest concern. Not only was her safety an issue, but I feared I'd have to take out her entire class of first-years if anyone caught sight of her dagger's power. Knowing Aelia, forbidding her to use it would only strengthen her resolve.

My thoughts flew to the matching dagger I kept hidden in my chamber, the one I'd wiped her memory clean of. As far as Aelia knew, Aidan had only gifted her one dagger all those years ago. I'd waffled for days about the second... If *he* knew I was in possession of such a weapon and had kept it a secret—

I squeezed my eyes closed, refusing to visualize the consequences of my betrayal. As it was, I feared for Gideon. Had I known the secret those daggers held, I never would have entangled my friend in the matter.

Forcing my weary lids open, the glint of the silver bangle on my wrist caught my eye. It was a damned shame Aelia's dagger had no effect on these cursed manacles. It was the first thing I'd tried when I had the mystical blade to myself.

And now there was another dragon, with not just any rider aboard. Dragging my hands across my face, I heaved out a sigh. Perhaps I should send word... The moment he sees Aelia on Solanthus he will undoubtedly set his sights on her. When had my life become this tangled web of deceit? Why had I ever agreed to any of it?

Because you had no choice. Phantom's feminine voice streaked across the tangle of thoughts. Even in hiding across the river, she often wiggled her way into my mind. Most often when I needed her most.

What would you know?

More than you think, my friend. Fate is the unseen current that pulls us inexorably forward, guiding our steps and shaping our paths, even when we believe we're the ones holding the map.

So you are saying that no matter what I do, we are all doomed?

That, I cannot answer, Reign. I only know that your fate is written in the stars and that destiny is often the path we discover in a vain attempt to avoid the inescapable.

You're remarkably sullen, yet poetic today.

I've heard of the new dragon hatchlings, and it pains me not to meet hi—them.

The sorrow in her tone reached all the way to my depths, wringing and twisting my insides. I wished Phantom could be free, but I simply couldn't risk it yet. Given the strength of our bond, she'd inevitably come to my rescue and the truth would emerge.

One day, Phantom, I promise. She and Solanthus would make quite a pair, indeed. I wondered of the disposition of the slate dragon. Given that of his rider, he'd surely be a handful. And Aelia would be his first target when he set his sights on her dragon at the term-end battle.

"Well, are you going to congratulate me or just stand there staring?" Aelia's voice snapped me free of my somber thoughts. She appeared before me, her bright silvery blue eyes radiating light and a sparkle of mirth as she regarded me expectantly.

"Well done, princess," I whispered, that elusive smile only she could conjure spreading my lips. "But don't get too cocky, you still have five more trials to pass."

"Professor, even your dark mood couldn't dampen my spirits today."

"I'm glad to hear it."

Rue and Symon rallied around their friend, each taking an arm. "Come on, Aelia, we're going to celebrate," the female cried.

"Celebrate?" I quirked a brow.

"All of Flare team passed, so Heaton has granted us a day off tomorrow," Rue explained.

"Isn't that generous of him?" I couldn't disguise the hint of annoyance in my tone. He was much too lenient on his squad, and they'd ultimately pay the price.

"Aelia doesn't have to train this evening, does she?" The Lightspire male ticked his chin at me.

"Oh, please, let her have the night off, professor." Rue pressed her palms together, pleading. "She'll be back to work the following day."

My gaze chased to Aelia's, whose expression remained neutral. Did she truly wish to drink herself into a daze with her classmates? Perhaps it would be for the best for us to take a night off. I could sneak across the river and attempt to discover more about Aelia's dagger.

That Symon male pulled his arm from hers and laced it around her shoulders, brushing his finger over the rounded tip of Aelia's ear, earning him a squeal. My blood boiled. I fisted my fingers at my sides as my shadows rioted in a furious windstorm. Fuck, just the idea of one of those Light Fae males' hands on her had my murderous tendencies rushing to the surface, let alone being forced to witness it.

"Reign?" Aelia squirmed free of Symon's hold and stepped toward me. My shadows encircled her, weaving and twisting until they blanketed us both in eternal night. I drew in a sigh as the peaceful darkness swirled around us. Noxus, I missed the night. "Reign?" Her eyes darted up to mine.

Calling back my shadows, the dark tendrils released her, and I knotted my arms across my chest. "Yes, I'm fine, Aelia. Take the night off; I need a break as well."

A hint of disappointment clouded her eyes before she spun around to join her friends. I couldn't keep my traitorous gaze from trailing behind her, long after she'd disappeared from the hall.

"Damn it, Reign. You must move more quickly." The headmaster glared up at me from his desk. "I thought your freedom meant something to you."

Grinding my teeth, I searched for a calm I did not possess. Having to deal with this sniveling fool was grating on my last nerve. "It does," I gritted out. "I've already told you, Aelia's latent abilities are a complicated case." Not to mention those daggers.

"You spend practically every moment glued to the female. How have you not been able to determine the source of her powers?"

"There's something blocking her," I blurted. If I kept this up, pretending I'd learned nothing, he'd truly believe me an incompetent idiot and send me packing.

His pale mossy eyes widened. "A spell?"

"That would be my guess."

"Hmm." He drummed his fingers along the desk as he stroked his silver beard with his free hand. "Then I'll summon a spellbinder from the neighboring kingdom of Mysthallia. Surely, someone should be able to unravel the incantation."

"Possibly..."

His wild, light brows knitted. "What is the problem with that?"

I can't have you finding out the truth before I do. "It would alert others and call unwanted attention upon our court."

"That is a weak excuse, even for you, Darkthorn." He slowly rose from behind the desk, those watery eyes following every twitch of my hand. "Please don't tell me there are other reasons for your reluctance, professor?"

"Of course not," I ground out.

Draven crept closer, and a whisper of *rais* lit up his palms. "It would be entirely unseemly for an instructor of this esteemed Conservatory to engage in improper behavior with a student."

"I assure you it is not that," I growled. "I care nothing for the girl."

"I should hope not, otherwise your tenure at the academy would quickly come to an end, forcing you out into the Wilds to live out the rest of your banishment."

It took every ounce of restraint to slide my lips into a smile. "I would never dream of it." Threads of darkness coiled around my fingertips, eager to strike down this insufferable male. I shoved my hands into my pockets and took a step back.

"Good."

I turned toward the door, my mounting fury inciting my *nox* into a frenzy.

"One more thing, professor." He hissed my title like an insult. "I did not appreciate being caught unaware in front of the king about your dragon."

Curses. I'd been waiting for him to bring her up for days. I was surprised the old bastard postponed the discussion for this long. "There was no reason to bring her up. Once the mark of the banished was carved into my flesh, our bond was severed." I spun around, eyes narrowed. "As you can imagine, it is not something I prefer to speak about."

He dipped his head, almost reverently. "That is understandable. And you have no idea where the dragon is now?"

"I do not."

"That's a shame. I was so thrilled when our little Kin was chosen by a dragon, but every bit of excitement was drained when I set my eyes on the beast across the river."

"It's almost as if the gods were urging us to play fair. With each academy in possession of a dragon, the end of the term battle should find us on equal footing."

The headmaster grunted. "I wish to annihilate Malakar and his precious Citadel."

A chill surged up my spine at the mention of Arcanum's unhinged headmaster. I'd suffered under his tutelage for four long years. I'd never forget his words the day I enrolled. *At Arcanum Citadel, we achieve strength from darkness and power through pain. Those who survive the first year, I pity you. For at least the slaughtered will dwell peacefully in the arms of Noxus, while the rest of you will now have your souls forged in hell fire.*

"As do I." Without another word, I marched out of the headmaster's office, shrouded in a tempest of shadows.

Chapter Forty-Two

A *elia*

In the dim confines of Heaton's sprawling dormitory, my body moved to the blaring music, unencumbered by the restrictive battle leathers I typically wore. For the first time in forever, I felt free. Dark curtains had been hung across the windows, shielding us from the intrusive light and creating a mysterious, shadowy ambiance. The voluminous skirts of my gilded satin gown drifted on the invisible breeze created by my fluid movements. Rue laughed as I attempted a rather intricate spin on a pair of high heels I'd unearthed from my closet. My entire ensemble for the evening was discovered in the depths of my armoire. I'd had no previous use for the elegant attire, but Rue had insisted today was the day. We were to celebrate our victory after all.

All of Flare Squad was in attendance, including a rather sullen Belmore and Ariadne, along with a mix of other first-years. Belmore had made it clear from the moment I arrived that he had expected me to fail our first trial. Thankfully, I'd proven him wrong. The rest of the team danced around the room, most friendly enough. A blonde standing beside Ariadne glared in my direction. She looked vaguely familiar, but I couldn't quite place her. And with the goblet of honeyed wine in my hand and the thrumming beats of the music, I couldn't care less about anyone else.

Symon danced toward us and curled an arm around my shoulders. Another Fae male followed him over. I recognized the blonde from Burn Squad from hours on the training field together, but I couldn't quite conjure his name. He immediately darted between Rue and I and began to dance with my friend.

Sy shot me a conspiratorial wink. "Devin has had his eye on your roommate since the beginning of the term."

"Oh really?"

He nodded. "Along with at least a dozen other males."

I laughed. He was not mistaken there. My roommate attracted the opposite sex like Fae to honeyed wine. I'd spent more than one night alone in our chamber while Rue released some built-up tension with males of other squadrons, as she so colorfully described it.

"How about you, Miss Aelia? Is there anyone here at the Conservatory that sends your gentle heart aflutter?"

Heat swam up my neck, settling across my cheeks. Nestled within the shadowed, dim room, only one male came to mind. The one in which I was trying my damnedest not to think about. "No one yet."

"We will have to change that tonight. Surely, there must be someone you find at least moderately appealing." He waggled his light brows.

"Only you, my friend, but I would never hazard our friendship for one night of reckless abandon."

Symon mimed a stab in the heart and buckled over dramatically. "Oh, you wound me so."

Threading my arms around the back of his neck, I pulled him into the middle of the dancefloor where we found Rue and Devin. We danced and laughed, the hours passing by in a blur.

With my friends still ravaging the dancefloor, I crept away in search of something to slake the dryness in my throat. A table was set up along the back wall, filled with bottles of unfamiliar liquids. There was one I recognized. Reaching for the honeyed wine, I poured another goblet full.

This one would be my last for the evening. I'd slowly built up my tolerance with an occasional sip here and there at dinner over the last several months. Slowly sipping the sweet liqueur, I remembered the vow I made to have fun tonight—within reason, of course. It was the first night in which I didn't have class or private training the following morning since we'd arrived at the Conservatory.

As I caught my breath, a pair of pale blue eyes locked on mine from across the room. The female whispered to Ariadne then her gaze darted from me to Heaton, who stood in a corner opposite me. *Oriah*! That was her name. She was the girl who'd made a scene in a fit of jealousy at Heaton's last party.

Sy appeared beside me, tearing my thoughts from the envious female. Sweat glistened on his brow as he eyed the gilded goblet. "Take it easy, my little round-eared friend."

"It's only my second glass, and I feel completely fine."

"Good, then come back to the dancefloor!" Stealing my goblet, he placed it back onto the table and dragged me into the crowd.

Heaton had joined the circle of Flare team initiates, and a warm smile parted his lips as he took me in. "You look lovely out of those leathers, Aelia."

"Good one, Heat." Rue released a cackle and her brother's eyes widened as he snapped his jaw closed, crimson coating his clean-shaven cheeks.

"That wasn't what I meant— I'm sorry that came out completely inappropriately."

I waved a dismissive hand and returned the smile. "I understood what you meant. And cheers, it is nice to wear a dress for a change."

He offered his hand when the music morphed from chaotic beats to a slow tune. I placed my palm in his and attempted a curtsy as his head dipped. His warm hand moved to my lower back and pulled me flush against his tall form. Brilliant cobalt eyes lowered to mine. "I'm so proud of how far you've come this year, Aelia. You're truly a spectacle to watch."

A whisper of embarrassment thrummed in my chest. "Thank you." Curses! I snapped my jaw shut before deciding to indulge in the compliment. Heaton deserved it, after all. "You've been an incredible team leader, and I never could have made it this far without your guidance and kind approach. Sometimes I forget you're one of them..."

He chuckled. "I try not to be." The smile on his lips slowly fell away, and he heaved out a sigh. "But Professor Reign is right, I need to be tougher on all of you if you are to succeed. So I'd like to apologize in advance for the weeks to come."

"That sounds ominous."

"Hopefully, it won't be. Darkthorn has done wonders working with you."

"Umhmm." I dropped my gaze to the smattering of skin revealed beneath his dress shirt and the Light Fae mark engraved on his flesh. My fingers instinctively flew to my mark and its strange appearance. "I'd really prefer not to talk about the professor this evening, or really anything having to do with the academy to be quite honest."

"Fine by me." His smile widened, and I leaned my head on his broad shoulder as we swayed to the music.

When the song ended, Heaton's hand remained locked around mine. "Shall we have a break for a drink?"

I nodded. I was completely parched after all the singing and dancing. Heaton escorted me to the table where I'd left my goblet. After topping off my glass, he poured himself a generous swig of laegar.

"So the laegar doesn't affect you?" I asked as he took a big gulp of the potent draught, and I followed his lead.

"Not after three and a half years at the Conservatory." He smirked. "Sometimes it's the only thing that will get you through the night." The mirth vanished as quickly as it had come, replaced by a well of darkness.

"Is it that bad?" And I thought the first year would be the worst. I swallowed down another sip of the wine and the sweet taste lingered on my tongue. For some reason, it seemed even more saccharine than I remembered.

"The first year at the Conservatory, when the lives of your teammates are taken, you lose strangers. In the following years, you lose friends. It becomes difficult to bear the pain, so it's simpler to close off your emotions to all of it. But without the highs and lows, are you truly living?"

There was something about the anguish in his expression that compelled my feet forward. Before I could think better of it, my lips brushed his. It was only meant to be a comforting kiss, a token of my understanding of his pain, but the moment I pulled away, I regretted it. Because the fire in his eyes spoke of a desire I'd refused to accept.

"Heaton, I—"

Before I could get another word out, his mouth captured mine, his tongue parting my lips. The haze of the wine blurred my thoughts and slowed my reactions. It wasn't until his hand cradled my nape that I snapped out of the wine-fueled fog and pulled free of his hold.

"Heaton, I'm sorry, but I can't..."

The deep blue of his luminous orbs dimmed and disappointment darkened his features.

"I'm sorry, I just don't think it's a good idea. You are my team leader, and my best friend's brother."

He ran his hand over his mouth, as if wiping away the kiss,

and cleared his throat. "You are right. I apologize. I shouldn't have done that."

I threw my thumb over my shoulder in the direction of the door as my head began to spin. "I'm going to go…"

I thanked all the gods that he didn't offer to escort me this time. And still, a tiny, stupid part of me was disappointed. Did he not care enough to ensure I got back to my room safely because I rejected his advances, or did he merely trust in my own capabilities now?

I stepped out into the hall, dismissing the ridiculous thoughts, and my head began to spin faster. What in all the realms? Reaching for the alabaster walls, I leaned against the cool stone as I staggered forward.

"There she is," a female voice hissed.

I spun around and regretted it instantly as the hall turned topsy-turvy. I keeled over, my knees hitting the marble floor with a crash. Blinking quickly to focus my hazy vision, two females stalked toward me.

Oriah and Ariadne.

"What did you do to me?" I snarled, my head spinning so fast I could barely see straight.

Oriah loomed closer, a sinister smile stretched across her flustered face. "Just a little misthorn root. The Shadow Fae blossom will have you vomiting for days. Long enough for you to reconsider this flirtation with *my* Heaton."

"I don't want Heaton," I slurred.

"That's not how it appeared when you kissed him."

Oh, stars, why did I ever do that?

"I'm not interested in him like that, I swear." I attempted to stand, but the hallway spun on its axis, and I remained on all fours.

"Good," she barked before twirling around with Ariadne and marching back to the party.

There was no way I'd make it back to my dorm in this condition. "Please, can you get someone to help me?" My hand shot out, and a burst of white light exploded from my palm.

Oriah and Ariadne gasped as the bolt zipped over their heads. With my vision swimming, I wasn't entirely sure I could trust what I saw.

"The Kin has mastered photokinesis?" Oriah squealed.

"Not possible." Ariadne eyed me warily as I stared at my palms as if they belonged to a stranger. "How did you learn to do that?"

I hadn't... Not really. But I would certainly not admit that to these two.

"You know nothing about me, Ariadne. Maybe if you weren't so terrible to me all the time, I'd share some of my secrets."

The Light Fae scoffed. "Good luck with those secrets and finding the way back to your dormitory." She laced her arm through her friend's and disappeared down the hallway. I considered throwing another burst of *rais*, but with my vision so obscured, I didn't want to risk severely hurting one of them.

Muttering a string of curses, I flopped down on my behind and leaned against the wall. Closing my eyes, I attempted to clear my vision, but it was no use. I'd have to crawl back to my dormitory.

Chapter Forty-Three

A elia

Oh, gods no, anyone but him.

An entourage of shadows slipped up the floating staircase an instant before their dark master appeared. I paused on the step, my hands on the one below while my behind remained on an upper level, sticking up in an absolutely mortifying position.

Our eyes locked, and Reign's dark chuckle sent fire raging from the depths of my belly and across my cheeks. "What in the name of Noxus are you doing, princess?"

"Oh, you know, I thought what better way to end a perfect night than to crawl down a staircase?"

He crept closer, then crouched on a step a few down from mine. His shadows curled around me, welcoming me into their icy embrace. One slipped beneath my arm, forcing a giggle. My palm slid off the step, and I hurtled down the slippery slope, straight for Reign.

I crashed into his unyielding form, sending us both

airborne. His arms wrapped around my body, then his shadows bolstered the protective shield of his muscled torso as we rolled and rolled, seemingly forever. One of those wraith-like tendrils shot out and snaked around the banister, finally hauling us to a stop.

Oh, Raysa, help me. As if my head hadn't been spinning enough before. Pushing free of Reign's embrace, I crawled to the edge of the step and spewed the lingering contents of my stomach across the glass stairway.

"I've got you, princess." Reign's arm curled around my waist as he gathered my wild locks with his free hand.

My stomach heaved again, and embarrassment burned every inch of my skin. When nothing else remained, Reign pulled me up into his lap. I lay my head back and nestled it perfectly in the crook of his shoulder. It was as if that soft space on his flawlessly muscled form was made just for me.

"Gods, I'm so embarrassed," I muttered weakly.

"Don't be."

I could have sworn I caught a faint smile on his perfect lips, but I could have imagined it, as I was fairly certain I was now seeing double. Mmm, two Reigns... Now that almost made this all worth it.

"How much did you drink at that party?"

"Only two glasses. It wasn't my fault. Oriah poisoned my wine with misthorn root because I kiss—" I snapped my jaw shut before my loose lips got me into more trouble.

Reign's entire body tensed around me and his shadows began to vibrate. The rage was so palpable it was suffocating. His aura flashed a bottomless onyx and his fingers tightened at my hip. I hadn't even realized they were there until his grip grew punishing.

"You kissed Heaton?" he growled.

For Fae's sake, how did he guess it was him?

I tried to turn in his arms, to see his expression more fully, but he kept his eyes fixed straight ahead. That icy mask crawled across his countenance, and gods, I wanted to smack myself for being so stupid. "It didn't mean anything—"

"It always means something, Aelia," he gritted out, the tenor of his voice flat and completely devoid of emotion.

"So what if it had meant something?" A sudden burst of irritation eclipsed the embarrassment. Reign and I had been tiptoeing around this thing between us all term, and I was simply exhausted. "*You* rejected me. You made it perfectly clear nothing could happen between us, so you expect me to stay away from every other male?"

"Yes," he ground out.

I spun around in his lap to face him, despite the fierce whirl that scrambled my mind at the movement. "That's not fair. You are the most exasperating male I have ever met. You tell me we cannot be together and then you say something like that?"

A hard line slashed across his lips, his midnight eyes flashing. "Fate may deny me the right to possess you now, but make no mistake, Aelia—you belong to me. And I will be damned if I let another male lay claim to what is mine."

All the air evacuated my lungs in a move so swift it felt as if my entire chest would cave in. "How... how can you say things like that?"

"Because I am exhausted of fighting this, and even the fetters of my restraint have their limits."

Those endlessly profound, inky pools of darkness latched onto mine, and the tempest of emotions that lingered beneath the surface pulsed between us like a living, breathing thing. Shadows curled around my neck, then danced across my lips, the faint caress more powerful than any male's touch.

"Let's go to my room." My voice was rough and breathless. I barely recognized it as my own.

Reign slowly shook his head, his lower lip caught between his teeth. "We can't..."

"Why?"

"Because you will hate me after."

"I won't," I blurted. Stars, I sounded desperate. Not to mention the fact that I had just vomited and was in terrible need of a shower.

A vein pulsed across Reign's forehead, and I could practically see the internal torment carved into his brow. Gods, he wanted this as much as I did. How was that possible? The realization had me giddy, my breaths coming in haggard pants as my heart danced out a happy jig.

I thought I'd felt something before, but this... I'd never had this confirmation. "Please, Reign..." I whispered.

His head slowly dipped, the move nearly imperceptible, as if his internal struggle had reached some sort of climax. He cradled me against his firm chest and lifted me up as he stood. His eager footfalls cracked across the glass steps as he ascended the staircase. Wait a minute... Ascended?

As if he'd read my flustered thoughts, a grin slowly spread across his lips.

"I was going the wrong way, wasn't I?"

"Yes, princess. Your dormitory is on the eighth floor, so you needed to go up the stairs, not down."

I wanted to cry. Then again, if I'd gone in the correct direction to begin with, maybe I never would have encountered Reign. Fate was a fickle beast.

Reign's pervasive shadows morphed into massive wings and we soared up the remaining levels, then across the hallway of the eighth floor, the walls blurring around us. My stomach somersaulted at each thrust of his wings.

When we finally reached my door, Reign jerked to a halt and again my stomach lurched. He waved his hand over the protective rune and the lock clicked. That's right, the bastard had given himself personal access to my dorm from the moment I'd arrived. He whipped the door open, we pitched forward, and my hold over my delicate insides crumbled.

Oh, no, please not again.

As we crossed the threshold, another wave of nausea hit,

and I barely wriggled free of Reign's hold in time to race to the water closet.

A persistent thrumming across my temples forced my weary lids open. Glancing around the room, the familiar canopy of vines coalesced over my bed. I swallowed the dryness from my throat as memories of the night before flashed across my hazy vision.

Oh, goddess, Reign.

"Good morning, princess." The rough edge to his tone had my entire body snapping to attention, and all grogginess instantly vanished.

Rolling over, I dragged my hand through my knot of disheveled hair before facing him. Reign was sprawled out on the chair beside my bed, his massive form dwarfing the tiny seat. Had he really spent the entire night here?

I hazarded a quick peek over my shoulder at Rue's bed, which remained untouched from the night before. I hoped she'd had a fun night out with Sy's friend from Burn team.

"How do you feel?" Reign's question interrupted my wandering thoughts.

"Pretty awful," I murmured, pressing my fingers to my temples.

"You managed to rest peacefully through the night, so I'd venture to say the worst is over. The effects of misthorn root can last for days, but it seems to have already burned right out of your system."

I nodded slowly, afraid to aggravate my precarious state.

"They must not have doused your drink with much of it, or—"

"Let me guess, you have another theory to test?"

A smirk flashed across his scruffy jaw, and I was instantly transported to the night before, to the warmth of his body, the fierce desire in his eyes. He had finally given in. If it weren't for my stomach's upheaval, who knew what would have happened between us? "I always have theories where you're concerned, princess."

"Theories, but nothing in practice."

"No, I'm afraid not."

And just like that, I knew the moment was gone. Last night had been a fluke, a flash of weakness between us both that we dared not repeat.

"Well, if you are quite all right, I must prepare for my classes. Not all of us have the day off." He slowly stood, and perhaps I'd imagined it, but I could have sworn he was reluctant to leave.

I'd nearly forgotten the day off was only for Flare Squad. Reign had a whole slew of other students to attend to.

He ticked his head at the pale wooden table beside my bed. "I left you a glass of water and some biscuits. If you manage to hold that down, you can try for something of more substance in the next hour or so."

"Tha—" I cut myself off before finishing the words. "You know..."

His head dipped sharply before he marched to the door. Every nerve in my being screamed at me to stop him, to beg him to stay and force the truth of his feelings out. His confession played through my mind on repeat. *Fate may deny me the right to possess you now, but make no mistake, Aelia—you belong to me. And I will be damned if I let another male lay claim to what is mine.*

What in the stars did that mean?

"Reign," I blurted as he stood just inside the threshold, lingering.

He spun around, and those midnight orbs chased to mine.

With the intensity of their gaze, I floundered for a long moment before I steeled my nerves. "Do you think things could be different between us one day?"

"Only the gods know, Aelia." A rueful smile parted his lips before he whirled out, slamming the door behind him.

Hot tears burned my eyes, a mix of exhaustion and frustration forcing them to the surface. Why did it always end up the same with us? Pulling the covers back over my head, I curled into the silky sheets. At least I could spend the entire day wallowing in self-pity in the comfort of my bed.

Or perhaps, I shouldn't waste the opportunity to test some of own theories. Pushing myself up, I reached for the dagger I kept tucked away in my nightstand. The cool metal hilt brushed my palm and I ran my finger across the crystal embedded in the intricate design. A swirl of light followed the movement of my fingertip.

Again, my thoughts flickered to the night before, to the blast of energy that had nearly taken Ariadne and Oriah's heads off. How in Fae's sake had I managed that? I wanted nothing more than to ask Reign, but putting some distance between us would be the wise thing to do. At least for the day, anyway. Before I knew it, we'd be whisked off to the Shadow Fae lands for the Shadows Whisper trial—

Wait a second! The Shadow Fae bloom... its poison had been ravaging my system when I'd managed that burst of *rais*. What if Reign's theory was right? Whatever was blocking my powers was dampened by the misthorn root and allowed my *rais* to erupt.

This was good... very good. I simply had to find a way to diminish the effects of the block without poisoning myself every time. This was how I'd pass the trials.

Tossing back the coverlet, I slid to the edge of the mattress, ignoring the persistent pounding in my temples. Perhaps, I'd have to make a quick stop at the healer first.

The door swung open and my roommate bounded inside, a beaming smile plastered on her face.

"Well, it appears someone had a good night." I tossed her a wink as I pushed myself out of bed.

"I did," she crooned before flinging herself onto my mattress with a dramatic sigh. "Devin is just so swoony." I laughed, the sound vibrating through my skull and only intensifying the shooting pain. I must have winced because Rue's giddy expression soured. "Are you okay? What happened to you last night? Heaton said you left early."

I nodded, gnawing on my lower lip. I had no idea how my friend would react to news of the kiss. I hated the idea of jeopardizing our friendship, but I also preferred for her to hear the truth from me.

"You didn't hear anything?"

She shook her head. "Heaton was oddly tight-lipped about the whole thing."

I groaned and flopped back down on the mattress beside her. "I did something really stupid, Rue. I honestly don't know what I was thinking. He just looked so sad, and I kissed him—"

"You kissed Heaton?" she squealed.

"It was just a peck... or at least, it was supposed to be. I didn't realize he liked me that way, and then Oriah must have seen..."

"Oh, goddess."

"She and Ariadne poisoned my wine, and I ended up on the floor crawling back to our room—"

"Oh, Aelia! Why didn't you come get me?" She wrapped her slender arm around my shoulder and pulled me into her side. "That sounds awful."

I debated telling her about Reign coming to my rescue but decided to leave that part out for now. Everything between us seemed like one enormous secret and if I let out even the smallest detail, the dam would erupt.

"I couldn't very well crawl back into the party. That would have absolutely made Oriah's night."

"And Belmore's." A giggle burst through my friend's lips before she could smother it.

"I suppose it was pretty funny now that I look back on it." At the time, I was completely mortified.

"How are you feeling now?"

"Better, but I could use a draught for my headache."

She sprang from the bed and darted toward the door before I'd gotten the entire sentence out. "I will run to the healer to get it for you. I'm so sorry I wasn't there for you last night, Aelia. But once you're feeling better, we can spend all day locked up in our chambers eating bon bons, and I'll regale you with my sexploits with Devin."

I nearly choked on a laugh as my friend twirled around in a happy circle. "That sounds absolutely perfect."

Chapter Forty-Four

A elia

I stood at the precipice of destiny, my entire life seemingly leading up to this one moment. Which was completely insane. It was only the second Ethereal Trial, and yet, it felt like so much more. The training field sprawled before me, morphed into a brilliant display of light and shadows. Our task today was simple: to navigate through a labyrinth that constantly shifted between solid and ethereal states using light and shadow manipulation.

Drawing in a deep breath, I attempted to still the wild thrashing of my heart. For the past several days, I'd been ingesting small amounts of misthorn root in a, perhaps, foolish attempt to dampen the spell holding my *rais* hostage. The side effect had been unpleasant, but now four days later, I managed to function without spewing the contents of my stomach on a daily basis. And my reluctant *rais* was blooming.

Now, I only hoped it would be enough to get me through this maze.

Are you ready, Aelia? Sol's voice soared across my subconscious an instant before the flap of his mighty wings whooshed overhead.

I suppose I must be, right?

You are more than equipped to handle this trial, little Kin.

If you say so.

Just remember the true peril is not from the maze itself, but rather from its other navigators.

Right. Because today, one member from each of the eight teams would run the labyrinth at the same time. The first one out would receive a generous bonus to their score, while the last one would be disqualified and sent home.

"First-years, are you ready?" Headmaster Draven's voice boomed across the field. He stood at the top step of the Hall of Glory with our professors surrounding him. I couldn't keep my treacherous gaze from scanning through the rainbow of robes for a certain Shadow Fae professor. With the exception of class, he'd kept his distance as of late, which I'd convinced myself was a good thing. I needed the extra time to train with Sol anyway. Flying with my dragon had become my new favorite pastime.

Draven pointed to the azure sky above and traced the air with his fingertip. A gilded sundial appeared, the light illuminating half of the circle. "Initiates, you will have thirty minutes to complete the trial or forfeit your spot at the Conservatory."

Rue appeared beside me and tugged me into her arms. "Good luck, today, Aelia. I know you can do this!"

"Thank you," I murmured softly, hoping none of the other Fae would hear.

She darted off as quickly as she appeared, vanishing into the crowd of students gathered to watch the show. All eight of us were lined up now, each to enter the labyrinth at a different point. With how quickly the walls moved, I wouldn't be surprised if we all ended up in the same spot once we'd entered.

As we were each from different teams, the rule of conduct did not apply. We were free to best each other by any means possible.

I glanced across the line and met a familiar pair of light blue eyes and short, blonde hair. Lucian. My fingers instinctively dropped to my dagger, brushing the metal hilt. I hadn't seen the Fae male who had attacked me this close up for months now. Every time we were in proximity of each other, he seemed to disappear. Today, that wouldn't be possible.

His lip curled into a sneer, eyes narrowing as he regarded me. I had a feeling that whatever, or whomever, was keeping him away from me no longer mattered today.

"Initiates, the time starts now. May Raysa be with you!" A horn erupted following the headmaster's words and the scene blurred before my eyes.

Forcing my feet forward, I crossed the labyrinth's threshold and a wave of power skimmed across my skin. The marvel of magical architecture pulsed with life, the ethereal walls crafted from *rais* and *nox* transitioning from solid forms to mere wisps of mist.

I took one step, then another, the walls slipping away as fast as I blinked. The path underfoot glowed faintly, lit by an internal luminescence that pulsed in rhythm with my heartbeat. How in Noxus's name was I expected to navigate this thing?

A murky cloud of shadows loomed ahead and the hair on my nape bristled. I slowed, gingerly maneuvering around the corner.

"Out of my way, Kin!" A female with plaited silver hair barreled past me, knocking me to the ground. An instant after she disappeared into the whispering shadows, a scream erupted. My heart lurched up my throat, but I crept closer all the same, keeping my back pinned against the wall of light. As I loomed closer, a pit appeared, concealed by shadows. "Hello?" I shouted into the void. "Are you okay?"

No answer.

Calling on my *rais*, I summoned a flicker of light in my palm, then dropped it down the bottomless hollow. I followed it down, deeper and deeper, until the flame was swallowed up by the darkness. The girl was gone.

An unexpected pang seared my chest, but I shoved it down and forced my legs to keep moving. If I didn't want to suffer a similar fate, I must find the end of this moon-cursed maze.

The thick scent of magic permeated the space, calling to my own unenthusiastic abilities, as I followed the gilded path. Thanking all the gods I'd seen the Fae female fall, I avoided the shadows when they appeared, trailing only the light. Bright bursts of light solidified paths, locking them in place, while deep shadows caused the walls to dissolve, opening new routes or closing old ones with a whispering hiss.

I wandered through the meandering shadows and glittering light for what felt like hours, but when I hazarded a glance at the sundial overhead, only a quarter of an hour had passed. Stars, there wasn't much time left and I was no closer to discovering the end of this maze than the true cause of my finicky *rais*.

Turning a corner, I hit a solid wall of alabaster and muttered a string of curses. Muffled voices seeped from the other side, one I clearly recognized because it starred in my nightmares for weeks after Lucian and Kian's attack.

"Forget the Kin," a male voice hissed. "Let's get out of here. You already saw what happened to Rutelia."

A prickle of goosebumps cascaded across my flesh, and suddenly, I was extremely thankful for the solid wall between us.

"She was weak and compulsive, and I am neither. I'll find the Kin and still make it out in time. If you doubt your own prowess, then go."

"I hope to see you in the winner's circle, Lucian."

"Coward," he muttered.

I refused to linger to overhear more. I needed to find a way out of here before I crossed paths with Lucian. Doubling back,

I hit yet another immoveable wall. "For Fae's sake," I hissed. A sliver of shadows coalesced from the ether and unease slithered through my insides. Spinning around, I darted down another path.

The shadows followed, a familiar presence pushing against my own powers. I stopped midstride and whirled around, fully expecting to find my moody professor lurking in the hazy mist. But only his dark minions remained. They slithered closer, and this time I didn't run.

A tendril of night slipped around my neck and another wave of goosebumps rippled across my flesh. "Use your *rais* to slip through the walls, princess. You're wasting precious time." Reign's rushed whisper brushed across the shell of my ear.

"Where are you?" I hissed.

"Not inside the maze, if that is what you are thinking. That violation would be a grave one, and I would be a fool to risk it. Now stop the chatter and do as I say."

The shadow glided down my arm then hovered in the air expectantly.

"Okay, okay, I'll try." *Wonderful, now I'm speaking to a shadow.*

Spinning back in the direction of the wall where I'd overheard Lucian and the other Fae male, I raced across the golden path. The immense barrier of pure, immoveable alabaster stone towered over me. Reign's shadow henchmen followed, zipping up and down the wall beckoning me closer. Couldn't they just shadowtravel me to the end of the maze? That would certainly make things easier.

"There you are..." Lucian's voice raised the hair on my nape. He stood only yards away on the other side of the wall which was no longer solid. Only a whisper of light stood between us now. Pressing his hands together, a sphere of brilliant *rais* pulsed between his palms.

Curses, not now!

Slivers of darkness curled around me, inciting a spark of

energy in my depths. "Right, I understand. I'm supposed to use my *rais*. Now, get off me." I tried to yank off the ghostly bindings, but my fingers slipped right through the shadows. "Oh, for Fae's sake!"

The annoying little creatures of darkness whirled around me, faster and faster until they practically vibrated as Lucian loomed closer. The hair on my arms prickled and streaks of energy coursed across my flesh. The flare of power blossomed, pure *rais* pulsing from my core and expanding to my fingertips.

My head whipped back and forth between Lucian and the towering structure, and my hands moved of their own volition. Sparks of golden light flared along the tips of my fingers and liquid lightning coursed through my veins. I threw my hands out and a wave of pure light exploded from my palms, vibrating the air with an intense cacophony of wails. I clenched my teeth as the sharp keening sound ravaged my eardrums. The wall trembled, quaked, and a few shards of alabaster came loose, white dust dribbling on my nose. I glanced up and Reign's shadows zipped by, pummeling into me.

I staggered back an instant before an avalanche of alabaster rained down. Shards of stone and rock pounded to the ground and the earth trembled beneath my boots. I barely managed to get the radiant orb up in time before I was buried in the rubble. Through the safety of the shield, I watched as the enormous wall crumbled, a mixture of shock and awe battling it out in my insides. From the corner of my eye, I caught Lucian scrambling away as the storm of boulders and debris hit the ground.

Once the dust settled, I rubbed the fine soot from my eyes and peered through the gilded shield encircling me and beyond the wreckage at my feet. *What the stars?*

Row after row of the mystical labyrinth had toppled over. Nothing but piles of ash remained of the luminous maze.

Chapter Forty-Five

A *elia*

"Are you absolutely certain I can't get you anything from the banquet hall?" Rue stood in the doorway of our chambers with Devin and Symon waiting just outside.

My stomach was in knots after the trial, and the idea of forcing food down only made it grumble in disapproval. "No, I'm not hungry." I slid to the edge of the mattress and tapped my toes against the cool tile.

"You would think after exerting all that *rais*, you'd be starved."

I released a noncommittal grunt. "No, just exhausted."

"Okay, if you're sure..."

"We could always bring you back some of those honey biscuits you love." Sy waggled his brows.

"No, really I couldn't eat a bite."

"Fine, we'll let you rest." My roommate finally left with the males trailing behind her.

My *rais* was suddenly all anyone could talk about. The entire academy was abuzz with rumors about the lowly Kin who annihilated the luminous maze. I barely made it back to the dormitories without being rushed by curious students. I wouldn't have if it wasn't for Reign who'd picked me up off the field and whisked me to my chambers in a cloak of shadows.

Then he'd forbidden me from leaving the room until he returned.

It had already been over an hour.

The tapping turned to aggressive bouncing, and before long, the entire mattress was shaking from the force of my nervous twitching. Pushing myself off the bed, I refocused the anxious energy into pacing.

Aelia, those frazzled nerves are interrupting my beauty sleep. The grumpy dragon's voice filtered across my subconscious.

Sorry, Sol. But you know, one would think a creature as ancient and all-knowing as you would have some insight as to that little spectacle of light from this morning.

Yes, one would think that.

My dragon had been uncharacteristically silent since the disaster. More than that, I could feel something different across our bond, as if he were purposely trying to shield something from me.

You're certain you have no idea what happened today?

I already told you I was out hunting when I felt the burst of power. It did not come from me, little Kin. It was all you.

That's not very helpful, Sol.

Believe me, Aelia, if I could provide answers for you, I would. Now, try to relax so that I may rest. My body is still growing and is in need of the respite.

I'll try.

As I sluggishly strolled the length of my room in an effort to slow the rapid flutter of my heart, my feet guided me toward the nightstand. After the trial, I'd secured my dagger in its hiding spot. Well, I suppose it wasn't exactly hidden well, but the lock on the door was spelled shut, according to Reign, so I never thought to worry. The moment my hand closed around the familiar hilt, the lingering unease began to dissipate.

But now... Surely, the headmaster would be curious about my sudden surge of powers. Where could I hide it? Could one even conceal such a powerful weapon? Even with my meager abilities, I could feel the energy pulsating from the artifact.

The door whipped open, slamming against the pale timber, and I nearly jumped right out of my skin. Reign stalked toward me, his shadows rioting in a frenzy of darkness. "Good goddess, Reign!" I shrieked. "Are you trying to scare me out of my wits?"

"No, I am trying to impress upon you the urgency of this situation." His hands were clenched at his sides, his aura a sleek obsidian so dark I could barely see around it.

"What situation?"

"Princess, do you have any idea what you've done?" He signaled out the window toward the field behind the Hall of Ether where the maze once stood. "You demolished an ethereal construct created by the combined efforts of every Light Fae professor at the Conservatory. That sort of prismatic manipulation takes years to master, and you brought it all crumbling down with a flick of your wrist."

"Well, it wasn't just a flick—"

"Aelia!" he barked. "This changes everything. You will never again be an anonymous Kin female with questionable powers. Everyone is looking at you now. You've caught the attention of the entire academy, not to mention the king."

"King Elian knows?"

He nodded, his face cast in shadows. "I just left the headmaster's office. A number of first-years were pulled from the rubble, one of whom was the son of a dear friend of the king."

"Oh gods..." My limbs began to shake, and I staggered to my bed before my knees gave. "I k-killed other first-years?"

Reign loomed closer, that dark energy pressing into me. "It wasn't your fault."

My head snapped up to meet his weary gaze. "It *was* my fault." Curses, I should have told him I'd been ingesting the misthorn root. "How many died?"

"Five. Four first-years and one of the groundskeepers who got caught in the blast."

A gasp erupted and I clapped my hand over my mouth. "I—I did this to them."

"What are you speaking of?"

I choked on a sob as vacant eyes filled my vision. The other Light Fae first-years may not have been kind to me, but not all of them were monsters.

"Aelia!" Reign's hands descended upon my shoulders before he gave me a rough shake. "Tell me, now, what you believe you did to cause this."

"I've been ingesting small amounts of the misthorn root since the night of Heaton's party."

The moment that name spilled from my lips, Reign gritted his teeth, a tendon fluttering beneath his stubbled jaw. "You've been doing *what*?" he roared.

"I was simply testing a theory."

"Aelia, that was so incredibly reckless!" He dropped to his knees in front of me, the rapid rise and fall of his chest so violent, I was scared for him. "You had no idea what that could have done to you. What if you'd been killed?"

"But I wasn't," I hissed. "It worked. It dulled the spell bottling up my *rais*."

"And nearly destroyed the academy."

"Don't exaggerate. It was only one field…"

"And now Draven is going to be on me—" He dragged his hands through his hair.

"On you?"

"To keep an eye on *you*," he growled. "You know how he is. I'm his lapdog, right? This vast flux of *rais* is inexplicable, and he *will* want answers. That task will fall on me, Aelia."

A chill skittered up my spine as memories of the Light Fae

Reign so brutally murdered in the Hall of Luminescence my first week at the academy rose to the forefront of my mind. Draven had forced his hand. Would the headmaster call for my life? Would Reign deliver?

"Misthorn root," he mumbled before he leapt to his feet and paced a quick circle, his footfalls so heavy one would think he'd been the one to take all those lives. His jaw ticked with every loop, the tension radiating from his entire form, suffocating.

He finally stopped his manic pacing and whirled toward me. "You do understand how *rais* and *nox* work, right? They are a balance of each other, where one harms, one heals, one destroys and the other salvages."

"Right."

"Misthorn root is toxic to Light Fae but can serve as an amplifier to Shadow Fae."

I swallowed hard. "An amplifier?"

"Of *nox*."

"But I don't have *nox*."

"That we know of," he whispered.

"How could I be Shadow Fae? I'm barely Light Fae..." I tugged at the collar of my tunic, revealing the glittering engraving that appeared the day Reign appeared at my doorstep.

He inched closer and lifted a finger, pausing as if to wait for my approval. When I didn't utter a sound, he gingerly traced the pattern of swirls along my skin. I held my breath as pops of energy ricocheted between our flesh.

"Do you feel that?" The question whooshed out, along with the remaining air in my lungs. I'd asked him at least once before, but he'd always denied it.

"Mmm, I feel it princess." His eyes chased to mine and the fire of a thousand flames burned through those starlit orbs. He inched closer, still, until our bodies were flush. "I feel it constantly when I'm near you now."

The air thickened between us, tension crackling in the minute space between our lips. "What is it?" I breathed.

"I'm not certain..."

"But you have theories?"

A wicked grin split the perfect bow of his lips. "I always have theories, princess." His finger drew lazy circles across my chest and goosebumps rippled in its wake. My entire body was alight with a mere touch. How was it possible?

Shaking my head free of the lusty thoughts, I tried to focus. There was a reason he'd come, and it wasn't just to fondle the Light Fae symbol on my chest. "Where is your Shadow Fae mark?" I finally managed.

His expression turned absolutely feral as he took my hand with his free one and slid it down his torso, across the rippling abs I could feel, even over his tunic, and descended farther still. I tried to jerk away when he reached his belt buckle, but he kept my hand pressed against his unyielding form until I skimmed his hipbone.

"Here," he murmured, his voice husky and laced with desire.

I'd been so flustered at the sight of his bare form at the pond, I'd missed it altogether. My hand still rested just south of his hip bone, my fingers itching to explore the clear outline of his breeches. The ties of his leathers were only an inch away, and I knew with certainty if I dared to unlace one, he would allow it. We'd been dancing around this overwhelming attraction, each of us on a dagger's edge. It would only be a matter of time before we fell. It was as inevitable as the incessant sun breaking over the horizon, a certainty that could not be denied.

But I wouldn't fall today. There was too much at risk, too much unknown.

Reluctantly, I removed my hand from his smooth breeches and took a step back. I hated that he let me. "If I see anything unusual pop up on my skin, I'll let you know."

"Please do." His eyes narrowed and he loosed a deep breath.

"If we weren't in the middle of the trials, I would take you to Shadow Fae lands to test your powers more thoroughly. But for now, we must simply wait. And you must stop taking the misthorn root."

"But then I won't be able to access my *rais*."

"The lingering effects should remain for another day or two if you've been ingesting it for this long. Regardless, the Dusk and Dawn Duel is next, and you can win that one without your *rais*."

I eyed the dagger I'd dropped on my bed at Reign's unexpected appearance. I was proficient with my blade, but a duel with a broadsword was trickier. Especially if I drew an opponent larger than me. "I'm surprised you have such faith in me."

His hand slowly skimmed down my arm then strong fingers entangled with my own. "I've always had faith in you, princess. I told you from the beginning, I do not pick losers."

Chapter Forty-Six

R *eign*

"Have you discovered anything more about the girl?" Headmaster Draven lifted a silver brow as he moved beside me beneath the shade of the canopy.

It seemed as if the entire academy had gathered along the Luminoc River for today's trial. Everyone wanted to catch a glimpse of the magicless Kin female who'd managed to destroy the work of the university's elite professors with nothing but a twitch of her fingers.

Draven had been on my ass for days. It was only by the grace of Noxus that I hadn't siphoned the life out of the overbearing male. But he was essential to the plan. If it weren't for him, I would never have found myself at this prestigious university. So, I forced myself to suffer through his endless tirades.

"Nothing more than I've already shared," I gritted out.

I was beginning to believe I wasn't the only one keeping

secrets on this campus. The interest that Draven held for the girl was far more than common curiosity. He'd been adamant I tail her from the moment she arrived.

It had to be the prophecy. Father wasn't the only Fae with access to the divine seers, and as the headmaster of the academy which provided King Elian with his army, Draven must have had some inside knowledge typically shared only with a select few.

But I couldn't merely mention the ancient foretelling without giving myself away, or at least provoking suspicion.

"Why are you so concerned with the girl anyway?" I murmured as the space beneath the canopy grew tight with warm bodies. It was nearly time for the Dusk and Dawn Duel to begin. "Even before her performance the other day, you were wary of her. Why?"

The headmaster's pale ivy eyes narrowed as he regarded me. "That is none of your concern."

"I believe it is my concern when it affects me directly." Tugging back my sleeve, I flashed him my silver cuff and the ancient glyphs sparkled beneath the sunlight. "If I knew what it was about the girl you were trying to discover, I could perform my job more effectively." And finally get these damned mana-cles off for good.

"True enough, but—"

"I've been faithful to you for years, Draven. Whatever secret it is you are attempting to keep from the blessed light of day, I am more than capable of sharing its burden."

His lips twisted, the silver mustache dancing along the top of his mouth like an angry katerpillar. "It is not my secret to share. I've been tasked by the king. That alone should be suffi-cient explanation, Darkthorn. Now, do as you're told and keep an eye on the girl. I want you at her side at all times, now more than ever."

"As I have been. I cannot very well sleep with the girl—" *Noxus's balls what is the matter with my tongue?*

He stroked his long beard as he gazed over the rippling waves of the Luminoc River. The first-years filled the western bank, preparing to begin. The duel would be fought across the narrowest point of the river where a luminous bridge constructed of limestone and pure light had been created for the event. The contestants would be forced to battle with one half bathed in eternal daylight and the other in perpetual darkness.

I'd already forbidden Aelia from using her *rais* for this event, but I couldn't help but wonder what effect the smattering of *nox* would have on her powers.

"Perhaps you cannot *sleep* with the girl, as that sort of thing is expressly forbidden in the code of conduct, but maybe you could sleep beside her, as a guard of sorts."

"A guard?" My tone hitched a few notches.

"Yes, for her safety. Didn't you say there had been a few incidents with other students?"

There had been before I threatened them within an inch of their lives if they ever so much as gazed in Aelia's direction. "It's been under control," I replied.

"Then perhaps a situation should occur... one in which she's frightened into submission." A nasty gleam sparked within the dull green of his eyes.

"You want me to orchestrate an attack?"

"I'm simply asking you not to come to her rescue should one of the other first-years go too far."

Anger pulsed through my veins, clouding my vision.

"Can you do that, Darkthorn?" Draven's voice dribbled through the roar of my pounding pulse.

I forced my head to dip despite the fury flooding my veins. I would never let any of those sniveling first-years touch her. I'd simply have to find another way to convince Aelia that my sleeping in her chambers was for the best.

Which it clearly was not. Mostly for my sanity.

A shrill buzzer rang out, screeching through my thoughts.

Professor Litehaus appeared at the foot of the river and pushed his spectacles up his aquiline nose. "Welcome, first-years, to the Dusk and Dawn Duel. In today's trial, combatants must harness the strengths of their respective powers while exploiting the weaknesses of their opponents, adapting their strategies as the bridge slowly rotates, changing the distribution of light and shadow."

Turning my attention away from Draven, I scanned the bank for Aelia. My eyes latched onto her familiar form in seconds, like a magnetic field drawing me within her orbit. Splaying my fingers, I released one of my shadows. As always, it shot straight to its mark, whirling and winding around Aelia's neck, then up to the shell of that tempting rounded ear.

"No *rais* today, princess. Understood?" I threw my voice into my shadows.

She glared up at me from across the lawn, but her head dipped all the same.

"Our first competitors today will be Lucian Brightcastle and Aelia Ravenwood."

I hissed out a breath, every muscle in my body tightening. How in all the realms did she manage to draw him? Not only did the male despise her, but he was also one of the most skilled with a broadsword.

With my gaze still pinned to Aelia's, I offered what I hoped was a reassuring smile. Something I wasn't entirely certain I could pull off. Again, she nodded, but her apprehension was so potent I could practically scent it from here.

Aelia climbed to the pinnacle of the gleaming bridge that spanned an abyss of swirling mist, splitting the battleground between radiant daylight and deep, impenetrable shadow. She whirled around to face Lucian, broadsword held high. The arrogant Light Fae flashed a cocky smile. *I swear to the gods, I will use my shadows to tear that male limb from limb if he hurts her.* The bridge, a narrow ribbon of stone bathed in light, trembled slightly as the structure began its slow, inexorable rotation.

"Competitors you have five minutes to best your opponents or the trial will end in a draw. You may begin when the bell tolls."

I leaned over the railing that separated us from the Luminoc, my gaze intent on the impending battle. The bell rang out and silence descended over the crowd.

Aelia, light on her feet and eyes aglow with fierce determination, thrust her broadsword at Lucian. His smile melted away and his sharp features hardened with the resolve of an experienced warrior. As they circled each other, the light and shadows shifted with every rotation. Lucian used his large form to push Aelia into the shadows, where he must have assumed her light-based powers would wane.

Only I wasn't entirely certain that would be the case.

Lucian struck first, a blaze of light bursting from his fingertips, aiming to blind Aelia. She ducked low, the light grazing just above her head, and she countered with a sweeping kick directed at his legs. Lucian jumped back, landing partly in shadow, and his powers dimmed. Aelia seized the advantage, her own powers amplified by the brilliant daylight enveloping her and thrust her sword. She grazed his arm with her gleaming blade and earned a hiss from the male.

Lucian attempted to draw Aelia into the darkness once again. He feinted left and then surged right, deeper into the shadow, clearly hoping she would follow.

And she did. Each arc of her sword grew more brazen as if fueled by the night.

Her moves were mesmerizing, the grace and effortless ease with which she fought were pure poetry. Lucian grew sloppy and desperate, each thrust a wasted effort of brute strength.

As Lucian's steps faltered in the lesser light, his attacks lost more of their potency. Aelia, meanwhile, seemed to only strengthen with each shift of the shadows. As the Fae male lunged out of desperation, she easily sidestepped, and he nearly barreled over the railing. He spun around and snarled, pressing his palms together. A flare of light lit up his hands. Splaying his fingers, the radiant glow forced Aelia to shield her eyes from the blinding display.

No...

With her arm over her eyes, Lucian pressed his advantage. He lunged with his broadsword and my heart catapulted against my ribs.

"Aelia, move!" I hissed into my shadows, and my voice met their mark. She parried just in time, avoiding the brunt of the blow. She glanced down at her torn sleeve and blood trickled from her upper arm. Rage coursed through my body at the sight of the deep crimson, raging down to the depths of my dark soul.

My shadows vibrated with fury, writhing around me, desperate to be released. I drew in a deep breath, calming the beast below the surface as Aelia's eyes met mine. She was okay. The cut must not have been deep.

The battle continued, silver streaks of metal blurring the air. She thrust and parried again and again, until both competitors seemed utterly drained. Gods, when would the timer expire? Lucian leapt at Aelia, cornering her against the stone railing. She feinted left then right, but he mirrored her every move. He arced his sword over his head and brought it down with a lethal swoosh. "Watch out!" the shout burst from my lips before I could stop it. A radiant shield bloomed around her form and Lucian's blade bounced right off the protective barrier, mere inches from her neck.

Thank, Noxus. So much for not using her *rais*.

The shield disintegrated, and she pressed forward, Lucian staggering back along the bridge. Now bathed in shadows, he faltered again, the flicker of light in his palm fizzling away. Aelia arced her sword and dazzling light swept across the blade.

No, rais!

The burst of light slammed into Lucian, his eyes snapping shut from the intensity of the glare. Aelia didn't hesitate. With a graceful leap, she devoured the space between them, spun her sword around and jabbed the hilt into his chest. He hit the railing and flailed, and Aelia moved in, landing a firm push against Lucian's chest. The Fae stumbled backward over the balustrade and into the icy depths of the Luminoc.

Chapter Forty-Seven

A^{elia}

Drawing in a breath of much-needed air, I dropped the broadsword and gripped the railing to stare down into the dark, swirling waters. Lucian's blonde head bobbed along the rippling current, his muttered curses reaching all the way to my sensitive ears. Before he turned toward the riverbank, those icy blue eyes met mine. A chill surged up my spine at the depth of hatred in his gaze.

The Light Fae would not take that loss well. Losing against a powerless Kin would be unacceptable.

"Woohoo, Aelia!"

"You did it!"

The whoops and claps of my small but fervent personal cheering section drowned out the dread pooling in my gut. I turned to my friends and was surprised to find not only Rue and Symon cheering, but also a few of the other members of my team, and Heaton, of course.

I rushed down the ramp of the glittering bridge, its constant movement now halted, and leapt into Rue's waiting arms. Symon joined in next, then Zephyr and Silvan. Even Belmore and Ariadne offered curt remarks of congratulations.

"I'm so proud of you!" Rue crooned as she spun us around in a circle. "Not only did you best Lucian, you tossed his arrogant ass into the river." A burst of laughter pealed out, and I couldn't help but join my friend.

"You did very well, Aelia." Heaton patted me on the shoulder and offered a tight smile once I'd come to a stop.

I hated that things were strained between us. I only hoped in time it would pass. Heaton was an amazing team leader, one of the best on campus from what I'd seen—and not only that, he was also one of the few Fae here with a heart. "Thank you, Heaton," I whispered, as if I were saying something truly naughty. "I never could've done it without your unfaltering leadership."

A faint smile pulled at his lips. "I'm not sure I had much to do with it."

"You were kind to me from the start when others were not. That alone is worth my gratitude."

"It's a little early for celebrations..." That deep timbre snapped my spine straight. I whirled around to find Reign's smoldering gaze. "You've only passed three of the six trials."

"Arguably some of the hardest ones," Heaton interjected, taking a step in front of me.

Reign inched closer and his ever-present darkness blanketed my skin in his frosty touch. "The Shadows Whisper will be the most difficult, by far."

"And she will be ready for it." Heaton knotted his arms across his chest, throwing his shoulders back.

"Because of my help," Reign snarled.

I spun at my professor, suddenly feeling like a dragon chew toy caught between the two blustering males. "Because of both of you, but most of all, because of me."

Rue released a cackle and wound her arm around mine. "She's right, you know. I've never seen anyone more determined to succeed than this little Kin."

I smiled down at my petite friend, but kept my eyes locked on Reign as I said, "Thank you, Rue." I purposefully uttered the words he'd fought so hard to banish from my vocabulary.

The buzzer rang out, stealing the smile right off my face. Only one battle had been won today, and the rest of my team still had duels to endure.

Symon slid his arm around Rue's slim shoulders and steered her back toward the left bank where all the first-years waited. "We'll see you later, my little round-eared friend." He shot me a wink and traipsed off with Rue at his side. Heaton and the remaining members of Flare Squad followed after them.

Which left only me and my broody professor.

And silence.

A loud grunt and a splash turned my attention to the murky river. Lucian hauled himself from the water, then climbed over the balustrade, his sodden clothes clinging to him like second skin. I couldn't help the grin of satisfaction as he hit the ground, muttered a curse and stomped back toward the Hall of Glory.

"I wouldn't get quite so cocky, princess," Reign mumbled, following my line of sight. "You still have the remaining trials and the final battle. There are plenty of opportunities for Lucian to slip a blade between your ribs." He tapped the soft suede of my tunic just below my breast.

An embarrassing gasp escaped at the all too vivid picture he painted—and maybe a little bit because of the unexpected touch. "You seem a little too enthusiastic about the possibility."

He turned to me with a rueful smile. "Is that really what you think?"

I slowly shook my head.

"There is a reason behind my mentioning it, princess. It wasn't simply to frighten you."

"Then why?"

"With the trials reaching their pinnacle and the final battle so close, not to mention your dazzling display at the luminous maze, and now your victory today, I fear your enemies may not keep their distance much longer."

"My enemies?"

"The other jealous first-years." He raked his hand over his face then dragged it through his hair, yanking at the tips, as if I were the most frustrating thing in the world. "As the end nears, tensions rise. There's more to lose and, thus, higher risk becomes more acceptable. Like enduring my wrath..." His dark gaze flickered to Lucian as he disappeared up the steps into the grand hall.

My jaw nearly unhinged as I processed his words. "You threatened Lucian to stay away from me?" Then my thoughts flickered back in time to Kian and that alleged assault in the dormitories that had left him in the hands of the healer for nearly a week. "And you attacked Kian?" Though I phrased them as questions, not a doubt remained in my mind. "But why? Why would you risk your position at the Conservatory for me?"

"I didn't risk anything," he snarled and tugged me to a small alcove of trees along the river. "Do you truly believe Draven cares who I torment? Who I kill? Do you not remember the first day you arrived? Or how about on orientation day? Fae do not value life like you do, princess. The sooner you understand that the safer you will be."

Images of the dead Light Fae flashed across my mind and my gut twisted. I nearly fell for his distraction. "But why do it for *me*?"

His eyes flashed and those shadows whirled to life, a tempest of emotion in wraith-like form.

"You didn't even know me then," I pressed. I was fairly certain I meant something to him now—what exactly, I had no idea—but back then? I was no one of importance.

"*Noxus*, you can be nosy! Why does it matter? Perhaps, you caught my eye from the beginning... maybe, I cared what happened to you."

"Dragonshit!" I glared up at the liar, his aura darkening with each lie spilling from his perfect lips. *Well, that's a new development.*

He threw his hands up with an exasperated sigh. "Fine, you want the truth?"

"Please!"

"The headmaster tasked me with the duty of watching you."

The confession was more jarring than an icy dip in the Luminoc. All the air whooshed from my lungs and a pang lanced across my chest. That was why he'd shown so much interest in me from the start. "But why?" I finally managed.

"I honestly have no idea. Draven did not explain. He only said I was to keep an eye on you and report back."

"So, you've been spying on me all these months?" All the times Reign appeared when I needed him flashed across my mind. Gods, I was so stupid to think he might have actually cared. I was nothing but a troublesome task assigned by the headmaster.

"Clearly not well," he hissed. "Otherwise, Draven would have long ago found out about your daggers and our late night visits to the Court of Umbral Shadows. I've given him bits of information, only enough to keep his curiosity sated, but all of that went to shit when you blew up the luminous maze."

I attempted to focus on his explanation, but only one word of that entire monologue drilled into my head. *Daggers.* Plural. "Did you just say daggers?"

"Excuse me?"

"You said you hadn't told Draven about my daggers, plural, with an '*s*'. I only have one dagger." I tapped the sheath strapped to my thigh.

"Slip of the tongue." The dark aura evaporated, and I

couldn't make out a thing. Had he lied again? Was he simply shielding his aura from me?

Raysa, I hated this male. I couldn't decide what I should be more upset about: the fact that he'd been spying on me for months, or that he was possibly lying to me again. Could I have had more than one dagger? How would I forget something like that?

My thoughts retreated to Rue, and of how easily he'd wiped her memory of my dagger clean. He could have done the same to me...

Reign stepped closer, drawing me from my internal musings. I staggered back and hit the pale white trunk of one of the trees of the small copse encircling us. "It's better that you know the truth about Draven anyway. It will make what I'm about to tell you easier."

"Tell me what?"

"That you have a new bodyguard, princess. Per Draven, I am to stay by your side from sun-up to sunset."

"But the sun never sets."

A wicked grin parted his lips. "Exactly."

Chapter Forty-Eight

This was ridiculous, over the top, and completely unnecessary. I glared at my newest roommate stretched out on the settee beside the hearth as Rue watched our exchange in delight. Conveniently, my original roommate had a date with Devin tonight, which meant I'd have to suffer Reign's presence alone.

It had been difficult enough attempting to explain to Rue why our professor would be staying in our chamber for the foreseeable future. He claimed things would settle down after the term break, but I feared it was only an effort to appease me.

"Oh, how I wish I could stay for this!" Rue squealed and clapped her hands.

I shot her a scowl from across the room as she plucked the purse from her bed. "Then you should, really you *should*."

She clucked her teeth and zipped to the door with her bag tucked beneath her arm. "I wish I could, but Devin would just be heartbroken if I cancelled our date."

"Then don't cancel, just come back after..."

Her eyes glinted with mischief. "Why put up with the date at all if I don't stay to reap the benefits after?"

Reign's deep chuckle rumbled in the air. "She has a point."

I twisted my head over my shoulder and sneered. I never expected that he'd be so fond of my roommate's naughty humor. More than that, I was shocked she was suddenly so loose lipped around our foreboding instructor. Only a few hours together and they'd become the best of friends. She barely twitched at the sight of him anymore.

Two sharp knocks put an abrupt end to the discussion.

"That must be him!" Rue flitted to the door as if her luminous wings had finally emerged. Swinging it open with a smile, she didn't even bother to ask Devin to enter. "Have fun tonight!" With a quick wave over her shoulder, she abandoned me with the shadow devil.

Traitor...

Reign slunk off the divan, wearing a loose-fitting dark tunic and linen trousers. I'd never seen him so casual. After he'd escorted me to the banquet hall, he'd dropped me off at my chambers while he went back to his to pack a bag. He had returned in record time wearing this ensemble, which I assumed was his sleeping attire.

He eyed me warily, and gritting my teeth, I returned the scrutinizing gaze. "What?" I blurted when the silent staring reached uncomfortable levels.

"Nothing." He shoved his hands into his pockets and strolled around the space, taking in every nook and cranny. He remained at the doorway to the bathing chamber for a long minute before finally turning around. "Have you bathed yet this evening?"

A fiery chill skirted up my spine at the sultry edge to his tone, stealing all rational thoughts. "I have not," I finally breathed out. He'd only left my side for a quarter of an hour at most. He would have known if I had.

"Perhaps you should. It will help you relax."

"I don't need to relax. I'm perfectly fine." I slapped my arms across my chest and shifted my weight to one foot. As if this defensive stance could somehow protect me from his roving gaze.

"You don't seem fine, princess. Your aura is a riot of brilliant colors." He inched closer. "One would think my presence made you nervous."

"I'm simply happy—no—absolutely thrilled that you are here."

He smirked and loomed closer still, so that I was forced to back up an inch or tempt a duel with his nose. "You have an odd way of showing your happiness."

"You know what? You're right," I hissed. "I am upset, not because you're here, but because you lied to me for months."

"How did I lie?"

"All that time you spent by my side, training me, 'protecting' me from the other students, it was all because of Draven, not because you actually cared—" *Oh gods, someone cut off my tongue.*

"So that is what you're upset about?" His dark brows furrowed as if I'd just revealed the most ludicrous answer.

"You lied," I hedged. "That is what troubles me."

"Hmm." A harsh line slashed across his lips, and a long moment of silence descended. I nearly pushed past him to get to the bathing chamber simply to escape the endless quiet when he cleared his throat. "It may have started as a simple task, Aelia, but the more I watched you, the more it became clear just how extraordinary you are. Draven's caution was well-founded. You possess a rare blend of kindness and compassion, coupled with unparalleled courage and an unconquerable spirit—qualities that make you the most remarkable female I've ever encountered. And powerful, Noxus, let us not forget powerful." His hand slowly lifted to my cheek, and the backside of his calloused fingers brushed my skin. "And now, I simply cannot seem to stay away from you."

"Reign…" I growled and pressed my hand to his chest. Warmth seeped through the soft material and every nerve ending in my palm spasmed at the faint contact. His shadows slithered between my fingers, up and around my arm. "You must stop doing this…"

"Why?"

"Because you're making my head spin and my heart—" I snapped my jaw closed before I blurted something completely mortifying.

Reign's crawling shadows morphed into wings and propelled him to the opposite side of the chamber. I stared up at him in shock, the sudden absence of his presence leaving my body cold. This attraction between us was purely physical—outrageously out of control, but only a matter of hormones. I wasn't naïve enough to believe there was anything more.

"You're right," he murmured. "I need to get a hold of myself. I apologize, I only need some time to adjust to this new situation."

Of us spending every waking moment together? I wasn't sure I could ever be in his proximity and not feel him everywhere.

"If you do not wish to bathe, then I will. I could use a cold bath." He dropped his piercing gaze and stalked past me, moving straight into the bathing chamber without another glance.

The moment the door closed, I released a ragged breath. Remaining in close proximity to this male until the end of the term would surely be the death of me. I'd rather the risk of an attack by Lucian or Kian at this point.

"Aelia! Aelia, don't!"

A panicked voice snapped me from a fitful sleep. I jolted upright in bed and scanned the room, my mind muddled with the haze of slumber. When had I fallen asleep?

"Aelia, no!"

My heart catapulted up my throat as I recognized the voice. Reign. Leaping out of bed, I raced into the bathing chamber and slid to a halt only a foot from the bubbling pool, nearly slipping on a patch of moss crawling across the stone.

Reign lay beneath the gentle spray of the cascade, eyes closed, and brow furrowed with concern.

"Aelia," he murmured again. A vein across his forehead jumped, twitching in an erratic beat. "Please, Father, no. It cannot be her." He was dreaming... of me?

I crept closer, careful to avoid slipping on the slick moss and tumbling into the pool along with him.

"It's *not* her..." he muttered again. "It cannot be."

I dropped down to my hands and knees to make out his rushed murmurs, forcing my eyes to remain focused on his face instead of his bare form beneath the bubbling cascade. His head lay against the stone, eyes closed, but the typical serenity of sleep didn't relax his features. He wasn't simply dreaming of me; this was a nightmare.

His bare chest heaved, and a part of me felt guilty for not waking him. But I needed to hear more. I leaned closer, so close that my nose could graze the shell of his pointy ear if I breathed too deeply. His musky, frosted scent invaded my nostrils and heat pooled low in my belly. Raysa, my attraction to this male was *not* normal.

"Aelia, I'm sorry. I am so very sorry..."

My heart pinched at the sorrow in his tone before a whisper of fear simmered. What was he apologizing for? What could he have done to deserve such a heartfelt sentiment?

I pushed myself up, intent on getting as far away from this enigmatic male as possible, when a hand snaked out and wrapped around the back of my neck. My breath hitched as Reign's fingers dug into the hair at my nape.

"Aelia?" His lids fluttered and I released a stuttering breath. "What are you doing here?"

Heat raced up my neck and flourished across my cheeks. Oh goddess, I must look like a complete fool! On my hands and knees beside him as he lay naked in the bath.

I wriggled free of his grasp and leapt to my feet. "You called for me. I was sleeping and I heard your voice, and I just ran and then, I don't know, I guess you were sleeping too..." *Oh please, goddess, help me.* "I will wait for you in my bed." I clapped my hand over my mouth and muttered a curse. "That did not come out as intended." I threw my thumb over my shoulder. "I will be out there. Not waiting. Oh, just come out whenever. Or not at all." I spun around and my bare foot slipped on the moist moss. My legs slid out from under me and I hurtled headfirst into the shimmering pool.

The tepid waters blanketed my body, only adding to the rising heat. I kicked and struggled and broke through the swirling waters only to find a pair of dark orbs hovering over me.

"Are you all right?" Reign stood on a step, revealing the masterpiece that was his perfectly sculpted form. Muscled, flawless skin rippled as far as the eye could see, the rushing water just barely covering his manly bits.

Oh, for Fae's sake, how did this keep happening to me?

"Yes, I'm fine," I spat and waded toward the steps, my long dressing gown filling with water and only slowing me down. When I reached the ledge, Reign offered a hand, but I shook my head and warm droplets rained down from my sodden hair. "I can get out on my own."

"Clearly, I was only trying to be a gentleFae."

I snorted on a laugh. "That is quite comical coming from you. It is your fault I'm in this mess to begin with."

"My fault?" His dark eyes turned incredulous.

"Yes, you were the one crying my name in your sleep."

"How kind of you to come to my rescue, but as you can see, I'm just fine." He lifted to his tiptoes, and I could just make out the sharp V trailing down to—

Oh, goddess. I squeezed my eyes shut.

With my lids sealed, I felt my way up the steps until I reached the vanity. Hazarding a peak through slitted lids, I found a towel and wrapped it around my drenched and now partially translucent sleeping gown. When I finally lifted my gaze to Reign's, his eyes were locked on my peaked nipples. *Oh, the mortification.*

Without another word, I stormed out of the bathing chamber and slammed the door behind me.

Much too soon, I'd barely had enough time to peel off my sodden nightgown, Reign appeared with only a small towel wrapped around his narrow hips. My traitorous gaze trailed his movements as he sauntered across the chamber to the bag of clothes he'd left beside my closet. When he spun around, his eyes locked on mine, and a sly grin curved his lips.

"See something you like, princess?"

"I hate you," I snarled. "Just get dressed already!"

"I prefer to sleep in the nude, but for you I suppose I could settle on my underdrawers. Is that going to be a problem?"

"Yes, a big problem." I flopped onto the plush mattress and drew the coverlet over my head.

"Fine," he growled. I could just make out the soft whoosh of fabric coming over his head, and I released another breath of relief. "Now where do you suppose I should sleep?"

I could practically hear the smile in his tone. Why did he enjoy torturing me so?

"On the sofa, on the floor? Perhaps, you can ask your dear friend the headmaster to provide another bed if you'll be joining us until the end of the term. But right now, I really don't care, Reign, just please let me sleep."

He grumbled something I was thankful I couldn't make out, then a long minute of silence ensued.

"Goodnight, Reign," I finally called out, refusing to lift my head from the pillow. I didn't need to steal another look at his perfect form. As it was, the image would be perfectly ingrained in my mind for the rest of my sun-cursed life.

"Goodnight, Aelia, and sweet dreams."

CONSERVATORY OF LUCE — FORGED IN LIGHT · TEMPERED IN TRUTH

Chapter Forty-Nine

A *elia*

A week later, and I had passed the Celestial Glyphs Exam. I could create a glyph to temporarily heighten my senses, increase my speed and strength, and a host of other useful skills, but I was certain I would lose my ever-loving mind if I spent another second wrapped in Reign's all-consuming presence. This thing between us was spiraling, growing more uncontrollable with each minute we spent together. My focus should have been on the next trial and surviving the battle against Arcanum, but instead, I spent every waking moment trying not to think about Reign, about his scent infiltrating every inch of my chamber, about his pervasive looming presence bludgeoning through my defenses.

Worse, he'd been surprisingly tolerable temperament wise. He and Rue had become fast friends, and I wasn't sure what irritated me more, that she was suddenly infatuated with our moody professor or that he behaved so pleasantly around her.

And now with Draven's ever-present eyes on me, we hadn't found the opportunity to skulk across the river to test Reign's latest theory. The notion was completely absurd. How could I be half-Shadow Fae? I had no dark powers to speak of. Then again, I had no *rais* until a few months ago either...

Aelia, you must focus if you wish to survive the last two trials. Sol's voice dismissed all the wandering thoughts. Had he heard my whiney internal pining? How embarrassing. In the past few weeks, our roles had reversed. I'd gone from the maternal figure to the inept child who required handling. I couldn't explain how the tables had turned so quickly.

I forced my feet to move more swiftly as I crossed the training field to meet Reign, Pyra, and Sol. Today, we would be practicing defensive maneuvers. With all the focus on the last few trials, I'd had little time to fly. And with Sol's ever-expanding size, he'd been forced to roam farther out on his hunting expeditions to quell his insatiable hunger.

Pyra, the phoenix, eyed the towering dragon, her talons digging into the tall blades of grass kissed in morning dew. She let out a screech as I approached, her beady eyes darting between Sol and me.

"Are you sure she's up for this?" The last thing I needed was the creature spontaneously bursting into flame and taking my professor-turned-bodyguard along with her. I may have been frustrated with the male, but I was not keen to watch his fiery death either.

"She'll be fine." Reign patted the enormous bird's feathered neck, the deep crimson and sleek onyx gleaming beneath the luminous rays of the morning sun. "The question is: are you ready?"

"Of course, I am." I didn't exactly have a choice. The Skyrider Flight trial was tomorrow, and from what I'd heard from Heaton, it was yet another difficult event. Then the final one was the worst yet, the dreaded Shadows Whisper.

"Aelia, I do not mean to frighten you, but these last two

trials typically have the highest death rate." Goosebumps prickled my flesh at the intensity in his tone. "You must be prepared."

I've got this, little Kin. Sol's deep, rumbling voice echoed through my mind. *I've never lost a rider in the trials.*

"I am," I replied, slamming my hands on my hips to glare up at my professor. I had to admit some of Sol's bravado had seeped into my bones. He was a dragon for Fae's sake. With the powerful beast as my mount, I should have no trouble besting the other first-years.

"You are familiar with the rules, then?" He cocked a dark brow.

"No... not exactly," I murmured.

"The teams will be divided in half which means there will be about forty of you up in the sky at once. It will be as close to a practice session of the battle with Arcanum that you'll have. It will be chaos. Anything goes. Even students from the same squad will not be punished for accidentally knocking out a teammate."

Wonderful. In addition to Kian and Lucian, I'd have to keep my eye out for Belmore too.

"I suggest you try not to use your *rais* unless absolutely necessary. I have no doubt that Draven will be watching you. He's already suspicious enough..."

"Suspicious of what, exactly, Reign?" I threw him a narrowed glare. "Why do I still feel as though there is more you are keeping from me?" Sol loomed behind me, his faint breaths whipping the hair atop my head.

Reign crept closer, completely unintimidated by my dragon, his midnight irises pinned to mine. "He is suspicious of who, or what, you really are. And I must admit, he is not the only one."

"And you're certain there is nothing else you haven't told me?"

His lips pressed into a thin line, his shadows swirling so

quickly around his form I could barely discern his aura. "Nothing concrete."

"Reign..."

His hands closed around mine, tugging them away from my hips. "You told me once you trusted me. Is that still true?"

I nibbled on my lower lip as I considered my response. I trusted him with my life, and yet I was certain he was keeping secrets from me. "I trust that you will keep me safe."

"Then that will have to do for now." The hint of a smile played across his lips. "Come now, mount that big dragon of yours."

Sol chuffed happily behind me and dropped to his belly. The earth rumbled beneath my boots and Pyra released a sharp screech, her wings fluttering nervously. "Sorry, girl," I murmured before I crawled up Sol's nubby leg, carefully avoiding all the jagged spikes. By the time I reached his back, my breaths were coming in ragged pants.

Perhaps, I did need a bit more practice with my dragon before the final battle. I'd allowed myself to become complacent along our joy rides simply because of what he was.

"Just follow my lead," Reign called out from below.

I couldn't help the hint of satisfaction as I towered over my professor and his much smaller mount. It may have been petty, but it was all I had.

Pyra's dark wings glistened beneath the harsh rays of the sun, bathing the feathered beast in a golden glow. She darted across the campus, twisting and turning, until it appeared as if flames flickered across her form. What she lacked in size, she more than made up for in speed. I could see why Reign chose her upon his arrival at the Conservatory.

Gods, there were still so many questions. Though I spent nearly every moment with my professor, I couldn't say I'd learned much of anything about him. What had he done to be banished? Why had he accepted this role at the Conservatory? I'd attempted on more than one occasion to pry the information out, but I'd been met with nothing but narrowed glares and tight lips.

Sol banked left hard, trying to keep up with Pyra, and I nearly slipped off his shoulder. My fingers locked around the wing bones that served as makeshift hand holds. Squeezing my thighs, my muscles burned with the exertion of keeping myself in place, but somehow, I stayed on.

Damn it, Aelia, focus. Gritting my teeth, I resolved to have my questions answered tonight in the privacy of my chamber. It was the least Reign owed me after all the lies.

As Pyra shot off ahead of us, I turned my thoughts back to the flight, to the shimmery blue stretched before us, and the feel of the powerful dragon beneath me. Sol leisurely flapped his enormous wings as the phoenix flew toward the border with the Shadow Court. Was Phantom close by watching Reign? Sol claimed he always knew of my whereabouts, was that always the case? I wondered if my dragon would ever have the opportunity to fly with Phantom.

I'd rather spend an eternity in solitude than be forced to associate with that ill-tempered female. Just like that, Sol's voice invaded my thoughts.

Wait a second, you know Phantom?

Of course, I do. There are very few dragons left. I make it a point to know the survivors.

But wait, how did you meet her? When you were out hunting?

No, I have yet to cross her in this lifetime. But I've had the displeasure of being acquainted with her for very many years.

Clearly, there was something to this story I was missing.

So why the animosity in your tone?

Sol veered to the right, the tempered flapping of his wings growing more agitated as he soared past the Conservatory grounds and banked so that he flew right over Pyra. *I do not wish to discuss our past, Aelia. I have been more than discreet when it comes to your mental pining.*

Heat flushed my face and a rush of shame blossomed low in my belly. Oh, Raysa, he'd heard me. How much did he know?

Everything, little Kin. I know everything.

Well, that's Fae-freaking-tastic.

Do not fear, Aelia. Your secret is safe with me. But Reign on the other hand...

What?

Plumes of smoke drifted from his wide nostrils, and a grunt rolled through his throat, vibrating the sleek scales beneath my thighs.

Please, Sol, tell me what you know.

It's not what I know, but rather a feeling. I only want you to be cautious around the Shadow Fae. He, much like his cold-hearted mount, are not to be trusted.

Chapter Fifty

A*elia*

"For Fae's sake, what is the king doing here?" The question popped out before I could muster the sense to contain it.

You've caught his attention, Aelia. Sol's deep grumble seeped into my scattered thoughts. He stood behind me like all the other skyriders lined up on the field in front of the Hall of Enlightenment.

It was time for the Skyrider Flight, the penultimate trial.

I scanned the field and the throng of Light Fae gathered. A nervous flutter battered at my insides, and it only escalated as I caught sight of Reign standing between Professor Lumen and Professor Litehaus. His dark gaze chased to mine for only an instant before Lumen spoke, drawing away his attention.

"Don't be nervous," Rue whispered. "You're going to do just fine."

"You've got a dragon, little Kin." Symon ticked his head

over his shoulder at Sol. "Of all of us, you should have the least to worry."

"Umhmm," I mumbled, scanning the verdant field once more.

Forty first-years lined the field, four or five from each squad, depending on how many were left. Rue, Sy, Belmore, Ariadne and I were on deck for Flare team, each of us in the finest gilded armor the academy had to offer. According to Reign, it wouldn't help us if we fell, but it should provide some protection from blades and ethereal beams of *rais*.

Farther down the row, I could just make out the foreboding outlines of Kian and Lucian from Scorch Squad. Kian's dark gaze flickered in my direction, his silver hair illuminated by the first rays of the sun. A gruesome scar marred his face, running from his forehead down across his upper lip. Had Reign inflicted that wound? A part of me already was certain of the answer. Behind Kian stood an imposing gryphon, and beside him, a ligel, Lucian's skyrider. The half-lion, half-bird of prey was enormous, reaching nearly to Sol's shoulder. How had I never seen that creature before?

"Noxus's dick, when did Lucian's skyrider get so big?" Sy hissed, his gaze following my own.

"Maybe he's imbuing it with *rais*," Rue offered.

"You can do that?" I squealed.

"Sure, if he's mastered light infusion."

Stars, there was still so much I didn't know. Not that I particularly needed Sol to grow any larger. As it was, we could barely find enough for him to eat.

Headmaster Draven clapped his hands and a swirl of brilliant light burst from his palms, illuminating his sallow features. "Welcome, students, to the Skyrider Flight. Today's trial will test your abilities to control your mounts while facing an array of obstacles and live adversaries. This trial will come as close to the final battle with Arcanum Citadel as you will have the opportunity to experience. It is imperative you treat this exercise as if it were the real thing. We must defeat our enemies across the river this year."

Whoops and shouts echoed across the field, the loudest coming from King Elian and his Royal Guardians. What I wouldn't give to know what was really happening across the border. Was the peace between the courts truly as frail as rumored?

Why were these two elite universities so important?

A myriad of questions spiraled as the headmaster droned on about the importance of the event. I forced myself to focus as his speech began to detail the rules.

"The in-flight battle will last for thirty minutes." An immense floating sundial appeared just overhead. "Your goal is simple: ground your opponents by any means possible. You must remain within the gilded arena for the entire time or you will be disqualified." He paused and pointed up to the glittering golden boundary drawn across the sky. "Points will be given based on time remaining in the competition. The last student to remain mid-air will win, giving their squad one hundred bonus points. The first Fae down will cost their respective team one hundred points. Therefore, it would behoove you to play as a team, but as you know, today, all rules regarding the code of conduct within teams will be waived. May the strongest first-year triumph"— Draven's gaze drifted to mine for an instant before rising over my head to Sol—"and may Raysa be with you all."

Another wave of applause and the crowd roared. Again, the upperclassmen had gathered to watch the events. Hundreds of students filled the edge of the field, huddled behind the canopy beneath which stood the fine professors of the Conservatory, Reign included. Beside them, the King and his guards stood beneath a radiant awning of pure white light. Clearly, this would be quite a spectacle.

King Elian's unearthly turquoise gaze flitted in my direction. The cold blue skimmed over my skin and rested just over my head at the dragon poised behind me. His aura darkened, a twinge of deep green swirling through the brilliant alabaster. Envy... I was certain of it. The King of the Ethereal Court was jealous of *my* skyrider.

"Does King Elian have a dragon?" I whispered to Rue.

She slowly shook her head. "Not anymore. From what I understand, his was killed in the Two Hundred Years War. According to the history books, the king was trying to save his older brother and was nearly slaughtered himself."

"His brother?" How could I have been so ignorant about Fae history? They truly taught us nothing in the Kin schools, just as Reign had alluded to many times.

"Yes, King Alaric had been in power for many decades before him. My parents often speak wistfully of the former Light Fae royal. His death was a great loss to our people."

The blare of a sharp horn put an end to my friend's words and pivoted our attention back to the headmaster. "Students, mount your skyriders."

Rue reached out, squeezing my hand. "We stay together at all costs."

I nodded quickly, Symon echoing my movement. "Together."

My roommate's fingers tightened around my own. "Good luck, Aelia."

"You, too."

Symon snuck between Rue and me and pulled us both into a hug. "We've got this, ladies. Flare Squad for the win." He squeezed us so tight a nervous laugh tittered out.

Once he released us, he stepped toward Griff, the beast nervously pawing at the ground. "Just don't fall."

"Don't be an ass," Rue hissed.

As my friends turned toward their skyriders, dread pooled in my gut. "I love you, both," I blurted before I lost my nerve.

Both Light Fae whirled around, their eyes wide as if my

sentiment were completely out of this world. A slow smile melted across Symon's face. "Cheers, my friend."

As Sy leapt onto his mount, Rue darted over, pulling Windy with her, despite her skyrider's reluctance to being nearer to Sol. "Love isn't a word much used in the Fae vocabulary, Aelia. Don't take it personally."

"Oh..." How sad. If there was one thing I always remembered about Aidan, it was his soft murmuring before I fell asleep as a child. *You are so loved, estellira.* My hand drifted to the medallion tucked beneath my leather armor as warm thoughts of my adoptive father filled my mind.

"It's barely even used with family. And honestly, I've only ever heard my parents say it to each other a handful of times my entire life." She shrugged.

Not to interrupt this poignant moment, but it's time, Aelia. Sol's gruff voice lanced through my thoughts and spurred me to action.

He was right. It was time.

With one last parting hug, I patted the dagger at my hip to ensure it was secure and clamored up Sol's leg. As I moved up the jagged limb, one of Reign's shadow minions curled around my throat.

"Good luck, princess. Whatever you do, do *not* fall."

"Thanks for the tip, Faehole."

"My, my, that curse was almost a grown up one. You better mind that tongue, princess, especially around the king."

"I'll try my best." I reached the summit of Sol's massive back and shimmied down his spine until I found my seat at the crest of his long, reptilian neck. "Do you have any worthwhile tips, professor?"

"Yes. Avoid direct confrontation with the others for as long as possible. You are the biggest target and the other first-years will have their sights set on you. I know you and your delicate mortal sensibilities will be hesitant to strike, but you must. Remember, it is you or them, Aelia."

My real name in that deep timbre of his, even through the murky whisper of his shadows, plucked a chord buried deep beneath the surface.

"Sol has the power to incinerate each and every one of your opponents. Don't forget that."

A gasp spilled out at the callous truth to his words. "It would be a slaughter," I breathed.

"Better them than you," he repeated.

I wouldn't. I simply couldn't. Half of my team was out there, my closest friends.

Reign is not wrong, Sol interrupted. *I could exterminate the majority of the playing field at your command.*

"I don't command it," I shot back out loud to be sure he heard.

Just know it can be done, if necessary.

Noted.

Another horn blared, the shriek sending my heart shooting up my throat.

That's the warning bell. One minute to go. Sol's massive wings beat the air into a frenzy, and my stomach dipped as we catapulted into the serene blue.

From the corner of my eye, I could just make out Sy and Griff on one side and Rue atop Windy on the other. We'd vowed to stay together, and I only hoped we'd be able to keep our word to each other.

"Let the trial begin!" Draven's voice boomed across the flight field.

Chapter Fifty-One

A*elia*

Chaos exploded before the last word fell from Draven's lips. Blasts of light illuminated the sky as radiant shields and solar flares burst from the ether. I was barely able to summon my own protective barrier as one of the first-years from Scorch team zipped by on his hippogriff and shot a blistering ray in my direction.

Sol banked left, angling his wings toward the earth, and avoided the brunt of the flash. More importantly, my shield held. Without the steady dosing of misthorn root, I'd feared my *rais* would remain hidden. Apparently, the thrill of battle had coaxed it to the surface.

"Incoming!" Rue shouted as another Light Fae barreled toward us, a torrent of prismatic light hurtling through the sky. Again, Sol managed to maneuver his massive form out of the way, but he was nowhere near as fast as Griff or Windy. The weapons made of pure *rais* sailed just over my head, and I released the breath I'd been holding.

After what felt like only a few minutes, a sharp screech echoed across the mid-air arena and my head whipped over my shoulder toward the sound. A female had been thrown from her skyrider and plummeted to the ground.

"Someone help her!" I shouted toward the mass of first-years from Burn Squad. She was their teammate.

Rue threw me a pity-filled smile when no one moved.

Except for her ligel. The creature dove after her but with an injured wing, it just wasn't fast enough.

Another horn blasted, this one a lower pitch, with a decidedly more somber tone. I already knew what it signified without dropping my gaze to the lush field below. The Light Fae female was dead. A mournful, beastly cry ricocheted through the chaos, only exacerbating the tightness in my chest.

What will happen to her skyrider, Sol? My thoughts flitted through the bond.

The ligel will mourn her loss for the designated mourning period of two weeks. If it does not bond with another during that time, then its soul will be recalled to Noxus's arms. Very few skyriders survive the death of their bonded.

That's so sad.

It is, little Kin.

Once the mournful cry subsided, the cacophony encircling me resumed, reaching a fevered pitch. Shouts, snarls, screams, and the clash of metal ripped through the air around us. Teeth, claws and wings flashed, and utter bedlam ensued.

If this was only a trial, I couldn't imagine how fierce the battle with Arcanum would be.

Let's move, Aelia. I would prefer to avoid these beasts if I cannot use my fire against them.

Only if they're a direct threat, Sol.

Fine. I could have sworn the big beast grumbled. He was just as bad as the Fae with their complete disregard for life.

"We're going to circle," I shouted at Rue before Sol's tremendous wings beat the air, propelling us higher up. As we ascended, I summoned my *rais* and drew the voice amplification celestial glyph across my chest. A swirl of light traced the movement of my fingertip as I formed the foreign loops and dots. "Can you hear me?" My voice boomed over the thundering flaps vibrating the sky.

Rue threw me a thumb's up from a dozen yards below, and I watched just long enough to see her draw her own glyph. At least that would help us hear each other over the chaos. I hazarded a quick glance over Sol's shoulder to see if Symon was doing the same, but instead I found him battling one of the first-years from Blaze Squad. Gritting my teeth, I prayed to the goddess to keep my friend safe, to keep my entire team safe, even the ones I didn't particularly care for. None deserved to die.

We circled for endless minutes as I watched the sundial. *Move faster*. Oh, please just let this blasted trial be over already.

Incoming! Sol's voice ricocheted through my mind in full blast. He swooped low, forcing me to clutch onto his wing bones to keep from tumbling down his neck. A deep growl rent the air, and I twisted my head over my shoulder to find Lucian on his monstrous ligel darting toward us. The creature's wings battered the air, and my heart catapulted up my throat.

"Go faster!" I cried out.

All you had to do was ask.

Now is not the time for jokes, Sol!

With one powerful beat of his wings, my dragon sprang forward, and my stomach smashed against my spine. Wisps of dark and light hair lashed against my face as the winds battered my body. Just overhead I could make out the edge of the radiant sphere, the topmost boundary of the flight arena. We soared higher and higher, until the air was so thin and icy, my lungs struggled to continue pumping. My head started to spin, and my thighs clenched around Sol's shoulder blades.

Please don't pass out, please do not *pass out.*

With a quick glance over my shoulder, I could just make out Lucian and his ligel falling back. *Thank the gods.* With Sol beginning to slow, I drew in a breath and relaxed my bone-crunching hold of the protrusions along Sol's wings.

Draw yourself a warming celestial glyph. It will protect you against the cold air.

Right, good thinking, Sol. I traced the air with my finger and a spark of warmth filled my chest.

As we continued to climb higher, the battle unfolded below, the frenzied melee of students across the sprawling campus. Already, more than half of the first-years had been eliminated. I glanced up at the floating sundial and already a quarter of an hour had passed. Only about twenty or so skyriders remained within the glowing parameters of the arena. I heaved out a breath and the puffy white clouds danced, twirling across my vision. *Oh, no.* Curses, I definitely should have spent more time flying at higher altitudes with Sol.

Bring us down. I'm not feeling very well.

Altitude sickness. You'll get used to it over time.

Maybe, but right now, I need to be closer to the ground or I may end up splattered against it.

Understood, little Kin. Hold on.

Angling his wings toward the earth, we began the descent. I narrowed my eyes and scanned the remaining competitors for Rue and Symon. My heart beat out a frantic pulse until my gaze landed on the familiar chestnut hippogriff and silver Pegasus.

Each of my friends battled other first-years, blasts of blinding light radiating all around them. Rue had conjured light spears and was hurling them in rapid fire at the male from Spark team. Symon and the female he sparred with flew circles around each other, their skyriders hissing and screeching.

The hairs on my nape prickled an instant before a shadow curled around my ear. "Aelia, watch out!" Reign's warning came an instant too late.

I spun around as Lucian dropped from the sky and landed

atop Sol's back. My dragon released a roar of indignation as the Light Fae scaled his prickly spine and staggered toward me. "There's no one to protect you now, Kin," he snarled.

Releasing my dagger from its sheath, I stood up, facing Lucian and flashed him my blade. "I'm afraid you've got this all wrong. You are the one in need of protection."

"So arrogant for a lowly half-breed." He unsheathed his sword and staggered closer.

I almost laughed. He had no idea how right he was... only my other half was decidedly not Kin. Reign's shadow hovered in the air between us, a barrier of delicate smoke dancing on the blustering winds. I sprang forward, my blade clutched tight in my fist. A whisper of energy surged through my palm, calling my attention to the crystal encrusted within the hilt. A flicker of light flashed within the prism before it was swallowed up in shadow.

Lucian leapt at me, thrusting his sword, but his balance was off and he missed my chest entirely. Instead, his blade nicked my shoulder armor and rebounded off. I gritted my teeth and pressed forward, my own legs shaky as I scaled Sol's uneven spine.

I cannot buck him off without risking you falling. Sol's voice hissed across the wind.

I figured as much. Don't worry, I'll get him off.
Please be careful, Aelia.

Pushing aside the warmth flooding my heart from Sol's apparent concern, I slashed at Lucian's chest, and he leapt back with a snarl. His boot landed on a jagged spike, and he let out a howl as the barb pierced the sole. "Noxus's nuts!" he roared, staggering back.

Gritting his teeth, he twisted his head over his shoulder, clearly searching for his skyrider. The ligel circled, staying well away from Sol's reach.

"Just admit defeat and I'll let you go unharmed."

"Never," he ground out. "I will never run from you."

Raysa, why were Fae so gods' damned stubborn?

"Why must we kill each other when our enemy is across the river?" And to be quite honest, I wasn't even certain the Court of Umbral Shadows was our enemy...

"This is just how it is, Kin. You wouldn't understand because you did not grow up at court. You have no idea how our world works, which is exactly why you do not belong in it."

A feral growl ripped from his lips, and he lunged.

My radiant orb flickered to life an instant before his blade arced down. The broadsword bounced off the shield and sent him staggering back. I pressed my advantage and sliced at his chest with my dagger. He dodged the hit and parried, our blades clashing in a dark symphony. We pranced back and forth across Sol's perilous spine, each move a dance with certain death.

Sweat trickled down my spine despite the icy air, and my muscles burned from the strain. How much longer could I continue this mid-air battle? Fighting atop dragonback was nothing like my days training on the field with Aidan.

With my thoughts distracted by the past, Lucian sprang forward. His massive biceps curled around me, pinning my arms to my sides as we fell. A sharp sting lanced across my back as I landed on a cluster of spikes. I hissed out a curse, but somehow, I managed to keep hold of my dagger. I thrust it into Lucian's belly, and a cry rang out. Warm blood seeped onto my hand, and I released my blade as nausea clawed its way up my esophagus.

The Light Fae released me, sitting up to survey the wound. I crawled backwards, shimmying my behind along Sol's spine as Lucian struggled to pull my dagger from his gut. The ligel circled again, an ominous growl renting the air. "It's not too late," I shouted. "Just go!"

"No!" He wrenched the dagger free, gripping it in his hand, before slamming on top of me once again.

"Aelia!" Reign's shadow suddenly appeared again, carrying my professor's frantic voice.

Lucian had me pinned to Sol's vertebrae, his massive weight driving the spikes into my back. Blinding pain shot up my spine and stars sailed across my vision.

Cold metal pressed against my throat and a pair of icy blue eyes bore into me. "This is how you die, Kin, at the edge of your own blade." Lucian sneered down at me, the hatred in his eyes all-consuming.

The glint of the crystal in the familiar hilt caught my eye. The flicker of light grew brighter as he pressed it against my chest and the medallion hidden beneath my tunic warmed. Radiant energy coursed through my flesh, igniting my veins in fiery heat.

Sol, drop us!

No, absolutely not, Aelia.

I'm not asking. If you don't spin us off your back this instant, Lucian will kill me.

You'll die anyway.

I won't. You'll catch me.

Aelia... we've never practiced—

Lucian moved the blade to my throat and I bit back a scream as warmth oozed down my neck.

Do it now!

The sneer on Lucian's lips vanished as Sol's wings pumped, and the enormous dragon flipped over.

"No!" Lucian's hands flew out, wildly grasping at nothing.

I felt it the moment Sol's spikes dislodged from my skin, tearing from my flesh.

And we fell.

Chapter Fifty-Two

R *eign*

A howl ricocheted through the air, the heart-rending sound like a feral beast gutted from spine to sternum. I watched in pure horror as Aelia fell, my heart and lungs failing me in the same instant.

"Get a hold of yourself!" Draven's sharp reprimand tore me from the chaos in my chest. "What is wrong with you? The king is watching." His hand curled around my forearm, and it was only then, I realized the primal cry had come from my own lips.

My shadows had morphed into wings, and my feet were already hovering a foot from the ground. If it wasn't for Draven's hold, I would have already shot into the sky and had Aelia safe in my arms.

"Let go of me!" I snarled.

"You cannot save her!" Draven's eyes lanced into my own, searching for an answer even I could not provide. I only knew Aelia had to live.

"Just try and fucking stop me." I ripped my arm free of his hold and launched myself into the endless blue. My wings pumped, beating the air in a wild fury.

I'm coming for you, Aelia.

Aelia continued to fall in what felt like slow motion, her delicate form floating on the breeze, twisting and turning. An aura of pure luminous light encapsulated her body, the glow so splendid it seemed to radiate from the goddess herself.

Noxus, I hadn't completely lost my mind, she—she *was* slowing.

Silence blanketed the arena and everything else stopped, including my own manic wingbeats. All eyes drifted skyward to the powerless Kin who'd managed to captivate the attention of the entire Conservatory.

An enormous flash of gold streaked across the sky, permeating the glittering orb, and massive talons curled around Aelia's body, snatching her right out of the turbulent blue. *Thank the gods.* Solanthus released a blood-curdling snarl as his wings angled toward the earth with his rider safely in his clutches and he slowly descended.

I followed behind him, nestled in shadows so as to not attract more attention than I'd already garnered. A wild roar of applause pierced the tense silence as the golden dragon deposited his rider onto the lush lawn.

My boots hit the ground an instant later, and my legs propelled me toward her. Fuck the rules, fuck everything. My heart remained suspended, unmoving, frozen in time until I reached her. Nothing else mattered but holding Aelia, confirming she was alive and well.

Gods, when had this happened? How had this happened? She'd become everything to me, the center of my entire world. The notion of life without her had become completely unacceptable, despite the cost. I would tell her everything... I had to.

"Aelia!"

Her motionless form was sprawled across the sea of green,

nestled within the rays of warm sunlight. I slid to the ground beside her, my heart a mad battering ram that echoed across every inch of my being. Her eyes were closed, porcelain skin awash beneath the brilliant sunlight. I pulled her into my arms and cloaked us both in shadow. Her blood slickened my hands and pure, unadulterated fear lanced across my heart.

Solanthus released a frustrated growl, plumes of smoke lifting from his nostrils.

"I will tend to her," I snarled right back.

Pressing my hand to her cheek, I caressed her icy skin. "Aelia, please, come back to me, princess. *Please.*"

Her lids fluttered, dark sooty lashes brushing the soft flesh beneath her eyes, and hope alighted in my chest.

"Aelia, it's me. I'm right here."

"Reign?" Those lids finally lifted, lively eyes meeting mine, and my heart tapped out a frantic beat. "Did I pass the trial?"

A rueful chuckle expelled through my clenched lips. "Yes, princess, you passed. You nearly gave me a heart attack falling from Solanthus's back, but yes, you passed."

"Oh, good." Her head lolled against my chest, and I swept a tangle of errant dark locks behind her ear. "And Lucian?" she muttered against my tunic.

I scanned the field for the bastard who was bound for Noxus's arms. If he wasn't dead already, he would be by morning. "I'm not certain."

Squeezing her tight against me, I reveled in the feel of her warmth in my arms, but my sticky fingers reminded me of a more pressing matter. "We will worry about him at another time. Now, I must get you to the healer."

"Right now? Can't I just sleep?" Her lids drooped, and that suffocating fear once again ignited.

"No, Aelia. Elisa must see to your wounds."

"Fine," she grumbled, and a reluctant smile threatened to cross my lips at that relentless stubborn streak.

Cradling her against my chest, I stood, my shadows swirling

tight around us. From the corner of my eye, I could just make out Rue and Symon racing in our direction. I'd deal with them later. Right now, I needed to tend to Aelia. Her teammates could come visit her at the healer.

My *nox* skimmed the surface of my skin, eager for action. Sitting, watching, and helplessly waiting had been pure torture. The silver cuffs around my wrists heated, singeing my flesh as *nox* overpowered their mystical hold and we catapulted through the shadows.

"I'll watch over her, Reign. Go get some rest." Elisa hovered over Aelia's bed in the small chamber. Her eyes were closed, skin still much too pale for my liking. She had lost quite a lot of blood and some of her wounds were already infected. Dragon scales were known to carry toxins often poisonous to Fae.

I stretched out my weary muscles and sank further into the chair. "No, I'm fine."

"You've been here all day. Surely, you must be hungry or thirsty."

"I said I'm fine," I snapped.

Elisa's expression pinched and a hint of remorse sailed through my conscience. Of all the Light Fae I'd encountered in my time here, she was the most decent one. She'd befriended me from the start when the others dared not cast a glance in my direction.

"I regret my tone," I gritted out.

The female's eyes widened to the size of glistening moons. Gods, how I missed the moon, the stars, the cool night on my skin...

"It's been a very long day. The stress of the trials must be getting to me."

"No need to apologize."

Technically, I had not.

She dropped into the chair beside me, her countenance pensive. "You have been very involved in the training of your acquisition. I'm certain it is quite taxing to devote that much of yourself."

"Mmm." I nodded, my gaze fixed to Aelia, to the steady rise and fall of her chest. I just wanted her to wake, to see those vibrant eyes, to hear that sharp tongue. Gods, watching her fall and being powerless to intervene had been the cruelest form of torture. And still, one trial remained, and then the battle against Arcanum. Against Ruhl...

"Are you familiar with the cuorem?"

"Excuse me?"

She leaned closer and whispered, "The cuorem bond? Have you ever heard of it?"

My brows slammed together, her words like a vice grip around my lungs. The cuorem...twin flames. I searched my memories for what little was known about the Fae mate bond. *A profound and mystical connection believed to exist between two souls, making them perfect counterparts of one another.* A true cuorem hadn't been seen in decades, possibly longer. I wasn't aware of a single Fae from my lifetime who'd experienced the connection.

My thoughts flitted back to my days at the Citadel studying Fae mythology. *The cuorem is not merely a romantic or emotional attachment; it is a cosmic and spiritual link that ties two souls together across time and space. It is said that those bound by the cuorem are predestined by the gods themselves, their spirits eternally entwined.*

Oh, Noxus... when I kissed Aelia all those weeks ago, I'd felt something. I had ignored it, tossing it out of my mind as nothing but an infatuation, lust. What if I'd been wrong?

It suddenly occurred to me I hadn't spoken for too long. "Why—why would you say that?" I stammered.

She shrugged, her eyes darting between us. "Because I've never seen you like this, Reign. It's been three years since we met, and I've never once observed you looking at any other female the way you look at Aelia. As if she's an extension of you, the reason for your breath, for every beat of your heart."

She wasn't mistaken and remarkably observant for a mere healer. I'd never felt anything like this in my thirty years on this earth. Shaking my head, I muttered, "It's not possible. She's not Shadow Fae." The lie tasted bitter on my tongue. Because perhaps, a deep, dark part of me had suspected all along.

"Stranger things have happened, I'm sure."

I shook my head again, unwilling, no, unable to accept that answer as the truth. There was no denying the hold Aelia had on me, but a cuorem? It would mean only one thing... Not only was Aelia Shadow Fae and my soulmate, the one created specifically for me by the gods, but she was also the child of twilight, the one spoken of in the prophecy.

A child of twilight, born from the dance of light and dark, shall emerge with the power to reshape destinies. From the celestial embrace and the shadow's whisper, a harbinger of cosmic balance shall be brought forth.

A fateful choice awaits her - to heal or to harm, to nurture or annihilate. Her every step shall resonate through realms, influencing the very fabric of existence.

When the child of twilight shall come of age, her choices, guided by the celestial and obscured by shadows, shall determine the fate of worlds. Whether she becomes a beacon of hope or a harbinger of oblivion, the child of twilight shall be the catalyst of an epochal choice - to bring forth a new dawn or plunge all into eternal dusk.

And it was my duty to kill her.

Chapter Fifty-Three

elia

"Are you certain you're well enough to compete?" Rue regarded me skeptically from her bed, her lively, floral dressing gown a perfect match to her darting eyes.

"Of course, I am." I pushed the coverlet back and slid to the edge of the mattress. I glanced past Rue to the leather divan where Reign typically slept. I ignored the pang in my chest at finding it empty. Still, his shadow minions remained, hovering in the dark crevices of the chamber.

Despite sleeping in our room every night, I'd barely seen the volatile male in the past three days since the semi-disastrous Skyrider Flight. I'd passed the trial, thankfully, but I had nearly died in doing so. Reign watched me constantly, but always kept his distance. Even when we trained, he seemed distant, his thoughts elsewhere.

And I hated how much I hated it.

"And anyway, even if I wasn't completely healed," I huffed

out, "what choice do I have other than to compete in the final trial?"

"Perhaps you could ask Headmaster Draven for an extension?"

I snorted. "That's laughable."

"Yes, I suppose you're right."

"And besides, I couldn't possibly abandon Flare Squad now. We are in second place among all the teams. If we score well today, we could win the Ethereal Trials."

"I know, I simply cannot believe it. We must find a way to defeat Scorch Squad." She clapped her hands and sparks of *rais* kindled between her palms.

"At least the finale is finally upon us." I pushed my weary bones out of bed and ignored the spasms that raced along my back. Though the healer's *rais* had worked wonders, Sol's poisonous scales had left their mark. Which he felt awful about. "By tomorrow, we will be one step closer to the end of the term."

"Thank, Raysa." Rue smiled and practically leapt out of bed. She cast a quick glance over her shoulder before crossing into the bathing chamber. "Where is your moody bodyguard this morning?"

I shrugged. "He's been conveniently absent the past few mornings. You would have noticed had you spent more nights in our chamber." I shot her a cheeky grin.

"That is true, but someone must enjoy these last few days. Sex is a perfect way to dispel the building tension. You should try it sometime." She threw me a wink over her shoulder as she sauntered into the bathing chamber.

"I actually never have."

Rue spun around so fast, she was nothing but a flash of blonde. "Excuse me?"

"I have never had sex with a male."

"Aelia! You are joking, right? I assumed you hadn't been with many but none at all?"

My lips pursed as my roommate regarded me as if I were an abomination.

She crept closer and took my hands in her small ones. "I did not mean to sound so surprised, Aelia. What a female does with her body is her own choice. I only thought—"

"I know. As would anyone."

"I have a new mission in life once we pass the term: to find you a male worthy of your virginity."

A rueful laugh burst through my pursed lips.

"Or you could simply settle on Professor Reign. Scorching hot is way better than worthy, don't you believe?"

I threw my head back as she cackled, joining in on the light moment of mirth.

Perhaps one day... if I survived the next few.

As Rue disappeared into the bathing chamber, a depressing thought wiggled its way into my mind. If I died in the last trial or the battle with Arcanum, I'd meet Noxus in eternal rest without having ever experienced being with a male. Did I truly want to die a virgin?

Reign's heated gaze filled my memories, then his ghostly fingers danced across my flesh eliciting a swell of goosebumps. Heaving out a breath, I marched to the closet shoving thoughts of my professor to the far recesses of my mind. My dire sexual status was not what I should be focused on.

As I shed my nightgown, I fingered the medallion hanging from my neck, my thoughts flying back to the mid-air battle. I'd felt something when the crystal from the hilt came in contact with my necklace. How could I have forgotten?

With only my underthings on, I raced to the bedstand that housed my dagger. Reign had recuperated it for me from Lucian while I'd been with Elisa. From what I heard, The Fae-hole was still recovering at the healer, some of his mysterious wounds not attributable to our mid-air battle. I was fairly certain my professor had something to do with it, but neither one of us had brought it up.

After all the chaos, I'd completely forgotten about my dagger. I also hadn't mentioned the incident to a certain temperamental professor. Perhaps, I should have... Yanking the dagger out from the drawer, I ran my finger across the gleaming crystal. A flicker of light kindled, but nothing like what I'd seen the other day. Bringing the hilt up to the medallion, I pressed it against the golden pendant.

The metal immediately grew warm and a buzz of energy skimmed my skin.

The creak of the chamber door whipping open sent my heart soaring into my throat and my arms across my exposed torso. "Reign!" I cried when I took in the broody Shadow Fae filling the doorway.

"Good gods, Aelia!" he barked, slamming the door behind him. *Behind him*! It didn't even occur to him to remain outside.

"You couldn't even knock?" I hissed as I spun around, shielding my front only to reveal my nearly bare backside.

"It isn't as if I haven't already seen—"

"Just stop it! Close your eyes and let me dress."

"Fine." His footfalls echoed across the chamber, and the leather settee squealed as he sank in. "My eyes are closed," he grumbled. "And for the record, you are Fae, and you've been living amongst us for months now. You should have gotten over this nudity issue by now."

"Fae you," I hissed.

An unexpected chuckle pursed Reign's lips, and it dawned on me, it was the first time I'd heard him laugh in days.

"What's gotten into you lately?" I asked once I was dressed in my fighting leathers. "You can look now."

He swiveled around on the divan and faced me, but I remained on the opposite side of the chamber, keeping my distance. Nothing good ever came of us being too close. "Nothing," he muttered, his eyes not quite meeting mine.

I hazarded a step closer. "For someone so intent on protecting me, you've been decidedly absent."

"I'm never far."

His words rang true. Though he had been physically removed, his slithering shadows had been a constant.

"What have you been doing?" My feet propelled me toward him, despite my brain knowing better, as if my body couldn't help but be close to him.

"Draven has had me preoccupied."

"With what?" A prickle of fear raised the hair on my arms. At least my epic failure in the last trial shouldn't have brought more unwanted attention. Except for maybe that gilded orb...

"Nothing that concerns you." His expression shuttered and I took it as my cue to put an end to this discussion. Gods, the male was so infuriating.

"Oh, there you are." Rue appeared from the bathing chamber with only a flimsy towel wrapped around her slender torso.

Reign's gaze flitted toward her, but a bored expression descended across his handsome face before it pivoted to meet mine once more. A trickle of satisfaction quickened my pulse. Rue was stunning, and without clothes? What male wouldn't ogle?

"Are you prepared for this evening's trial, Aelia?" Reign's question drew my thoughts to more important matters. The final trial. With my scores so far, as long as I did better than average, I would pass.

"Of course."

Rue swung her arm around me and threw Reign a beaming smile. "We're going to slay, Professor Darkthorn."

"I look forward to it." He rose from the sofa, eyes intent on mine. "Rue, do you mind? I need to speak to your roommate in private."

"Of course not. I'll throw on my clothes and go visit Devin before the trial."

"Again?" I squealed.

"Never can get too much of that tension out." She tossed

me yet another wink before disappearing into the depths of her closet to dress.

Reign stalked closer, and his smirk turned downright sinful. "She's not wrong," he murmured. "It could be a good exercise for you... to dispel some of that built up *rais*."

I gasped, and Reign's smile only grew more brazen.

"Well, you've made it clear we can never be together," I whisper-hissed, "so is there someone else you have in mind, professor?"

The smile slid right off, replaced by something lethal. He erased the distance between us, his shadows whipping into a whirlwind of pure night, wrapping us up. His hand wrapped around my neck, fingers gently grazing my throat. "No one is to ever touch you, do you understand?" he rasped.

"No one but you?" I choked out. "Only you refuse to—"

"There are other ways to release the tension, princess." With his hand tightening around my neck in a possessive hold, he grabbed my free hand and pressed my palm to the apex of my thighs.

Another sharp release of air pushed between my clenched lips.

He guided my fingers just below the laces of my leathers and exerted pressure. His bottomless orbs fixed to mine and a tempest of desire swirled beneath the surface. His aura was so dark, it was pure, endless night. "Do you need me to help you?"

I slowly shook my head as heat pooled between my thighs. I had touched myself there a handful of times in my life, but never like this. Never in front of smoldering eyes. I'd never felt the need, the desire so overpowering it felt as if it wasn't satiated, I'd explode.

My hips tilted, eager for the pressure my own palm exerted, urged on by his. Good gods, was I mad? Was I really going to allow this to happen? I rocked against my own hand, an unnamable force building at my core. It was nothing like I'd ever experienced before. Energy blossomed, stemming from that spot between my legs and rushing to the base of my spine.

"Eyes on me, princess."

My gaze snapped to meet his, to drown in those endless obsidian pools. I wanted nothing more than to be lost in Reign, to forget about everything else. He was this all-consuming force I simply couldn't fight anymore.

Icy fingers crawled across my tunic, the dark tendrils of *nox* spiraling around my breasts and raising my nipples to sharp peaks. The faint touch through the soft suede was pure torture. One shadow broke off and curled around my waist, moving farther down until it slipped beneath the waistband of my leathers and skimmed my most sensitive area.

I gasped, the frosty, airy touch against my heated skin sending fiery sensations through every inch of my body. Good gods, who knew his shadows could do *that*?

Those ghostly fingers ran across my center, teasing and torturous until the pressure grew to an overpowering crescendo. "Reign," I groaned, those fathomless spheres locked on mine.

"Let go, princess, I've got you." The jagged edge to his tone compelled me over the edge.

My head fell back, and pure pleasure throttled my veins as I climaxed with stars dancing across my vision. My breaths were ragged, my heart and lungs struggling to resume normal functioning. Goddess, I'd never felt anything like that before.

A sharp slam snapped me from the lusty oblivion, and I blinked quickly, drawing free of Reign's hold to face the door. His shadows dispersed, revealing my now empty chamber. By the gods, I'd been so wrapped up in the moment, I'd completely forgotten about Rue.

Reign must have followed my line of sight because he muttered, "She didn't see anything. We were completely covered in my shadows."

I whirled on him and jabbed my finger into his obnoxiously hard chest. "Don't ever do that again."

A frown carved into his jaw. "Give you a tiny bit of pleasure? The least you deserve in all of this?"

"I don't want pleasure! Not like that," I amended. I wanted to feel *his* hand, his fingers against me. The traitorous thoughts sent my stomach into somersaults, the lingering aftershocks of my pleasure still vibrating my entire being. I staggered back, moving away from him. "I have to go..."

"We're not finished here, Aelia."

"Then, what? What do you want from me?"

"I'm only trying to protect you, damn it!" He threw his hands in the air and a storm of shadows zipped across the room. "In a few hours you will be on Shadow Fae lands, and I fear whatever is blocking your powers is coming undone. If anyone discovers who you are—"

"Who am I, Reign? It's clear you have an idea. All of your theories and conjectures... You're a clever male, that much is clear. What is it you know that I do not?" I closed the distance between us, too riled up to understand or even contemplate the risk. "Tell me!"

"I cannot!" he roared.

"Why?"

"Because if I admit it to you, it will become real. And I cannot accept that, Aelia."

Genuine fear pulsed in his eyes, encircling his form in an aura of bright sapphire and deep navy.

Lowering my voice, I pressed my palm to his chest. His heart beat wildly beneath my hand, a mad hemmingbyrd fighting with every last breath to survive. "Please, Reign."

A torrent of shadows curled around his imposing form, and he disappeared.

Chapter Fifty-Four

A dense canopy cast the ominous Sombra Forest in perpetual twilight, shadows stretching and morphing on a light breeze coming off the Luminoc River. I stood between Rue and Symon, every nerve ending intensely aware. The air was thick with whispers—each shadow a voice, each murmur a potential deceit or hidden truth.

My fingers curled around the scroll that had appeared on my bedside table this morning.

The final trial: The Shadows Whisper

Objective: Traverse a dense forest where shadows communicate secrets and lies within the time allotted. Competitors must discern truth from falsehoods whispered by the shadows using their powers to illuminate the truth.

How did one illuminate the truth?

I would have asked one of our professors, but the moment

383

Rue and I had gotten dressed, hoods were dropped atop our heads and we were whisked away only to re-emerge from the darkness a moment ago.

In Shadow Fae lands…

Beyond the circle of first-years gathered, Arcanum Citadel loomed in the distance, towering spires of obsidian stretching high into the endless night sky. Memories of the last time I'd found myself on this side of the Luminoc assaulted my senses. I scanned the murky forest for my professor, but he was nowhere to be found. And with the abundance of shadows slinking around every corner of the woodland, it was impossible to tell at this distance which were his. If any at all.

"Raysa, help us," Symon muttered. "Do you feel that? That emptiness?" He pressed his hand to his chest.

Rue nodded, so I numbly followed her lead. But it was a total lie. Instead of the void the others felt, I'd never felt so whole. There had always been some sort of trickle of energy when I set foot in the Court of Umbral Shadows, but never anything like this.

An unnamable force ignited in my core, slowly inching across my skin, through my veins. It was a prickle of awareness that sprang from the base of my spine and blossomed in my chest. My hand instinctively moved to the medallion beneath my tunic. The usually cool metal was warm beneath my fingertips, pulsing with life. Echoing the steady vibration was the dagger at my hip. The crystal seared through my leathers, warming the skin beneath.

Good gods, what if I *was* Shadow Fae?

As we waited in the ever-thickening silence, I scanned the lurking shadows, desperate to feel some sort of connection. I called to them, summoned the dark minions in my mind. The energy coating my veins flared, but not a whisper of darkness emerged.

This was crazy. Reign was driving me completely mad.

His original premise was much more likely. My *rais* was

blocked somehow, and the spell cast was unraveling the more time I spent on Shadow Fae soil. That must be it.

The blare of a horn sent my pulse skyrocketing.

"Let's do this!" Rue pressed her palms together, and a faint glow lit up our murky surroundings. She took off a second later, winding through the thick copse of sprawling trees.

"Rue, wait!" I had to warn my friends about the gloomwhisper. Surely, the dark beast would be out tonight. I sprinted after her with Sy at my side. "We have to be careful. There are creatures out here..."

She twisted her head over her shoulder. Belmore and Ariadne along with Kian and Lucian were only a few yards behind. "I'm more concerned about the other first-years than the monsters lurking this side of the Luminoc."

Dark fingers of night curled between us as we ran. "They're coming for you," they hissed. "Trust no one, or you will not survive."

The menacing whispers echoed through the stillness, elevating the rapid pounding of my heart.

"Did you hear that?" Sy whisper-shouted.

I nodded slowly. "We cannot become distracted by their words. They're only trying to trick us."

"Right." Rue marched forward, leading the way through a dark thicket, hands still aglow.

"Do you know where we're going?" The darkness closed in around us, the canopy of trees overhead so thick, not a sliver of moonlight squeezed through. If it weren't for Rue's light, I was fairly certain I'd be unable to discern the tip of my nose.

"I have a general idea," she called out over her shoulder.

Another shadow circled, tickling the sensitive shell of my ear. And where Reign's shadows lit me up inside, these had the exact opposite effect.

"Aelia... oh, little Kin, you will never prove your worth among the Fae. You are nothing..."

I swatted at the dark wraith as its words hit a nerve, wishing

I could slice my dagger across its ghostly form. Then it would see how worthless I was.

Ariadne raced past us with Belmore at her heels. The forest split ahead, a sharp V in the thick terrain. She paused for an instant at the crossroads before veering to the right.

"Which way should we go?" asked Symon.

"To the left." Rue raised her palm, lighting up the pathway.

"Are you sure?"

My roommate nodded. "Heaton said to always move East. There's a clearing in the center of the Sombra Forest which marks the end of the trial. The sun is in the west, in the Court of Ethereal Light, so if we simply keep moving away from our center, we will find our way."

"I think we should go this way." Symon pointed along the gloomy path down which Ariadne and Belmore disappeared.

"Why?" I inched closer to my friend. Unlike Rue, I didn't feel the magnetic pull toward the sun.

"I just have a feeling."

Shadows curled around Symon's back, writhing around his form.

"It's the shadows! They're only trying to manipulate you."

"What in all the realms are you talking about?" Sy stared at me as if I'd grown a second head.

"Don't you hear their whispers?"

He slowly shook his head, light brows furrowed.

"Don't you see them?" I pointed over his shoulder.

Sy spun around, squinting through the interminable night. "See what?"

Oh, stars. Grabbing my friend by the arm, I dragged him to the left path where Rue waited.

"You're sure it was Heaton that told you to go east and not some trick of the shadows?"

Her head bounced up and down. "Heat told me yesterday when we spoke of the upcoming trial."

"Then we go east, and we do not deviate, despite what our guts tell us."

"Fine," Symon grumbled. "You're lucky your ears are so cute, little Kin, or I would have abandoned you long ago." He threw me a cheeky grin, and I dug my elbow into his side.

We trudged through the unnerving forest for what felt like an eternity. Unlike in the other trials where the timeframe was clear, today we had no ticking timer, no idea when this event would come to an end. Worse, I was fairly certain we were moving in circles.

The twisting paths grew thicker, the trees more ominous, jagged branches reaching and scraping as we passed.

"Oh, goddess!" Rue came to an abrupt stop and clapped her hand over her mouth, pointing down a murky trail. "Is that Phoebia?"

Tipping my head back, my gaze traveled to where she pointed and up the enormous trunk until it settled on a body hanging over a large limb. Waves of blonde hair cascaded over the female's head, her slender form wrapped in thick, strangling vines. Dark purple veins crisscrossed her exposed flesh, and a sickly green pallor coated her skin.

"Oh, gods, how awful." I squeezed my eyes closed.

"Aelia, help me!"

My ears perked up at the familiar deep timbre. "Reign?" My legs were moving toward the sound before I could stop them.

"Aelia, where are you going?" Rue called out.

But I didn't slow, I couldn't. Not when Reign's voice sounded like that. Pain. Desperation. Agony.

"Aelia, please. Help me!"

I sprinted through the woods, jagged twigs lashing across my face until tears filled my eyes. "Reign! Where are you?"

"Over here! Help me!"

Pumping my arms, I willed my body to move faster. My legs ached, my muscles screaming from the strain, but I kept going. Jagged branches slashed at my face, biting into my skin as I raced through the forest. The faint sound of rushing water reached my ears, barely perceptible over the wild thrumming of my pulse. I pushed myself harder, faster. "I'm coming, Reign!"

My boots pounded the earthy terrain, moving so quickly they were nothing but a blur. The sole of my shoe slid forward, and my arms shot out to steady myself. Within a fraction of a second, I glanced down to see the thrashing waters of the Luminoc at the edge of the cliff I precariously wobbled upon.

No, no, no!

My hands scrambled for purchase, clinging onto a looming branch as one foot slid over the edge. Wrapping my fingers around the thick limb, I dragged myself back onto solid ground. My lungs heaved, constricting from the strain.

For Fae's sake, I nearly plummeted over the ledge.

Heavy footfalls pounded behind me, and Rue and Symon emerged from the darkness. "Aelia! Are you all right?"

I exhaled a sharp breath and nodded. "Just barely."

Symon's head swiveled over his shoulder, and his smile of relief twisted. "Emily?" His brows furrowed as he stared into the encroaching forest. "What is she—"

"No!" I shouted. "It's not her."

He spun at me, panic in his eyes. "How do you know about Emily?"

"I don't. I only know that I just followed a voice that clearly wasn't real and nearly fell to my death."

His light eyes were wild, pain cutting into his handsome face. "It sounds so real, Aelia. Are you certain?"

Confirming the wicked shadows writhing between us, I dipped my head. "It's only an illusion, a trick of the shadows. I'm sorry."

Gritting his teeth, he released a shaky breath.

"Who is she?"

Sy shook his head, the haunted look in his eye stilling my tongue.

"And we've gotten completely off track," Rue grumbled, eyeing the river.

"I'm sorry, I thought it was Reign..."

She squeezed my shoulder and offered an encouraging smile. "It's all right. I know it's not your fault." Weaving one arm through mine and the other through Symon's she dragged us back into the foreboding depths of the forest.

CONSERVATORY OF LUCE

FORGED IN LIGHT

TEMPERED IN TRUTH

Chapter Fifty-Five

elia

"We must be close to the end now." Rue signaled us forward as muffled voices filled in around us.

We'd only run into a few other first-years so far, but now they seemed to be everywhere. Or was it only the shadows' whispers?

"Child of twilight you will not succeed. You will perish like all who tried before you..." The ominous whispers continued, a deafening song with an endless tune. "Princess, they are coming for you..."

Every hair on my nape stood at attention, and the burgeoning power in my core grew more restless.

"You cannot hide in the shadows for much longer, princess. They will find you..."

"Ugh, just shut up!" I clapped my hands over my ears and squeezed my eyes closed. When I finally reopened them, the voices had stopped, and two pairs of wary eyes stared back at me.

"Are you okay, Aelia?" Rue's bright irises twinkled with the faint moonlight, highlighting the concern in her eyes.

"Yes, sorry, it's the shadows, they simply haven't stopped since I set foot on this Raysa forsaken land."

Her hand clasped around mine and she tugged me forward. "Come on, we're almost there, I can feel it."

A sharp crack resounded, sending goosebumps up and down my spine, and Kian and Lucian dropped from the sky. Or rather, from an enormous tree.

"This is the end for you, Kin," Kian snarled, the sliver of moonlight catching on the grisly scar across his face. "We will not have the likes of you sullying our great academy for a single day longer."

"Oh, get out of our way, you imbecile," Rue growled right back.

"Why must we fight each other?" Symon added. "In a few days' time, we'll be pitted against the Shadow Fae. Can't you save your damned energy?"

"You know that's not how it works, Lightspire," Lucian hissed. "You're an embarrassment to your family, associating with the likes of her."

"Oh, fuck off, Lucian," Sy barked, and flames flickered across his fingertips. "Or I'll shove my light up your ass. Maybe it'll loosen you up a bit."

"Please, let's not fight," I hissed. "We're nearly at the end, and all of this can be over."

Kian shook his head. "It will never be over until you've been banished from Conservatory grounds. You do not deserve the title of Royal Guardian, even if you end up patrolling the border of the Wilds to protect your precious Kin."

I'd had about enough of this arrogant male. I'd tried to reason with him, attempted to understand his closed-minded ways. Clearly, the time for playing nicely was over.

I drew my dagger in one hand and summoned the swirling energy, the power begging to burst free. A light flare exploded from my palm, sending Kian and Lucian hurtling back. If I hadn't enclosed Rue and Symon in a glittering orb an instant before, they would have suffered a similar fate.

The males landed on their behinds across the small clearing, both muttering curses.

"I am not a lowly Kin," I growled. "I deserve to be here as much as the rest of you. You can accept that or die trying to kill me."

Kian and Lucian pushed themselves off the ground and exchanged a dark glance. My power blossomed, fiery *rais* filling my core. Before the light daggers sailed from their palms, I expanded the radiant shield around all three of us. Their weapons bounced off the glittering orb and disintegrated within the murky earth.

A sharp hiss ricocheted through the forest and the tiny hairs along my arms rose. Oh, no. Heavy footfalls crashed through the trees an instant before the gloomwhisper appeared. The massive beast, its monstrous body ethereal and shifting, emerged from the darkness.

"What in all the realms?" Symon shrieked as the monster stalked toward us.

"Gloomwhisper!" I cried as I shoved my friends back. "Don't let its talons touch you, they're poison."

Rue and Symon wore matching questioning expressions, but they nodded all the same as we staggered back toward the ring of trees. My fingers tightened around the hilt of my dagger and the crystal grew warm against my palm. The Shadow Fae creature loomed between us and Kian and Lucian. From between its shadowy form, I could just make out the terror carved into the males' faces before they darted between the trees.

Cowards.

"Get out of my home, Light Fae," it hissed.

"Happy to," Sy replied. "We were just leaving, actually."

Its shadowy talons shot out, the wraithlike appendages solidifying as it struck out at Rue.

"No!" I charged and sliced my dagger through its arm.

The ghostly limb disintegrated beneath my blade, a screech ripping from the creature's mouth.

Symon summoned his light and tossed a volley of glowing orbs in rapid fire.

The gloomwhisper hissed and shrieked as the light pierced his smokey form, but he continued toward us all the same. His clawed hand reached for us again, and I arced my dagger for another attack. The blade cut through its smoky torso, and its screams echoed through the thickening tension of the forest.

"How is that working?" Rue cried out.

"No idea." Ignoring my friend, I continued battling the twisted tendrils as Sy and Rue launched waves of luminous energy at the creature.

Though my blade clearly affected the monster, they didn't stop him. With every limb severed, another grew in its place.

"Try its eyes," Rue shouted over the cacophony of hissing.

Now, how would I reach its eyes? The beast stood over ten feet tall. Gods, I wished I had wings like Reign. Scanning the clearing, I found a massive tree at the edge of the circle. If I could lure it closer, climb the trunk and jump down like Kian and Lucian had done, I could, in theory, strike with enough force to reach its head.

"Rue, Sy, this way!" I motioned toward the giant tree, and the three of us sprinted toward it with the gloomwhisper on our heels.

As if my teammates had read my mind, they began their assault, waves of *rais* flowing from their outstretched hands as I shimmied up the tree.

"Hurry, Aelia," Rue called out. "It's difficult to sustain our *rais* without the sun."

Of course, I knew that. As Light Fae, we should all experience that dampening of our powers.

Only, I did not.

Once I reached a sturdy branch, I crawled to the edge with my dagger between my teeth. Just below, the enormous creature made of unearthly shadowstuff writhed and clawed at my friends. Smoke and solid darkness coiled around Rue, as it pulled her into its deadly embrace.

"Rue!" Symon cried out, reaching for her as she disappeared into the beast's shadows.

With a quick prayer to Raysa *and* Noxus, I leapt from the tallest branch with my dagger poised to strike. The gloomwhisper's luminous eyes lifted as I sailed through the air, an instant before I struck. It let out an unearthly howl and swiped at my torso with a jagged claw.

Its talon ripped through my leather armor, and I bit back a squeal as it sliced through the flesh beneath. Arcing my arm in a furious strike, I jabbed my blade between its glowing eyes.

Another shriek pierced the chaos of my thundering heartbeats, and the gloomwhisper disintegrated beneath me.

Chapter Fifty-Six

A *elia*

A silly giggle erupted from my lips as I sipped the honeyed wine, the sun's rays kissing my bare shoulders. Sprawled all around me were the remaining first-years, everyone too drunk on wine and other spirits to bother with each other today. Of the hundred-and-sixty students that had entered the Conservatory at the start of term, less than a hundred remained. Flare Squad had done surprisingly well with thirteen of us still standing. Scorch Squad had won the Ethereal Trials thanks to Kian and Lucian abandoning us against the gloomwhisper, but at least my friends and I had survived.

Though I knew the greatest challenge of the term was yet to come, I resolved to enjoy this brief respite. Tonight was the Winter Solstice, the Night of the Longest Shadow, a time for great celebration. Then, in three days' time, we'd battle Arcanum Citadel.

And more would die.

I dismissed the grisly thought and swallowed another big gulp of wine.

"I still cannot believe how you destroyed that gloomwhisper," Symon purred, clinking his glass against mine. "My little Kin is all grown up."

"Shhh," I hissed. I'd sworn my friends to secrecy about my dagger. Though neither understood the ramifications quite like Reign had, they vowed to keep my secret, with an oath and all.

"To Raysa!" Rue crashed her goblet against mine, then Symon's, then anyone else close enough to reach.

Thanks to Elisa's miraculous healing touch, along with a few other healers who had been brought in from the king's personal staff, all the remaining first-years were in peak condition once again, myself included. The gloomwhisper's claw had only skimmed my flesh, so the healing process had been greatly shortened this time around. Or at least, that was the most plausible answer Elisa had conjured.

A part of me feared it was my Shadow Fae side emerging.

Now back on the right side of the river, the flourishing power had been tempered.

That familiar presence pressed upon me, and I lifted my gaze in time to find my temperamental professor stalking toward the field. My traitorous heart staggered at the sight of him, at the straining of each perfectly sculpted muscle of his torso beneath his dark cloak, at the entourage of shadows. This was the first I'd seen of him since his disappearance the night before the final trial.

In which, he'd abandoned me.

I held onto the bitter sentiment, stoking the building anger. I couldn't do this back and forth with him any longer. I simply would not.

I opened my mouth to say as much but the broody Faehole stalked right past me without so much as a glance. I twisted my head over my shoulder and followed his dark form until it reached the headmaster and King Elian. The pair stood beneath the entrance of the Hall of Glory. The royal's icy glare darted in my direction, his frosty expression sending goosebumps rippling across my arms.

"Why do you suppose the king is here again?" Rue asked. She must have followed my curious gaze.

"I heard he never left," replied Symon. "His Ethereal Royal Highness has been observing the final two trials."

All the air swept from my lungs in one glacial blast. What if he'd seen my dagger? What if that was why Reign had been summoned?

The goblet slipped from my hands, sending the glass tumbling to the ground and the rosy wine spilling across my lap.

"Oh, curses," I muttered. "I better go clean this up—"

"No, don't go!" Rue whined. She flashed me her hand and a toothy grin. "I can blast you with some heat and get you all dried up in no time."

"But I don't want it to stain..." I motioned at the dark tights lamely.

"You can send them to be washed tomorrow, or better yet, you can simply ask for a new pair."

"But that would be so wasteful."

"You can take the Kin out of Feywood, but you can't take Feywood out of the Kin." Sy shot me a smirk, and I retaliated with a smack to his head. "Ow," he whined.

"I'll be right back, I promise."

"You better." Rue waggled a long finger. "Besides we must prepare for the Winter Solstice soon. I haven't decided on my gown yet, have you?"

I shook my head. I hadn't even taken a glance. Until last night, I wasn't certain I would survive the trials.

I was. Sol's voice ricocheted through my mind, and I instinctively searched the skies for his massive form. Nothing but pale cerulean stretched until the border of the Court of Umbral Shadows where darkness prevailed.

Where are you?
Hunting. I must be prepared for the battle.
Can we just not talk about anything bad for one day?
Certainly, Aelia. Tomorrow, we train.
Deal.
Be safe, little Kin.
You too, Sol.

Once our connection was severed, I marched toward the Hall of Glory, my gaze intent on the heated discussion taking place atop the marble steps. If I wasn't certain I'd get caught, I would have drawn a celestial glyph to amplify my hearing.

The moment I neared, Reign's eyes chased to mine, and the males went silent.

I dipped my head as I approached, then sketched my best attempt at a bow once I stood in front of the king. "Excuse the interruption, your Ethereal Highness," I murmured. "And to you, headmaster, but I need to speak to Professor Darkthorn. It's urgent."

Reign's eyes narrowed, his perfect lips twisting. "I'm afraid that's not—"

"Go ahead, Darkthorn," the headmaster interrupted. "We'll continue this conversation later."

"But headmaster—"

"I said go."

With a grunt of frustration, Reign spun toward me and cocked a dark brow. "What is it?"

I pushed past the pang of hurt at his tone and held onto the anger from earlier. He was lying to me, keeping things from me, and generally acting like a complete and utter Faehole. "Not here," I hissed.

Then spinning past the foyer flooded with Raysa's glorious, shimmering light, I trudged toward the suspended glass staircase. Winding past the first step, I led Reign into a small nook beneath the landing.

"Why did the king summon you?" I whisper-hissed the moment his imposing form filled the hidden alcove.

"*That's* why you dragged me here?" Pure venom laced his tone, and it only snapped my spine straighter. If he thought he could intimidate me with that growl, he was sorely mistaken.

"Yes, *professor*. Why else would you think? It isn't as if I forced you here to have my way with you."

The hard set of his jaw softened, and a twinkle of starlight flickered through the darkness. "Shame... that would have been much more interesting."

"Don't you dare," I snarled before smacking my palm into his unyielding chest. "You cannot keep distracting me with those twinkling eyes and that damned wicked smirk."

"I didn't know my eyes twinkled at you." That stupid smile only grew more ridiculous.

"Reign! Tell me right now why the king is here and if he knows about my dagger."

The grin vanished and darkness melted over his features. "He does not. But you've piqued his interest. Clearly, Draven has been blathering on about you and the proph—" He slammed his jaw shut, the crack echoing across the silent space.

"The what?"

An expression of pure torture descended over his countenance, a scowl slashing his lips.

"I swear to all the gods, Reign, if you do not tell me what is going on, I will walk away and never return. I will jump on Sol's back and force him to fly me to the other end of the continent where no one will ever see me again."

A long moment of silence fell between us, the tempest of emotions raging across the dark depths of Reign's eyes billowing with each haggard breath. A vein across his forehead twitched, and he released a frustrated sigh. "There is a prophecy about the child of twilight..."

Child of twilight? Where had I heard that phrase before?

"A child of twilight, born from the dance of light and dark, shall emerge with the power to reshape destinies. From the celestial embrace and the shadow's whisper, a harbinger of cosmic balance shall be brought forth.

A fateful choice awaits her - to heal or to harm, to nurture or annihilate. Her every step shall resonate through realms, influencing the very fabric of existence.

When the child of twilight shall come of age, her choices, guided by the celestial and obscured by shadows, shall determine the fate of worlds. Whether she becomes a beacon of hope or a harbinger of oblivion, the child of twilight shall be the catalyst of an epochal choice - to bring forth a new dawn or plunge all into eternal dusk."

I stared, jaw nearly unhinged as Reign recited the prophecy, word for word. Once he finished, he stood motionless, dark gaze pinned to mine.

"And you believe I am the child of twilight?"

"It doesn't matter what I believe, but what Draven and the king do."

"That's why the headmaster had you spying on me..." The pieces of the mysterious puzzle began to fall into place, and a whisper of dread filled my gut. The tension grew thicker, the silence more ominous. Until an insane bout of laughter bubbled out. I keeled over as a fit of hysterics cramped my belly.

"Aelia," Reign growled. Squeezing my hands, he forced me to straighten. "This is serious."

"It's not me, Reign. It can't be. How could I be this child of twilight destined to destroy Aetheria? It's completely absurd."

"Is it though?" He reached for my dagger and freed it from the sheath at my hip. Dragging his finger across the crystal, the flicker of light danced before the darkness consumed the flame.

"There you two are!" Rue's voice sailed around the corner, and I snatched my dagger back and tucked it into the sheath.

She waggled her brows as she regarded us. "Did I interrupt something important?"

"No," we snapped in unison.

"Oh, goodness."

Symon turned the corner an instant later, wine sloshing over the rim of his goblet. "Come ladies, I am here to escort you to your chambers to begin the preparations for the Winter Solstice."

"How much time do we really need?" I glanced between my friends. Reign had already melted into the shadows like a big coward.

"Well, it will take at least a few hours," said Rue.

"Then there's the obligatory pre-celebration in my room," Sy added.

"So yes, it is time to begin." Rue slid her arm through mine and jerked me away from Reign. "Professor, I take it you will dress in your own room this afternoon?"

"I don't—"

"Aelia will be more than safe in our capable hands. Right, Sy?"

"Of course." He laced his arm across my shoulders so that I was sandwiched between my two friends.

"We will see you tonight, professor!" Rue wiggled her fingers over her shoulder before towing me up the steps.

Chapter Fifty-Seven

A*elia*

"Oh, I don't know, Rue, it seems like a bit much..." And still, I could not tear my eyes away from the looking glass. I did not recognize the female before me. All thoughts of the prophecy, of gloom and doom, of the final battle flew right out of my mind.

The exquisite ballgown molded perfectly to every curve of my body as if painted on by the goddess. The fabric spun of a shimmering gold satin sparkled with countless tiny lights, creating an ethereal effect as if adorned in stardust or woven with the essence of light itself. The embroidered bodice of the dress was intricately detailed with a plunging neckline that fit my figure perfectly and accentuated an elegance I never knew I possessed.

"You look absolutely radiant, Aelia."

"One hundred percent agree," Symon interjected. "I would not change a thing."

I curled a long lock of wild blonde hair around my finger, the errant strand refusing to remain in the elaborate updo Rue had concocted. I studied every inch of the gown, unable to look away. Goddess, if I was trying not to call attention to myself this certainly was not the appropriate dress. I appeared bathed in a celestial glow, every exposed millimeter of my skin iridescent beneath the sunlight streaming in from above.

Finally tearing my gaze away from my reflection, I focused on my friends. Rue was stunning in a deep crimson gown highlighting her petite form with her pale blonde hair in elegant waves, while Sy looked handsome as always with a pristine double-breasted surcoat in pure white with matching trousers. Both had already helped themselves to honeyed wine, their eyes glistening with mirth.

"So what exactly will we do at this grand celebration?"

"Besides drink heavily, stuff ourselves with culinary delights, and dance our asses off?" Sy grabbed my hand and twirled me in a quick circle until my head spun.

"Yes, besides all that," I laughed.

Rue released her goblet and lifted a finger. "First, a grand ceremony will be held in which a chosen Fae, often one of the most promising students at the Conservatory, ignites the Eternal Flame using the last rays of dawn. The flame symbolizes the return of the sun and the triumph of light over darkness and is essential to the celebration of the Winter Solstice. The sacred bonfire is kept burning throughout the night, and its light is said to ward off evil spirits and bless those who bask in its glow."

"Wow..."

"And then everyone gets soused on the grand assortment of Fae spirits," Symon interjected.

"That's when the fun truly begins." Rue waggled her light brows just as two sharp knocks echoed across the chamber. "Speaking of fun, that must be Devin." She clapped her hands before flitting toward the entrance.

Rue yanked the door opened, and my heart flip-flopped at

the sight of the male obscuring the doorway. "Oh, it's for you, Aelia." She bounced back to her side of the chamber as I stood frozen, unable to rip my eyes away from Reign's daunting form.

His hair was pulled back in a tie at his nape, with a few tousled wisps having come loose, framing a face marked by strong, angular features and that piercing, intense gaze. The long, black cloak that cascaded from his shoulders was fastened at the front with ornate silver brooches featuring intricate designs. Though he stood perfectly still, the luxurious, heavy fabric somehow flowed dramatically with each inhale, adding to his imposing presence. The high-collared tunic beneath made from rich, dark material molded to each muscular dip and valley of his torso, emphasizing his strapping build. His chest lifted on an inhale, and the elaborate embroidery of the dark threads of his tunic caught the light, shimmering beneath Raysa's watchful eye.

"Noxus, princess, you look more glorious than the goddess herself," he whispered on an exhale. His shadows curled around us, an icy veil of darkness shielding us from the obtrusive light streaming in overhead.

I teetered forward on the high heels Rue forced me to wear, my legs moving to Reign of their own accord. In that brief moment, all of his sins were forgotten. My hand jutted out, reaching for him as if in a trance. My fingers landed on the ornate brooch, brushing the cold metal. "It's... beautiful," I murmured.

He inched closer, his frosty breath skimming the shell of my rounded ear. "It's made of infernium vein."

My heart jolted, punching my ribcage. Infernium vein? As in the non-existent metal that forged the blade of my dagger?

"Come on, you two." Rue barreled through Reign's shadows, drawing me back to the present and to Devin now standing in the hallway waiting.

Symon wrapped his hand around mine and tugged me out the door. "It's time to celebrate!"

"In the midst of this great celebration, we must not forget why we come together to commemorate the Winter Solstice." The headmaster's voice boomed across the field behind the Hall of Glory, which had been transformed into a spectacle of glittering lights. A cascade of warm golden hues and flickering candlelight bathed the enchanted space. Twilight. It was a rare sight on this side of the Luminoc River. "It is said that the first Fae emerged during a Winter Solstice, the Night of the Longest Shadow, born from the union of the frost-covered earth and the fire of the celestial heavens. And so, we light the Eternal Flame to celebrate the return of the sun and the triumph of light over darkness."

Wild applause rang out across the lawn, every student and member of the Conservatory staff in attendance. And beside the headmaster, stood King Elian and his entourage of Royal Guardians. His unexplained presence only exacerbated the flutter of nerves in my stomach.

Sol, where are you?

In Mysthallia, land of the spellbinders. I find their livestock more pleasant than those in Aetheria. Do you need me?

No, just checking in.

Enjoy tonight, Aelia. You've earned it. And should you need me, I'm only a quick flight away.

Just the sound of Sol's voice quieted the nervous clatter. *You're right, and I will.*

"...Miss Aelia Ravenwood, please come forward."

My gaze snapped toward the headmaster as the mental connection was interrupted.

"Aelia, go!" Rue shoved me toward the dais.

"What?" I croaked.

"You were chosen to light the Eternal Flame." My roommate parted the crowd, shooing everyone out of my way.

Reign was by my side before I took the first step, his

shadows whirling in a maddening fury. "No grand show of your *rais*, do you understand?"

I nodded quickly as Reign fell back and the throng dispersed, and I found myself in front of an immense pyre. King Elian's scrutinizing gaze raked over me, an overpowering energy skimming my skin. Could he sense the dagger hidden beneath my skirts?

"Congratulations, Miss Ravenwood," Draven drawled. "This is an incredible honor."

Sketching a bow, I dipped my head before the royal and the headmaster. "It is truly." I barely restrained the *thank you* before it burst free. Being indebted to Draven, or worse the King of Ethereal Light, was surely tantamount to a death sentence.

Spinning away from the two commanding males, I faced the enormous pyre and the entire student body beyond. The air prickled with anticipation. Somehow, within the hundreds gathered, I found him. My gaze instantly latched onto that dark, mercurial one, as if drawn to him like the sun.

Darkness clouded Reign's aura, a whirlwind of emotions streaking through the nebulous orb surrounding him. Still, he slowly dipped his head, and a reassuring smile crossed his lips. Pressing my hands together, I summoned a hint of *rais*, only enough to light a meager flame. My palms glowed and power extended to my fingertips. On a soft exhale, I released the flames, setting the pyramid of wood ablaze.

A roar of applause shattered the tense silence and the strained set of my shoulders relaxed. Whoops and laughter exploded across the lawn, boisterous music resounding from every corner.

I rushed off the platform, eager to disappear into the crowd. The moment I descended the steps, I was surrounded by Flare team. Heaton pulled me into a hug then handed me a goblet teeming with honeyed wine. "Congratulations, Aelia! You have truly impressed me." He pressed a chaste kiss to my cheek before releasing me. Rue and Symon embraced me next, each shouting their congratulations.

"Now we drink, then we dance!" Symon shouted.

"No, dance first!" Rue cried out. "I've already had plenty." She took my hands and spun me in a circle as the field transformed into a dancefloor.

Laughter and happy chatter echoed through the air, and a tangle of giddiness and relief filled my chest. I had survived. I'd made it this far, and I certainly was not giving up now. Reign was right. He did not choose losers, and I would succeed at the final battle, just as I had in everything else so far.

As if my thoughts had conjured my broody professor, Reign emerged from the dense horde, students fleeing at the terrifyingly beautiful sight of him and his ominous shadows. I, on the other hand, could not seem to look away or get my feet to move an inch.

Those dark minions circled me, wrapping me in their icy cold, and a chill raced up my spine. Reign's eyes latched onto mine, the starlight kissed in eternal night, and all the air abandoned my lungs. It took me a long moment to formulate words, let alone an entire sentence when he looked at me like that. "Are you going to tell me more about the prophecy now?" I finally forced out.

He shook his head, lips thinning. "No, Aelia Ravenwood, not tonight. Tonight, I am calling in my favor in return for the vow."

That tether around my heart constricted until my pulse slowed. I gaped, desperate to force my traitorous organ to keep pumping.

"Agree, Aelia, or the unbreakable binds of the vow will kill you."

"What are you asking of me?" I rasped out.

"To forget about all of it for one night. To forgive me for everything that I have done and everything I may do in the future. To give us this one evening together without any constraints from the past."

My chest ached, the tightening mystical binds growing more taut. I heaved in a breath, but the pain only intensified. "Reign, how can you ask that of me?" Gods, I should have been furious. He could have asked anything, but why this?

"Because it is the only thing I want and know I can never have otherwise." The pain in his eyes mirrored my own, a scorching, blinding ache that knew no bounds. How could I forget it all?

But a vow with the Fae was binding. I had no other choice. I had to agree or forfeit my life.

And goddess, I wanted to agree. I wished for nothing more than to spend a night with Reign unhindered by our circumstances or the chaos around us.

"Okay," I murmured.

A heart-stopping smile melted across his lips as he offered his hand. "I, Reign Darkthorn release you, Aelia Ravenwood from this vow in exchange for one unforgettable evening. Now that your end of the bargain has been completed, I will take your secret with me to the grave."

The pain in my chest vanished, the steel knots around my heart unraveling. All the brewing anger I felt a moment ago disappeared. I drew in a breath and leaned into his touch. "I must say that was the last thing I expected for you to ask, professor."

A mischievous smirk curled the perfect bow of his lips. "I am pleased that after all this time together, I haven't grown predictable."

I snorted on a laugh. "Never."

His fingers tightened around my own, and he tugged me closer. Rings of impenetrable shadow closed around us, shielding us from watchful eyes, and when he lifted me in his arms, I knew exactly what would come next.

Chapter Fifty-Eight

Brilliant light gave way to the darkness, and my head finally stopped spinning when we emerged from the shadows and appeared in... Reign's chamber?

Unlike every other space across this grand campus, not a shred of light touched the surface. Cool darkness prevailed, originating from the corners and sweeping across the enormous space. A massive four poster bed stood in the center, bathed in liquid night. Starlight danced across the canopy and swathes of gauzy onyx material cascaded across the structure carved from pure obsidian.

Reign carefully released me, so slowly that I skimmed over every inch of his torso on my way down. Once I was on my feet again, my knees wobbled, whether from nerves or the shadow-traveling, I'd rather not consider. My palms skimmed his cloak, then found the intricately carved brooches.

"How are these made of infernium vein?"

He shrugged. "I'm not certain, but this cloak has been in my family for generations."

"Your family?"

His expression shuttered once again. "You promised, Aelia, one night, no discussion of the past or future."

My head dipped, and I exhaled a sharp breath. "Then what shall we do?"

A twinkle of mischief lit up those bottomless orbs. "Something I've dreamt of doing for months." His lips captured mine with the fury of a storm unleashed, a passionate tempest that swept away all thoughts of resistance and left only the raw, electric intensity of the moment.

I gasped for breath as his mouth ravaged mine, clinging to him as if he were the very air I needed to survive, the only thing anchoring me in a world that had narrowed to the intensity of this moment, this fiery kiss.

He lurched back, ripping his mouth from mine, and ice cascaded down my spine. "Wait..." he rasped. "Before this goes any further, I want to be clear. Your vow does not require anything of you beyond forgetting for one night what has since happened between us. It does not obligate you to any of this—"

I pressed my finger to his lips. "For Fae's sake, just be quiet and kiss me."

His mouth melted into a smile beneath my finger, and he drew the offending digit into his mouth. His tongue glided across the sensitive skin, and an embarrassing moan erupted from my darkest depths as I watched him.

"Mmm, I love it when you make those sounds, princess."

I withdrew my finger and caressed his cheek, the rough stubble tickling my palm. "Do you, now?"

"Oh, yes." He backed me toward his bed, and I stumbled when the back of my legs hit the footboard. His mouth descended over mine once more as he splayed me across the silky coverlet. "You have no idea what you do to me, Aelia, or how many times I've imagined making you mine. Gods, I've never felt anything like this."

"Neither have I..." The breathy admission against his lips was oddly startling. After everything we'd been through, I should be furious, despite the vow. But none of it mattered. With Reign, it felt as if the depth of my feelings were endless. The connection we shared was soul-deep, ingrained in my very bones.

His lips continued their assault, moving from my mouth along the curve of my jaw. He nibbled the sensitive skin of my lobe, and my back arched at the thrilling sensations. "Mmm, princess, those ears." He ran his tongue over the rounded tip and a faint groan rumbled in his throat. "They're so..."

"Perfect," I finished as I caressed the sharp point of his ear.

His eyes chased to mine and held. For an endless moment, he simply watched me as his fingers distractedly twirled a few strands of blonde-streaked hair. "I cannot believe I found you..." His words fell away, darkness carving into his jaw. I opened my mouth to ask what had brought on the sudden melancholy, but his lips captured mine before I could formulate the question.

Reign's shadows coiled around us, the icy tendrils tickling my heated flesh. The opposing sensations of fiery heat and frosty chill set my body ablaze. He deepened the kiss, the hunger in his assault growing ever more ravenous. I, too, couldn't get enough. I clung to his arms, hitched my dress up to wrap my legs around his hips, desperate to annihilate every shred of distance between us. Heat pooled below the billowing skirts of my gown. A need like I'd never experienced before blossomed deep in my core.

As if Reign could feel my burning desire, he nestled his hips between my legs and rocked against the ache between my thighs. Another groan escaped at the fiery sensations. My heartbeats no longer thrummed only for me, but rather for him, matching the manic pace vibrating his chest. "Reign..." I murmured.

"I know, princess. I feel it too."

"What is it?"

His lids slid closed and his lips dropped to my neck, then moved farther down until his tongue twirled across the glittering swirls of the Light Fae mark. He lifted his gaze to mine, something unreadable flashing across the midnight depths. "I honestly do not know."

His mouth descended lower still and anticipation tightened my core. His tongue slowly swept across his lips then over the swell of my breasts, spilling over the corset of my gown. "Oh, princess, you taste like the sweetest nectar of the gods."

A nervous giggle burst free. "I bet you say that to all the Fae ladies."

He snorted, his mouth curving into a scowl. "Not a single one."

A silly smile parted my lips. "It's a pity we only have tonight," I muttered.

"It's a damned shame."

"Because tomorrow, I will require you to explain yourself. All of it."

His gaze dipped, and a look I'd never seen from the arrogant professor flashed across his sculpted jaw. Regret? Remorse? Sadness? I had no idea, but a swirl of unease ignited in my gut. "I swear it."

Well, that was unexpected.

His mouth captured mine once more, tossing all thoughts of argument to the farthest recesses of my mind. All I could think about was Reign and every single point of contact of our flesh. Jolts of energy sparked between us, each touch sending tremors of desire racing through every inch.

I suddenly needed this gorgeous, ridiculous gown off. I needed him to touch me, for his shadows to blanket my bare skin. I wriggled beneath him, trying to squirm free of the oppressive corset, but the laces were knotted tight. As if he'd read my mind, or perhaps he'd noticed my struggle, he slowly shook his head.

"What?" I panted.

"As much as it pains me to say, I believe it will be safer for us both if we kept our clothes on this evening."

Heat burned my cheeks and my thoughts instantly flew to my virginal status. Did he somehow realize after his shadows had that very close encounter with my lady parts? Was he worried I would get attached? It was only one night, after all.

"What if I die tomorrow?" The desperate question escaped before I could stop it.

A murderous gaze flickered over the lusty haze, and his lazy smile twisted into a scowl. "Never say that, Aelia. Do not even think it."

"It's a possibility... and if I choose to give myself to you tonight, you really have no say in the matter."

A rueful smile melted away the frown. "You are truly testing my restraint, princess. I am not a good Fae, I am far from kind or selfless. I take what I want with no remorse. But I do not want to be that male with you."

"I've never been with a male," I blurted. *Good goddess what was wrong with my lips?*

Reign's eyes widened before a flash of understanding, then lust, darkened his gaze. "Noxus, you are truly evil," he muttered, his eyes to the sky. Returning his gaze to mine, he framed my face with his strong hands, and I leaned into his touch, reveling in the scent of frosty air that blanketed his skin. "I pray to all the gods that one day I may be that Fae for you, because you are mine. You and I are meant to be, as certain as the stars that grace the night sky across the river and the dawn that follows, inevitable and eternal, but not tonight, princess."

"Why?"

"Because first you must know the truth... all of it."

A crack like thunder vibrated the entire building, and the bed trembled beneath us. Reign leapt up, his shadows alive and in a frenzy, his eyes wild in panic. He jerked me off the mattress, and my skirts billowed, the shimmery glow illuminating the entire room.

"They're here!"

Chapter Fifty-Nine

"Why are they here already? We were supposed to have three more days!" I paused midstride as we approached the glass staircase and tossed my heels over the banister.

Sprinting down the sleek steps, I cursed my cumbersome, trailing skirts, with Reign by my side. The halls were empty, the sound of our pounding footfalls matching the erratic tempo of my heart. All the other first-years were on the lawn, celebrating the Winter Solstice. They were drunk, chaotic, unruly. Oh, goddess, it would be a bloodbath.

"Damned Malakar likes to keep his students on their toes. He likely sprang this upon them too."

"Malakar?"

"The headmaster of Arcanum Citadel."

Right. And of course, Reign would be familiar with his tricks because he'd attended the elite Shadow Court academy.

A cacophony of screams and cries echoed just beyond the

safety of the Hall of Glory. They grew louder with each step, sending ice surging through my veins. Oh, please let my friends survive this.

Focusing on the wispy strands that formed the bond between my skyrider and me, I searched for his comforting presence. *Sol, I need you!*

What's happened?

Arcanum began the assault early. They're here.

Curses. Where are you? Are you somewhere safe?

I'm with Reign, but I'm on my way to the battlefield. I paused in the grand foyer, steps away from the gilded front doors I'd crossed through only a few months ago, proving my worth at the Veil of Judgement.

No, Aelia. Stay where you are until I arrive.

I can't, Sol. The rest of my team is out there.

Steel bands encircled my arms, my shoulder blades smashing into a muscled torso. Rings of shadow curled around my form, tightening and constricting until I could barely breathe.

Sol!

Don't resist, Aelia. It's for your safety.

"What are you doing?" I shrieked at Reign.

"I'm sorry, princess, but I agree with Solanthus." His warm breath tickled the shell of my ear, his strong arms holding me tight against his body. "You cannot go out there. I will not lose you."

"Reign, this is madness! It's the final battle. If I do not fight, I will not pass the term, and I won't be allowed to remain at the Conservatory."

He spun me around, his shadows still coiled tight around me. "Fuck the Conservatory, Aelia, fuck this battle. Don't you understand that there are much more dangerous factors to consider?"

"No, I don't! Because you haven't explained *anything*." Gods, I wished I could move my hands because I would slap the idiot. "You tell me of this prophecy, then you disappear... Why do you think I am this child of twilight? And why hasn't anyone else heard of this prophecy but you and Draven? What more aren't you telling me?"

"I told you I would explain everything when I could, but right now, I must go out there." His arms fell away, but those shadows remained, relentless steel bands, pulsing and tightening.

"Reign, no!"

His brows furrowed, lips twisting as he leaned in and pressed a kiss to my forehead. "I'm sorry, Aelia, but I've only just found you, and I'll die a thousand deaths before I let him have you." Those smoldering midnight orbs remained locked on mine for an endless moment before his murky shadows swallowed him whole.

"Reign!" I shrieked in vain, wriggling and squirming. Searching my core, I found the well of power pulsing at my center. Radiant light poured through my veins and blanketed the swirling shadows. Sharp hisses vibrated the air as the *rais* and *nox* collided in a tangle of vibrant energy. No sooner did one dark wraith disappear than another emerged in its place.

Squeezing my eyes closed, I searched the bond for my traitorous skyrider. *Sol! Where are you?*

Moving fast. I'll be there shortly.

A thought wiggled its way into my mind, only stoking the building anger. *How did you and Reign conspire against me? I thought only bonded skyriders could speak telepathically.*

I told Phantom to deliver the message.

What? But I thought you hated her.

I never said that. I said I didn't trust her. But it was an emergency and concessions had to be made.

About a hundred more questions sprang to mind, but I vowed to broach them later. The sounds of battle loomed just outside the walls, shouts and screams vibrating the grand hall. Right now, I had to find a way to reach the dagger strapped to my thigh. Luckily, my fingers were the only part of me not currently constrained. Inch by inch, I tugged at the layers of gilded satin until my leg was bared.

Reign's shadows wriggled and hissed as if aware of what I was attempting. Splaying my two freed fingers, I reached for the hilt. *Got it*! Gingerly sliding it up my leg, I sought a firmer grasp. The sleek metal slipped from my fingertips and clattered onto the floor.

No!

Frustration bubbled in my core, a rush of anger and betrayal sizzling beneath the surface. How could Reign do this to me? Raysa, I was so tired of all the secrets, all the lies. A wave of power surged, and light exploded from my fingertips, a stream of *rais* that wrapped around the dagger and lifted it off the ground. I gawked as the weapon materialized in my hand, the crystal warm against my palm.

Without wasting a second, I slashed the blade across Reign's shadow minions. Screeches and furious whispers echoed around me, and for an instant I wondered if Reign could feel the pain of his shadows. Good, he deserved it for his treachery. Tossing the errant thought to the back of my mind, I sprang forward and raced through the gilded doors, prepared to face judgement once more.

A cloud of menacing darkness loomed over the Conservatory eclipsing the ever-present sun as the swarm of Arcanum students filled the sky. My breath hitched at the unearthly sight. There must have been at least two hundred Shadow Fae skyriders against our measly count.

I scanned the melee for any sign of Rue or Symon, but a knot of pure black encompassed the light. From this distance, I couldn't make out a thing.

As I raced toward the battlefield, a dark shadow streaked overhead. A wave of dragonfire lit up the murky sky and swallowed up two Light Fae skyriders. I watched in horror as the hippogriff and gryphon plummeted to the earth in a blazing inferno, their shrieks sending goosebumps across my arms.

Raysa, protect us.

Sol! Where are you?

Five minutes out. Where are you?

Still safe.

Aelia...

Just get here as fast as you can.

Clenching the dagger in my fist, I sprinted toward a mass of Light and Shadow Fae battling on the ground. I'd have to limit use of my blade for emergencies, or to make a kill strike. My stomach revolted at the idea. These were only students, like us, forced to train and fight for their king and court.

The air was thick with smoke and the oppressive weight of shadows, the sun barely a whisper in the sky as I stood on the field, heart pounding. I could feel the darkness pressing in, encroaching on the halo of light that pulsed from my core.

I drew a deep breath, feeling the familiar surge of *rais* flood my veins, a warm, glowing fire that danced along my fingertips. Just ahead, the Shadow Fae emerged from the darkness, their forms shifting and melding with the night, eyes gleaming with hatred. A tall male with eyes like black ice stepped forward, and the air around him seemed to ripple with dark energy.

Gods, he was beautiful in a terrifying way. And oddly familiar...

He lunged and I raised my hands, summoning a beam of pure, radiant light that cut through the darkness like a blade. He hissed and his shadows recoiled, their forms dissolving into wisps of smoke, but he surged forward, undeterred.

He moved with an eerie grace, his attack swift and relentless. I dodged a swipe from his umbral dagger, spinning to deflect another blow with a radiant shield that flared to life just in time. The impact sent a shiver through my body, but I held firm, pushing back with a burst of energy that sent my attacker reeling.

"You're stronger than I expected, for a lowly Kin," the male's voice echoed, cold and mocking.

My brows slammed together, fury coiling deep in my core. "Fae you," I gritted out.

He lunged again, and I barely had time to react, raising my arm to block his strike. His power was overwhelming, a crushing force of darkness that seemed to swallow the light. I gritted my teeth, summoning every ounce of my *rais* to push back. For a moment, we were locked in a battle of wills, light and shadow swirling around us in a chaotic dance.

With a cry, I unleashed a wave of blinding light, forcing him to stumble back. I seized the moment, channeling my *rais* into a spear of light that I hurled straight at his heart. He darted to the right and the ethereal weapon sliced across his upper arm. Eyes wide, he glared at me as he clutched his wound.

"Until we meet again, Aelia Ravenwood." The Shadow Fae male let out a low whistle and the thunderous flapping of wings vibrated the thick air.

The slate dragon dropped low from the sky and the male leapt up, catching one of its enormous talons. I watched in awe as he scaled up his massive leg as the dragon drifted higher. Stars, I needed to learn to do that.

A flash of gold upon the horizon caught my eye, pivoting my attention to the serene blue of Mysthallia to the west.

It's about time you joined the battle.

Sol's roar reverberated across the field as he swooped closer, and everything else went still. For a long moment, all eyes focused on the enormous golden dragon soaring ever closer. He released a torrent of dragonfire and Shadow Fae skyriders scrambled across the flight field.

From just overhead, a familiar voice broke through the uproar. "Aelia!" Rue waved as she zipped by on Windy. Beside her flew Griff with Symon aboard.

Thank the goddess they were safe.

Sol landed with a ground-shaking thud, his nostrils flared as he flattened his body to the ground so I could climb up his leg.

"I'm glad you finally made it."

And I am not pleased to find you in the middle of this disaster.

"Where else would I be?" I bit back.

Reign was supposed to keep you safe.

I'm alive, aren't I?

Where was my professor? In all the chaos, I'd nearly forgotten about him. Or at least, I'd pretended to.

Once I was firmly seated on Sol's back, his wings pounded the air and we catapulted into the gloomy sky. Smoke and shadows blanketed the pale blue, casting the battleground in darkness.

We must get Arcanum to retreat. It's the only way to win. Sol's voice streaked through my frazzled thoughts.

Okay, and how do we do that?

Like this.

Solanthus, the Sun Chaser, flexed his wings and darkness once again reigned supreme, those massive leathery appendages blocking out what remained of the sun's glittering rays. With a spine-tingling shriek, he bored down on the tangle of skyriders.

Griffons, ligels, hippogriffs, all scrambled at the sight of the monstrous golden dragon.

"Hold the line!" A shout came from across the aerial battleground an instant before the Fae male I'd fought earlier appeared atop the slate dragon.

Oh, for Fae's sake. *Do you know that dragon, Sol?*

Mmm, unfortunately.

How about the rider?

My inquiry remained unanswered as Sol's earthshaking roar vibrated through his entire body, making my thighs quiver. He surged forward, straight for the dragon in question. Scorching flames filled the air as the beasts clashed mid-air.

Snarls and deep growls blasted over the chaos of combat, and I gripped onto Sol's wingbones with everything I had as he dodged sharp talons and torrents of dragonfire. The two wild creatures were relentless. Squeezing my thighs until my muscles burned from the strain was all I could do to keep seated.

"Surrender, Kin!" A shadow curled around me, delivering the message. "You are sorely outnumbered, and half of the first-year Light Fae have already fallen. Arcanum Citadel has won the battle."

"Never," I hissed back.

Dark orbs pinned to mine, and that familiar twinge deepened. "You prefer to die, then?"

"I am not the one dying today."

"Arrogant words for a lowly Kin."

"I am *not* a lowly Kin," I snarled. "I am Light Fae!" Splaying my fingers on one hand while keeping a firm hold of Sol with the other, I released a solar flare. The radiant energy smashed into dragon and rider, alike, sending both hurtling back.

"Aelia, watch out!" Another shadow danced across my ear, the familiar icy touch a comforting one. Reign emerged from the shadows between us an instant later, Phantom's immense onyx form blotting out the other rider.

The slate dragon spun around, maw wide open and nostrils flared. A tornado of pure night whipped through the wind, speeding straight for me.

Reign leapt from Phantom's back, his shadows morphing into airy wings. He landed atop Sol and jerked me behind him. "No, Ruhl!" he shouted at the approaching rider. "Not her!" My eyes snapped to Reign's profile. "I'm sorry," he murmured, glancing quickly at me before turning away. Darkness curtained those piercing irises. "For everything."

"Are you out of your mind, brother?" The Shadow Fae male loomed closer, his dragon hovering only a few yards from Sol.

Brother? What the actual Fae?

"Not her," he hissed again.

"What is the matter with you?" Ruhl snarled. "Do you have any idea what father will say?"

"I don't give a fuck."

"That's what you've been doing all this time?" His dark brows furrowed, a thin line slashing across his mouth. "Instead of doing Father's bidding, you've fallen for the girl?"

My mind spun as I attempted to process the Shadow Fae's words, but everything was happening too quickly. My heart kicked at my ribs, my lungs tightening with each ragged breath.

"Who are you?" I blurted, peering around Reign and pinning the Fae male in my sights.

"Who am I?" A sinister chuckle pierced his lips. "Oh, Reign, you haven't told her?"

"Shut your mouth, Ruhl!"

"And miss this opportunity? Absolutely not." He spun his wicked gaze on me. "I am Prince Ruhl of Umbra, heir to King Tenebris of the Court of Umbral Shadows."

All the remaining air vacated my lungs, and stars danced across my vision. Gods, this wasn't happening. It couldn't be...

"And the male standing so protectively in front of you is my eldest brother, Prince Reign."

EEK! I'm sorry, that really was an evil cliffhanger!! But, the next book in the Courts of Aetheria, Crown of Flames and Ash, will be here before you know it! And you can preorder it now! I have it tentatively scheduled to come out in November, but I hope to bring that date up. In the meantime, if you join my VIP mailing list (https://shorturl.at/2zXPK) or my Facebook group, GK DeRosa's Supe Squad, you'll get a sneak peek at Chapter 1 of the next book along with the prequel short story!

And while you're waiting for the next book, check out all of my complete series from the world of Azar. Start with the super fun paranormal reality TV show dating game Hitched: The Bachelorette :)

Guide to the Courts of Aetheria

Court of Ethereal Light

King Elian of Ether

Light fae, beings associated with illumination and radiant energy, possess a variety of magical powers aligned with the forces of light and positive energy through *rais*.

Light Fae Abilities

1. Photokinesis:
The ability to manipulate and control light.
2. Healing Light:
The power to harness light energy for healing purposes.
3. Luminous Wings:
Only extremely powerful Light Fae can sprout ethereal, radiant wings that allow them to fly gracefully through the air.
4. Illumination Sight:
The ability to see beyond the visible spectrum, allowing Light Fae to perceive things such as auras, energy patterns, or hidden magical forces.

5. Solar Empowerment:

Drawing strength from sunlight, Light Fae experience enhanced abilities, increased vitality, and heightened magical powers when exposed to sunlight.

6. Prismatic Manipulation:

The power to control and manipulate prisms and rainbows.

7. Radiant Shields:

The ability to create protective barriers or shields made of radiant light.

8. Solar Flare Burst:

Unleashing bursts of intense solar energy, powerful Light Fae could create blinding flashes or focused beams to repel adversaries.

9. Light Infusion:

Infusing objects or individuals with radiant energy.

10. Harmony Induction:

The ability to radiate an aura of peace and tranquility.

11. Illuminate Knowledge:

The power to gain insights, visions, or access to hidden knowledge through the illumination of light.

Court of Umbral Shadows

King Tenebris and Queen Vespera of Umbra

Shadow fae, beings associated with darkness and shadows, possess a range of magical powers aligned with the forces of shadow and concealment through *nox*.

Shadow Fae Abilities

1. Umbrakinesis:
The ability to control and manipulate shadows.
2. Shadow Travel:
The power to traverse through shadows, allowing mature Shadow Fae to move swiftly from one shadow to another.
3. Cloak of Invisibility:
The ability to wrap themselves in shadows, becoming invisible to the naked eye.
4. Umbral Constructs:
The power to shape shadows into solid, tangible forms.
5. Fear Induction:
The ability to manipulate the fears and anxieties of others.
6. Eclipse Manipulation:
Control over celestial events, particularly eclipses.
7. Shadowmeld:
The power to merge seamlessly with shadows, becoming one with the darkness.
8. Umbral Blades:
Conjuring weapons made of solid shadow.
9. Whispering Shadows:
The ability to communicate through shadows.
10. Nightmare Weaving:

Crafting illusions and dreams that induce nightmares.

11. Corruptive Touch:

The power to taint or corrupt objects with shadows, extremely rare.

Also by G.K. DeRosa

Dark Oblivion

Acknowledgments

A huge and wholehearted thank you to my dedicated readers! I could not do this without you. I love hearing from you and your enthusiasm for the characters and story. You are the best!

A special thank you to my loving and supportive husband who always understood my need for escaping into a good book (or TV show!). He inspires me to try harder and push further every day. And of course my mother who is the guiding force behind everything I do and made me everything I am today. Without her, I literally could not write—because she's also my part-time babysitter! To my father who will always live on in my dreams. And finally, my little hellions, Alexander and Stella, who bring an unimaginable amount of joy, adventure and craziness to my life everyday.

A big thank you to Sanja Gombar, for creating a beautiful book cover, to Samaiya Beaumont for the lovely header designs, character art and all the swag. I could never come up with all the ideas that you do! And a special thank you to my dedicated beta readers, Rachel, Daniela, Tess, and Amanda and of course Sarah (the best VA ever!) who have been my sounding board on everything from cover ideas, blurbs, and story details. And to my ARC readers who caught spelling errors, and were all around amazing.

Thank you to all my family and friends, author and blogger friends who let me bounce ideas off of them and listened to my struggles as an author and self-publisher. I appreciate it more than you all will ever know.

~ G.K.

About the Author

USA Today Bestselling Author, G.K. De Rosa has always had a passion for all things fantasy and romance. Growing up, she loved to read, devouring books in a single sitting. She attended Catholic school where reading and writing were an intense part of the curriculum, and she credits her amazing teachers for instilling in her a love of storytelling. As an adult, her favorite books were always young adult novels, and she remains a self-proclaimed fifteen year-old at heart. When she's not reading, writing or watching way too many TV shows, she's traveling and eating around the world with her family. G.K. DeRosa currently lives in South Florida with her real life Prince Charming and their little royals.

www.gkderosa.com

Made in the USA
Columbia, SC
21 April 2025

56892949R00269